Dark Romance

Lost In the Chase

Danni Marie

Book Cover Design: *Ainy*

Editor: *Chloe Marler*

First Edition – October 2025
Cover Design: Ainy Designs
Editor: Chloe Marler
Publisher: Danni Marie
Printed in the United States of America

Registered with the United States Copyright Office.

DEDICATION

For the girl who questions her worth.
The one who smiles through silent panic
attacks and crippling anxiety.
The one who shows up for everyone but can't
find the strength to show up for herself.
The one who blends in so well, even she
forgets who she is.
The one who gives everything...
and still feels like it's never enough.
Just know:
You are not broken.
You are not alone.
You are beautifully created.
Wonderfully you.
And you are worthy of being loved.
This story is for you...
Because you're not lost.
You're simply in the chase of becoming the
best version of yourself.

<u>TRIGGER WARNINGS</u>

This novel contains mature themes that may be disturbing or triggering to some readers. Please proceed with care.

- Sexual coercion
- Abuse
- Exploitation
- Trafficking involving teenagers (ages 16 and up)
- Childhood trauma
- Murder/death
- Physical violence
- Captivity
- Cancer
- Hospital scenes and settings
- Medical procedures/graphic details
- Emotional trauma
- Panic attacks
- Post-traumatic stress disorder (PTSD)
- Bondage
- Discipline
- Dominance
- Submission
- Sadism
- Voyeurism
- Explicit sexual content
- Non-consensual touching/assault references
- Psychological manipulation/gaslighting
- Alcohol/substance use
- Strong language

A GENTLE NOTE TO READERS
REGARDING TRIGGER WARNINGS

These elements are not written for shock or entertainment. They are deeply tied to the male protagonist's backstory and essential to understanding his emotional journey, his scars, and the man he becomes.

I want to be clear. I do **NOT** condone, romanticize, or glorify abuse in any form. This is a fictional story that explores survival, pain, healing, and ultimately, the power of love.

If you are a survivor, please know that you are seen and your story matters. I wrote this with sensitivity, empathy, and care. If you are in a tender place or need to protect your peace, please honor that. You deserve to feel safe at all times.

And if you choose to continue reading, I want to thank you gently for trusting me with your heart. I spent a year pouring myself into this story, and I truly hope it stays with you long after you turn the last page.

With love and understanding,
Danni Marie

♩ ♫ <u>**PLAYLIST**</u> ♩ ♫

- **No Vanity - Jxdn**
- **Streets - Doja Cat**
- **Every Breath You Take - The Police**
- **Lavender Haze - Taylor Swift**
- **Say Yes to Heaven - Lana Del Rey**
- **Somewhere Only We Know – Keane**
- **Cinnamon Girl – Lana Del Rey**
- **Good For You – Selena Gomez**
- **Busy Women – Sabrina Carpenter**
- **Revolving Door – Tate McRae**
- **Down Bad – Taylor Swift**
- **I Can Do It with A Broken Heart – Taylor Swift**
- **Think About Me – Jxdn**
- **Wicked Games – The Weeknd**
- **Call Out My Name – The Weeknd**

PROLOGUE
<u>FIFTEEN YEARS AGO</u>

The metal bites into my wrist as I fight with the last ounce of strength left in my body. My skin is raw where the chains cut deep… blistered and torn, but I keep pulling. Keep struggling. Keep fighting.

It's useless.

Duct tape seals my mouth shut. The bitter taste of glue clings to my tongue… sour, chemical, vile as I try to scream. But nothing comes out. Just muffled, desperate cries. My legs are bound, rope cutting so deep it feels like it's fused to my bone. Every involuntary muscle twitch slices deeper, sending pain throughout my severed body.

The air is thick not just with mildew and humidity but with something darker.

Decay.

Secrets.

Death.

It clings to the walls, heavy and still, like the room itself is watching me, waiting to claim me as its next victim.

God, I wish I hadn't seen it. I want to rip it from my memory. Burn it. Destroy it with my bare hands.

But I can't.

Everything I saw completely shattered me. Crushed what was left of my soul and ground it into dust.

If I had just stayed home. If I had listened to her. If I had made my little brother fall asleep next to me on the couch, put on a movie, and held him tighter.
Maybe none of this would have happened.

Maybe this wouldn't be my final breath.
My last thought of him.

I'm a terrible brother.
All I feel now is regret.
Because when I go, he'll be alone.
My brother.
He'll be dumped into the foster care system, left with no family. Just him and the aching memory of me and Mom. But who knows? Maybe he'll get lucky.
Maybe he'll end up with a good family.
One that gives him the kind of life we never had.
A future.
A sliver of hope.
Anything would be better than this.

The doorknob rattles.

A sharp clatter slices through the silence, electrifying my teenage nerves with panic. My entire body tenses in unfiltered terror. I stop breathing. My lungs seize. My heart slams against my ribs, like it's trying to outrun death itself.

God, I wish I could escape.
Run straight to my brother.
Hold him. Tell him everything's going to be okay.
Tell him we will be okay.
That Mom is just out late tonight…
Even if she's not.
Even if we're not.

The door creaks open, slow and deliberate, like the groan of a coffin lid waiting to bury me.

This is it.

Heavy boots scrape the floor. Slow. Measured. Almost predatory.

"All right, boy," a voice growls with a Russian-accented, low and rough like gravel under tires. "What the fuck am I going to do with you? "A cloud of cigar smoke hits my face. It burns. Stings my eyes. Crawls down my throat like poison.

I shouldn't be here.

I'm sixteen.

I should be in my room with headphones on, sketching out dreams I thought I had time to chase. Wondering what college I'll get into.

What girl I'm taking to prom.

Worrying about my future… not fighting to survive.

But unfortunately, it looks like I won't get that far.

The room is pitch black, but I can smell him. Sweat. Expensive cologne. Whiskey and leather.

The scent of cruelty, if it had a body. He steps closer. Too close. I can't see his face, only his shape. Big. Solid. Menacing.

I brace for pain. A punch. A kick. The slam of a metal bat.

But it doesn't come. Instead… he laughs. A slow, amused chuckle, like he's flipping through options in his head. Like I'm not a person. Just a toy, he hasn't decided how to break yet.

A hand grabs my collar and yanks me up. Hard and jolting, sending agonizing pain radiating through my sore body.

His eyes are soulless. Solid black. Black as oil, deep as the darkest ocean trench. My vision spins. Blood rushes to my head. I try to cough, but the tape turns it into a choking gasp.

"I was going to kill you," he mutters, breath inches from my face, reeking of liquor and ash. "But you know what?" A jagged grin slices across his face… teeth too white, too perfect. Like they were stolen from someone's corpse. "You're not bad on the eyes, son." A chill needles down my spine. It sinks into my bones, freezing me from the inside out.

No… No, please God no.

"I might have some use for you." His grip tightens until I feel my collarbone creak. I'm a deer in a wolf's mouth…There is nothing I can do or say to escape this fate.

My fate.

"You wanna see your brother again?"

I nod. Fast. Too fast. My body shakes with it. His fingers loosen just barely.

Then he leans in. His lips brush my ear, fear throbbing through my body. "Then listen closely. You want to keep him safe? You want to provide for him? You want him to live another day?" The following words drip like venom, and I can't help but shed a tear. "You are going to walk down that hall. Take a left and you will see a red door. Go in… and you'll know what to do." He chuckles again. It's not even laughter. It's the sound of something inhuman, like he's choking on his victim's blood.

He leans in closer, voice slick with cruelty. "Oh, and son, think of it as a gift… from one man to another." Then he shoves me back.

My knees slam against the floor. Pain radiates through my ribs. *Please. Please let this be a nightmare.*

"Do we have a deal, boy?" he growls, voice laced with venom. "You can take your mother's place since she still owes me."

I go still.

My mother's place? What does that even mean? How long will I belong to him? What exactly will he make me do?

A heartbeat later, cold metal kisses the skin of my throat.

A knife. I don't move. I don't breathe. Then… I feel it. A trickle of blood dripping down my neck.

"But if you don't…" he whispers, his breath hot and
sour against my cheek, "I'll slit your
throat and be done with it."

I nod. *What other choice do I have? It's the only thing I
can do.*

His smile stretches wider, warped and twisted. In one
swift motion, he rips the tape from my mouth and cuts the
ropes. Pain sears through me. My scream collapses in my
throat.

"I own you now," he says, unlocking the chains on my
wrist. "And son… if you try anything stupid, I'll gut your
brother in front of you… just like I did your mother."

Time stops. He said it out loud. So now it's true. The
crack in my chest splits wide open into a cavern of unescapable
pain I'll never crawl out of.

He shoves me toward the hallway. The lights flicker.
The walls moan. The floor beneath my feet feels alive.

Watching.

Listening.

Waiting.

Am I at a motel?

"Make sure to get a tip, son. She's our best customer, so
don't disappoint her." Then he winks and slaps my back like I
just won the lottery. *What was that about?*

I stumble forward with my quivering legs, barely able
to hold myself up from the last 24 hours. The hallway stretches
like a tunnel to hell. The air is heavy with cigarette smoke,
body odor, and something else I'm not familiar with… The
carpet sticks to my bare feet. The wallpaper peels in curling
strips, like secrets clawing their way out. Then I see it. The red
door. Splintered wood and chipped paint. Deep crimson with a

gold doorknob. It looks like it's breathing. Alive. Waiting to
gobble me up and never let me go.

> *I don't want to go in.*
> *But if I don't… he'll kill my brother.*
> *Or worse… sell him.*
> *Make him do this.*
> *He's just a child and the only family I have left.*
> I reach for the knob. My hand trembles so hard that it
> can barely grab the damn thing.

I turn it… dreading what is behind this cursed door, or worse…
who.

> *Wake up.*
> *Wake up.*
> *Wake up.*

I step inside. Perfume hits me, sending nausea straight
to my gut. It's floral, sickly sweet. Suffocating, like someone
poured it over the room to mask the filth beneath it.

The lights are dim and have a tinted gold hue. Velvet
curtains pool in the corners. A heart-shaped bed sits center
stage, wrapped in crimson just like the door. A table holds two
glasses of white wine. A golden lamp flickers beside it. It
should feel romantic, but it feels like a prison.
And in the center of it all… her.

She's naked. Maybe thirty. Dark caramel skin glistens
with oil. Chocolate curls streaked with sun-kissed highlights
sensually draped over her bare shoulders. She's beautiful, the
kind that lures the sailor close. Not to love him, but to watch
him drown at the bottom of the sea.

> *Am I next?*

The thought curdles my stomach as her eyes crawl over
me, slow and possessive like I already belong to her. "You
must be new," she says, voice like honey. "I'm a regular. So,
you'll be seeing me a lot… if you do well." She smiles. Not

kindly. She stands with her arms crossed, undressing me with her eyes. And somehow, it makes me cover myself... even though I'm fully dressed.

"My husband has his fun with his secretary, and well..." She trails her fingers slowly around her nipples, a wicked smile tugging at her lips. "I have mine."

My face goes hot, and my throat locks, and my ears ring. She stands, moving toward me. It's slow and taunting, like she's ready to pounce.

No. Please... stay over there.

Her body sways with practiced grace, every movement calculated. Her full breasts rise and fall with each step, unapologetic and commanding. Her confidence is petrifying. She doesn't just own the room... she owns me, and I never gave her permission. She extends her hand. Like we're meeting at a damn charity fundraiser.

"Nice to meet you," she purrs. "I'm Emily Woodrick. After tonight... I'll be your favorite client." I stare at her hand like it's a snake ready to strike. Maybe it will.

"I... I don't think this is right," I stammer. "I don't want—"

She cuts me off. "It's cute that you think you have a choice." Her voice turns ice cold. "I pay you to please me. So really... It's a win for both of us. You get sex and you get paid." She laughs with sarcasm. "Isn't that what every guy wants?"

No.

Not me.

I was waiting.

Waiting for the right one, waiting to give all of myself to someone who truly saw me.

Loved me.

But now... who would want someone like this?

Someone broken. Someone damaged. Someone too far gone.

She steps into my space. Close enough that I feel her heat, which is shocking, considering her heart's frozen solid. The scent of honeysuckle and bourbon wraps around me like a noose.

God, I wish it were a noose.

"I'm… I'm a virgin," I whisper. "I don't know how to—"

Her eyes flash… sharp, emotionless, and strangely eager. "Where have you been my whole life?" She says in a flirtatious voice, inches from my face.

You have to do this if you want to survive.

Shut it off.

Shut the emotions off.

Shut it all off.

She leans in, her breath brushing my lips. "I can teach you all my tricks." Her tongue drags along the seam of my mouth. Then she kisses me. Soft. Sweet and poisonous. But all I can taste is bile. It's rising fast, burning my throat.

I think I'm going to throw up.

Her hand slips lower, finding me.

Shit.

She wraps her hand around my shaft through my sweatpants like she's done this a hundred times.

No.

Stop.

No.

My body betrays me.

Please stop.

I don't want this.

She feels it harden in her hand and smiles. "You're adorable," she breathes. "So innocent." Her smirk grows as she traces my shoulder. "Let's change that."

I close my eyes, forcing my mind to reset, to go numb, to detach. Anything to disassociate from what's about to happen. She leads me to bed like a teacher walking a student to the front of the class.

And I realized… I thought that night I was going to die. I prayed for it. Because death?

Death would've been mercy.

But instead… I walked through that red door. And I never came back out the same.

I didn't die that night. I disappeared. And the boy he chained up?

He never made it out.

Only the monster did.

CHAPTER ONE
<u>15 YEARS LATER</u>
LILA

"What have you done to me?" I mutter, narrowing my gaze at the stranger in the mirror.

Why did I ever agree to this?

Aster squeals beside me, doing a little victory dance. "Oh my gosh… You look like pure, drop-dead sex in heels."

I shoot her a side-eye. "Just because it's Halloween doesn't mean you get to dress me like a pornstar."

"Oh, yes it does," she teases, giving me a cheeky swat on the butt with a wink. "Besides, you're the hottest Rapunzel I've ever seen." She steps back, admiring her handiwork. "Who knows? Maybe your Flynn Rider will come along tonight…smolder and all… and sweep you off on a ride that'll make you forget all about that tower."

I grab a silk pillow from her bed and launch it at her. She dodges with a laugh, disappearing into the bathroom. Left alone, I run my fingers along the edge of her vanity. Even her makeup brushes look expensive. Gold-handled, soft-bristled. The kind I'd never buy for myself.

I turn back to the mirror and let out the breath I feel like I've been holding since I stepped into this costume. My fingers trail over the sparkly lavender corset Aster expertly laced me into, hugging my figure in all the right places. The ruffled skirt sits daringly high on my thighs, shorter than anything I'd wear on a typical day.

Yet somehow… it feels enchanting.

My long, golden waves cascade over one shoulder in a loose braid, delicate purple flowers woven through the strands.

A tiara rests atop my head, its golden frame encrusted with crystals that shimmer like tiny fragments of stardust.

Aster even worked her magic with my makeup. My green eyes are lined just enough to appear wide and doe-like, my cheeks dusted with a pink hue and a hint of shimmer. My lips are painted a deep mauve, full and inviting.

Not that I'd ever invite someone to use them.

Maybe it's the oil accentuating my legs. Perhaps it's the mischievous chameleon perched on my shoulder, daring me to step out of my comfort zone. But for the first time, I'm not just playing dress-up. I'm not the invisible girl in the background.

I look like I belong in a story worth telling. Transformed. Bold. A woman finally ready to be seen.

And it's all thanks to her.

Growing up, Aster Sikes was my saving grace.

When I turned ten, my parents poured their life savings into transferring me to a prestigious boarding academy. My dad even took a job as a janitor there to receive a tuition discount. My mom had dropped out of school to raise her younger brother after their parents died in a car crash. My dad aged out of the system, growing up in an orphanage without a proper education.

They gave up everything for me.

So, I worked. I studied. I earned scholarships and did everything I could to lighten their burden. But no matter how hard I tried, my classmates never let me forget where I came from. They mocked my thrift-store clothes. Snickered when I ate lunch alone. Wrinkled their noses like poverty was contagious.

I learned to make myself invisible until Aster found me and pulled the invisibility cloak off.

Aster Sikes is everything I'm not… unapologetically cool, effortlessly rich, and totally magnetic. Her father runs

Sikes & Co. Renewables, the clean energy empire her grandfather built, and her parents turned into a global force. The company builds solar panels and wind turbines, powering everything from luxury homes to entire cities in over sixty countries. Forbes features them so often, they might as well have their own column.

We met when we were paired for a science project, and from that day on, we were inseparable. We were both only children, so finding each other felt like fate, like we'd stumbled into sisterhood. When Aster stood beside me, the bullying slowed. She got detention for fighting kids twice her size and gave me her designer hand-me-downs. The pastel, princessy outfits her mom insisted she wear, but she never would. She thought dressing me up might shut the bullies up.

Sometimes, they still whispered. But I didn't care anymore because I wasn't alone.

Aster made me feel seen. Accepted. Wanted. Her family became my second home. Her parents treated me like I belonged, even though they were billionaires, while mine barely scraped together enough to buy groceries. And now, fifteen years later, she's still my person.

I fidget with the hem of my skirt, tugging it down like I can shrink myself back into the shadows. I'm used to blending in and fading into the background. But this costume? It makes me stand out. It makes me visible. And I'm not sure if that excites me… or terrifies me.

"Don't do that, Lila!" Aster's voice snaps from the bathroom. "I know exactly what that beautiful little brain is thinking. You look freaking amazing. Now hold your head high and strut that twenty-six-year-old body with confidence!"

"Okay… I'll try," I murmur.

"You better! Be honest… do my boobs look amazing or what?"

She struts out, confidence oozing from every inch of her. I laugh, taking her in. "You look so hot. Total Halle Berry Cat Woman vibes."

"It better! Do you know how hard it was to squeeze into this latex? Someone better make me purr loud enough for Gotham to hear."

I giggle, shaking my head, secretly wishing I had even half her ease around people.
She's poured into a black, skin-tight bodysuit that hugs her like a second skin. Her shoulder-length black hair sways as she moves, cat ears perched atop her head. Smoky eyeshadow makes her amber eyes burn gold in the light.

Aster is everything I am not. She is the moon to my sun, night to my day, the fire to my quiet flame. One look, one touch, and she has people at her feet, while I'm stumbling over my insecurities, just trying to disappear into the shadows. Yet somehow, she convinced me to step out tonight. To take up space. To be seen. To dress in a way I'd never dare. To become someone, I never allowed myself to be. And I can't shake the feeling that tonight will be different. That maybe… just maybe… I'm about to meet a version of myself I've kept locked away.
The part that's been trapped in a tower, waiting for a single moment to break free.

As we descend Aster's grand staircase, my fingers glide along the cold marble railing, our heels clacking in sync with my pounding heart. Aster moves past me, leaving behind a trail of her luxurious perfume, a captivating blend of vanilla and rose that lingers in the air like a love potion.

She grabs her custom-made shoulder bag, a shimmering masterpiece designed to look like a pile of gold and silver jewelry. It's the perfect match for her Cat Woman ensemble, bold, dramatic, and obsessed with everything shiny. Of course, she didn't find it. So naturally, she had it made.

Aster doesn't do anything halfway. She pours her entire heart and soul into every detail. And because of that, she doesn't just wear the costume… She becomes it, like she stepped straight out of the movie.

She arches a brow at me, confusion flashing across her face. "Lila, where is your purse? You need to carry something to hold your taser, pocketknife, and pepper spray."

I roll my eyes. "It did not match my costume. Besides, where are we going that I would need all those weapons?"

She laughs, strutting over to the foyer table and picking up a blush-colored box topped with a white lace bow. With a mischievous grin stretching from ear to ear, she sets it down in front of me.

"Open it," she says, practically bouncing with excitement.

"No way. Aster, you really didn't have to get me anything! You already dressed me from head to toe."

"It's just a little something to complete your costume… I couldn't resist."

I tear into the box and burst out laughing, doubling over and crossing my legs as I try not to pee from laughing. I'm gasping for air, completely losing it. "Stop. You did not get me a cast-iron skillet shoulder bag."

"Oh, I did," Aster says proudly. "And it's stocked with goodies in case we run into any crazy-ass guys tonight."

Still giggling, I wrap my arms around her neck. "You're insane, but that's why I love you."

She hugs me tight, then suddenly squeezes my sides, making me shriek. "Loosen up, woman! Tonight is about fun."

"Stop!" I squeal, trying to wiggle free. "You know I'm ticklish!"

"Exactly why I did it," she grins, relentless. "I'm tickling the nerves out of you."

As we make our way to her blacked-out Mercedes G Wagon, my legs feel weak with nerves.

Okay Lila... You can do this.

I usually never agree to attend events or parties. She is a celebrity, not me. I am just an ordinary girl with a simple routine. Work. Go home to my tiny apartment. Cook. Bathe. Read. Write. Sleep. Repeat. That's my life. Safe. Predictable.

This version of me? It isn't who I am. It has never been. But tonight… I want it to be, just for one night.

Her world is an extravagant whirlwind of shopping, traveling, interviews, and fashion shows. But truthfully? I've never envied it. I crave a quiet life. She thrives in chaos. I find comfort in stillness. But she promised tonight would be low-key. Just a simple Halloween party.

I hesitate, my hand hovering over the door handle, seriously considering backing out.

Come on.

Come on.

Open the damn door.

I close my eyes and yank the door. I climb up into the G-Wagon, my pulse echoing in my ears. The doors click shut behind me, soft but final, like I've just sealed away the girl I used to be.

It's just a party, I tell myself.

Just a few hours of socializing.

But something stirs deep in my chest. Not fear. Anticipation. Like my skin knows something my mind hasn't caught up to yet.

What I do know is this... I've stepped out of my tower tonight, ready to explore the new world waiting for me. And the girl in the mirror? She's done hiding. Not from herself. Not

from anyone. Tonight, she steps into the spotlight. Head high. Heart racing. Fire pulsing through her veins. Ready or not…
Here I come.

CHAPTER TWO
LILA

The interior oozes luxury. Diamond-stitched leather seats mold to my every curve, while chrome accents and sleek digital displays give the dashboard a futuristic, high-end appearance. The suede steering wheel, as soft as freshly shaved legs, is sensually teasing the driver. Soft ambient lighting casts a warm, elegant glow throughout the cabin.

This is not just a car. It is pure seduction on wheels, perfectly fitting Aster's bold personality.

As we make our way down the long, grand driveway, I glance back at the mansion. The glow from the windows feel safe like a lifeline I could still grab onto.

I could still turn back…

I could curl up on the couch with my heated blanket, a bottle of wine in one hand and my favorite novel in the other.

That would be predictable. So even though I want to turn back… I won't.

Settling into my seat, I watch as tree after tree blurs past, doubts swirling in my mind.

Do I really have the guts for this? What if people laugh at me? What if it's all a setup, a prank to remind me I don't belong? Are they being nice… or is there some hidden agenda meant to hurt me?

My mind drifts back to tenth grade, when the star lacrosse player asked me to the homecoming dance. He'd heard I had a crush on him and used it to his advantage.

I was thrilled until we arrived.

He led me to the center of the dance floor, then pulled out his phone to record, called someone over, and smiled.

His ex-girlfriend.

At least, that's what I believed. But the moment she stepped into the circle of flashing lights and laughing faces, I realized the truth. She wasn't his ex. She was his real girlfriend. And I was nothing more than a joke. Just a pawn in his cruel game of emotional chess.

The crowd pressed in, their laughter slicing through me like shards of glass straight to my heart. My chest tightened, making it hard to breathe. My vision blurred. My stomach twisted as shame burned hot against my skin. I wanted to disappear.

"You really thought I'd take you?" He froze, soaking in the crowd's attention, then let out a low chuckle. "That's cute." His eyes dragged down my body with slow, deliberate cruelty. "I'd never date someone who lives in a… shithole."

Then he started toward me, achingly slow, like he was savoring the moment. Like he was feeding off my humiliation, and without warning, he smashed an egg on my head. "So run back to the trash… where you belong."

Let's just say Aster had no idea about any of this until later, and now he can't have kids, thanks to a hospital visit for severely damaged testicles, courtesy of her. I smirk at the memory. My best friend is a total badass.

But then my leg starts bouncing, nerves creeping back in as the unknown of tonight settles over me.

Aster notices and cranks up the music, trying to drown out my anxiety with my favorite tunes. My heart skips when pop punk blasts through the speakers.

"I knew you would be freaking out about the party," she says, smirking. "So, I had the playlist queued up and ready to go just for you."

My worried expression melts into a grin, and I place my hand over my chest. "You really do know the way to my heart."

"Or the way to get you horny before the party," Aster teases. "Maybe you will actually get laid tonight."

"Aster!" I sputter, turning red.

She laughs, throwing her hands up as if she is innocent. "I am just looking out for you. You are always so tense… and need some cock… I mean to loosen up." I can't help but chuckle at her vulgar mouth.

"I am not clueless, you know. I have been with one guy…" I mutter defensively. "Plus, Clint took me out the other night and it was… uhhh, nice." I plaster a large fake smile across my face.

"Ew, Lila, you're kidding. That frat guy from college? He is a douchebag and thinks he is better than everyone because his daddy owns a few clothing stores." She rolls her eyes and makes a gagging noise. "I bet that prick is compensating for a pencil dick."

I spit out my water mid-sip, and we both break into high-pitched laughter. "Okay, okay… you're probably right," I admit, still catching my breath. "But he's connected to Heartford Cyphers International, the company I've been dreaming of working for years. So, yeah... I might as well play the game."

"Lila, whatever helps you sleep at night… but getting laid multiple times a week? That's what really relaxes the body."

I pause, her words echoing in my head.

Maybe she's right. What if I actually had an orgasm and let this built-up anxiety go? But every time a man has touched me, it's ended in disappointment. Empty. Forgettable.

Still, something inside me aches for more. Emotionally? Physically? Sexually?

God… I don't even know. All I know is I've never felt truly satisfied.

I shake my head, snapping back to reality. *Focus, Lila. Tonight is about fun. Nothing else.* I crank up the volume, letting the music drown out my thoughts. The rhythm takes over, and I start nodding along, dancing in my seat, scream-singing along to "No Vanity" by Jxdn.

Aster watches me for a long moment, a slow smirk spreading across her face.

"Lila, you're insane," she laughs. "And you're definitely a Gemini."

"What's that supposed to mean?" I ask, still jamming to the tunes.

"Well, I've always heard Geminis have two sides to their personality. A sweet side like an angel…" She shoots me a sideways glance, her voice dropping just enough to tease. "And a wicked side that's full of spice… and a touch of darkness."

I pause, taken back by her words. "What do you mean?"

"Oh, babe… I think you know exactly what I mean," she says with a wink, turning her eyes back to the road.

I glance at her, breathless, and my lips part as a strange realization settles over me. *Do I really understand what she's hinting at? Is that how she sees me? Sweet one minute… sinful the next? Can I really be both? Maybe I've always been.*

Aster whips around the winding road, making the car ride feel like it'll never end. I watch her navigation screen, my eyes fixated on the estimated arrival time ticking lower and lower.

Five minutes.

Four minutes.

Three minutes.

With each second that disappears, my heartbeat quickens. Aster must sense it because her fingers find my hand, squeezing reassuringly. Finally, the navigation chimes: "You have arrived at your destination."

Right on cue, she makes a sharp left toward a monstrous black gate. I blink up at the towering iron structure, its gold accents glinting under the moonlight. Aster grins. "Welcome to our playground for the night."

"This place gives me the creeps," I murmur, shifting uncomfortably in my seat.

She laughs, her eyes flashing with wicked delight. "Good. That's the goal! It's Halloween, after all. Maybe you'll find a big, strong man to protect you."

I roll my eyes, but can't help the shiver that runs through me. She scans a QR code, and the massive gate creaks open, swallowing us whole. I glance behind us as the iron bars slam shut again, locking us inside.

Well, it's too late to back out now.

The road ahead twists into darkness, flanked by twisted oak trees whose branches stretch like skeletal fingers overhead. Flickering jack-o'-lanterns cast eerie red and orange glows along the path, their twisted faces carved into wide, sinister grins.

I should have stayed home.

Figures loom between the trees, their hollow, masked faces appearing and disappearing in the shifting shadows. My stomach twists. One moment, they're part of the bark … and the next, they're closer, like they're waiting for the perfect moment to rip open our doors and drag us into the dark, eerie forest.

My hand fumbles for the door lock. "Uh, lock the doors… like *now*."

Aster snorts. "Relax, Lila. They're just actors." But the way the darkness shifts around them feels too real. The road curves and then…

I see it.

I grip Aster's arm. "Holy. Shit."

Before me rises the kind of mansion you only see in fairy tales or daydreams; it's Gothic and grand, with towering spires that reach the night sky. Moonlight spills across the stone, casting shadows over balconies and arched windows. The whole place feels like a whisper from another era, as if Juliet herself is waiting on a balcony for her Romeo. It's beautiful, yes, but in the way a graveyard is beautiful. Quiet. Reverent. Unnerving.

The music thrums through the ground, a steady, pulsing bass that vibrates in my chest.
At the center of the courtyard stands a fountain, but it's no ordinary sculpture. It's Michael Myers.

A monstrous stone figure of the slasher icon looms over the entrance, his knife raised mid-swing, his blank, emotionless face staring straight ahead. Thick red water drips from his hands, splashing into the basin below, as if blood itself is pouring from the blade. My pulse skips.

Aster smirks, eating up my every reaction. "Creepy enough for you?"

I gulp. "I think I just unlocked a new fear… can we turn around?" I say sarcastically, but deep down, I mean it.

She chuckles, completely unbothered. "There's no way to escape now."

As we pull up to the valet, I spot a sea of luxury cars stretched across the massive lot. Rolls-Royces, Lambos, Aston Martins… each one probably worth more than my entire existence.

Aster looks just as stunned. "Damn. I swear, I had no idea it was going to be this packed."

I let out a nervous laugh. "A small celebrity party, huh?"

She shrugs and casually tosses her keys to the valet. He's dressed in a sleek black tux, his face hidden behind a glowing, neon orange mask. Two giant X's cover his eyes, and a sinister grin stretches across the lower half.

"This place is going to be the death of me." I tighten my grip on Aster's arm as if she's my lifeline. We climb the grand steps and slip through the towering vintage doors, straight into my own personal hell.

The air inside explodes with sound and color. Ghostly strobe lights pulse, casting shifting shadows across the towering walls. Overhead, a grand chandelier glows with a kaleidoscope of colors. Men in tailored costumes – Armani, Dior, Gucci, maybe even Versace. The smooth bastards sip whiskey with practiced ease, their eyes tracking every woman who passes like predators waiting to pounce.

The women drip in diamonds and lace, their corsets cinched tight, waists sculpted to perfection. Expensive perfumes hang heavy in the air, sweet, luring, and seductive, each scent oozing pheromones that pull in anyone close enough to breathe them in.

Aster locks onto a Jack Sparrow look-alike across the room. "Damn. That man is delicious."

I roll my eyes. "We need drinks before you start dry-humping Johnny Depp."

She smirks, dragging me toward the U-shaped bar. The setup is pure luxury. Antique gold barstools line a sleek white marble countertop, gleaming under chandeliers that flicker like candlelight. Above, cobwebs and glittering spiders drape from the crystal fixtures.

It's giving Dracula with a trust fund. Whoever owns this place definitely bought it with Mommy and Daddy's money.

Aster grins at the bartender. "Two of your finest shots."

The woman wears a fitted black turtleneck and a sleek, matching skirt; her sheer tights catch the light as she moves. The same mask the other men wore covers her face, except hers glows neon pink. Without a word, she pours two shots into crystal glasses. I grab mine and throw it back. The burn hits instantly.

Aster's eyes widen. "Damn, girl. That was hot."

I grin and down the next two without hesitation. A wave of exhilaration surges through me, my social anxiety numbed by vodka. The alcohol floods my veins, and suddenly, I don't care anymore. I grab Aster's hand. "Come on! Let's dance!"

We push through the crowd, bodies pressing close, sweat slicking skin. The bass pulses through my veins, the room spinning in a haze of neon lights, fog, and heat. I run my hands up my body, fingertips grazing the curve of my waist before gliding to my throat. My movements are slow. Teasing. Lost in the rhythm. A light sheen of sweat clings to my skin. It should feel dirty… but in this environment? It feels downright sexy. I'm not just dancing… I'm coming undone, and for once, I don't want to stop it.

And then a firm presence presses against my back. Hard. Unyielding. Dominant. An unfamiliar thrill creeps up my spine. The space between us is nonexistent. His body fits perfectly against mine, and the thin fabric of my costume does little to conceal the fact that…
Oh.

My breath catches. His arousal is pressed against me, heavy and unmistakable.

A dark spark ignites low in my stomach, the kind of ecstasy that's both dangerous and alluring. I glance over my shoulder, and…

Dark blue eyes. Sharp jaw. A wicked smirk. *Oh God, calm down. It's just a man. A hot, hard, Batman-shaped man. …Yeah, I'm screwed.*

My pulse stutters. He's watching me like he's already marked his territory upon me. A lazy smirk tugs at the corner of his mouth, confidence radiating from him. I swallow hard, heat crawling up my neck.

"Uh… hi, and you are?" I manage, my voice is weaker than I want it to be.

The smirk deepens. "Isn't it obvious?" His voice drops into a low, gravelly whisper, one that sends heat straight to my core.

"I am Batman."

My lip's part, an involuntary laugh slipping out. "Is that supposed to be an impression of Bruce Wayne?"

I don't know if it's the liquor buzzing through my system or his sheer presence that has me lightheaded, but something about him disarms me. **I really haven't had much experience with relationships… or men in general.**

He lifts a hand, trailing a single fingertip along my bare arm, sending goosebumps across my skin.

Oh God, it feels good to be touched.

"It was supposed to be… Did you like it?" His smile melting away my nerves.

I nod, completely breathless, like I just ran a mile. I should step away. But I don't. His touch is electric, leaving a scorching path.

"Want to dance, sexy Rapunzel?"

I nod again before I can stop myself. His strong hands find my hips, molding to them like they belong there. I press closer, my chest brushing against his firm, solid frame. He's at least six feet tall, and with my height at 5'7 in these heels, he's getting a perfect view of my cleavage.

Or, at least, I hope he is.

His dark blue ocean eyes flicker down.

Mission accomplished.

A side smirk tugs at his lips, his fingers tightening just slightly against my costume fabric. People swirl around us, bodies moving in time with the music. Couples grind against each other, lost in their own worlds.

His hands guide my movements, leading me through the seductive rhythm, his grip firm, possessive, and dominant. And I feel it again. The press of him. Thick. Hard. Unapologetic. He knows I feel it… knows that I know, but he doesn't pull away, doesn't shift. We stay locked in place, eyes locked, breath tangled, my clit throbbing for attention.

What the hell is happening… to me?

I squeeze my thighs together, trying to smother the ache. "So, Batman…" My voice comes out winded, laced with something dangerously close to need. "Who are you under the mask?"

His smirk deepens, but he doesn't answer.

I narrow my eyes. "So, do I know you? Are you famous? I mean, this is a celebrity party."

His gaze locks onto mine, amusement flickering behind those welcoming eyes. Then, he does something that nearly short-circuits my brain.

He leans in. Closer.

And closer.

So close… his breath ghosts along my jawline, down my neck.

My stomach tightens. My pulse quickens. *Yep, it's the alcohol or the fact that I haven't had sex once and need it... like BAD.*

He doesn't touch me, but honestly, he doesn't have to. The alcohol has me needy and ready for this man. "If I tell you..." His lips brush just close enough to tease the shell of my ear. "Will you go on a date with me?"

The world tilts. For a second, I forget how to respond, to form sentences. Everything inside me screams yes. But before I can answer...

My body goes cold. Numb. The lump in my throat is so big I can't swallow. A sharp vibration buzzes against my wrist, coming from my smart watch. My heart rate. I glance down at my watch.

125 BPM.

138 BPM.

152 BPM.

No, please not right now. I'm finally having fun...

But fate doesn't care. And sadly, I can't control the panic attack any more than I can control the weather.

My chest tightens. I can't speak. My head becomes foggy like I'm about to pass out. My hands shake. The excitement was too much. Too fast.

Who would ever want to be with someone like me, who has this crippling anxiety? I'm broken... a mess. No wonder I'm alone. I need to get out of here. I need to escape... Now.

I jerk away from him. "Uh... excuse me, I need the ladies' room," I blurt, slipping from his grasp before I can talk myself out of it. I push through the crowd, my vision swimming, my breath shallow.

Aster is too busy swapping spit with Jack Sparrow to notice my disappearance. I don't stop moving until I reach a grand staircase in the center of the entrance.

I don't know if I'm allowed up here. But honestly, I don't care. I need air. I need a moment to breathe.

I take the stairs two at a time, like I can outrun it. But anxiety always finds me. Hallway after hallway of locked doors with fingerprint access. I keep going.

At this point, I will take an attic entrance… Anything.

At the end of the corridor, a single door stands ajar. I grip the handle, my breath still uneven, and push it open. Relief washes over me.

Finally.

I step inside and close the door behind me, my heart still hammering in my chest. I press my palm over it.

Slowly, the rhythm of my heart starts to calm, and I take a deep breath, trying to compose myself. Then, I lift my head to take in the room.

My insides twist. My lip's part, but not a sound comes out. The sight before me is something that will be etched in my mind forever.

What. The. Actual. Fuck.

CHAPTER THREE
LILA

My watch buzzes. A sharp vibration against my wrist, reminding me that my heart is racing. But this isn't panic fueling my adrenaline. It's something else. Something forbidden. Something unknown.

"Streets" by Doja Cat pulses through the speakers, thickening the tension in the air and cloaking the sound of my entrance. I linger just beyond the doorway, concealed by the corner's shadow, unnoticed.

Unlike the rest of the museum-like mansion, this bedroom oozes dark sexual desire but feels emotionally cold. Nothing about it suggests intimacy, only indulgence. It's bathed in shadows, where elegance and darkness blend into something dangerously beautiful.

A towering black upholstered headboard dominates the space, its luxurious bedding a siren's call, luring anyone reckless enough to sink into its embrace. On the nightstand, a crystal vase overflows with fresh, full, and almost too vivid red roses, which stand out against the moody palette.

Above the bed, a skylight allows a sliver of moonlight and stars to seep in, casting silver streaks across the silk sheets. Velvet curtains cascade in dramatic waves behind the bed, framing the space like a stage because that's what this feels like.

A private performance. And maybe, for this moment… it is. This is a room built for pure seduction. A hideaway from reality.

And at the center of it all, a brunette bombshell, dressed in a slutty maid costume, kneels before a masculine silhouette. Her black-and-white lace mini skirt barely conceals the curve of her ass, and her dark brown curls bounce with each movement. I freeze.

What is she doing?

Is she okay?

Oh no… what is he doing to her?

I step closer, the shadows shifting, revealing the scene with sharper clarity. His head tilts back, eyes closed, mouth slightly parted, his expression dripping with pleasure. He is dressed as the Phantom from *The Phantom of the Opera*. But his mask isn't the usual plain white; it's custom, extravagant, black, adorned with intricate gold roses. It hides both eyes, most of his nose, and half his mouth, but leaves just enough to reveal the faintest curve of a dimple on the left.

Rich bastard. It's probably real gold.

The mask conceals most of his face, deepening the mystery… but my eyes drift lower. Helplessly hungry. Hungry for more.

His white dress shirt hangs open, framing a bare chest that glistens with sweat under the flickering candlelight. His black vest is pulled back, like it's been shoved aside, ready for what's to come next.

The tie around his neck loosened as if someone had tried to rip it off but gave up halfway. But it's the ink that stops me cold. A tattoo sprawls across his chest… bold, dark, commanding. I can't make out the design.

The lighting is too low. Too shadowed. But I see enough to know it's not small. Not subtle. Thick lines curve over muscle, disappearing beneath his shirt like secrets hiding in plain sight. There's something emotional about it.

Grief?

Sadness?

Pain?

My eyes narrow, trying to piece it together, desperate for just a little more light. But the shadows are greedy, and the sweat sliding down his chest only blurs the lines more. Still, I can't look away.

It moves with him as he shifts. My breath catches. Whatever the tattoo is… it means something. I can feel it.

His leather-gloved hand flexes at his side while the other grips the back of the brunette's head, guiding her each and every controlled movement. My gaze drops, and my eyes widen.

His black dress pants are resting at his ankles.

Damn, no underwear?

The realization slams into me, sending heat racing up my spine.

Shit… She's giving him head… just my luck.

Lila, this is wrong. You need to get the hell out of here.

But I don't move. My chest rises and falls in perfect rhythm with her movements. My legs are frozen, my shocked eyes lock onto the scene unfolding in front of me. Every part of me knows I should turn away. I should leave. But the wetness pooling between my legs says otherwise.

No, no, no. This isn't happening… not here, not now.

My tongue flicks out to wet my lips as I bite down on the corner of my mouth, heat rushing through me. I've never done that before. But God, I can't stop imagining what it would feel like to do it to him.

My gaze trails along the sharp line of his jaw, the stubble only enhancing every perfect angle. My pulse quickens as I take in his veined arms and the way his neck muscles flex with every stroke she gives him. And the way his muscles tense beneath the sheen of sweat?

It steals my breath.

A surge of need flares within me as I watch his body respond to her, but my body is responding to him. His tall, dominating presence fills the room, swallowing the space, smothering me like he's my personal sauna. His dark, slicked-back hair gleams under the moonlight, and my entire body ignites with want. Then he lets out a low, throaty moan. Deep and raw as his head falls back. And I feel it… everywhere.

He's intoxicating.

Everything about this moment feels surreal. Dreamlike. Drawn into the seductive rhythm, I lose myself. My fingers move before I can think, tracing the softness of my lips, then dragging lower down my neck, over my breast, teasing along my curves before grazing my thighs.

What kind of person does this make me? Watching a stranger like this, letting myself be consumed by a need I can't even understand. But my body doesn't care about right or wrong.

It only wants him. Is this how far I've fallen? Deep down, is this really who I am?

The heat between my legs pulses, demanding attention. My fingertips skim the delicate ruffles of my skirt, dipping beneath the lace of my thong. Aster had insisted I wear something sexy tonight. "Just in case you get lucky," she'd teased.

I'll have to thank her later.

I caress the thin material, then slowly shift the thong aside as I slip my fingers in. The teasing stroke against my clit sends a shiver through me, my body betraying every ounce of common sense I have left. I don't even realize I'm moving, thighs parting slightly, the pressure of my hand against the lace growing bolder.

Across the room, the Phantom throws his head back again, his Adam's apple bobbing as another groan rumbles from his throat.

I surrender to seduction, my body no longer my own as I close my eyes and listen to his panting. My fingers slide lower, dipping into my wetness, exploring, teasing,
Until a soft-whispered moan slips past my lips.

I freeze.

The music thrums through the speakers, but time stops in my mind. The brunette is still lost in her task, unaware of my intrusion…

But he isn't.

My gaze drifts up. And then I see them… Piercing through the shadows. Ice blue eyes locked onto mine. *Watching me.*

CHAPTER FOUR
LILA

The heat in his gaze locks me in place, pinning me like prey beneath a predator's stare. There's something about those eyes - the color, crystal blue, and their devastatingly unforgettable quality.

They feel familiar… *but where have I seen them before?*

My breath stutters. My heart hammers so violently, I swear he can hear it. My eyes widen in panic, the heat of humiliation crashing over me like a wave I can't outrun. He sees it. He knows. I slap a hand to my forehead, desperate to hide the shame already written across my face.

What the hell is wrong with me?

And yet… his expression isn't what I expect. The phantom isn't shocked. Not angry. Not mortified. Not disgusted… If anything, he looks entertained.

Should I apologize? And ruin their moment… probably not the best idea, Lila.

His eyes trail over me, taking in every inch as if he were savoring the view. It's an unspoken, seductive dare pulsing between us. He doesn't stop. Doesn't pull away from her. Doesn't act embarrassed, unlike me. His stare lingers like a touch, slow and ravenous.

"That's it… suck my cock like the filthy slut you are." He growls, the rough demand slicing through the dark.

I can't help but gasp at the vulgar words spilling from his mouth, but something about them, something in the way he says it, makes me like it. She's the one on her knees, doing the work, yet his eyes never leave mine, like every sinful word is meant for me.

My thighs clench. A spark ignites low in my belly, and the need building between my legs swells into something so intense, it feels almost dangerous. His jaw flexes, the sharp cut of it tightening as he thrusts deeper into her mouth. His leather-gloved hand fists her hair, controlling her every movement. But he's not looking at her. He's looking at me.

Why do I feel like I'm the one being touched, when it's her body under his hands?
This is wrong. So fucking wrong.

My fingers twitch against my thigh, but I refuse to move. I refuse to be that girl.

The one who comes undone from just a look. But that damn tattoo has a grip on me, a chokehold I can't shake.

Ugh… I want to kiss his neck, to trail my lips down to the sweat-glazed curve of his chest where the ink lies. And then my body betrays me.

My fingers brush over the swell of my breasts, lingering like they're waiting for permission. But none comes. Still, they keep moving. Lower. Slower. Bolder. Each breath quickens as they trace over my ribs, skimming the curve of my waist, until they find the edge of my thong. I hesitate, just for a second.

Then I slip beneath the lace, my fingertips trembling as they make contact.

A slow, aching circle. Then another. Desperate. Relentless. I bite back a moan. No. *You can't, Lila*... But I can't stop.

I match him. Stroke for stroke. His chest rises and falls in sync with mine, the strain etched into every tense muscle, every slow, deliberate breath.

"Fuck, that's it. I like when you do that," he grits out, his grip tightening as his hips snap forward, thrusting harder, rougher. A strangled gasp catches in my throat. I can't see him fully, but from the way she reacts, from the wet, obscene sounds filling the room, I can picture exactly how big he must be. And the thought sends a fresh wave of heat pulsing between my legs.

I bet he'd fit perfectly inside me.

His ice-blue gaze pierces straight through me, darkening and sharpening as he drinks me in, like he's memorizing every detail. The way my other hand skims along my body. The way my breathing shudders with every needy movement.

I shouldn't want this. But I do. More than I've ever wanted anything.

The coil inside me tightens, pleasure building to an unbearable peak. A soft moan escapes my lips before I can stop it, swallowed by the music thudding through the speakers. But he hears.

Oh, he hears. And he likes it.

His smirk curves slow and wicked, his body tensing as his pace quickens. His moan turns into a growl, low and sultry, as he finally lets go and comes undone right in front of me. And I fall with him.

My release slams into me so hard my knees nearly buckle, my thighs trembling as wetness pools between them. My body pulses, every nerve alight, the pleasure so overwhelming I forget how to breathe.

For a few blissful seconds, I float in the aftershock, caught in a haze of euphoria and disbelief. Then, reality slaps me in the face.

What the hell did I just do?

My stomach lurches, mortification crashing over me like a tidal wave. I yank my hand out of my underwear, frantically smoothing my dress, my braid, anything to feel human again.

From across the room, he laughs.

Not loudly. Not mockingly. But a small, knowing chuckle slips past his lips, as if he's just won some silent game I didn't even know we were playing.

My jaw drops.

Did he… laugh at me? Excuse me?

Embarrassment flares up my neck. My eyes narrow. My nostrils flare.

Oh hell no.

I roll my eyes, spin on my heel, and bolt. My heart is pounding, my face on fire, and I can still feel his eyes on me like he branded me with that smirk.

What was I thinking? Watching him and touching myself. God, I'm never showing my face again. I need air. I need out. Now. And the fact we did that… without even touching? No. Nope. Absolutely not. What the hell is wrong with me? He laughed. He actually laughed.
What an absolute dick. But…

God, the way he looked at me. Like he owned every inch of me with those gem-like eyes. No. Stop it. He's a stranger. A cocky masked stranger who gets off on being watched. This isn't me. I don't do this. I'm leaving. I'm forgetting this ever happened, I have to… right?

The endless hallway of doors blur as I rush out, my pulse still erratic, my body still humming from what just happened. But even as I leave, one thought lingers in my mind, stubborn and taunting.

I liked it, and so did he. And honestly… I have a feeling this isn't over.

Practically fleeing through the hallway and down the stairs, I miss the last step and crash onto the cold marble floor.

Maybe I'm losing it. Maybe that didn't just happen, and the severe panic attack made me hallucinate the whole thing. That can happen... right?

Pain jolts through my tailbone as I sit mulling over my thoughts. "Ow! Son of a …." I hiss, wincing. I groan, pressing my palms against the slick surface, my dignity officially in shambles. "This night cannot get any worse," I mutter under my breath as I stand on my shaky legs.

"Lila, where have you been? I've been looking for you everywhere! They're about to start the game out back!"

"Hell no. Nope. I'm done for tonight. I'm calling an Uber." I huff, still trying to steady myself.

"But if you're the first one to make it through, the owner will grant you any wish!" Aster says, helping me to my feet. "Come on, you have to do it with me! It'll be so much fun!"

I roll my eyes as she grabs my hand, pulling me toward the back doors. "What is he, a genie?"

Aster grins. "More like a devil. No one's ever actually won."

Beyond the pool, in a sprawling field, rises a fifty-acre hedge maze. It's massive and threatening, like something ripped straight out of the *Goblet of Fire*. Above the entrance, a large white sign drips with blood-red paint, each letter oozing like fresh wounds:

HAUNTED MAZE
ENTER IF YOU DARE.

I grab two shots from a passing waitress and throw them back immediately, hoping the burn will wash away the lingering heat still pulsing through my body. *News flash... It doesn't.*

"Well, I called it. I've already died from embarrassment tonight, and this is my funeral," I mutter.

Aster cackles, looping her arm through mine. "Funeral or not, you're still going in." The cold night air bites at my skin as we step outside.

Thank goodness. I need to cool off after what just happened.

The towering hedges loom ahead, fog spilling from the ground, curling around my ankles, and in the distance, flickering lanterns barely cut through the shadows.
A shiver crawls down my spine. It's not from the chill but something else. It's part thrill, part fear. Part of the night itself. But then… A feeling. The same one I had upstairs. That unsettling pull, like I'm not alone. Like those ice blue eyes are slicing through the dark, finding me again.

My breath catches, each heartbeat pounds harder than the last. I don't know where he is, or who he is, but I can feel him. His presence coils around me like smoke, thick, smothering, impossible to ignore. I take a step toward the maze, and something inside me awakens. He's here. Somewhere in the dark. Watching. Waiting. Hunting.

Or maybe he was never here. And perhaps the monster I felt breathing down my neck… was me. And I'm just compartmentalizing my anxiety.

CHAPTER FIVE
LILA

The haunted maze looms ahead, daring me to step inside. I tug up my corset, making sure my B-cup chest is snug and secure, just in case this game involves running. Kicking off my heels, I leave them by a pool chair with the other guests' shoes, sling my skillet-shaped purse across my chest, and straighten my posture.

I'm ready for anything or anyone who might try something funny. The shots I downed earlier swirl in my head, fueling my bolder, more competitive side. A warm buzz hums through my veins, syncing with the pulsing energy of the crowd.

You don't get to be valedictorian by being passive. You fight for it. And I'm fighting for this wish… I need it… she needs it.

I whip my braid over my shoulder and grab Aster's arm, a spark of determination igniting in my chest. "Let's do this damn thing!"

Aster looks me up and down with a slow smirk. "Mmm. I like this, Lila," she says, holding up her hand.

I grin and slap my palm against hers in a loud, satisfying high five. *That's going to hurt tomorrow.*

The crowd surges with anticipation at the maze's entrance. To the right, a stage stands, complete with a DJ table and oversized speakers. Just then, a familiar figure in a Batman costume steps onto the stage and approaches the microphone.

No way… Is this his party? His house?

His face remains masked, but I'd recognize those deep blue eyes anywhere. Even with the shifting dance floor lights, their intensity is unmistakable, sending butterflies fluttering through my stomach.

Aster nudges my arm, catching the look on my face. "Wait… is that the guy you were dancing with earlier? *Damn, that body is hot,*" Aster says, raising a perfectly arched brow.

I nod, biting back a sheepish smile. "Yeah… but I totally screwed it up. I, um… had a panic attack."

Her eyes widen. "Oh no, Lila! Are you okay? What did you say?"

"I told him I had to go to the ladies' room," I groan. "Then I dipped and never went back."

Aster gasps dramatically. "Girl… no! You can't ghost him mid-seduction!"

"Trust me, I didn't want to," I mutter, the heat rising in my cheeks. "But I made a total fool of myself. The panic attacks… they control me. I don't control them."

"Umm, so go back over there and play it cool," Aster urges. "Say something came up, but now you're back. Act confident. Seriously, who could resist you, especially looking like a five-course meal?"

"Aster, I literally can't. I'm too nervous. I'm going to… shit myself." I cross my legs, trying to soothe the storm swirling in my stomach. A giggle slips out of both of us, cutting the tension just enough.

Until I glance at the stage, and there he is. His gaze already locked on mine.
The air thickens, too heavy to swallow. Then… a slow, sexy smirk curves across his mouth. And it doesn't end there, he winks.

Oh, the things I bet that mouth could do to me.

Heat slams into my core.

I glance around, expecting some other girl to wave or wink back. But no. His gaze is fixed only on me.

Wait, was that for me?

Aster grips my arm, squealing. "Shut up! Did sexy-ass Batman just wink at you?"

"Play it cool! He's still watching!" I yank her down before she can start jumping like an overexcited fangirl.

On stage, his lips tilt into a full-on smile, perfect teeth and all, letting everyone see just how dangerously charming he is. He knows exactly what he's doing. The kind of smile that's all confidence, all game.

Then, in a deep, gravelly voice, he begins: "Ladies and gentlemen, welcome to the haunted maze, where your worst nightmares come to life."

His voice, God, that voice is hypnotizing. "The master of this mansion will grant the winner of this obstacle course one favor. However, nothing comes without a price..." My stomach clenches.

A favor? I thought it was a wish... with no strings attached. Damn it, Aster. Always roping me into some crazy shit. But I need this. This favor could change everything for my mom... for us.

He pauses, letting the suspense simmer in the silence, the entire crowd holding its breath, waiting for what comes next.

"The objective is simple: reach the exit first. But beware, this is no ordinary maze. Creatures lurk in the shadows, waiting to capture you. If they manage to zip-tie your wrist, you'll be escorted out, and you're eliminated. However, if you can escape the zip-tie, you're free to keep going."

Fan-freaking-tastic. A fight-or-flight game? Perfect setup for a panic attack, which will land me straight in the emergency room. Great.

I fidget with my fingers as he continues, my buzz beginning to fade, fear creeping in. "When the fireworks sound, we will have our winner." His smirk grows sharper. "Good luck…
And may the odds be ever in your favor." He says it in a perfect Capital accent, imitating Effie Trinket from *The Hunger Games*. I snort.

Of course, he would.

Then, without another word, Batman disappears into the maze.

Wait. Is he playing too? Or will he be one of the monsters waiting to grab me in the darkness? Hmm. I sure hope so. The thought hits me like a freight train. A sudden warmth pulses between my legs. I imagine his hard body against mine again, this time pinning me down, zip-tying me in the shadows, whispering in my ear. *Shit. I really need to get laid.*

The crowd surges forward, and I take a deep breath, steadying myself. Aster and I grip each other's arms, refusing to let go. *We started this together, and we're damn sure finishing it together.*

The entrance looms ahead, the sign draped in blood-red roses and sharp, tangled thorns, woven so seamlessly into the hedges it looks like the maze grew around it. We step through… into a world of shadows and towering green shrubbery. All around us, people scatter in every direction, swallowed by the dark.

"Which way do you think we should go?" I ask, glancing around the four-way stop.
Aster doesn't answer. She's deep in thought, a furrow forming between her brows. I nudge her lightly. "Alright, spill it. What's on your mind?"

She hesitates. "Do you… Do you think I'm a bad person?"

I frown, gripping my skillet-shaped purse a little tighter. "What? No! Why would you even ask that? Did someone say that to you? Because I will use these weapons."

Aster lets out a soft laugh, shaking her head. "No, no one said anything… but good to know you've got my back."

"Then what's up? Why did you ask that?"

She sighs, her voice dropping. "Because if I won, I'd probably wish for something stupid. A car, maybe. A trip. Something materialistic. But you, you're different. I can see you wishing for something selfless. Like donating to charity or buying your parents a new house. I just… wish I could be more like you sometimes."

A lump forms in my throat. *She wants to be like me? I've always wanted to be like* her.

"Oh, Aster… I've always wanted to be more like you," I whisper, reaching for her hand. "You're unapologetically yourself. You walk through life with this fierce confidence, like nothing can shake you. I think that's why we're so perfect for each other… we balance each other out."

I see tears forming in her eyes as she begins to fan her face. "Ugh, don't make me cry. I'm going to mess up my makeup," she mutters, voice shaky. "But I love you. I really needed to hear that. Sometimes I look stronger than I actually am." She looks down at the ground as we curve deeper into the maze.

I squeeze her hand gently. "I know, and you know I'm always your person. You don't have to carry everything alone."

She nods, a soft smile tugging at her lips. "Yeah… I know." Then she glances over at me. "Now spill. What are you going to use the wish for if you win?"

I don't want to say it. If I say it, it becomes real.

I look away, blinking fast, trying to shove the words back down. But they claw their way up my throat, relentless and aching. Finally, I whisper, "I haven't told you yet because I was waiting for the right moment… but my mom had a mammogram a few months ago." Aster's face falls. "They found a lump."

The words hang between us, heavy and suffocating. She swallows hard. "Lila…" I force a breath, but it shudders on the way out.

"They did a biopsy. It's stage four." My voice cracks, and suddenly, I can't stop. "They say she has a little time left... A year, Aster. That's all they're giving her."

Aster stops walking. Her hands tremble before she grips my arm like an anchor, grounding me. "Why didn't you tell me?"

I let out a broken laugh. "Because if I say it out loud, it becomes real… and I can't let it be real." My heart cracks as the truth finally settles in. "Aster, I can't lose her. I can't sit here and watch my dad fall apart a little more every day, pretending to be strong when I know he cries himself to sleep every night. I can't even look at her without seeing the ticking clock strapped to her chest, counting down the last moments of her life."

My voice wavers. "She goes back to the doctor next week to talk about treatment options, but she doesn't want chemo. She doesn't want surgery. She just wants to live this next year as herself." My throat tightens, pain clawing its way through me. "And I can't—I just can't—" Tears slip down my cheek before I can stop them.

Aster reaches up and wipes them away, so gently, like I'm the fragile girl she met back at the academy. "You're my sister, Lila." Her voice is fierce, unwavering. "And my parents? They love you like their own daughter. If you don't win this, I'll talk to them. We'll figure something out. Perhaps we can arrange for her to be transferred to a high-end Oncology hospital. There must be something we can do."

I nod, grasping onto her every word, clinging to this tiny flicker of hope. Aster pulls me into a hug, holding me like she's trying to piece me back together. Like she can feel the weight of my grief pressing in on me, threatening to crush me, and she's trying to hold me up.

I squeeze my eyes shut, pressing my forehead into her shoulder, letting myself breathe, just for a second. Just to stay upright. We sniffle and wipe our faces, both of us pretending we're strong enough to keep going.

Aster forces a determined smile, her eyes still glassy. "Alright," she says, "let's win this thing for your mom!"

Then suddenly, the roar of a chainsaw rips through the night, followed by a blood-curdling scream. We freeze, still wiping tears from our faces. My stomach knots, my pulse hammering against my ribs. "Ummm, this is fake… right?" I attempt to laugh, but it comes out thin and breathless.

"It better be. If not, I'm prepared." Aster unzips her purse and whips out a taser, swinging it in the air like she's auditioning for an action movie.

I take a quick step back. "Damn, Aster, watch it! With the kind of luck I'm having tonight, you'll accidentally take me out before the maze does."

She rolls her eyes as we continue to make our way to the finish line. "Okay, but seriously, what happened earlier? When you ran down the stairs like a bat out of hell?"

I stiffen. "Uhhh… well, I walked in on—" The words die in my throat. We round a corner, and at the end of the narrow path stands a figure straight out of a horror movie.

Tall. Cloaked in black. Still as death, just waiting for his next victim.

The long, pointed beak of his plague doctor mask tilts slightly, those cold, black lenses locked onto us. The tattered edges of his heavy robes shift in the breeze, but he doesn't move. Just waits, patient and calculating, like he already knows how this ends. In one gloved hand, he grips a long wooden staff, his fingers curled tightly around it. In the other, an old lantern flickers with an eerie green glow, casting a sickly light that illuminates the leather straps across his chest and the hand-stitched seams of his gloves. A silent executioner.

I swallow hard, my throat dry as sandpaper. This isn't just a costume. It's a nightmare that has come to life… And he's standing directly in the path we chose.

Aster lets out a shaky breath. "Nope. Nope, nope, nope. RUN!" she shrieks. I don't hesitate. I grab her arm and bolt, my bare feet pounding against the damp ground, my lungs burning as we take a sharp turn, then another. The maze twists and shifts, the hedges seeming to close in around us. The wind howls through the leaves, carrying whispers that I swear are voices.

"Is he chasing us?" I gasp, barely able to get the words out.

Aster steals a glance over her shoulder. "No… I don't see him. Maybe he—" A bloodcurdling scream cuts through the night. We skid to a stop. My pulse riots, thundering in my ears.

"That was the first victim," I whisper, barely able to breathe.

Beside me, Aster exhales a shaky breath. "Looks like the game just started."

Then…

At first, it's faint. Barely audible over the pounding of my heart. But then I hear it again. Footsteps. Slow. Deliberate. One after the other, crunching against the ground with a terrifying calm. They're close. Too close. Getting closer.

"Oh, fuck no. I did not sign up for this," Aster hisses, clutching her purse like it's a weapon. "You know I'm chicken shit when it comes to scary stuff." She barely takes a step back before it happens. A shadow surges from the dark, its form broad and its movement swift.
Black-gloved hands clamp around her waist, yanking her backward with terrifying force.

"Lila!" she chokes out, her gasp sharp and strangled as her body jerks in panic. She thrashes, kicks, and claws to get free, but he's too strong. Too silent. Too intentional.

"Aster!" I scream, reaching for her. But it's too late. The figure twists her around and pins her arms, dragging her deeper into the maze. She fights, cursing up a storm, but the zip tie around her wrists is already tightening.

"Go, Lila! Win this for your mom!" she shouts, thrashing wildly against him. Then, mid-struggle, she grits out, "Sir, I can tell you've done this before… and you clearly picked the right victim."

I can't help it… I laugh and roll my eyes, even now. Classic Aster.

I hesitate, my feet rooted in place. That's when I see them. The gloves. Black. Leather. Tight against strong hands that just took her. Goosebumps coat my skin…

Is it him? The Phantom? Why didn't he take me?

Aster thrashes on the ground, kicking at his shins, but his grip doesn't budge. He hauls her up with terrifying ease and slings her over his shoulder like she weighs nothing.

Aster's going to love being manhandled by this guy… assuming we live to laugh about it.

His head tilts. Observing me. Like he's ready to chase me. Expecting me to run. Waiting for fear to kick in but… The way my body reacts is absolutely sickening.

Why… Why am I turned on?

A pulse ignites deep inside me, heat coiling low in my stomach.

Lila. You can't want this… Not now. Not ever.

I shake my head, legs stumbling into motion. To run. To escape this craving, I don't understand. *Go. Just go.*

I take off into the maze, my breath coming in shallow gasps. My heart is a caged animal, thrashing to escape. But something is wrong. I should be terrified. Instead… I feel something else.

A need. A thrill. Like I want him to chase me. Like I want to be caught.

A chilling laugh echoes from somewhere ahead, laced with wicked amusement. I freeze. My watch vibrates against my wrist, my heart rate spiking, but not from fear. No, this is something entirely different. I force myself to move, pushing deeper into the twisting passages of the maze. Then, another sound. Leaves rustling. Footsteps. Not behind me. Ahead.

CRUNCH.

CRUNCH.

CRUNCH.

Then… Silence. My breath stalls in my throat. I know someone is there. I turn slowly, my body thrumming with the knowledge that I'm not alone. I come face-to-face with a grotesque carnival clown mask. The twisted red grin stretched wide in a deranged, frozen expression. Bloodshot eyes bore into mine, hollow and crazed, like something ripped straight from a horror movie.

A gloved finger, smooth black leather, traces the curve of my lips. My breath hitches.

"What's a lost little princess doing all alone in the dark?" His voice is distorted, warped by a voice modulator, making it impossible to recognize. Deep. Mechanical. Predatory. "Did someone break you out of your tower?"

He stands over me, unmoving. Watching. Waiting for me to react. To run. To tremble. The panic rises. My pulse pounds. My body screams at me to move. But I don't. *Why the hell does this feel good? Is it because this could be Batman? Could it be the Phantom? There's no way it could still be the alcohol… can it?*

A slow, terrifying realization coils around my spine, sinking its claws deep. *Is this who I am? Is this what I crave?*

A chill rushes through me, colder than the night air, more unsettling than the creatures lurking in the shadows. Because for the first time, I don't know whether I want to run…

Or be caught.

CHAPTER SIX
LILA

The clown inches closer, inhaling deeply near my neck, as if savoring my scent. My pulse pounds erratically. This isn't passion, it's pure, bone-chilling terror. "Who knew you'd smell so good, considering you live in that shithole on the West Side?" He sneers, his voice dripping with twisted amusement behind the grotesque mask.

What the hell? How does he know that?

My heart hammers as I twist sharply, but he's quicker. With a vicious tug at my braid, he yanks me down against the hard ground. *Well, that's going to leave a bruise.*

I thrash wildly, kicking and screaming, but he's heavier than he looks. His strong hands slam me face-first into the damp, cold earth. The chill seeps through my costume, raising icy goosebumps across my skin.

He fumbles with a zip tie, trying to pin my wrists behind my back as he flips me onto my side. *Well, he's definitely* not *kinky.*

Adrenaline surges, hot and wild. I spit venom. "Is this some sick joke, you piece of shit? Who the fuck are you?" He straddles me, trying to gain control… But I twist hard, my legs snapping up. My knee cracking against his head.

Lila: 1. Dickhead: 0.

He grunts, but I don't wait. I scramble upright, chest heaving, rage and fear tangling like live wires in my veins. Then he laughs, low and dark, distorted through the modulator. "Oh, Lila. I know you very well… and you know me."

My blood turns cold. *He knows my name.* He circles me like a wolf, ready to devour his prey. *So, he really* does *know me*… And that realization scrapes across my skin like frostbite.

Gripping my purse tighter, I slip my fingers inside, unzipping the "frying pan purse" Aster rigged with hidden weapons. I stay low, undetected in the shadows, and feel for the essentials, pepper spray… pocketknife… Then… bingo.

The purple taser.

I wrap my fingers around it, steadying my breath, waiting for his next move.

"Oh, I'm hurt," he drawls, placing a hand over his chest. "You don't recognize me?" A chilling laugh slithers through the modulator. "Princess?" That single word freezes me deep within my bones. "Or should I say… phony princess?" He rips the tiara from my head and hurls it into the abyss.

My spirit cracks under the weight of his words, splintering like glass. I keep the hard-core facade intact, pretending I'm untouched. But truth is… it hurts more than I want to admit. It feels like high school all over again, like I'm the punchline to some cruel joke. A toy.
His toy.

I know I'm not a princess. I'm far from it. The house I grew up in should've been condemned, and we lived off peas, cornbread, and milk to make ends meet. So, to be dressed like this… yeah, I get why he called me a phony princess. Because that's all I am. A fake. And honestly? I can't even argue with him. He circles closer, voice laced with pure hatred.

"You mooch off Aster and her parents, pretending you matter, when everyone knows you're just a desperate charity case. Her family only puts up with you so they can write off the money they throw at your family for a tax break." My pulse quickens. My mind spins, flashing through faces, exes, creeps, admirers. Every one of them a breadcrumb trail leading to this moment.

"Think harder, princess," he sneers, voice dripping with mockery. "You've turned me down again and again. And I don't like being told no. So I dug a little deeper, tried to figure out what makes you tick… but instead, I found out who you really are." He leans in. "Trash." The light bulb flickers on.

Ohhh… I've turned him down multiple times. That prick. Now I know exactly who you are. And you just picked the wrong girl to piss off.

I back away, but he mirrors every step, a sinister dance of rage. Steadying myself, I grip the taser, a dangerous smile flickering on my lips. "Hello… Clint." Without hesitation, I jam the taser into his ribs and press the button. Sparks burst forth, and he convulses violently before collapsing with a satisfying thud.

"LILA, YOU DUMB BITCH!" Clint roars, twitching in agony.

In one swift move, I straddle him and rip off his hideous mask, revealing a smug, entitled face beneath. Disgust flares inside me. "Aw, you're just as ugly as I remembered." He glares but is still groaning in agony from the most powerful moment of my life.

I feel… in control for the first time in my life. Well, except for that moment with the Phantom. But I'm still not convinced that was even real.

He's rambling now, desperate to say anything that'll save him… *Newsflash, asshole… nothing's going to save you.*

I tilt his chin up to me and sneer, "That's for touching my lips and neck without permission, you creep." Slowly, I bring the taser toward his crotch. His eyes widened with pure panic. *Just what I want…*

"Lila—wait!" he begs.

My voice drops dangerously low. "And this is for calling me a dumb bitch."

"NO! PLEASE! I WANT KIDS!" His voice shatters, filled with terror.

My laughter is cold and mocking. "You? Offspring? The world doesn't deserve that punishment."

Sweat beads on his forehead. "LILA, PLEASE! I—I CAN HELP YOU!" His desperation turns to sobs. "D-Do you want a job? I can get you into Heartford Cypher International! I'm good friends with the CEO and his right-hand man!"

Heartford.

The company I've dreamed of joining for years. The one that once changed my life… and just might save it again.

I lift the taser slightly, my fingers tightening around the grip. Skepticism churns in my gut. I'm not sure if I can trust him. "Don't screw with me, Clint. I've got more weapons in here than patience."

"I swear!" he exclaims, frantically grabbing his phone. "Look, I'll email the CEO now! I'll recommend you and put in a good word… just spare my balls! Please! I'm adding you to the email right now!"

My phone vibrates once, then twice. I glance down. *It's real.*

A message sent directly to the owner… the one I've tried to contact hundreds of times.

An opportunity to become the rescue I once needed. This company didn't just change my life; they gave it back to me. Months of struggle, countless rejected applications, and all it took was threatening a sociopath's manhood?

A satisfied smirk curves my lips as I step back. "See? Was that so hard?"

Clint exhales shakily. "Shit, I really thought you'd do it."

"Trust me, I was tempted, but watching you squirm like a pathetic little man-child was way more satisfying."

He looks around anxiously. "You won't tell anyone, right? I don't need this shit on social media."

I twirl the taser playfully. "Pull that again, and your balls will trend worldwide."

He chuckles nervously. "Whoa, seriously, chill."

I narrow my eyes. "Wait, why are you even working here in the maze tonight?"

He shrugs. "Didn't Aster tell you? The party's hosted by Beck Heartford, the CEO… the one I just emailed. It's a fundraiser for cancer research and those who can't afford treatment."

Beck Heartford. And the fundraiser is for cancer? Is this fate, or am I being punked right now?

My throat tightens.

The city's most sought-after bachelor and the brilliant mind behind the company dismantling sex trafficking networks around the world. Who wouldn't *want a man like that? I'm here to help my mom… but maybe, just maybe, I can help myself too by letting him do whatever he wants to me.*

Lila. Snap out of it, you horny slut.

I ask, voice casual despite the excitement coursing through my body, "Oh, is he… umm, here tonight?"

Clint perks up. "Yeah! I'm surprised you haven't seen him. He's dressed as Batman. He's like a damn golden retriever. Super nice guy."

My heart pounds violently as I remember the man who once asked me out. His masculine body pressed against mine on the dance floor, his hard desires unmistakable.

Oh God, I'm so stupid. I literally asked if he was a celebrity. He probably thinks I'm an idiot. And running off mid-panic attack? Yeah, that didn't help. I know I don't deserve someone like Beck... But that doesn't mean I don't want him. And tonight? I'm barely holding it together beneath all the chaos.

My knees weaken as excitement and confusion collide, a storm pulsing beneath my skin. An unexpected heat pools between my thighs as I think of him.

He is here tonight, and I watched him enter the maze... Is he hunting? Possibly hunting me? And what about the Phantom...

My head spins.

Could they be the same person? Is the Phantom just another adrenaline-fueled illusion? Is he a figment of my imagination?

"Lila?" Clint's voice cuts through the haze. I nod sharply and turn toward the darkness of the maze.

An exhilarating realization coils within me. Tonight just became complicated, and I might enjoy every twisted second of it. I take off in a sprint, heart pounding, blood thrumming. It's not the light guiding me... It's the heat pooling low in my belly. The thrill. The want. The chase.

"Where are you going?" Clint yells behind me.

I don't look back. "To hunt."

CHAPTER SEVEN
LILA

I sprint through the maze, my breath coming in ragged gasps, my mind racing faster than my feet.

The real question is, who am I looking for? And why? Batman? The Phantom? ...Both? No. Stop it, Lila. This isn't healthy. Stop thinking with your vagina. I'm looking for Beck... Yeah, Beck. For my mom. He can help her. He knows people. He's powerful. That's the reason I'm trying to find him. Nothing more. End of story.

But then there's the other issue. The one I'm fighting internally.

Why does my pulse spike at the thought of the Phantom? I mean, is he even real... or just the shadow of my own darkness, finally seeping out? And why the hell does my body still hum from the way he looked at me, like he saw straight through my clothes and straight into my soul?

Something about him keeps pulling me back into that moment. It wasn't like anything I've ever experienced... No, he wasn't like anyone I've ever experienced. I don't know him. But I want to.

I want to go back to that room. To take him in slowly. To memorize every detail so I'll never forget. Oh God, and to be the one to touch him. To feel him unravel beneath my hands. I want him to want me. To be pulled to me the way I'm pulled to him. But honestly, it was probably all a fever dream, just panic mixed with being horny. Maybe my body craved something so badly, it made him up.

I shake my head, forcing the thoughts away.

Focus. He's not real.

When I win this, I can ask Beck Heartford for anything. He could get my mom into a world-renowned treatment center. The kind of facility and medications that only celebrities and billionaires have access to. There's always medicine for people like them. Just not for people like us… We're the ones no one notices. The ones no one cares if they live another day. Just another passing face on the street. But Beck… he can pull strings. Maybe even fund an experimental trial, if one exists. He could be the reason she gets another day. *And I need her to have another day.*

But at what price? What will I have to do? Damn it! He sounds like Rumpelstiltskin.

You never really know his intentions when he makes a deal. Is it to help… or to gain something for himself? Will I owe him more than I bargained for if I win this little maze game?
Or am I just trapping myself in a maze he built… one I'll never escape?

A twisting battle of logic and desire rages in my head as I push forward, my bare feet pounding against the damp ground. Then… A break in the maze. I skid to a stop at a four-way split.

In the center, a stone table glistens under the moonlight, lined with rows of crystal shot glasses and handcrafted cocktails. *Oh, thank God… This should shut my brain up.* A gift for the competitors, no doubt. Or a trap. Either way, I don't hesitate.

I grab the first shot.
This is for my mom. Nothing more. And Beck? He's probably just another rich asshole
who doesn't give a damn.

Adrenaline pulses through me. I throw it back as if it's water. Then another. And another. The smooth liquor burns down my throat, drowning out the noise in my head. Heat stirs low in my belly, humming through my limbs. A feeling that is new and unfamiliar. Thoughts blur. Logic slips.

Shit. That's good. And definitely expensive.

I turn to walk away and throw a wink at the drinks, feeling the buzz. My body thrums with a reckless energy. I glance up at the sky, searching for constellations to guide me, but all I feel is the intoxicating rush of power.

I'm going to win this. My mom will grow old with my dad. She will watch me walk down the aisle to the love of my life. She will watch my kids grow up. She can't give up… I can't give up. We have never had much, but we have always had each other, and I wouldn't trade it for all riches in the world. My parents are my lifeline. She's not going to die. I won't let her.

Determination burns through me like a second shot of liquor. I take off again, weaving through the maze… left, right, right, right, left.

Aster got caught. But I'm not Aster. I'm Lila fucking Anderson, and I won't let that happen to me.

Then… A sound. A howl ripping through the dead of night, stretching long and guttural, bouncing off the hedge walls. I freeze mid-step, my breath hitching. Silence. Then, another howl. Closer this time.

A slow, creeping chill slithers up my spine. I swallow hard. "Hmmm… maybe Jacob from *Twilight* will come find me," I whisper to myself. The words barely left my lips before a giggle bubbles up, slipping past my mouth before I can stop it.

Shit.

The shots are really working now. I feel powerful. Reckless. Invincible. A little too invincible. I need to move. That stupid giggle of mine probably echoed through the maze just like the howl, giving me away. I take another step, but the moment I round the next corner, I stop cold.

At the end of the narrow corridor, a figure stands, still and unmoving. His mask glows bright red in the shadows. A flickering light in the distance catches him just right, casting his silhouette. Tall. Towering. Unmistakably male.

Oh.

I can't make out the details; he's too far away. Too wrapped in shadows. But I feel him. He isn't just viewing me. He's absorbing me. His presence is suffocating. Electric. An intensity that coils around my lungs, stealing my breath.

Maybe he hasn't seen me yet… Or perhaps I want him to.

My stomach tightens, my thighs pressing together on instinct. A twisted thought slithers through my mind.

What if I let him catch me? What if I let him tie me up?

We stare at each other. Neither of us moves. The space between us feels too tight, too tense, too charged. And then the unexpected happens… A hauntingly beautiful hum drifts through the air. Pulling me in like a siren's call, wrapping around my senses and dragging me into a trance. I forget how to breathe. How to move. How to think.

Who knew a hum could be so sexy? God help me… I think I can fix him. I can fix the man behind the mask if he really is a monster.

The sound is close. Low. Smooth. Like he's done it a thousand times. Each note flows from him effortlessly, like muscle memory… like sorrow turned into a melody. The tune is tragic. Elegant. Familiar.

I have heard it before, but what is it?

My stomach twists, and my heart races with anticipation.

Why is he humming? Is this a game? Or is it his warning? A declaration... that I've already lost.

He takes one step forward, just one, and it shatters my spiraling thoughts. I snap. My body reacts before my brain can catch up. I bolt. Sharp right. Left. Another left. The hedge walls blur around me, twisting and shifting, every turn a gamble.

Maybe I will crash into his big, strong, dominant arms... Lila, this is not the time.

The chill in the air cuts through my skin like a thousand tiny knives. The ruffled glittering skirt clings to me, my bare feet freezing and damp from the dewy ground. My braid whips behind me as I push forward, lungs burning, throat raw.

Still, I swear I hear footsteps. Heavy. Slow. Taunting. He isn't running. He doesn't need to. He's letting me run... letting the exhaustion catch up to my aching body. I turn another sharp corner and meet a dead end.
Gasping, I slam myself into the shadows, pressing into the maze wall, chest heaving.

"Dammit!" I mutter under my breath, shivering violently. "Why don't they put this kind of thing on the invitation? I would've worn more clothes!"

Oh no... I said that out loud. My mouth is always getting me in trouble.

Stillness within the maze is eerie. But a shift in the air catches my breath. Everything stills. My senses sharpen. I feel it... the same suffocating presence I just experienced. Somewhere beyond the twisting hedges, he lurks. Patiently waiting for my next move. And I swear, whoever he is, he's nearby.

My body betrays me, responding with an unexpected heat that blooms beneath my skin. Blood courses through me like molten lava, and I realize, to my embarrassment, that my expensive lingerie that Aster made me wear is completely soaked.

Bracing my hands against the shrubbery, I lean forward, letting my head drop as I try to gather myself. My mind clouded with filthy thoughts of this masked man devouring me in ways I've never experienced before.

What is wrong with you? Are you sick?

A tingling sensation spreads across my upper arms, trailing up to the back of my neck and back down again.

Shit! I really am sick! Am I having a stroke? Why am I tingly?

I lift my head slowly, and in my peripheral vision, I catch a faint red glow… waiting for me to acknowledge his presence.

"You should never turn your back when you're being hunted." His voice is smooth and dark, wrapping around me like smoke, thick and impossible to ignore. Each word is laced with something deadly, and yet… I can't help but feel drawn in. It's like his scent is a pheromone crafted to torture me. Sandalwood. Spearmint. The hint of leather.

I feel the soft pressure of his gloved fingers on my arm, tracing a slow, deliberate line from my shoulder to the back of my neck. My breath catches, my mind screaming at me to pull away, but my body stays frozen, gripped by something more profound than fear. This touch, though unfamiliar, feels almost like destiny.

Slowly turning around, I come face-to-face with the masked figure. The same LED mask that the other employees wore. It has two glowing red X's over the eyes and a sinister, gleaming grin. He's dressed in a sleek, all-black suit that sharpens the outline of his muscular physique, accentuated by the eerie red glow. Unlike the others, he has added a black turtleneck beneath, making him look both expensive and warm.

My mind is screaming at me to run… to get as far away from this sick bastard as possible. But my body? My body betrays me, rooted in place, soaking up every sensation. Like it craves this twisted game of cat-and-mouse. Like I want to be toyed with… or maybe, just maybe, I want to toy with him.

He leans in closer, the glow of his mask illuminating my face. His fingers press firmer against the back of my neck, anchoring me in place. "I'll give you a head start, princess," he whispers, his voice silk and sin.

Then he vanishes. No footsteps. No rustle. Just gone, like he was swallowed by the night as if he was never there.

I stumble back, chest heaving, heart slamming against my ribs, my watch buzzing as it alerts me that my heart is racing. But is this fear, or is it the excitement of playing his game? The silence is deafening. And somewhere, deep within the maze… he hums again. Slower this time. Louder. Like a promise. He didn't just let me go. He wants me to run because the hunt… his game… has only just begun.

CHAPTER EIGHT
LILA

How? How did I even end up here, sprinting through a maze that feels endless? This whole night, it's like an out-of-body experience.

Will it ever end? Can I really pull this off? One thing I do know is that he will not beat me.

I creep through the godforsaken maze, my body trembling uncontrollably, every muscle screaming with exhaustion. I'm barely able to stand, but pure determination keeps me moving.

I'm close. I have to be.

I've made sure to only move forward. Never once looking back. But then, something catches my eye. In the far-left corner of the haunting hedges, a soft glow breaks through the darkness, faint, but unmistakable.

Could it be the finish line?

The hedges stretch fifteen feet high, impossible to see beyond. Anxiety coils in my chest. Strangely, I haven't run into any creatures. No chainsaws. No screams. Nothing. Just silence.

Unnerving silence. The kind that settles right before a tornado hits.

Is he the tornado? Waiting to flip my world upside down.

This feels like a trap. Or maybe that's the point. Reverse psychology. Make it look like a trap, so I hesitate, freeze, and turn back when, in reality, the finish line is right through there.

Nice try, stranger in a mask. I see you. And I'm not playing by your rules.

The glow becomes more distinct. My heart lurches, bracing for the fireworks to go off.

I did it, Mom. You're going to be okay. We're going to be okay.

Following the swirling path, I make a sharp left, and then I see it. A winding path lit by flickering lanterns leading to a stone gazebo, carved so beautifully it could've been torn from the pages of *Pride and Prejudice*. It feels sacred, like a hidden portal to another world, tucked away behind the maze walls, far from everything else.

A place to breathe. A place to hide. A place to think.

Moonlight spills over the dome, vines of blooming lilacs cascading down the pillars. Stars shimmer above like scattered diamonds as clouds drift lazily past. And for a moment, it feels like pure magic. The most peaceful place I've ever seen. A place I could hide away from everything, wrapped in a blanket, lost in books and dreams. But nothing. No voices. No celebration.

Just the wind howling through the hedges and the chattering of my own teeth. The warmth from the liquor has vanished. My skin is covered in goosebumps from the cold. My nose is running, my feet ache, and my legs tremble beneath me.

I'm so close… and yet still so far away.

I glance around. No sign of him either, just me and the serene sight before me. I move toward the gazebo. Each slow step feels like a risk, but I can't help it. The architecture pulls me in. I take a deep breath, the scent of lilacs filling my lungs. My fingers brush against the stone pillar to steady myself as I climb the steps.

"HOW THE FUCK DID YOU GET IN HERE?" The modulated voice slices through the silence from behind.

Oh God.

I freeze. I turn, heart slamming in my chest.
He's there. The red mask. And he's not just angry, he's
outraged.

His chest rises and falls with sharp, furious breaths,
rage radiating off him like heat. " I-I'm sorry," I stammer. "I
thought this was the exit…" He doesn't move. Just studying
my every breath like he can hear the fear in it, and he's
probably enjoying every second of it. But little does he know,
seeing him standing in front of me, chest heaving and body
rigid with wrath, doesn't terrify me. It thrills me. I want to
know why he's angry. I want to know who he is behind the
mask. Is he a monster? Hell, I don't even know what his face
looks like, and still, he's irresistible. Tempting. Dominant in
all the ways that make my pulse race.

A wicked excitement coils low in my belly, pulsing
straight to my clit. And suddenly, something takes over.
Something dark. Hot. Sensual. And because of it, I want to
taste the fury on his skin. Devour every inch of this
maddening, masked man. I want to toy with him the same
way he's toyed with me.

"It's beautiful," I murmur, eyes still locked on the
gazebo, voice low and soft with wonder. I lean against the
pillar, letting my fingers brush over a lilac bloom before
lifting it to my nose. "I didn't mean to trespass," I say, voice
smooth but honest. "I know what it's like to have a place that
feels private. Untouchable. Yours." My gaze flicks toward the
shadows, searching for him. "I wasn't trying to take it from
you," I add, a little slower this time, breath catching on the
edges of the words. "I just wanted to feel it… even for a
second."

He doesn't respond.
I wish I could hear his thoughts…
"I'll go," I add softly.

The tension in the air is suffocating. And yet… electric. Something pulses between us, and I feel it everywhere. My body reacts like it knows him.

This has to be Beck… I mean, it's his house and his maze, so this must be his special place.

I go to take a step down… And then he grabs me from the shadows. "No. Don't you dare fucking leave!"

His voice lowers, the modulator dropping it to something dark and sinful. The sound alone could make me cum. "I found you," he whispers in my ear, his tone low, possessive, controlled.

It feels like time stops. The glow of neon red pulses between us like a heartbeat, and for a moment, we're the only two people in the world. We stand beneath the gazebo, lilac blooms swirling around us in the wind. Moonlight cuts through the dark, finally revealing him. And I truly see him. Not just the mask. Not just a shadow cloaked in designer Armani. But something more.

He isn't just a danger lurking in the maze. He's the pull in my chest. The ache I can't explain. A need that wraps around my ribs and refuses to let go. It's not just lust. It's something deeper. Something scarier. Like this man behind the mask was meant to be mine. As if my soul had recognized him long before my mind could process it. Like I was meant to find him here in the dark, and now that I have, I never want to let go.

It feels like that moment with the Phantom. The heat. The intensity. The way my soul felt stripped bare. But this is different. That moment was a fantasy, blurred by my imagination. This is real. I can touch him. Feel the heat radiating off his body. The wind tugging at his black hood. The tension coiled in every muscle. The gravity that pulls us closer.

He backs me against one of the pillars, his body not quite touching mine, but close enough to burn. His gloved hand hovers near my waist, the other brushing my neck, and the air in my lungs is nonexistent.

Every inch of me is trembling, aching for something I don't understand. I should push him away. Run. Scream. But instead, I tilt my chin up and breathe him in. Because beneath the mask, beneath the fury, I feel it. He doesn't want me gone. He wants me right here. And God help me… I don't want to leave.

My purse hits the ground as I gasp, startled, but the sound is swallowed by the tension. He yanks me down the stairs by the arm, spinning me until I'm pressed against the wall, chest to chest, breath to breath. His grip tightens. It isn't just fury holding me in place. It's want.

"You're not going anywhere," he growls, his voice a rasp of raw need. "Not until I say you can." His masked face is inches from mine. I can't see his eyes, but I feel them dragging over every inch of me. I should push him away. But instead, I lean into his anger.

"What the hell is your problem?" I demand, my voice shaking but not from fear.

"You went through a gate marked DO NOT ENTER."

"What are you talking about? There was no gate," I snap, breathless. The air between us crackles with tension, his energy wrapping around me, coiling tighter with every second.

He steps even closer. I feel his gaze drop to my lips. Warmth pours off him like a fever. "Right," he growls. "So, the gate just walked off on its own?" His breathing is sharp, uneven. But it's not just anger. It's something more profound. Raw. Feral. Like he's fighting the need to touch me. Claim me. And I'm standing here, trembling… wanting him to lose that fight.

Is he unraveling for me the same way I'm unraveling for him?

My own anger flares. "Don't accuse me of lying. I hate that!" I move closer to him like a challenge, letting my alter ego rise to the surface. My lip catches between my teeth, slow and intentional. He sees it.

Good.

"Don't… don't do that," he says, completely breathless.

"Do what?" I tease, fingers brushing across his shoulder like he did to me. "You found your princess… so now what? Going to punish me? Zip-tie me?" I say, voice dipped in melted sugar.

His mask tilts, but no words come. He's still, as if he's processing what's happening. Frozen, like he's afraid to touch me.

That's new.

"How did you find me so fast?"

"You can't hide from me, princess." His voice lowers, his glove lifts, brushing my jawline. "Not when you shine so brightly in the dark."

Damn him.

Goosebumps ripple down my spine. He knows exactly what he is doing to me. I swallow hard, my heart pounding in my ears. Something shifts. A strange new confidence rises in me. One I have never felt before. Maybe it is the adrenaline. Maybe it is the lingering liquor. Or maybe it is just him.

I flutter my lashes at the glowing mask and bite my bottom lip as I trail a finger down his torso, slow and deliberate, drifting lower. He pulls away before I can keep going and pushes me up against the gazebo. Then his leather glove clamps over my mouth. "What did I say, princess?

Don't fucking do that again." He pauses, the silence stretching like he's weighing his next move. His voice dips lower, almost amused. "Hmm... maybe I should punish you."

Oh shit... Please.

His gaze drops to my chest, watching it rise and fall with each rapid breath. I'm no longer cold; my entire body is burning, hot and ready for him. "Wait a second... are you turned on?" he teases, and I can almost hear the smirk in his voice. I pause, unsure of what to say.

Do I admit it?

I seize his hand from my mouth, boldness surging through me as I push him back against the maze wall. My lips hover near the cold surface of his mask, breath brushing between us.
My palms rest on his chest, right over his heart, which is pounding like it's trying to break free.

"I think you're the one who's turned on," I whisper, letting a smirk tug at my lips. "Your heart's practically trying to escape your chest." My hands trail lower, slowly, deliberately, until they reach the length straining against his expensive pants. My hand molds to his bulge as I firmly feel the hard erection, and I audibly gasp...

He's huge. What am I doing? This isn't me.

"It looks like I was right... Beck."

He doesn't correct me. Doesn't say yes. Doesn't say no. Just stares. He doesn't respond when I say his name, but something shifts in the air. Something unreadable.

Did I say the wrong thing? Is this not Beck?

His fist clenches at his side, knuckles straining beneath his glove. Then slowly, he exhales and releases. His fingers wrap around mine, the one still resting against his hard cock. He guides my hand upward, controlled and slow, until the back of it meets the cool surface of his mask, as if he is kissing it.

"My turn to treat you like a princess," he murmurs. But something has shifted. The words land cold. Icy. There's no warmth in them. No softness in his tone. His body tells me more than his voice ever could. The way he stands, the tension in his jaw. It feels like I've just declared war without meaning to… and he's already planning his revenge. But maybe I'm overthinking it. Maybe he was just shocked that I figured out who he was before he had the chance to tell me.

He peels off a glove, each movement dripping with seduction. His bare hand, rough yet devastatingly perfect, grazes down the front of my corset. He pauses just before our skin connects, like he's emotionally struggling with himself.

"Why did you stop?" I whisper, breathless. Then his hand returns. And the second our skin touches, it's like I've won the maze. Fireworks explode inside me, sparking through every nerve, igniting something wild and electric that I didn't know I was capable of feeling.

I want this man. Not just the mask man but whoever he is underneath it.

His fingers slip beneath the layers of my skirt, trailing fire until they find the delicate lace of my panties. I should pull away. But I don't.

I don't want this man to stop touching me… Like ever.

His fingers slip beneath the fabric and into my wetness. "Damn, you're soaked," he murmurs, his voice smooth as silk, even through the modulator.

A soft moan escapes me. "Mmmmhmm." I tilt my head back, lips parted as heat floods my veins. His fingers move with maddening control, like he's learning my body with a purpose. When he finds my clit, he doesn't rush. He moves in slow circles, coaxing, teasing, dragging me closer to the edge with every stroke.

"Oh God," I breathe, unable to hold it in.

No one has ever touched me like this. No one has ever made me feel like this. And the fact that it's him makes it even more perfect.

"Shit, princess," he groans, like he's barely holding himself together. But I don't close my eyes. I want to see him. Memorize every detail. His touch. His breath. The rhythm of his hand.
The way the moonlight hits his shoulders. I want to burn it all into my memory. He moves his finger from my clit to my entrance, slipping inside of me with deliberate pressure. My knees nearly giving out as I almost collapse in his arms.

I steady myself against him, clutching his suit like a lifeline. If I could see his eyes, I know they'd be locked on mine, reading every pathetic part of me. Knowing damn well, I'm practically a virgin.

He goes still. His voice lowers, unreadable. "Are you a virgin...?" I cut him off.

"No," I whisper, breathless and aching. It's not a lie. I have been with someone. One time. But it never felt like this. "So please… just touch me."

A low chuckle rumbles from behind the mask. "Well… since you said please," I swear he's smiling under there.

His finger begins to move, slow and deep. In. Out. Rhythmically. He slips in another one. My head tips back against the gazebo as I surrender to the pleasure. I don't just feel him inside me… I feel seen in a way I never have before.

"Yes, right there. Don't stop," I groan, my voice thick with need. But suddenly, he pulls his fingers out of me and grabs my wrist with a firm grip, spinning me around and pressing me against the gazebo.

What the hell?

One gloved hand pins me in place, the other, wrapping around my wrist, holding me still. His plastic lips hover near my ear, his voice low and commanding. "Looks like I've caught you, Princess… and now you're mine."

With a smooth shift, he gathers both of my wrists in one hand and pins them above my head.

He really waited until I was about to finish… What an asshole!

With his other hand, he grabs something out of his pocket.

Shit. Shit. Shit. The zip ties.

The restraints around my wrists bite into my skin as he locks my arms behind my back. "You're a dick!" I snap. "You could've at least let me finish first!" He doesn't speak. "Are you mad that I figured out who you are?"

Still nothing. But his hands tighten the restraint again. *I guess that's a yes.* "Ouch—that hurts!" I hiss. But then... a strange sensation pulses through me. It hurts. And yet... I like it.

God, what is wrong with me? I should be furious. I should spit in his face and run away. But instead, I'm still craving more of him. He's an asshole. A mystery. A menace. And somehow, I still want him.

He doesn't respond. He's already leading me out of the gazebo with firm, silent steps. His grip on my arm is tight but not cruel. My heart is hammering. He leads us through the maze with unsettling confidence, like he knows every twist and turn by heart. For a moment, guilt tugs at me. What I'm about to do isn't exactly fair… But I don't care.

This is for my mom.

"So… are you mad at me, or is this your version of foreplay?" I ask, my voice edged with frustration. He says nothing. Just keeps walking. Silence stretches between us, thick and heavy.

He probably feels pretty damn good right now, like he's already won this twisted game.
But what he doesn't know is that I came prepared.

When I ran into Clint right after the taser incident, I made a decision. If I got caught, I knew I wouldn't win with strength alone. I'm smaller than these men. So I'd have to outsmart them. Use what Aster stashed in my purse to my advantage, and it might be my only shot. And now… It's time to play my cards. But I have to play this perfectly. It's dark. I can't see shit. But I hear voices. Music. We're close. I feel it.

The bass rumbles through the ground, shaking up through my muddy, bare feet. His grip clamps tighter around my left arm as he walks beside me. But luckily, my right hand is free, perfectly positioned to reach the pocketknife hooked to my thong.

God bless Aster. I've never used a weapon in my life. But right now? This little knife might be my only chance at freedom. My mom's freedom from cancer.

I look up at him, and he slowly turns his head to look at me as we freeze. His body language is off, like he has something on his mind.

He's distracted… I must do it now.

"Beck, please forgive me for what I am about to do… and please hire me after all of this." A thrill buzzes through my veins, sparking adrenaline, and I yank my arm from his grip and take off in a sprint, weaving through twisting paths. A few guests rush past me, their laughter and urgency mirroring my own as we all weave through the maze, desperate to find the exit. The fireworks haven't gone off yet, so the game isn't over.

The knife is still tucked in place. With trembling fingers, I pull it free from my waistband and angle the blade. One quick slice, and the plastic around my wrists gives way with a sharp snap. I'm free. No hesitation, I take off in a full sprint, and I don't dare look back.

My breath is gone, and I'm pretty sure I have frostbite, but after two rights and one left, a sign greets me above the exit. Blood red letters read:

YOU MADE IT, BUT AT WHAT COST?

Umm. Okay? That's freaking creepy.

I step through, and fireworks crack overhead. The song "Every Breath You Take" by The Police echoes through the night, but it's not the regular tempo. It drags, low and haunting, like a funeral march. The Red Mask is nowhere to be seen, but God, I feel him. In the stillness. In the shadows. In every ragged breath I can't seem to catch.

He isn't gone. He is waiting. Watching and letting the game unfold. And somehow I know the real hunt hasn't even begun.

CHAPTER NINE
LILA

It's been thirty-six hours since my world flipped upside down, and I still don't know if I'm happy about it… or furious. I don't like change. I crave consistency. But something inside me has awakened, and she's clawing her way out, ripping through every wall I've built to keep her contained.

"Are you ready, Princess?" His voice is low and commanding, laced with heat. Those ice blue eyes pierce through the black and gold rose mask, locking on mine like he already owns every inch of me. "Ready for your punishment?"

My breath catches, and my heart stutters. I nod, speechless, entirely at his mercy. The belt comes undone in one smooth motion, the sharp sound slicing through the air like a warning. Then he flips me onto my stomach, swift and controlled, molding my body to the bed like it belongs there.

"You disobeyed me," he growls. "And for that… you'll have to pay." His palm drags over the curve of my ass, firm and slow, sending a shiver down my spine. Every nerve sparks under his touch. "I told you not to bite your lip." His voice dips, a dark whisper against my ear. "And you did it anyway." His bare hand lands with a sharp slap that makes me gasp.

I glance over my shoulder, eyes meeting his, and sink my teeth into my bottom lip, slow, teasing, defiant. "Oh? Like this?"

He grins, all dangerous edges and perfect teeth. His jaw flexes, the stubble from his five o'clock shadow catching in the moon's glow spilling through the skylight, as if the stars themselves are bearing witness. Butterflies explode in my stomach, and slick heat pools between my thighs.

"You're asking for it," he chuckles low and primal. The belt hisses through his fist as he steps back, eyes burning into me.

"Hmmm. Maybe I am." The way he looks at me, dark, hungry, says everything. This punishment won't be gentle. And I'll beg for every second of it.

Yes. Please keep going… don't stop.

Then…

RING. RING. RING.

Wait.

No.

Shit, shit, shit.

I bolt upright, yanking off my sleep mask in horror. *I just had a wet dream. A filthy, deliciously detailed wet dream.*

And it was about him. The Phantom.

The one who laughed at me, after we basically eye-fucked across the room. God. What is wrong with me?

I groan, flopping back against my pillow, already hating myself for every second of it.

No. Absolutely not. Dreaming about him is off-limits. Completely. Hell! He probably wasn't even real!

My phone buzzes again. I grab it off the nightstand, trying to suppress the leftover heat still pulsing through my body. "Umm, hello?" I croak.

"Lila, what are you still doing in bed?" Aster's voice explodes through the speaker. She doesn't even give me time to respond before continuing, "You sound flustered… Wait— do you have a guy over?"

"Aster!" I gasp. "You know I would've texted you!"

"Well? Spill. What is it?"

I lower my voice, like someone might actually be eavesdropping from inside my empty apartment. "Ummm… I had a…" I mumble.

"You had what?"

I glance around, then yell, "Okay! I had a wet dream!"

"Oh. My. God," she squeals so loud I have to pull the phone away from my ear before she causes permanent damage.

"And the worst part?" I groan. "It was about the Phantom. The one I watched…"

"No way. Shut up. I knew you were a kinky bitch," she squeals again. "Did you get his number? Did you see him again after the party?"

I sigh, already disappointed in myself. "Nope. Honestly, it felt like an out-of-body experience. I had way too many shots..."

"If this Phantom of the Opera brought that side out of you and you masturbated to him getting off—"

"ASTER!"

"I mean… that's what you did, Lila. But honestly? I kind of hope he's real."

We both burst into laughter. "Well, when you put it like that, it sounds like I need therapy," I say between giggles, "and probably need to get laid."

"Oh my God, yes. Can you please pick out something or someone…yummy at the sex club this weekend?"

"Girl, what? Are you nuts? I've never even been to a place like that," I say, shaking my head. "But… I'll think about it."

"You better. But hey… ummm I didn't just call to harass you about your sex life. I wanted to check on you." Her tone softens. "You said your mom has her appointment today. How are you holding up?"

The laughter dies. My chest tightens. My voice catches. Reality slams into me like a thousand bricks pressing down on my lungs. Silence lingers as tears slip down my cheeks, one after another. She hears my sniffles. "I'm… trying to be strong. For Dad. For Mom. But I'm falling apart, Aster. I can't do this…"

There's a pause. She doesn't rush me; she lets me cry. Then I hear her sniffle too. Even though she's a badass… when it comes to me, she's a big baby. If I'm crying, she's crying. If I'm mad, then she's angry. And I wouldn't change it for the world… but she'd kill me if I ever told anyone.

"You can do this. Lila, you're the strongest person I know," she finally says, softly. "And I love you. Your family is my family. I'll be beside you every step of the way. Do you want me to come? I'll drop everything right now and head that way."

I wipe my face with my sleeve. "I think I'll be okay. But I'll let you know if I need you."

"I love you."

"Kisses," I whisper.

"Kisses, babe."

We hang up, and my throat knots, making it hard to swallow as dread creeps in. This is the appointment. The one that gives life or death its whole, brutal meaning. The one where my mom decides if she's going to fight… or surrender.

I sit up and take in my tiny, rundown studio apartment. It's not much, but it's mine. The hardwood floors are scuffed and splintery. The stove only works half the time, and I usually take the stairs because the elevator is always broken or stuck. I can't really afford anything else… not that I'd ever give up this view.

My flat is shaped like an "L," with soaring, exposed-beam ceilings that make it feel bigger than it is. One full wall is made entirely of floor-to-ceiling windows, offering a panoramic view of New York City.

I'm on the top floor. Seven stories up. In a building that probably should've been condemned twenty years ago… and could honestly collapse at any moment. But at night, the city glows. The skyline twinkles like a thousand tiny stars.

Seeing real stars in the city is rare here. So I settled for the next best thing. The floors creak, the walls are thin, and the radiator barely works, leaving my limbs practically frostbitten in the winter. And of course, there's a constant draft from the windows.

But it's beautiful. And it's mine. A place I can finally call home, and it's exactly what I need in this season of my life. My full-sized bed sits in the far corner, pressed against the glass. The best seat in the house.

I slide my pink fuzzy house shoes on and shuffle toward the kitchen, my stomach churning with nerves. I load the coffee machine with decaf and tap my fingers against the counter, waiting for the beep. My phone lights up. Still no notifications, no emails.

No call from Heartford.

No mysterious "wish granted" announcement.

Just… nothing.

Silence.

I groan and drag my hand through my tangled hair.

Even with Clint's recommendation, they still don't want me. What's wrong with me? Why am I never enough?

My mind drifts to the first day of boarding school. I was ten. In gym class, I finally worked up the courage to join the dodgeball game, hoping that just this once, I might make a friend. But the team captains refused to pick me. Even after everyone else was chosen, I was still standing there, alone, cheeks burning as my limbs grew heavy and tears began to fall while they laughed.

All I wanted was to join in on the fun. To not be invisible. To feel like I mattered.

But I didn't matter. I was a crumb on their designer shoes because my uniforms were secondhand. Because my dad was the janitor. Because my mom worked in the cafeteria. Because I really didn't belong in their world.

Is that why they haven't called me? Because I don't belong?

I remember walking home, the weight of my backpack dragging me down, feeling like my ten-year-old heart would never recover from that moment. I was humiliated. I convinced myself that the principal only allowed me to attend the prestigious school because they felt sorry for me. And maybe they did.

And maybe Heartford doesn't want me because they investigated my past. Perhaps they found out. Maybe they see me as baggage. A risk. Someone who could damage their reputation because of that night.

The night that changed everything. The one that started my panic attacks.

A lump rises in my throat. I can't swallow. My chest tightens, my heart pounds.

Breathe in for four. Hold out for four.

I press a hand to my chest, waiting for my smartwatch to vibrate in rhythm. The panic simmers, retreating just enough for me to think clearly. I walk over to the full-length mirror and take in my broken appearance.

Okay, Lila. You've got this.

Your mom needs you today. Your dad does, too. You don't have time to spiral out of control. Today, I wear a brave face. *The reflection staring back at me isn't perfect. Not polished. But it's strong enough to show up. And right now? That's enough.*

CHAPTER TEN
LILA

The bus dropped me off fifteen minutes ago, and I'm still frozen like a damn statue outside the skyscraper hospital. This could be the place where my mom either recovers or dies.

My heart sinks into the pit of my stomach, and my mouth goes bone dry.

Lila, move. They're probably waiting for you in the waiting room.

I stare at the sign above the automatic doors, reading it over and over, like it might suddenly say something different.

Memorial Kettling Cancer Center.

They need you. You can do this.

I try to lift my left foot, but it's like an anchor chained to my leg. I'm sinking. Fast. Screaming for help but drowning in silence. So, I do what I've always done. I cut the emotional chain. I flip the switch like I'm Elena Gilbert from *The Vampire Diaries*. I shut everything off. Numbness is safer.

I step into the lobby and instantly regret it. The place reeks of antiseptic, death, and slow goodbyes. The scent crawls over my skin, cold and smothering, sending shivers down my spine and dread straight to my stomach.

I think I'm going to be sick.

My coffee threatens to rise, but I force it down, same as the tears burning behind my eyes. The lobby is beautiful. Too beautiful for a place so cruel. The modern furniture could be in a home decor magazine, all clean lines and soft edges. But what catches my eye and twists my insides is the botanical garden planted at the center of the lobby. Sunlight pours through the floor-to-ceiling windows and gleams on the trees as life blooms in a place built for endings. *What a fucking paradox.* Grand fixtures hang high, and the glow keeps moving, brightening the craft tables, the café, and the little gift boutique.

Laughter echoes from the far side of the room. I glance over, completely appalled by the sight. Families are playing board games, finger-painting, and smiling as if this were some summer camp, not a place where people wait to hear if they're going to live or die.

How are they so happy? Is this what I'm supposed to look like when I put on a brave face? This is bullshit.

I cross my arms and glare around the room. Then I see them in the corner, near the elevators. Mom's hunched over, fidgeting with her fingers. Her dirty blonde, shoulder-length hair falls in messy waves around her pale face. Her eyes are rimmed red and shadowed beneath, like she hasn't slept or stopped crying in days.

Dad sits beside her, looking smaller than I've ever seen him. He's lost weight. His dark hair has always been a mix of salt and pepper, but now it appears entirely gray. He pulls her close and presses a kiss to her temple. His shoulders shake as a tear slips down his face. I freeze again.

I can't do this. I can't sit here and wait for her cancer to eat her from the inside out. Why hasn't my wish been granted yet? Why hasn't anyone called? After this appointment, I'm going to Heartford Cypher International to raise hell. I don't care if it sounds desperate. Beck will wish he had called the second he sees me. Freaking rich prick. They love to play heroes until it's time to pay up.

I suck in a deep breath and slowly cross the lobby, forcing each step forward. "Mom! Dad!" My voice cracks as I reach them. "I'm so sorry I'm late. I… I got caught waiting on the bus."

Mom lifts her head and tries to tame her hair with her fingers, like she's suddenly trying to look composed. Dad wipes his eyes, like the act alone could erase the pain etched into his face.

We're all wearing glass masks… seconds from shattering.

Mom reaches out and pulls me into a hug, wrapping me so tight I forget how to breathe. "Oh, honey, it's okay," she murmurs into my shoulder. "We were running behind, too, so I called. They pushed the appointment back thirty minutes." She brushes my hair from my face, offering a small smile that doesn't quite reach her eyes. "We'd better head upstairs so I can get checked in." I force a smile.

Grabbing both Mom and Dad's hands, we make our way to the elevator. I press the glowing up arrow. The silence between us is heavier than words. "How are you feeling?" I ask, my voice light, my eyes searching hers for something, anything, hopeful.

"I'm okay," she says gently. "Just a little tired today. But it'll get better."

We step into the elevator. Dad presses the button for the tenth floor, and something inside me snaps.

I jerk my hand away. "Oh, really? It'll get better?" I snap, louder than I intended. "How exactly? By sitting around doing nothing?"

"Lila—" Dad flinches. "She doesn't want the treatment," he says, voice low and calm. "We've been through this. She doesn't want it to change her."

"She doesn't want it to change her?" My voice breaks. "What does that even mean?"

Mom says nothing. Not because she's cold. Because she's hurting too. And somehow… that only makes it worse.

My anger falters and collapses into something softer. Something worse. It's not anger.

It's fear.

Tears fill my eyes, blurring the glowing floor numbers above the doors.

"You're just… giving up?" I whisper. "You're going to leave us? Without even trying?"

A breath shudders out of me. "Don't you… Don't you want to see Dad walk me down the aisle someday?" My voice cracks, and I can barely get the next part out. "Mom… I want to watch you… love my kids… the way you have loved me."

It hurts to say the words, like they're knives in my chest. "I don't know how to do this without you," I whisper. My voice cracks with every word. "I don't want to be brave." The sobs break free, choking me. "I just… I want my mom."

Ding.

The elevator doors slide open. I can't breathe. I don't wait for them. Tears blur my vision as I run through the hallway, searching for the bathroom like it's the only thing keeping me from drowning.

I burst into the bathroom, grip the sink with both hands, and lean over, sobbing so hard my body shakes. My tears hit the tile floor, one by one, like they're trying to echo how broken I am.

I look up.

Wow, I look terrible.

My hair is a mess, my eyes red and swollen, my cheeks blotchy like I held it together just long enough for someone to ask if I was okay.

Well… I guess skipping makeup was the right move.

I turn on the cold water and splash my face, again and again, until the sting fades and my chest stops burning. It helps.

Barely.

I stare at the girl in the mirror. Cracked. Pretending. Holding the mask tight enough to keep it from falling… but my arms are tired. I can't keep holding it much longer. Then my stomach lurches.

I slap a hand over my mouth and make it into a stall just in time. My world is falling apart, and I can't do anything to stop it. I feel helpless.

After throwing up my coffee, I lean against the cold wall, breathing slowly.

In for four seconds. Out for four seconds. In for four seconds. Out for four seconds.

I wipe my mouth, flush, and stare at myself in the mirror again. It's not a perfect reflection. But it's someone trying. Someone holding it together, just enough.

I dry my hands, take one more steady breath, tug at my clothes, and I step back into the waiting room. The low hum of voices surrounds me, families whispering, nurses tapping on keyboards, the distant buzz of machines.

Then…

"Alice Anderson."

My mom's name.

My watch vibrates on my wrist, warning me that my heart rate's too high. *Don't fall apart, Lila… not today.* But it's too late… the panic attack has already settled in, waiting to demolish me one second at a time. I look down at my watch.

118 BPM.

133 BPM.

148 BPM.

My breathing turns heavy. Cold tingles crawl from my hands up to my neck. I feel every pound in my chest, and it only fuels the panic.

Oh my God, I'm going to have a heart attack.

The knot in my throat chokes my words before they can even form. Mom walks to me and takes my hand. Her other hand brushes down my arm, her thumb resting over the watch like she can soothe it through sheer love.

Damn it. My heart.

I take a deep breath in through my nose as we walk together toward the nurse. She sees right through my glass mask.

The watch goes quiet, not because I steadied myself but because she did. My heart rate settles, and the grief returns. I should be the one comforting her. She is the one stepping into the unknown. And still she worries for me, holding my mask when I can no longer hold it.

This.

This is why I can't lose her. She is my comfort. My rock. My home. And I don't know who I'll be or what I'll become… if she's gone.

CHAPTER ELEVEN
LILA

The scent of lavender hangs in the air, soft and ghostly, rising from the sleek black diffuser on the windowsill. It's supposed to be calming… maybe for the patients. Maybe for the doctor himself. Maybe to mask the sting of reality as he delivers yet another slow-motion wrecking ball to someone's world.

He sits across from us, middle-aged and maddeningly composed. Crisp shirt. Clean-shaven. Eyes unreadable. He doesn't look like the kind of man who says, "You're dying." But that's exactly what he's about to do. And he's done it before. This is his normal. He wears the white coat of death as if it were just part of his uniform.

What a horrifying kind of normal.

"It's stage four triple-negative breast cancer," he says, as if reading a headline from the morning paper. The words fall like lead, heavy and suffocating. My throat closes and tears burn the rims of my eyes, ready to fall. I reach for Mom's hand and squeeze it tight. Her skin is thin and cold. We sit in stiff chairs facing the physician's desk, the room uninviting and bright. Everything feels clinical. Distant. Chilling.

"And… what does that mean?" My voice is barely above a whisper.

The doctor doesn't flinch. Doesn't blink. He types on his keyboard—click, click, click—and then rests his fingers on the desk, tapping.

Tap. Tap. Tap.

A steady, slow rhythm. Too steady. It mirrors the pulse pounding in my ears, only calmer. Like he's tapping out my heartbeat but on mute. My panic is screaming.

His fingers don't stop. He turns the monitor screen toward us.

"It's one of the most aggressive forms of breast cancer," he explains. "It spreads fast. It doesn't respond to traditional hormone or targeted therapies." We knew it was cancer, but this…

He gestures to the screen. A chart glows with tangled lines and highlighted cells. "Most treatments target hormone receptors. Think of them like locks. The medicine acts as a key." He looks at us. "But triple-negative breast cancer has no locks."

No locks.

No keys.

No cure.

My stomach drops. The room spins as my anxiety takes hold of me. I can't breathe. My voice shakes. "How long…?"

He glances at the chart again, then lowers his eyes to the paper in front of him. And for the first time, he actually looks sad. Human. "Eight months," he says softly. "The cancer has already metastasized. It's spread to her lymph nodes."

I thought I had a year with her, but now four months have been ripped away from me.

Mom's fingers curl tighter around mine. She's still here… for now. She looks down at her lap. Defeated. A single tear falls onto her jeans, leaving a dark splotch on the faded denim.

I inhale deeply, the lavender curling through my nose. It's sweet and floral, with a hint of earth and medicine, and I try to let it calm me before I shatter in front of her. The world tilts. I feel it. Slowing. Her mask has shattered into a thousand tiny pieces.

Eight months.

Eight months until Dad is left to sleep in a bed that's half-empty for the rest of his life.

Eight months until I can't call her to hear her voice or tell her I didn't eat ramen for dinner.

Eight months until I lose her.

I feel my heart folding in on itself, like paper crumbled up into a ball.

And Beck.

Damn him.

He made a promise. I won fair and square, and still, he ghosted me as if my mother's life meant nothing.

I grit my teeth.

If he's not at the company when I walk out of this room, I swear I will burn his damn house to the ground. I don't care about the job anymore. And I don't care if I ever get another one. Because honestly... what do I have left to lose?

Cancer's already taken it all.

I shift in my seat and wrap my arm around Mom, pulling her into me. Her fragile body crumbles against mine. Then the sobs come... low, shattering cries that don't even sound like her. I stroke her hair, whispering promises I'm not even sure I can keep.

"I'm here, Mama. I'm not going anywhere." She's always been my strength. Now it's my turn to be hers. Dad places a hand on my back, rubbing slow circles. His other hand trembles in his lap. He doesn't say a word. He's breaking too, but in silence. He is still holding onto his glass mask... barely.

The doctor clears his throat. "There are some options. A few experimental trials, new chemo combinations, and immunotherapy. But there are no guarantees."

Dad's voice cracks. "Alice doesn't want treatment. She said... she wants nature to take its course. No chemo. No pills. No side effects."

I turn to Mom, watching as she stares down at the floor, completely defeated. She still hasn't spoken. "Mom?" I whisper. "Is that really what you want?"

For a second, I think she won't answer. But then... her red-rimmed eyes rise to meet mine. She looks at the doctor. Her voice is barely audible. "What treatments are... available?"

Hope. It swells in my chest so fast it hurts. The doctor nods slowly. "There's a new trial we're running. A chemo drug designed to revert cancerous cells to healthy ones, in combination with a double mastectomy and follow-up radiation." She flinches, and I see the flicker of fear cross her face.

It's too much. Too big. Too expensive.

"And... how much does it cost?" she asks, already knowing the answer is too much for us to afford.

The doctor clicks through his file, eyebrows drawing together.

Then... "Well, it appears... It's already been paid for."

We all freeze.

Dad blinks. "Excuse me?"

"I'm looking at it right here," the doctor says, tilting the screen. "Payment processed this morning. The total amount: fifteen million dollars."

Fifteen. Million.

My jaw goes slack. I exchange a wide-eyed look with Dad.

"That… can't be right," Mom whispers. "We didn't pay that."

But I already know.

My heart stutters.

Beck Heartford. This must be him. This is the wish. The one he never called to confirm. He did it quietly. Anonymously. But… how did he know?

It doesn't matter. I don't care what it costs me. I will do whatever it takes to keep her alive.

I clear my throat and force a casual shrug. "Could be a medical grant. Or maybe the Academy pitched in. Some kind of scholarship fund. Who knows?" I meet Mom's eyes and smile softly. "It's here. It's real. All you have to do… is say yes."

Dad turns to her, emotion tightening his voice. "Alice… do you want to do this?"

She looks between us, and something shifts. Her eyes brighten. Her spine straightens. For the first time since we walked in, she doesn't look like she's dying. She looks like she wants to live.

"I want to watch my girl become a wife and loving mom," she whispers. "So yes. I want to try."

The room blurs with tears as I leap from my chair and wrap my arms around her. "I love you."

She clutches me back, holding me like she's afraid to let go. "I love you too, sweetie. I'm going to be alright."

My phone rings as it tears through the emotion. I glance down. A number I don't recognize. I hesitate.

Could it be…? No way…

I swipe to answer. "Hello?"

A bubbly voice floats through the speaker. "Good morning! Is this Ms. Anderson?"

"It is."

"Hi! This is Jasmine with Heartford Cypher International. Mr. Heartford would like to meet with you for a formal interview. Are you available Monday morning?"

My parents are watching, holding their breath, but something about this feels off. Eerie. Too perfect.

But I can't contain my excitement, and I practically jump out of my skin. "Yes! Yes, absolutely!"

"Perfect. Monday at nine o'clock in the morning. Just let the front desk know you're here to see Mr. Heartford, take the elevator to the top floor, and I'll be there to greet you. Any questions?"

"No, ma'am. That sounds amazing. Thank you so much!"

I hang up, slowly turning to face my parents. "I have a job interview," I say breathlessly. "With Heartford. Monday morning."

They jump up and pull me into a tight hug.

Dad kisses my forehead. "We are so proud of you. You have worked incredibly hard to get that interview."

If only he knew I tased a man and blackmailed him… whoops.

The doctor clears his throat again. "So… we're moving forward with treatment?"

Mom grabs my hand and squeezes. "Yes. We are."

"Excellent. We'll need to start Monday morning at nine o'clock."

I blink. My stomach drops.

Monday. At the same time. Of course, this would happen.

"I can cancel the interview," I say quickly. "I'll be here."

"No!" Mom says firmly, turning to me. Her voice is soft but firm. "You've always wanted to work at Heartford. Don't miss it… not for me."

"But Mom…" Tears sting my eyes.

"Absolutely not. I want to watch your dreams come true. I want to help you plan your wedding. I want to watch you walk down the aisle in some ridiculous dress you'll regret later but love in the moment." She smiles, voice cracking. "So promise me, Lila. You'll go."

I nod, swallowing the lump in my throat. "Okay, I promise." But as I look at her alive, full of hope for the first time since the diagnosis, something inside me curdles. Because this doesn't feel like a miracle, it feels like a transaction.

Fifteen million dollars. A second chance at life for my mother. An invitation for me to step inside the world's most powerful company. All at once? This isn't a coincidence. It's a contract. And I never signed it.

Beck Heartford's name is on the building. His voice made the offer.

But it's the three masked figures who have me questioning my sanity.

Three unforgettable encounters. Batman danced with me, making me feel safe and wanted. The Phantom, who awakened a darkness I didn't know I craved. And the Red Mask, who hunted me through the maze and left me in a trance, I haven't escaped.

My mind drifts to that night, the one that was my undoing. The night I've never recovered from. The way Batman's strong hands held me close, our bodies grinding together as if we were the only two people in the world…

I never wanted to leave the dance floor. I never wanted to leave him, especially after finding out he was Beck.

But then I walked in on a scene that left me speechless and completely captivated. The Phantom's eyes had me mesmerized. Sharp, crystal blue, all-consuming. The ink etched across his chest burned into my memory, igniting something deep and forbidden in my core.

And then the Red Mask, the one that grazed my skin, a touch so light it scorched and left me branded. His breath ghosted against my ear, slow and deliberate, like he knew exactly what it did to me. And that hum.

Low. Dark. Almost primal.

It vibrated down my spine and into the hollow of me, echoing long after he vanished into the night.

Damn it, Lila. You're with your parents. Focus…

But I can't.

They haunt my memories.

In the maze, it was Beck in the Red Mask who whispered in my ear. It was him who hunted me in the dark.

Or was it?

I thought it was him. I wanted to believe it was him because it would make sense.

But what if it wasn't? What if it was the Phantom? No. He's not real. He can't be real. He's a figment of my imagination… right?

The panic attack must've made me hallucinate. He couldn't have been real.

Unless… they're all the same person.

I know Beck is Batman. But the other two? Are they him too?

The Red Mask.

Batman.

The Phantom.

Three faces. Possibly one man.

My pulse roars in my ears.

Did I trade my soul for a miracle… or did I sell myself to a monster wearing three masks?

I don't know who I'm walking into on Monday. I don't know what I've agreed to. All I know is this: something darker than cancer has wrapped itself around my life, and somewhere in the distance, I swear I hear it again.

That melody. That voice. That sultry hum, a quiet threat, creeping like ivy through my chest and stealing my breath. Calling me. Claiming me. As it always has. I think it's already too late to run.

CHAPTER TWELVE
LILA

I'm curled up in my cozy bed, wrapped in the cream knit blanket my mom made me for college graduation, and it still smells like her: warm vanilla and a hint of her bar soap, clean and familiar.

She's okay. She's going to be okay. So, stop worrying tonight. Go to sleep.

But I can't. As I waste away in my bed, I stare out the wall of windows while the city hums beneath the night sky. Planes blink overhead, flying in and out of the local airport, each one carrying people whose stories are still moving forward, while mine feels frozen in time.

I'm twenty-six. And somehow, my personal life feels like it belongs to someone twice my age. Stalled. Stuck. Wasting away in here.

I'm supposed to be resting. After the week I've had with Mom's diagnosis, the fifteen-million-dollar miracle, and the job interview of a lifetime, numbness would make sense. But I'm not numb. My mind isn't spiraling over the cancer or how I should be preparing for my meeting on Monday. It's locked on *him.*

Yet, I don't even know which one of them I'm fixated on. But there's a fire beneath my skin, molten and alive, pulsing and burning for more. Something in me has awakened. Something I can't quiet or name. A need that coils deep. Maybe for someone. Maybe just… a touch.

I pull my knees to my chest, fingers gliding over the satin of my pink tank top. The soft fabric is a poor substitute for the touch I crave, but it will have to do for now. My arms tighten around myself as I rest my head against my knees, trying to hold it all in. Trying to hold her in. My reckless, untamed alter ego, the one dying to get out.

I want strong hands trailing the curves of my body. Warm breath skating across my skin. A kiss.

Yes… a kiss.

God, I haven't been kissed in years. And lately, I feel like I've aged a decade, like I've forgotten how to flirt, how to be wanted. How to want.

I really am lacking. I feel old. Pathetic. Lonely. Like the world moved on without me, and I forgot how to catch up. How to date. How to even talk to people anymore. Maybe I should try a dating app. I do want to get married someday. But how does someone like me get there… when I don't even know how to start?

The city lights blur through the glass, and my mind drifts back to the party, to the forbidden bedroom where the lights flickered like this.

The Phantom.

The king of the room where she knelt before him, taking him into her mouth inch by inch. Where everything in me shifted. The same skylight where moonlight poured over him, casting him like the star of the show. Then he leaned back, eyes closed in ecstasy, muscles flexing as he gripped the back of her head, guiding her rhythm.

God, the way his chest rose and fell. The ink stretched across his sweat-coated skin. And the way he watched me. Watched me touching myself from across the room.

Damn it, Lila. He's not real. It was the panic attack. A dream. A hallucination. Why do I keep thinking about him? Is it grief? The stress with Mom? Is it my anxiety unraveling? Or… Is it because I really want him to be real? No, that can't be it.

But the ache between my legs says otherwise. I glance around the room like someone might be watching.

Ridiculous.

I roll my eyes and let out the breath. I didn't realize I'd been holding since he slipped into my thoughts.

"Okay, Lila," I whisper, barely audible. "This is the only way to get relief…" I say it quietly, trying to make myself feel less crazy, less alone with the need simmering under my skin.

I slip a hand beneath the blanket, my fingertips gliding down the length of my bare skin, slow and tentative, until they reach my stomach. My knuckles graze the fabric as I lift the waistband and slide inside. Warmth greets me. The slick heat pulses between my thighs.

"Oh…" It feels… good. I haven't touched myself since the night I lost my virginity… and didn't cum. So I had to finish the job myself. Back then, I was innocent and knew I needed to fix the way I felt. Tonight, it's about something else entirely. I thought I just needed a release, but this feels deeper. Like a connection. To him. The imaginary man in my head.

I'm really losing it.

A soft breath escapes as I find the delicate bundle of nerves, already aching for more.
His eyes flash behind my lids. Those light blue gemstones, aching and unblinking, burning into my soul like they've always belonged there, like they've claimed me long before I ever saw them.

What would it feel like if he actually touched me?
A moan curls in my throat. "Mmm."
RING. RING. RING.

I freeze, my hand still, hoping the annoying sound will stop. Then it does. Thank God. I continue circling my clit, the pressure building...

RING. RING. RING.

"You've got to be kidding me!" I groan, blindly reaching for my phone on the nightstand. "Dammit, Aster!" I answer with a growl.

"Woahhhh. Someone woke up on the wrong side of the bed! What the hell is wrong with you?" Aster's voice slices through the line, sharp, smug, and wildly amused, since I never get flustered with her.

"If you must know," I huff, "you just ruined my orgasm, and I was so close."

A beat.

"Who are you and what have you done to my best friend! First the wet dream, now this? That party really turned you out. You horny little slut." Her voice is half scandalized, half proud.

I laugh despite myself. "Maybe I'm finally taking your advice. But I know you didn't call just to kill my vibe… what's up?"

"Well, actually… You never told me if you wanted to go to the sex club with me tonight. And judging by what I just interrupted, it might be in your best interest."

I bolt upright. "Oh no. No, no, no. The last time I went anywhere with you, I ended up watching a stranger get sucked off, got chased through a haunted maze by some red-masked monster who might be my future boss, and also the guy I grinded on during a dance. And now I'm fantasizing about someone who doesn't even exist. So… no. Hard pass."

"Aww, come on, Lila," she whines. "Don't be a party pooper. It'll be fun. No haunted gardens, I swear. Just drinks, music, and hot people doing hot people things. And hey, maybe you'll finally get off tonight. There's plenty of boy toys to play with."

I bury my face in my hands. "Aster, how do you always manage to drag me into this shit?"

"Hey, I can't help that chaos finds me, and we are a package deal! Lila, just think of it as a celebration. You survived this week. You earned it."

God help me… I'm considering it. "If I do go," I say slowly, "what do I even wear? I've never been to a place like this."

"You know that bag of clothes I gave you? There's an outfit in there that's perfect for tonight. The black lace Dior two-piece. Wear it with your strappy black heels, hair down, soft curls. You'll look incredible."

"But—"

"No buts! I just texted you the address. Be there by eleven. A few people are meeting us."

I glance at the clock. 9:30 p.m.

"Aster!"

"Lila!" she mocks in return.

Guess I'd better drag my ass out of bed to shower and shave, since there's a chance I might get lucky tonight.

"Okay, fine. You win. I'll see you soon. Kisses."

She makes an obnoxiously loud smooching sound and hangs up.

I lie there, staring at the crack in the ceiling, tracing it like a roadmap to nowhere. Just like my romantic life. One dead end after another.

The buzz still hums beneath my skin, a quiet aftershock. My thighs ache. My chest rises and falls too fast. I'm chasing something I don't understand. Is it arousal? The need to feel wanted? The need to see them behind my eyelids, the three who flipped my boring world upside down? Maybe tonight I'll finally stop thinking about them.

And tonight, I'm done pretending. I want someone to wreck me. Wreck me in ways I've only dared to dream about.

I swing my legs out of bed and walk to the closet, searching for the clothes Aster gave me last week. When she hands over outfits, you'd expect a trash bag full of everyday hand-me-downs like a normal person. But of course not. Aster folds designer couture into oversized Louis Vuitton, Dior, and Gucci shopping bags like she's running a luxury boutique.

I dig through the nearest one and find the outfit instantly. I knew exactly which one she meant, mainly because when I first saw it, I thought, *Where the hell would I even wear this… I guess you found a place.*

I hold up the top and admire its beauty. It looks like confidence stitched into fabric. Stunning. Fearless. Everything I'm still trying to find in myself.

I peel off my oversized T-shirt and toss it aside. The hardwood floor is cool beneath my bare feet, smooth and grounding, reminding me that I really am doing this. I pace the room, heart thudding, adrenaline kicking in as I try to get ready. Fast but careful. Because tonight might actually matter.

One thing is clear. The maze was the spark that lit the fuse. The moment everything inside me shifted. The night I realized I craved more, emotionally and physically. And tonight feels like the invitation. Like a whisper daring me to take the next step. But just as I begin to lean into it, a memory surfaces.

I was eight the first time I almost drowned. Slipped beneath the surface of the community pool, lungs screaming, arms flailing. After they pulled me out, I swore I'd never go near water again. But Mom... she wouldn't let fear win.

"Walk straight into the fire, Lila," she'd said gently. "That's how you take its power away."

So I did. She signed me up for swimming lessons even though I was petrified.
I learned to float. To swim. To trust the water again. And eventually, I learned to love it.
Now I swim laps when I'm stressed, and honestly, after the week I've had, I should probably be doing that right now.

Water is where I think. Where I reset, where I find balance. And maybe this is just like that. Only now it's not the water calling me. It's them. The masked men. The ones who drown me with their presence. The ones who saw the fire in me before I ever dared to touch it. Tonight isn't about danger. It's about reclaiming the fear of rejection. The fear of the unknown. The heat that's been building in my core. It's about proving I can want more and survive it. I deserve more. I deserve a love that consumes me.

CHAPTER THIRTEEN
LILA

I stare out the Uber window, completely in awe of the sex club. I don't know what I expected. Something grimy, maybe. Dark. Sketchy. Smelly enough to make me cringe. I pictured it tucked into some rundown part of town, like where I live, somewhere with flickering streetlamps and drunks stumbling in and out, chasing whatever escape they could find.

But holy hell. I forgot this is Aster's place.

Of course, it's nothing like I imagined. She blows my mind with everything she does. I mean, really, why would I expect anything less than jaw-dropping perfection?

The building rises like something out of a Gothic fairytale, just like the mansion from the Halloween party. This place is regal. Dramatic. Unapologetically grand. It wasn't built for people like me.

Four stories of ivory stone rise toward the sky, adorned with ornate columns and intricately carved balconies befitting royalty. Marble statues stand guard at the second-floor windows, watching over the entrance like silent protectors of whatever darkness may lie within. But unlike the polished mansions of the Upper East Side or the sleek glass towers uptown, this place doesn't care about being modern. It appears to have stepped straight out of the early 1800s. The building screams romance.

And yet… every window is tinted and blacked out. No light. No glimpse inside. Just panes of glossy glass swallowing the night, like the building itself is hiding something. Or maybe someone. But I can't help but feel connected to it… to her. It feels just like me. Soft, welcoming, and polished on the outside, but no one sees through my windows. They don't see the part of me I keep buried deep within.

The contrast is unnerving. This historic masterpiece, cloaked in secrecy, like a cathedral built for sin. My pulse kicks up. This isn't some underground warehouse or velvet-curtained lounge. This is indulgence. Luxury. Power. And the rich? They walk in without shame, not caring who sees because this is their world. This is where they belong, while the rest of us, the "normal" ones, sit on the outside, wondering what's inside.

And it's just sex. Something anyone can have anytime, without spending a dime. Yet somehow, they still flaunt it and make the rest of us feel like we're missing out.

What a messed-up system.

And here I am falling right into the trap. I grab the door handle and hesitate. My hand freezes midair, hovering just inches from it. The last time I felt this way was outside Aster's house, right before that Halloween party. I was unsure then, clinging to fear of the unknown.
But tonight feels different.

There is still fear, but there is fire too. Confidence. Curiosity. Fear will not get me anywhere. It will not get me laid. And it will not help me find the parts of myself I have been too afraid to face.

"Ma'am, I said we have arrived..." The driver's voice cuts through my thoughts, and I realize I am still sitting in the Uber.

"Oh. Right. Thank you so much," I say, handing him cash. I don't hesitate for long, because this time, I am not the same girl who wants to turn back. I am ready.

The car door creaks open, and I step out. Cold air brushes my thighs, and I inhale the crisp breeze, the scent of fall grounding me as I try to steady my emotions. Goosebumps erupt across my legs, my teeth beginning to chatter. Of course, I forgot my jacket.

The sheer top clings to me like a second skin, each thread of floral lace revealing more than I have ever dared to show. The off-the-shoulder neckline dips dangerously low, framing my chest like I am gift-wrapped for the holidays and ready to be opened. The sleeves are loose and flowy, softening the look and giving it just enough of a feminine edge that screams Lila. And the skirt?

It's practically lingerie. A temptation disguised as an invitation. The mesh ruffles sway with each step, teasing the tops of my thighs. My legs are long and freshly shaved, slick with shimmer oil that makes them look even longer, like something off a runway. My waist is cinched, the kind that begs to be gripped. Perfect for a man to pick me up and toss me onto a bed, no questions asked. And for once, I don't feel invisible.

I feel like I did at the Halloween party. Seen. Wanted. Sensual. Which is terrifying, considering that night ended in a bit of a disaster. And yet, here I am again, swept right back into the madness. All because of her.

Aster stands near the entrance, leaning against the brick wall like she owns the night. One hand on her hip, head tilted, a single brow raised as she eyes me like I'm a piece of meat she's about to devour.

"Damn, Lila." She grins, pushing off the wall. "You look like you walked out of a wet dream. Just know I'd absolutely hit that. I'm not saying I'm into girls… but for you? I'd consider a personality shift."

I giggle, my cheeks flushing. Usually, I'd argue when she says things like that. But tonight, she's right. I look hot… and I know it. "You told me to get laid so I could relax," I say, pulling my skirt up to show a little more skin. "Well… It's happening. Tonight."

"Ohhh, I like this, Lila." She whistles, circling me. "Lace? Legs? That hair? Babe, you're about to make grown men forget their morals and their damn names."

My golden waves tumble over my shoulders, catching the glow of the streetlights. "Good. Maybe they'll finally know what it feels like to crave something they can't touch. Because tonight I choose who I want."

I adjust my top and push up boobs I don't really have. But the way Aster's eyes linger? I might believe it's working.

"You're not just showing up tonight," she says. "You're making an entrance."

"Damn straight. I learned from the best," I say with a wink.

As we reach the velvet curtain, my pulse pounds. Courage buzzes through me, but anxiety still lingers at the back of my mind.

Please, not tonight. Don't let a panic attack ruin this.

I feel myself starting to dissociate, the noise and lights blurring at the edges, my breath catching in that familiar quiet panic.

She notices. Of course she does.

Aster steps in without a word and wraps me in a bear hug, pulling me tight against her chest. "Please know that I'm so proud of you," she whispers. "You're doing an amazing job in every area of your life, even if it feels like your world is falling apart." She squeezes tighter, and honestly, I need it. I need her. I need this moment.

I rest my head on her shoulder, eyes burning, a tear threatening to fall. And if it does, I know I'll lose the edge I worked so hard to build up for tonight.

I can't let that happen.

So I blink it back and say, "Aster, don't lie to me. The only reason you're hugging me is to feel me up and get a better view of my tits."

Then it happens. That sound I love. Her laugh, loud, unfiltered, contagious as hell. The kind of laugh that could brighten anyone's day, even mine. Even now.

"Come on. They're waiting!" Aster grabs my hand, dragging me past security, who barely glance at us.

Of course, they know her. She's probably here every other night.

Inside, the first floor pulses with energy. Neon strobe lights slice through the shadows, casting flashes of electric blue and hot pink across the room. Pole dancers twist and arch on glowing platforms, their bodies glistening under the pulse of the lights. They wear the sexiest lingerie I have ever seen. Thongs that barely conceal anything, breasts of all shapes and sizes on proud display. And those heels? Skyscraper tall. They move in them like they were born to, effortless, seductive, powerful.

"Lavender Haze" by Taylor Swift throbs from the speakers like a cinematic entrance made specifically for me and Aster.

The energy slams into me, just like the maze. My skin tingles. My thoughts slip. And I'm practically high off the atmosphere. One beat, one pulse, and I'm back, back to that unforgettable night.

Aster grabs my hand and pulls me toward a roped-off VIP table, where four scrumptious men lounge across a black leather circular booth, sipping on liquor that probably costs more than my rent.

This is not good... because I want every single one of them.

Their eyes are locked on the pole dancers, then the crowd on the dance floor, hunting, scanning, waiting for the next woman to catch their attention.

But then they see us. And just like that, everything else fades. These men are practically drooling. Two of them can't take their eyes off Aster. The other two? They're devouring me like I'm dessert.

Aster leans into my ear, her breath warm against my skin. "Checkmate for us." Like this is just another game to her, and they're the knights already bowing to the queen as she makes her next move. It clicks then why she always loved chess so much.

Back in boarding school, she was the state champion. At the time, I didn't get the obsession, but now? It makes perfect sense. It was never about the board. It was about strategy. The power she holds. The thrill of getting inside her opponent's head, ready to sacrifice a pawn and pin the king.

Because in here? Aster runs the whole damn game.

They look us up and down like we are tonight's entertainment, but fun fact, they are ours. "Did you save us drinks?" She purrs, bending over the table as she snatches one of the glasses out of the hand of a dark-haired, caramel-skinned muscle god with the most perfect full beard I've ever seen.

He smirks, his brown eyes lighting up as she brings his crystal whiskey glass to her lips and downs every last drop without blinking.

She did not just do that.

It was hot. Tempting. A total power move that put the entire night in her hands. She leans back, licking the corner of her mouth like she owns the room. "Well, since you're all just going to keep staring at us with your mouths open…" She starts, flicking her gaze between the stunned men, "I guess we'll just have to find a better table to sit at."

She turns to walk away, but before she can take a single step, the bearded man grabs her waist and pulls her straight into his lap, his mouth finding her neck. "Hmmm, that's what I thought," she purrs, smirking as his lips trail up her skin. Then she turns to the other three, all still looking at me like they've never laid eyes on anything they weren't allowed to touch.

"Boys, this is my bestie, Lila," she says, twirling a curl around her finger. "If one of you doesn't fuck her or at least make her see stars tonight, I swear I'll cut your dicks off and toss them in the ocean. And well… I'll let the fish feast. Got it?" She shoots me a smug little smile like she just did me a favor, while I give her the most annoyed glare I can manage.

Oh. God. Way to be subtle.

I clear my throat, my voice barely above a whisper, unsure how to speak after… that. "Umm, is this seat taken?" I ask the tall, black-haired Korean hottie.

His chocolate-brown eyes lift to meet mine. They're warm and sweet, but something in them feels familiar. Like me. Like, there's another side of him he doesn't show easily. And when he does, he becomes animalistic. "By you, if you choose."

Oh my God. He has a British accent. Of course he does. Because obviously, I needed one more reason to spiral.

I can't help but stare at his side profile. He looks like he walked straight out of a K-drama. Sharp jawline, flawless skin, and that effortlessly cool male lead energy. And not just any K-drama guy. This man could absolutely play the emotionally unavailable heir to a billion-dollar empire who completely unravels the moment he meets her. The girl who crashes into him with her coffee, stains his expensive button-down, and then shyly offers to get it dry cleaned, unaware she just turned his entire world upside down.

And me? I'm a hopeless romantic. I could binge those shows for a week straight, no sleep, no shame, completely swept away by a man who doesn't even exist. Except this isn't some quaint café with stolen glances…

This is a sex club. And my best friend just threatened him. So yeah. Great start to a potential love story.

I watch his Adam's apple bob as he swallows his whiskey, and I can't help but gulp. If I get to choose who gets to pleasure me tonight, it's him. He's definitely my type. He could erase the Phantom. And Batman. And the Red Mask.

Damn. I really am screwed up.

"I'm… I'm sorry about Aster. Sometimes she's a little much."

He cracks a smile and runs a hand through his soft, tousled hair. "I've gotten used to her at this point."

We glance across the booth, and yep, Aster and the bearded guy are basically dry humping and making out like they're the only two people in the room.

"Is she always like this?" I say, floored by how effortlessly she fits into this world.

When I turn back, his eyes are still locked on mine. Unblinking. Steady.

Oh. Wow. He hasn't looked away once.

"You have no idea," he says, still not breaking eye contact.

Panic starts to rise in my chest, and my palms begin to sweat. How would he know what Aster's like… unless they've already hooked up? I'm not okay with her sloppy seconds.

"Wait, have you two?" I ask, hoping he catches what I'm really trying to say.

He chuckles, a slow, deep, sultry sound that rumbles from his chest. "God, no. She's not my type."

Oh. Cool.

Except now my brain spirals even more.

If Aster, the most beautiful, magnetic woman I know, isn't his type, then there's no way I am.

Stop thinking. Just feel. Just feel, Lila.

I toss back a shot. Then another. And one more for good measure. He watches, raising a brow, clearly impressed. "Let's start over. Proper introduction this time." I flip my hair with a wink. "Hey, I'm Lila. And you are?"

He grins, all white teeth and a wicked smile, and leans in. His voice brushes my ear, low enough to send a chill down my spine. "My name doesn't matter. Because after tonight, the only thing you'll remember is how I made you feel."

Oh shit. I definitely picked the right one.

"Hm. Let's see if you can live up to that," I say, lifting a brow.

He rises, extends his hand, and smirks. "Come dance with me." I grab another shot from the busty, shirtless waitress strutting by with goddess-level confidence.

The exquisite bourbon burns slow as it slides down my throat, grounding me in the moment, reminding me this isn't a dream. His hand swallows mine. Big, warm, steady.

This is real.

I glance back at Aster, who's finally taking a break from her full-blown makeout session to watch me get dragged away by this irresistible man. She dances in place like a total fangirl, cheering me. And then, because she can't help herself, she adds her signature flair. She sticks out her tongue and moves it up and down like she's licking an ice cream cone. Of course she does.

I roll my eyes, laughing as I follow the stranger onto the dark, kaleidoscope-colored dance floor. But once we step in, I realize something I hadn't noticed before. The floor is open, wide, like a stage.

And towering above us are balconies filled with people. The elite. Watching us move, watching me move.

I glance up, strangely enjoying the attention. I feel seen. In control. Desirable.

Is that a new kink unlocked… or just the alcohol? Yeah. Probably just the alcohol.

He pulls me close, his hands gripping my waist as I let him take the lead. Our bodies move in sync, slow and intentional. I slide my hands up his chest, feeling the hard muscle beneath his soft cotton shirt. He smells like cinnamon and spice, and everything nice and expensive.

This is the man I want to deflower me tonight. I need this. I want him to know I'm his for tonight. He can play with me if I get to play with him too.

I slip my hands under his shirt and hesitate just for a moment. Then, without breaking eye contact, I press my palms to his skin just above his belt. He tenses under my touch, his eyes dropping to watch me, swallowing hard, and nibbling on his bottom lip.

Oh, he likes it.

So I keep going. My hands skate up his toned abs to his chest. His skin is on fire. My own is flushed and aching.

Hmmm. I never knew I loved being in charge.

My clit pulses with desperation, ready for some kind of friction. Movement. Anything. People grind around us, making this scene even more invigorating and sexy.

He leans in. His lips brush mine, just a faint touch, like he's waiting for my permission. I lean into his ear. "So, you're a tease?" I say with a smirk.

"Only if you want me to be…" That beautiful smile on full display.

But I can't wait any longer. The Phantom woke something deep within me, and she's ready to come out and play.

I kiss him. The first man I've kissed in years. The kiss I've been dreaming of. He responds, and I can't help but lose myself in it. Our mouths swirl together, deeper, hotter, like we've been doing this forever. But something's missing. It's good. So good. But not soul-twisting. Not the way it should be.

Then a ripple in the air, a crackle of energy, like static before a lightning strike. The thing that was missing in the kiss? There it is. But it's not coming from him, it's coming from somewhere else.

The bass of the music dulls, muffled, like I've been dropped underwater. Bodies still move around me, hips grinding, mouths open in laughter and moans, but my world stops. My skin prickles. My breath halts. And then I hear it.

A hum. Low and velvet smooth. Enthralling. It threads through the crowd, yet it feels like I'm the only one who can hear it. The melody slides between bodies, curling down my spine, and wrapping around my throat like a noose made of silk. My eyes widen.

That sound. That damn sound. The same tune from the maze. The one that haunts my dreams. The one that pulled me into the darkness and has yet to let me go.

My breath stutters, heart skipping, lips still pressed to the stranger's. A scream pulses in my throat, trapped, trying to claw its way out.

He's here.

I feel him before I see him. Like the air itself bends to make room for him. Heavy. Overwhelming. Laced with fury, heat, and something far more lethal.

Possession.

My body knows before my mind does. I'm on fire for him, and I don't mean the stranger my lips are pressed to. Every hair on my skin lifts. My nipples harden beneath the lace. My thighs press together as wetness coats my thong.

I look up to the second-floor balcony. And there he is.

The Red Mask.

His sleek black-on-black suit is tailored to perfection, and his dominant silhouette radiates fury. His shoulders are tense, chest rising and falling like he's barely containing the storm inside him. His eyes are hidden behind the glowing neon mask, but I swear I feel them on me. Locked on me. A silent scream. A message only I understand.

And that message? He's livid. His leather-gloved hands grip the metal railing with a force that feels personal. I'd bet anything his knuckles are bone white beneath the leather from how tightly he's holding on.

He doesn't move. He doesn't have to. His presence alone demands obedience.

Well, good thing I'm not obedient.

And yet he's across the room, elevated above the chaos, untouchable but consuming me whole. The sexual tension pulsing between us is thicker than the air itself. I'm kissing one man, but it's him I'm aching for. The Red Mask. The one who doesn't even have to touch me to set me on fire.

My body tightens. My heart beats for the man behind the mask. He isn't just observing, he is claiming me, furious that someone else dares to touch what he believes is his. Then he tilts his head, a slow, deliberate gesture that feels like both a promise and a threat, as if he's already preparing for the chase.

The worst part is how much I want him to see me with the stranger. I want him wrecked, just like he left me. Strung out from the way his fingers made me feel beneath the lilac-covered gazebo. He pushed me to the edge and left me clawing for the release that he denied me. He made me feel things I've spent years trying to avoid… and I don't even know his name.

And now? I want him to burn for me like I burned for him in the maze.

The stranger's lips brush mine again, but my tongue is already moving, tangling with his. I arch into him, pressing my body against his hard length, letting the Red Mask see every inch of me with him. But in my head… I'm not kissing this man. *I'm kissing him.*

I jump, wrapping my legs around the stranger's waist. He grabs the backs of my thighs, and I let him feel all of me.

Let the Red Mask see. I want him to come down here. To lose control. To touch me. I take a moment to catch my breath, hoping to see a reaction, but…

He's gone. The balcony is empty.

No shadow. No mask. No hum. Just… silence. Like he was never there. Or worse… like he was and didn't like what he saw.

My heart stutters. My throat tightens. Was he ever really there? Or worse… is he still here, watching. Waiting. Coming for me.

God, I hope he is.

CHAPTER FOURTEEN
LILA

My heart pounds in rhythm to the music. My watch vibrates, warning me that my heart rate is sky high, but this isn't panic. I can't breathe because of him. Because of the way the stranger kisses me like he needs it to survive. Neither of us can catch a breath. I'm so thirsty. Craving something deeper, something real. But the stranger isn't quenching it. He's not the drink I need.

I need more. But more of what? The one that I'm imagining? Beck?

It makes sense that he's the Red Mask. It was his house. His maze. His gazebo. I watched him walk into the maze that night. It has to be him. I know it's him.

I pull away, breathless. His brown eyes are wild, dark with want, and I was ready to give in to him. Ready to be consumed. Until I felt it. That magnetic pull radiating from the balcony above. Until I saw him.

The red neon X's. The eerie smile glowing through the dark. He wasn't just standing there. He was dominating the entire room without lifting a finger.
Owning the space like it belonged to him…
Like I belong to him.

I drop down from his waist, my legs trembling. There's a damp spot on his shirt, right where my wetness seeped through my thong.

Well, that's embarrassing.

I glance away, humiliated, then meet his gaze again as he mimics my movements. "I'm… I'm so sorry," I whisper, horrified.

"Lila," he murmurs, leaning in so close I can feel his breath on my cheek. "Don't worry about that." His voice drops lower, velvety and hot. "Because by the end of the night…" His gaze flicks to my thighs, then back to my lips. "That wetness will be dripping down my face."

Fuck.

I smile, a little shy but playful. "If I'm going to be your dessert, can I at least know your name first?"

He hesitates, as if he knows this is a one-night thing, and letting me know his name makes it more real. "Come on," I tease, leaning in closer. "How am I supposed to scream your name if I don't know it?"

He lets out a low, soft laugh that sends butterflies spiraling through my stomach. "Shit, Lila. That's insanely sexy when you talk like that." Before I can get another word out, he kisses me. Slow. Teasing. Almost emotional.

"Pleaseee," I pout, fluttering my lashes like a bratty little tease.

He smirks, eyes dancing with heat. "Well, how the hell am I supposed to say no to that?" He leans in, lips brushing mine. "Call me Leon."

"Mmm, Leon… the name of a lion. Should I be scared? Or excited to be your prey tonight?"

He smirks, brushing his thumb over my bottom lip. "That depends. Are you the kind of prey that runs or begs to be caught?"

I freeze. I wasn't expecting that. He's the perfect book boyfriend; flirty, confident, gorgeous, but something still feels like it's missing.

His voice drops lower, thicker with heat. "How about I take you to the pleasure room and find out?"

"I'm listening…" I grab the front of his shirt and pull him closer.

"If I take you there, it's over. Your body will only know me."

"Wait. What exactly is the pleasure room?"

"It's where I focus only on you," he says, his tone dripping with sex. "I blindfold you. Every sense tuned to touch. The way my hands move across your body. The way my tongue curls around your clit."

My breath hitches. My thighs squeeze together. This man isn't him… but he can make me feel good tonight. And maybe that's enough. Who knows? Perhaps this is the beginning of something. Maybe it's our love story.

But what Leon doesn't know is that I've never really been pleasured by a man. No one's ever gone down on me. This will be a first. One I'll never forget. I've had sex once, and he finished in under a minute… so technically, I'm still a virgin in every way that matters.

I give Leon a teasing smile. "Umm… yes, please. Lead the way. And if you do a good job…" I lean in, lips brushing his ear. "I might just give you a reward."

Did I just say that out loud? Hell yes, I did. Not that I actually know how to please a man, but still.

He kisses my neck, then grabs my hand in a way that feels strangely emotional, leaving me confused. His fingers lace through mine as we move through the crowd of bumping, grinding bodies.

We step into the gold elevator, and I catch our reflection in the mirrored walls.
Oddly enough, we look good together. His fingers are still locked with mine. It feels intimate, more than just a one-night thing. But I'm probably reading too much into it.

He presses the button for Level Three. "Let me text Aster so she won't worry."

LILA: Hey, so it's happening.

ASTER: SHUT UP! You're lying.

LILA: Nope. He's taking me to the third floor.

ASTER: You lucky bitch. Want me to wait for you?

LILA: Hopefully I'll be in here all night… 😏

ASTER: If y'all get tired, there are hotel rooms on the fourth floor.

LILA: Noooo. This is not an intimate thing… just fun! Nothing more.

ASTER: Well, I hope Leon knows that. Call me in the morning and tell me everything!

LILA: I will. Kisses!

He wraps his arm around my waist. I press into his chest. "Are you ready?" he asks.

"Oh, Leon… you have no idea."

The elevator doors glide open, and my breath catches. Imagine if Versailles had a secret wing no one spoke of, a place built not for politics but for indulgence. That's what this feels like. A fever dream.

No way this is real. I must have stepped into one of my dirty fantasies.

Above us, the ceiling stretches like a portal to another world, a swirling galaxy hand-painted in vibrant hues of violet, midnight blue, and silver. The ceiling seems to pulse with life, stars glowing like a heartbeat above us.

The lighting is dim and intimate. Velvet circular couches made for two are draped with sheer curtains, offering glimpses of the shadows inside. Nearby, open lounge areas buzz with quiet conversation. The seating there is upholstered in soft ivory, trimmed with gold that curls like vines along the walls.

The scent of luxury hangs in the air. Expensive cologne, sweat, desire, and sex. And the bar?

It glows beneath a calligraphy sign that reads, "Versailles Kissed By The Cosmos." The marble counter glistens, sleek and sensual. Liquor bottles shimmer like stained glass, each one shaped like diamonds and precious stones. No prices. Just power. Everything here tempts. There are no clocks. No windows. No distractions. Only pleasure.

"This place is expensive," I murmur. "Really expensive. And what did you say you did again?"

He walks with confidence, like the world bends for him. People greet him with reverence, like he's someone famous.

Do I know him from somewhere?

Before I can ask, we reach the receptionist. "Room 302," he says.

"Yes, sir. Do you need anything else?"

He turns to me. "Lila? Need anything?"

I swallow the lump rising in my throat. "I think I'm good."

Nerves build in my stomach as I try to steady my breath. He smiles. "I'll be right back. Just heading to my office to get something special for you. Go ahead and get ready."

Office?

He vanishes.

I blink. "What does he mean, his office?" I ask the receptionist.

She glances up, confused. "Mr. Amour? He's the owner of the club… didn't you know?"

Dammit. How does this always happen to me? This is exactly like the maze. Will I be having wet dreams about him next week, too? Ugh. How could I be so stupid? He probably does this with every girl.

My voice sharpens. "Does he bring a lot of women up here?"

She hesitates, glancing around like she's debating whether to spill. "I don't know if I'm supposed to say this," she whispers, leaning in slightly, "but I'm a girls' girl… and from what I've seen, you're the first."

My heart skips.

Oh. I'm the first. And tonight, he'll be the first to pleasure me truly. This is starting to feel more emotional than I'd like.

I consider leaving, but something deep inside whispers, 'Stay.'

Perhaps I would like to learn more about Mr. Amour.

"Could you tell me how to get to my room?"

"Down the hall. Left turn. If you need anything, let us know. We're here to assist your deepest, darkest fantasies."

"Umm… thanks."

I'm doing this for myself. Lila, you deserve this.

I walk the long hallway, lined with ivory doors and gold accents, and stop at 302.

Don't be nervous. He will forget about you tomorrow.

My heart feels like it's about to leap out of my chest. My watch vibrates. My hands tremble as I reach for the crystal knob, slowly turning it, unsure of what I'm about to walk into. Then I step inside.

The room is rich and exotic, draped in the decadence of Versailles. A leather table dominates the center, its four restraints shimmering in the low light. Beside it, a tray glows with temptation. Glass vials of oil gleam, the way I want my body to glisten under someone's touch. Nipple clamps wait with the promise of a bite, a silk blindfold lies ready to steal my sight, and a jeweled paddle sparkles like it belongs in a palace. There is more, some I recognize and others remain a mystery, but together they hum with the promise of pain and pleasure entwined.

Oh God. I don't think I'm ready for this.

My chest rises and falls, quick and shallow. I slip off my heels and climb onto the table, the material cool beneath my skin. I lie back, open, waiting, still dressed in Dior. I'm not sure what's about to happen or what I'm supposed to do, but if he wants to restrain me, I'll let him.

The blindfold slips over my eyes. I tie it tight.

I'm doing this. I'm going all in.

Even if it's Leon touching me, it's not his face I see behind my eyelids. It's theirs. The ones who haunt me. The one with ice blue eyes that undress me without a single touch. The one from the maze. The red mask. The hum.

The door creaks open behind me. My heart stutters. Footsteps echo slowly across the room. Steady. Intentional. Unhurried. I try to breathe normally, but I'm failing miserably. "I thought you might've gotten lost," I tease, my voice light but trembling at the edges.

Silence. Only his breath, his presence. Then I feel it.

A leather-gloved hand brushes my ankle. Painfully slow. It trails upward, over my calf, my thigh, stopping at my hip. He's not speaking. Not rushing. Just exploring.

I should be scared. But I'm not.

"I need to tell you something," I whisper. "I've never done this before. I've never… been
pleasured. Not by anyone."
Still, no response. Then his other hand wraps gently around my wrist, fastening it to the restraint. The next follows firmly. Dominant but tender. My breath catches.

Wait. Gloves? Leon wasn't wearing gloves.

A chill blooms across my skin. And then I feel it. That pressure in the air. The pull. It's him. Not Leon. Not a stranger. Him.

The Red Mask.

He saunters around me, fingers grazing along my arm, my ribs, down my thigh, mapping me, claiming me without a single word. And I let him.

God, I want him to.

He stops near my head and tips my chin up. I wait, lips parted, for the kiss. It doesn't come. Instead, his breath grazes mine. Hot. Lingering. Torturous. He hovers, close enough that I feel it in my bones. And then…

He hums. Low. Velvety. Like a secret language only we understand. The same hum that echoed through the maze. The one that threaded through grinding bodies on the dance floor. The one that owned me long before this moment. And I know without seeing him. I know exactly who he is. And I don't want him to stop.

My body locks in place. I whisper, "Leon?"

Nothing.

Then a voice cuts through the silence. A voice I don't recognize, but one my soul already knows.

"Looks like I have caught you again, princess."

CHAPTER FIFTEEN
LILA

I don't move. I don't breathe. Because I want the Red Mask to stay, and I'm terrified that if I speak or react, he'll disappear.

Is this revenge for cheating in the maze? Did he let me win so I would owe him? Or is this payback for Leon and the dance floor?

His breath lingers just above my lips, searing me without ever making contact. God, I ache for the feel of his mouth. I crave the taste of him. He's teasing me, and he knows it. Knows I'm coming apart beneath him with every shallow, desperate breath.

This might be a dream. A hallucination. But I don't care. Because whatever this is, it feels more real than anything I've ever known. I'm still fully clothed, trembling with anticipation, already drenched between my thighs. "Touch me," I whisper, barely audible.

His gloved fingers trace the curve of my jaw, the leather cool and commanding against my skin. They drift lower, gliding over the curve of my covered breast and down my stomach, each movement a silent dance of desire, making my nipples hard beneath the designer fabric.
He pauses at my hips, where my skirt clings tight like a second skin.

He slips his fingers beneath the waistband. Slowly, with agonizing patience, he begins to slide the lace down my thighs. My red thong is revealed, and the air thickens. His breath deepens. A low growl rumbles from his throat, raw and unrestrained. Then his mouth caresses my stomach. Soft.

Warm. Torturous. He kisses lower, each press of his lips more possessive than the last.

I can't see his lips, but God, if I could... I know they'd be full and inviting. The kind of mouth meant to ruin you with a kiss.

My back arches. My head falls back. I'm lost in the sensation of the way his mouth moves on me. His hands return, slipping under the delicate fabric at my hips. He pulls my panties down, inch by inch.

I lie there, bare and quivering, exposed in every way that matters. Above me, he lets out a groan. Not of control, but submission. The kind of sound that says he's been starving for this. For me.

"Princess," he murmurs, voice dripping like honey laced with poison. "You're a masterpiece."

The words slice through me deeper than I expected, my heart latching onto him and every syllable.

No one's ever said that to me. Not like this.

Not when I'm half-naked, trembling, and completely exposed.

A moan slips out, needy and unrecognizable. "Please... touch me like I'm the only one who ever mattered."

What the hell is happening to me? I don't beg. I never beg. I'm not that girl.

My pulse pounds like a war drum in my throat.

"You have no idea how many times I've touched myself to the thought of you... like a damn teenager who never stood a chance," he says, voice low and wrecked with need. I can't help but giggle and nibble on my lip. "What did I say about that?" he asks, his tone clear but still cloaked in mystery.

He is no longer wearing the mask. I can hear him. Clearly, and God, I am so close.

If my hands weren't restrained, I would rip off this blindfold and never let him go.

But I can't help myself. I tilt my head in defiance, teasing him just like the dream I recently had. "Oh? Like this?" I whisper, biting down again and shifting my hips just enough to make sure he knows exactly what he is doing to me. My clit throbs from the tension. From the heat. From the sensation, but silence remains.

The air in the room is thick and smothering, humming with emotions I don't fully understand, and I don't think he does either.

Is he feeling this too, or is it just me again, trapped in my own head, hoping for something that isn't real?

He doesn't move, but I hear it. His breathing is shallow and labored, like he's caught in the middle of a decision he doesn't want to make, as if he's deciding whether to vanish into the shadows or consume me whole.

Then slowly, his leather-gloved hands rise and cradle my face. They're gentle. Too gentle for the storm in the room. He pulls me closer. So close, his breath ghosts over my mouth, warm and poisonous.

"I… I can't do this," he murmurs.

"Then what are you going to do to me?" I whisper, my voice trembling, the words barely holding together.

I try to pull back. His grip tightens. "Are you going to punish me?"

He doesn't answer. Instead, the room shifts. The speakers buzz softly, as if they've been listening to us this whole time. And then the first haunting note of "Say Yes to Heaven" by Lana Del Rey fills the silence. He still doesn't speak. But somehow, the song is his answer.

My chest rises and falls, syncing with the rhythm, with the weight of what's about to happen. Because the song isn't just playing. It's us. It's every unspoken thing between us. A yes without words.

"Fuck it," he breathes, ragged and desperate. Then he closes the distance, giving in at last, every ounce of restraint shattering as his mouth claims mine.

My first kiss in years wasn't with Leon. It was with him. And the moment our mouths meet, he makes it clear that this moment was inevitable. It's raw passion. Intense. Starved. Desperate.

He kisses me like he has been dying of thirst, and I'm the first drop of water he's allowed to taste. Like I'm the only thing keeping him from falling apart. His lips crush into mine with a force that's both brutal and tender, like he's punishing himself with every second of pleasure. Like he's kissing me to forget something or to make sure I never forget him.

His mouth moves against mine like he's famished. Like he needs this to survive. And maybe I do too. I part my lips for him without hesitation, welcoming his tongue, craving the connection to him. We crash together in a kiss that consumes.

This is what a kiss should feel like…

It isn't just hunger radiating from him. It's fire and ice, a storm raging beneath his skin. He's at war with himself, torn between wanting me and trying not to. His mouth tastes of spearmint and smoke, dark and clean together, already my newest addiction.

I hate cigarettes. But this? This… I don't mind.

I can't help but kiss him deeper, greedier for more. More of this. More of him. He kisses me softly at the corner of my mouth, then maps a path down my neck like I'm fragile. And something shifts. His touch slows. Softens. It turns gentle, almost hesitant. Almost… afraid.

"I want you…" I breathe. "Please. Take off the blindfold. Let me see you… all of you."

I feel it, the way his hands falter ever so slightly. He's not just pausing. *He's scared. But why?*

Then his voice cuts through the silence, low and frayed at the edges. "Trust me… You don't want to know me." A breath hangs between us. "I'm nothing but unworthy of you."

"Then show me. Show me every scar. Every secret. Every filthy, broken piece you think I won't want, and Baby, I'll show you how wrong you are."

I've never called anyone that before. But something about him makes me forget who I am. Makes me want to be his.

He doesn't speak. His breath catches, like he's shocked or stunned by my response. His hands tremble slightly against my skin, like my words cracked something open inside him. Like maybe… he wants to believe me. And then his mouth dips lower.

"Well then, let me show you what I know," he says, the smirk in his voice unmistakable. His breath ghosts over my sensitive skin as it throbs. "So, no one's ever kissed your sweet cunt?" He leans in, his breath warm and maddening as he hovers just above my clit.

"No," I admit, my cheeks burning.

"So no one's ever made you cum before?" His tone shifts. Softer now. Quieter. Like, he's not just asking to tease me. He's trying to understand me.

"I've had sex once," I whisper. "But… I've never had an orgasm. Not from anyone." Silence.
A beat.
"Damn it," he mutters, more to himself than to me, before leaning in closer. "Then, Princess, I'm not stopping until you're shaking." His hands hover just above my hips.

I can't see him, but I feel it. The way the heat of his palms pulses just above my skin. He isn't touching. He isn't retreating. He's suspended in hesitation. And for a moment, nothing happens. Only the echoes of our breaths fill the space. Only this invisible thread between us, pulled taut with anticipation. And then I hear it.

The slow slide of leather. First one glove, then the other, peeling away a layer of who he really is.

He took them off.

I gasp as his fingers graze my ribs, drifting lower to my hips. Warm. Bare. Human. Skin against skin.

Lila, this is real and not a dream.

His contact is hesitant. Careful. As if I might break. Or maybe he will. I lay there, waiting, frozen in place. Legs spread, bare and exposed, ready for whatever he wants to do to me. Every part of me is buzzing for what comes next. And then I feel it. His mouth. Right there on my clit. Wet, warm, intentional. It's not just pleasure, it's a jolt that shoots through my entire body. It's not just pleasure. It's a shock, as if my body has been waiting its whole life for this single touch.

My back arches, the world slipping away. His tongue moves with purpose, not greedy, not rushed. Every stroke feels like an unspoken confession, as if he's discovering parts of me no one else has ever dared to explore.

Heat spreads low in my belly. Pressure coils tight and deeper with each slow lick. My thighs twitch. My breath catches in my throat. He flattens his tongue and drags it through me like he is savoring every taste. A sound breaks from his throat. It vibrates against me, and I nearly come undone.

"Mhmmmm." It slips out before I can stop it. My hips lift without permission, desperate for more. But his strong, steady hands are already there. They press into my thighs, grounding me, holding me in place.

"Oh fuck…" he breathes. "If you keep this up, I'm going to cum in my pants."

A smile curls on my lips as I picture his face behind the blindfold. And somehow, that image alone makes my pulse race even faster.

No one has ever touched me like this. Like, I am everything he has ever wanted. Like I'm not just a body beneath him, but the wet dream he never thought would come to life. I'm the one restrained, but somehow still the one in control. The one with all the power.

Each swirl of his tongue builds something wild inside me, something alive. But when his lips close around my clit and he sucks, the gasp rips out of me. My head tips back. My pulse races. Heat spreads through me, every muscle tightening.

He hums against me, the sound sinful, sending vibrations through my clit that make me shatter a little more. It sinks into my skin, curling my toes, unraveling me piece by piece.

I want to moan his name. I want to give him that. But I don't know who he is… Well, not officially.

My hands clench the sides of the table. "Baby," I whisper, breathless. "You feel so good."

He groans again, louder. His mouth works faster now, his tongue tracing circles that make my eyes roll back. One finger slips inside me. Then two. He finds a rhythm that pulls moans from my chest and makes my thighs quiver. "Right there. Yes. Please. Don't stop."

My hands pull against the restraints. My skin glistens with a sheen of sweat. My legs lock. My lungs forget how to breathe. The world disappears, and all I see is the Phantom, caught in the moon's glow and imprinted on me like a memory I will never escape.

But with the Phantom in the back of my mind, while the Red Mask pleasures me, I am unraveling second by second.

Oh God, I think I'm about to black out from the pleasure.

And as I fall apart beneath his mouth, his touch, his whispered grunts, his fingertips drift across my thighs, lingering like a memory I cannot erase. I will never be the same.

And him… he will never be just a fantasy from the maze again. Because he's real, I've felt him and touched him. I don't know his name. I've never seen his face. But I've felt his soul. And now that I have, I'll never stop chasing it. He thinks he's pulling the strings, but I'm already his. And soon, the man beneath the mask?

He'll be mine.

CHAPTER SIXTEEN
LILA

My white baby-doll heels click against the concrete as I weave through the streets of New York City. It's eight o'clock in the morning, and of course, cabs are impossible to catch. So, I'm stuck walking if I don't want to blow my shot at Heartford Cyphers International.

Ever since Saturday, my mind's been in a fog, but I must snap out of it if I want this job.

Don't screw this up.

The wind whips my hair into a frenzy, every perfect curl completely disarrayed.

Perfect. Just perfect.

RING. RING. RING.

My phone buzzes in my purse, and I start fumbling around like a cyclone, bumping into strangers as I dig through the designer bag Aster got me for my birthday. A white Chanel shoulder bag that screams femininity.

Honestly, I should marry her; she spoils me more than any man ever has.

"Hello?" I answer breathlessly.

"What the hell! Why didn't you call me yesterday?" Aster practically screams through the phone.

"Well, I slept all day after the chaos… Saturday night."

"Bitch, you got laid… didn't you?" she squeals.

"Unfortunately, no. But I did get a little something, enough to keep me sane for this week."

"Wow. Leon must be really good with his mouth if that's all it took. It takes me forever to get off that way!"

Silence.

"Hello? You better have not hung up on me!"

"Aster ummm… you're going to think I'm crazy, but…
it wasn't him."

"Damn, girl. You're a dog! You went up with one man
and ended up with another?"

I can hear her clapping on the other end. I hesitate.
Because honestly? I do sound insane.
I exhale, trying to steady my voice. "It was the guy in the Red
Mask… from the maze."

The line goes silent. "Lila… sweetie, do I need to come
get you? Are you okay? Do I need to take you to the
hospital?"

"No, I'm serious! It was him. I felt him. Well… at least,
I think I did."

"What do you mean you *think* you did?" Her voice
softens, puzzled.

"I woke up on the massage table and found Leon in the
lobby. He said I was already asleep when he got there… so he
just let me rest."

"Lila… I'm worried. What if you dreamed the whole
thing?"

"Okay, but what if I didn't and the whole thing was
real? I mean, I smelled him, Aster. I tasted him. There's no
way it was a dream!" My voice wavers, like I'm trying as
much to convince myself as her.

"Okay, valid, but—" I cut her off before she could
finish. "Just give me a few weeks to figure this out before you
start calling your family doctors, okay?"

"Fine," she sighs. "But at least give Leon a chance. I've
never seen him with anyone. The guys say he's super picky.
He's never like this with anyone, and he texted me yesterday
to check on you. He seemed really worried after you left."

I pause. "But I'm taken—"

I hesitate, not finishing that statement.

She'll definitely think I'm nuts if I say that out loud. I'm emotionally taken but not physically… so I can't deny him the chance.

"Umm, never mind, but yes, I'll try. Send me his number and I'll call him."

"Yay! Great! Just know I love you, even if you're a little crazy." She giggles. "But I'm with your mom and dad now, so I'll keep you updated on her treatment. Good luck with your interview. Kisses!"

"Kisses. Tell them I love them and I wish I could be there."

I hang up and realize I'm standing in front of the towering skyscraper. Right there, above the revolving doors, gleams the official gold plaque:

Heartford Cyphers International.

The company I've wanted to be a part of since I was seventeen.

Since that night.

The night that molded my future.

The night I'll never forget.

My heart skips. My body starts to quiver. A cold sensation creeps up my spine and crawls to the base of my neck. My chest tightens like an elephant is sitting on it, stealing every breath.

I tighten my grip on my purse like it's the only thing keeping me tethered to reality.

No, no, no. Not again. Not now. Don't freak out. Don't freak out. Don't freak out.

I gasp, trying to pull in air, but it's like my lungs forgot how to work.

Shit. I'm hyperventilating.

The world starts to spin, and I feel lightheaded.

I'm going to pass out. I didn't even make it to the interview. How pathetic, Lila.

My watch vibrates: heart rate spiking, breathing irregular.

Who would want this? Who would want to put up with this? Is this why I've never been in a serious relationship? Is this why I've never been hired here? Did they see right through me on my application?

I dart through the revolving door, heading straight toward the reception desk. The woman behind it is flawless. Her bun is sleek, her makeup perfect in every way, and her outfit pristine.

*She looks ten times more polished than me…
And I'm the one here for the interview.*

"Um, ma'am? Can we help you?" she asks, eyeing me up and down.

I smooth my hair and adjust my dress, trying to act normal, even though it feels like my nerves have been electrocuted as panic flows throughout my body. "Yes, could you tell me where the bathrooms are located?" I glance around, looking for a sign, but I see nothing.

"I'm sorry, we don't offer public bathroom access. It's reserved for customers, associates, and employees."

Ouch. That one stung. She doesn't think I belong. And maybe she's right.

I swallow hard. "Actually, I have a nine o'clock interview with Mr. Heartford."

My eyes stay fixed on the granite counter, afraid that if I look up, it will show just how rattled I am. How easily my insecurities betray me. How deeply the fear sinks in that I don't belong somewhere this glamorous.

Her eyes widen slightly. "Oh… my apologies, miss. Take a left at the elevators, follow the long hallway, and the bathrooms will be on your right."

"Thank you so much," I mumble, already halfway down the hall, walking fast, more like escaping, desperate for just thirty seconds to breathe.

I burst through the bathroom door and grip the cold granite countertop, my fingers digging in like it's the only thing tethering me to earth. My chest heaves as I try to catch my breath.

In through the nose. Four seconds. Out through the mouth. Four seconds.

Again. And again. Trying to quiet the fight-or-flight storm destroying me from the inside out.

Lila, your heart monitor was clear, but your body feels scared. Your heart is safe. Your body is reacting, but you are not dying. I am grounded, present, and healing from this.

My heart rate starts to calm. The erratic skips settle into a steady beat.

I glance down at my watch, checking my vitals. Sinus rhythm. Oxygen back to 99%. "Oh, thank God," I whisper, my voice barely audible over the hum of the fluorescent lights. "I can do this. This doesn't define me."

I repeat the words like a chant, trying to anchor myself. Trying to believe them. "Well, I know one thing you can't do." The sound of urine hitting the toilet follows. A male voice echoes through the bathroom, casual and sarcastic, like he belongs in here. *What the hell?*

"Ew! You perv! Get out!" I whip around, scanning for him.

"I swear I have a taser and I'm not afraid to use it! This is the women's bathroom, so get out!" I yank the purple taser from my purse and slowly move forward, heart racing, as I inch around the wall separating the sinks from the stalls.

"You can't use a urinal in that dress," a voice says, cool and calm, like this is just another Tuesday. I freeze, holding the taser out in front of me, ready in case he decides to make a move.

But he stays where he is.

He stands with his back to me in front of the urinal, completely unfazed. The quiet sound of urine trickling confirms it. He's tall and broad, dressed in a navy suit so perfectly tailored that it hugs every sculpted muscle as if it were stitched into his skin. And that's when it hits me.

I ran into the wrong bathroom. In my rush to calm down, I didn't even look at the door. Now I'm standing here, breathless and armed, while some ridiculously attractive man is just trying to relieve himself.

"Well, now who's the perv?" he says, and I know if I could see his face, it would be wearing a full-blown shit eating grin.

As if I'd barge in here to get an eyeful of him.

I cross my arms over my chest, still holding the taser. "Oh, please. If I wanted to see a skinny hot dog, I would've gone to the food truck outside."

He chuckles, low and cold, and I don't wait for another word. I snatch my purse off the counter and storm out.

What a prick.

But honestly? He got my mind off the panic. So weirdly, I'm kind of glad it happened. I stomp to the elevator and catch my pouty reflection in the mirrored doors.

I look like a hot mess.

I push my blonde curls back into place and smooth the fabric of my soft, blush-pink blazer dress. The tailored fit hugs my waist so effortlessly. The white ruffled hem brushes the tops of my thighs, and delicate pearl buttons run down the front, adding a touch of vintage charm. White ruffled cuffs peek from my wrists, giving it a romantic, almost doll-like finish. I grab my lip oil from my purse and glide it across my lips.

Well, this is as good as it's going to get.

I step into the elevator and press the button with a shaky finger. Top floor. The doors close behind me like a coffin sealing shut.

My heart flips in my chest. My brain is in absolute chaos.

I'm about to see Beck again for the first time since the Halloween party. Or... what if I already saw him this past weekend? He could've been the man between my legs... and I'd have no idea, while he sits there thinking about the taste of me on his lips. What if he looks at me and says, "Who the hell are you?" Even worse, what if he smirks and says, "I remember everything." Was it him in the Red Mask? Had it always been him? And if it is... then is he playing games with me?

I feel sick.

What if I blow the interview? What if I get the job? What if I make a fool of myself and end up working side by side with the guy who left me wrecked in every way?

UGH.

CHAPTER SEVENTEEN
LILA

The elevator lurches to a stop.

Lila, confidence is key. If I walk in with my head held high, as if I know what I'm doing, it's more likely I'll get the job... Right?

I also need to make sure Beck doesn't think I'm sad about him ghosting me this weekend, if it was him. I square my shoulders, run my fingers through my curls, and tug the blazer into place like it's armor.

Showtime.

"Twentieth floor," the robotic voice announces. The elevator doors glide open with a soft chime, and I step out like I've just crossed into another realm.

My lungs forget how to breathe. It's... stunning. No. Intimidating.

Wow. He really does like to go all out.

Above me, thousands of lilac-colored flowers cascade from the ceiling like a frozen waterfall. They hang in delicate clusters, suspended by golden wires that curl and twist like spun sunlight. The blooms look almost real. Soft. Ethereal. Haunting. Arranged as if they'd been captured mid-fall, frozen in time. They remind me of that night in the maze. The gazebo. A nightmare dressed in a fairytale.

It's the same flowers. But why? Is that a coincidence? Or a clue?

The walls rise around me, towering slabs of white marble veined with smoky gray, polished so perfectly they catch and bend the light like mirrors. The air smells clean, cool, and fresh, with a hint of cut flowers. Like purified air, only the wealthy can afford.

Honestly, I've never felt so small in an empty room.

I clutch my Chanel purse tighter. My heels click across the marble, letting it be known that someone is here. Everything reverberates off the walls, like you couldn't even whisper a secret without someone hearing it. Everything gleams. Everything screams: *You don't belong here.*

And still, I keep walking. Because somewhere behind one of these doors is Beck Heartford. Whether he remembers me or not, whether he's the Red Mask or just another billionaire with a God complex, I'm about to find out.

The receptionist desk sits at the far end of the grand hallway, and the woman behind it looks like she was designed to be here. Flawless dark chocolate skin. Amber eyes flecked with gold. A sleek low ponytail. A white skirt suit tailored so perfectly that it had to be custom-made, and most likely was. She radiates poise.

She fits his world effortlessly. And me? I look like a hurricane in Chanel.

I approach, heart hammering like a war drum in my ears. My eyes drop to the floor. I don't want her to see how cracked I feel beneath this outfit.

"Good morning," I say softly. "I have a nine o'clock interview with Mr. Heartford."

Her face lights up. "Perfect. You must be Ms. Anderson," she chirps, voice so chipper it sounds like she's already had three shots of espresso.

Damn. I need whatever this girl's drinking.

"If you need anything, let me know," she adds, flashing a movie-star smile. "I'm Jasmine. Mr. Heartford's personal assistant."

Let's be honest… I can't compete with that.

I nod, forcing what I hope looks like a calm, confident smile. But inside, I'm already planning my escape route.

"If you're ready," she says, gesturing toward a pair of massive double doors, "you can follow me to his office. They've been waiting for you."

They? What does she mean by they?

My stomach flips.

She glides across the marble like she was born on Mount Olympus. Effortless. Regal. And I'm scurrying behind her, trying not to trip, trying to disappear into her shadow, coming in behind a goddess.

Yeah. That's not exactly a power move.

She opens the doors, revealing an expansive office space that resembles a setting from a luxury design magazine. More marble. More gold. Everything is big, bold, and breathtaking. And then I see him.

Beck Heartford. The man I've never seen face-to-face without a mask. The moment I've replayed a thousand times in my head. What I'd say. How I'd hold his gaze. How I'd pretend not to care. But it all vanishes. Gone. Just like that.

He's seated like a king on his throne, one leg crossed over the other, sipping tea like he owns time. He's wearing a white button-down, sleeves casually rolled to his forearms, and tailored brown dress pants that hug him in all the ways that should be illegal. A matching coat drapes lazily across the back of the couch, like even his clothes know they belong here. His sun-kissed skin glows against the crisp white of his shirt. And his hair.

God help me.

Golden, tousled curls. Effortlessly perfect. Like he just walked off a beach in Malibu.

I want to run my hands through it. Fist it tight and tug him closer until we're lost in the same heat that ruined me Saturday night.

It frames his face with a kind of reckless elegance. Boyish. But the kind that carries the risk of getting your heart broken because he's the type to accidentally friend-zone you just by being nice to everyone. And you thought his friendliness meant he was into you. It softens him, but not enough to dull the sharp cut of his jaw or the way his ocean-dark eyes pin me like prey. And honestly, I want to run to see if he would chase me.

It's the kind of hair that belongs to a fairytale prince. He lowers his cup and reaches for the documents on the table, still unaware of my presence.

"Mr. Heartford, this is Lila Anderson. She is your nine o'clock interview," Jasmine says. He looks up immediately, giving her his full attention.

"Thank you. Please let me know when my next interview arrives. That will be all for now," he says, not breaking eye contact for a second. She blushes.

Who wouldn't... I mean, look at him.

"Good morning, Ms. Anderson..."

"Please, call me Lila," I cut in quickly.

"Lila, it's great to meet you. Please take a seat and we'll begin."

My heart sinks to my stomach when he says my name. He has no idea who I am. Or maybe he does, and if that's the case... he deserves an Oscar.

"Before we get started, could you tell me what our company does?"

The question throws me, but I don't hesitate. "Yes, sir. I, um..." I clear my throat, suddenly hyper-aware of how loud my heartbeat feels. He's watching me closely, completely still, calm, and entirely focused on me. The pressure is unbearable. I glance down, twiddling my thumbs.

"Heartford Cyphers International is… a private cybersecurity and intelligence firm. You work with agencies like the Federal Bureau of Investigation, the Central Intelligence Agency, the International Criminal Police Organization, and international nonprofits. The company focuses on tracking and dismantling criminal networks."

My fingers tighten around the strap of my bag. His gaze doesn't waver, examining my every syllable, patiently waiting for my answer. "Specifically, sex trafficking rings, digital slavery markets, black market webcam operations, and cyber exploitation tied to sex crimes." I pause, trying to remember the next part without rambling.

"You build breach detection software and surveillance systems used in sting operations. You monitor the dark web to identify victims and gather intelligence. Sometimes even going undercover to… to help." My voice wavers, but I push through. "You use data. Hacking. Encryption. Digital forensics. Behavioral profiling. You find the patterns other people miss. But it's not just about data."

I glance up and meet his eyes, even though it makes my stomach twist. "It's about people. About finding the ones who get lost in all the noise. About saving them." I take a breath, and suddenly I'm not reciting facts anymore. "I know what it's like to feel powerless. To watch someone you love suffer and not have the tools to help. Mr. Heartford, I know how to fight. Quietly. Desperately. When no one's watching. And I believe that kind of perspective matters here."

I pause. My throat tightens. "I notice things other people overlook… because I've been overlooked. But that doesn't mean I can't be part of something bigger. Something that actually changes lives."

He stares deep in my eyes, and I can't read his reaction.

Did I say something wrong? Did I screw it up? Should I get up and leave?

Then he smiles. Not a polite smile but a real one. Warm and full, with a flicker of light in his eyes that sends butterflies plunging straight into my stomach.

"Wow," he says. "That was phenomenal." He leans back slightly, still watching me. "The reason I ask is because some people don't really understand what this company does, and it becomes overwhelming to them. So, we prefer to explain everything during the first interview. But it seems like we won't have to do that with you."

We? First Jasmine said we… now him.

I glance around. It's just him in this luxury office.

Does he have a rat in his pocket or something?

I straighten my spine.

"Yes, sir. I've known what this company represents since I was a senior in high school."

He rubs his thumb slowly across his bottom lip like he's thinking.

Sir, please don't do that in front of me. I can't control myself around you.

"What inspired you to pursue a career in this industry?"

My lips part, but no words come out. I glance down at my hands. They are trembling as the memory creeps in, uninvited. I lace my fingers together, trying to stop the shake, trying to steady my breath.

Tell him the truth. You can trust him.

"I..." My voice is so soft I barely recognize it. "Can I be honest with you?"

Beck nods once, slow and solemn. "Of course." His voice is gentle. His posture is polished and attentive, every inch of him focused like I'm the only thing that matters in the room.

They are warm and comforting, like we are the only two people in the entire building.

I swallow hard. "I was seventeen," I whisper. "Late for a shift at a coffee shop. I thought I'd save time by cutting through a back alley."

My nervous system is on edge, every muscle locked tight. It's hard to even say the words out loud because if I do, it makes it real. A reality. One I barely survived. "In that alley… I was taken."

The words hang between us. Too loud. Too quiet. Too final. He doesn't speak. Doesn't flinch. He just listens.

"I woke up in a room that felt wicked. The walls were damp. No windows. Just cracked concrete, the steady sound of dripping water, and this awful smell… like death was hiding in the corners." My voice catches. I force it out anyway. "It was pitch black. But I could hear him."

I bite the inside of my cheek to keep from falling apart in front of my potential boss.

Not yet. Don't fall apart yet.

"He had a Russian accent. Cool. Calm. Almost gentle. Like he had done it before. Like, I was not even a person to him. Just another girl. Another number." The next part clogs my throat like cement. But I say it. "Every second felt like it lasted an hour. I didn't know what was going to happen to me… but I knew what he wanted to happen. And I thought…" My voice cracks, breath hitching

"I thought I'd die there. Just vanish. Be forgotten." I pause. The silence sharpens around me. "He said if I didn't do what he told me, he'd ruin my family. He knew we were poor. Knew we had nothing. He used it to scare me, and I believed him. I was terrified. And alone."

Tears burn behind my eyes. I don't let them fall. "I did what he said. I walked down this motel hallway that reeked of sex and stale smoke. The carpet was sticky against my bare feet. The walls looked bruised. Like they'd been hit repeatedly. There were holes in the drywall. Jagged. New. Everything about this foreign place screamed violence. But the one thing that I will never forget is…"

A long pause. I force the words out like they're knives in my throat. "The red door."

Beck doesn't speak. His jaw is locked in place. I barely whisper. "I was seconds away from losing everything. My family. My virginity. My identity. Who I am. And then… your company saved me. I didn't even know it was real at first. I remember flashing lights. Men in bulletproof vests. Shouting in a language I didn't understand. And then he was gone, and I was saved."

I exhale, but it feels more like a collapse. "I still dream about it sometimes. The door. The hallway. His voice. I still panic, out of nowhere, like he's right behind me. My brain forgets I survived."

Silence. It's crushing. But I force myself to finish.

"That was the night I started having panic attacks. I never told anyone what happened. Not my parents. Not my best friend. I guess, it felt like if I said it out loud, it would crawl back into my life and retake everything."

I blink quickly, but a tear escapes anyway. "I guess I want to work here because if I can help someone escape their own red door, then maybe what I went through won't be in vain."

The silence stretches. Thicker than before. A thousand unspoken things fill the air.

Beck's expression doesn't change, but something in him does. His jaw tightens.

His hands lower to the table, as if moving too quickly might break something inside him. Then he sets his coffee down with care.

"Lila…" His voice is faint and somber. "Thank you for telling me that." He leans forward, elbows braced on his knees, and there's a softness in his eyes sharp enough to split me open.

"What happened to you should never happen to anyone. And the fact that you're here, in this room, telling me this…" He pauses, his throat working as he swallows. "That's courage most people will never understand. And the fact that you want to work here, with the pain you've gone through… that's exactly why you do belong here."

My chest caves in. I don't know if I'm about to cry or vomit or run out of the room. But then he adds, gently, like a promise: "You belong here. With this company. With us. With me."

CHAPTER EIGHTEEN
LILA

CLAP.
CLAP.
CLAP.

A slow mocking echo breaks the silence like a slap to the face. "Let's not be naive, Beck," a voice drawls. "She could be lying through her teeth. You know how manipulative women are."

I freeze. The voice doesn't come from Beck. It comes from behind him, somewhere deeper in the room. From the massive desk chair facing the wall-to-ceiling windows, back turned, silhouetted against the skyline. And then the chair turns slow and deliberate.

Well, there's the we I couldn't find.

He's been sitting there this whole time, eavesdropping, listening to every gut-wrenching word that took everything in me to talk about with Beck. My stomach drops through the floor as my mouth goes dry. The bastard was listening to my trauma like it was entertainment. He heard everything. Every word. Every crack in my voice. Every secret I swore I'd keep buried is now in the hands of a stranger. Not just Beck. Him. And the way he listened… quiet, calculating. He knows my weakness. And people like him? They use that kind of power.

Bile rises in my throat. I cross my arms, stunned.

Is he serious? How dare he even suggest I'd lie about something so raw. So real and painful for me to even talk about.

Beck sighs and rubs his forehead like he's already exhausted. "Lila, this is Kage. My best friend and my advisor."

And then our eyes meet.

Oh no.

The navy suit. The broad, muscular frame.

Great… It's him. The bathroom guy. Mr. Urinal. Maybe he won't recognize me… or my voice. Where are the hidden cameras? Because my life is clearly a joke.

And then it happens. That grin. That smug, jackass grin spreads across his face like he's been waiting for this moment. He knows exactly who I am.

"Ohhh, this is funny," he says, leaning back in his business chair. "We can't hire her."

Beck frowns, crossing his legs and looking completely caught off guard. "And why not?"

"Because," Kage says smoothly, "Ms. Anderson was spying on me in the men's bathroom this morning. She's a perv. How can a perv work at our company with what we represent?"

My mouth drops.

He did not just say that. Who the hell does he think he is?

And just like that, my other personality decides to make an entrance. I really did try to keep her contained, but I stand to my feet, ready to defend myself and fight this rich douchebag. "Listen here, skinny dick. I would never lie about my darkest secret. And if I wanted to look at you or make a move, trust me, I would have. But I didn't. And if you must know, I was trying to use the women's bathroom."

I emphasize *women's* with every ounce of attitude I have.

Oh God. I just said that. Out loud. To him. In front of my potential boss.

I sit back down stiffly, cross my legs, and take a casual sip of tea like I didn't just verbally attack the room. Silence. My heart pounds.

Kage narrows his eyes like he's deciding whether to argue with me or throw me out the window. Then, out of nowhere, Beck does the last thing I expect. He throws his head back... and laughs.

Is he laughing at me? At Kage? At both of us?

Kage scowls. "What the hell are you laughing at?"

Beck clutches his chest, trying to catch his breath. "Well, we have to hire her now."

"And why is that?" he snaps.

"Because I've never seen anyone stand up to you. And I've definitely never heard someone call you a skinny dick."

He breaks into another round of laughter. A smile tugs at my lips. I can't help it. I made him laugh. And God, does he look good when he laughs.

Shit. I want him.

After what we did the other night... I must make him mine. And that smile? It could melt me into a puddle.

Kage crosses his arms and glares out the window like he's plotting my potential death. "And what about the other thing?" He mutters.

Beck's brows draw together. "What other thing?"

"This is the girl who decided to cheat in the maze. We all saw it on the cameras."

I blink, wide-eyed, unable to process what I just heard.

Stop. No. This can't get worse. CAMERAS?! I tased Clint to get this interview. I practically fell to my knees for the Red Mask while he was fingering me.

The memory slams into me like a freight train. I slap a hand over my face in horror.

They saw it.
They saw everything.

My stomach drops. My face flushes red-hot. Beck turns toward me, his expression unreadable. "Wait… this is Rapunzel from the party?"

"Well, yeah," Kage says dryly. "Didn't you recognize her?"

I brace myself. Waiting for the judgment. Waiting for the disgust. Waiting for the moment he decides I'm not worth hiring, even after I told him my deepest inner pain.

Beck stands and walks toward me, his tall, muscular frame looming over where I sit.

This is it. I pissed off the golden retriever. He's going to revoke the money. Maybe even humiliate me for showing up, thinking I ever had a chance in a place like this.

"I searched for you everywhere after you disappeared," he says softly. "I saw you in the crowd and kept hoping I'd run into you after you won. But you were gone. Vanished like a ghost." His voice dips lower, almost like he's still trying to convince himself I was ever real.

He gently takes my hand and pulls me to my feet, standing close to me.

What is happening?

Then, like I've stepped into some twisted fairytale, he lifts my hand to his mouth and kisses it. Soft. Intentional. Familiar.

This confirms it. He is the Red Mask. That's what he did before he zip-tied my wrist.

My heart skips. Not because I'm anxious, but because I'm relieved.

I know it's him. But are we still playing his game? Should I run? Or should I tell him I already know?

"Please forgive me for not recognizing you," he murmurs. "That night on the dance floor, one of my contacts tore. I could barely see. But I didn't need to see you to know I wanted to find you again."

God. Only men in books talk like this. But he keeps saying and doing all the right things. Over and over and over.

I smile, eyes dropping to the floor, blushing like a schoolgirl. And then it's ruined by the villain in the room. Kage stands up, and the air shifts instantly. He slides his hands into the pockets of his navy suit and briskly makes his way toward us.

"That's enough of this bullshit. Stop thinking with your cock, Beck. Let's focus on the real issue."

My eyes drift to Kage's side profile as he snaps at Beck, and I'm completely caught off guard. My thighs twitch, warmth pooling low in my stomach. He steps in close. Too close. And for the first time, I really see him. And honestly, I wish I didn't because he is absolutely captivating.

Tall. Masculine. Dark brown hair, thick and tousled like he just casually strolled out of Fashion Week in Paris. Effortless. Sex on legs. A boy next door dipped in something dark and dangerous.

I haven't even seen his smile yet, but if I do? Go ahead and zip me into a body bag. And then his eyes. God. His eyes. They aren't the Phantom's icy blues that haunt my dreams… but damn, these will do.

They are a kaleidoscope of green and gold. Like moss and wildfire woven together. The kind of eyes that could make you confess sins you haven't even committed. And I hate that I notice all of it. Hate that my body is reacting to him. Because I just met this man, and he is already my archnemesis. I don't want anything from his arrogant prick. The asshole who just called me a liar and a perv.

And yet this perfectly sculpted man in Prada has no idea the power he holds over me.

I mentally clamp my jaw shut before I start to drool.

I mean… It wouldn't be the worst thing to get Eiffel Towered by these two. Aster did draw that out for me once when I asked what it was. She said it was the most erotic night of her life.

No.

No.

No.

Get it together, Lila. You're in trouble. They saw you cheat. Should I confess to it all? No. I can't do that. My mom needs treatment.

I stand my ground. "I didn't cheat."

"Yes, you did. This is your third time lying, Lila. This doesn't look good for you," the smug bastard says.

The way my name rolls off his tongue…

"No, I didn't. The only rule that Mr. Heartford said was to make it to the end of the maze… not how."

Kage locks eyes with Beck, his glare sharp enough to cut steel. "What the fuck. You didn't specify?"

Beck slides his hands into his pockets and shrugs, completely unbothered. "To be honest, I'd had a couple of shots. I was buzzing, so I may have forgotten to be specific. But even with that buzz, I couldn't forget you, Rapunzel."

My heart swoons as I smile at Beck.

Kage rubs his forehead like he's about to lose his mind. "Dammit. I can't be your friend anymore if I hear that shit one more time."

I chuckle internally because, weirdly, I like watching him squirm.

"Okay, so what would you like me to do, Your Majesty?" Beck says, with complete sarcasm on his sharp tongue.

Who owns the company? Because I'm not sure anymore, by the way they're acting.

"The price she'll pay for the favor is cleaning your house once a week."

Okay, so that's really not so bad. It definitely could be worse. But if the drama king had kept his damn mouth shut, I doubt Beck would have made me do anything. Not with the way he was looking at me. Not with the way he kissed my hand like I was his.

My heart pounds with frustration. I didn't spend years earning a cybersecurity degree to end up a glorified housemaid. But fine. I've had worse jobs.

"And since she tased and blackmailed Clint, our most loyal employee, she will work on his team. He will be her manager."

Damn. That is cold, but I guess I deserve that.

"Do you have any objections, Miss Anderson?"

I hold my tongue and glare at Kage. "Nope. That sounds perfect," I say, every word laced with sarcasm. I turn to Beck with a softer smile. "Thank you, sir, for the opportunity to work here. And thank you for taking care of my wish. I won't let you down."

He smiles and takes my hand. "We'll be in touch. Can I have your number? Not as an employee, but as what we were at the party."

Those words send butterflies swirling in my low belly. The memory of his hard length pressed against my backside makes my knees wobble.

Answer him before you drop to the floor.

"Yes. I'd love that."

Kage huffs, clearly annoyed. "Fuck. I'm done with this shit. Be here at seven o'clock tomorrow morning. Tenth floor." He storms out.

And damn, I like to watch him leave.

The door slams behind him like a gavel. Final. Cold. Unforgiving. But the silence he leaves behind? It screams louder than anything he said.

And I can't stop thinking about the way he looked at me like he knew me. Not just from the bathroom. Deeper than that. His anger felt too sharp to be about a job. Too personal. Like I crossed a line I didn't even know was there. Was he in the maze? Has Aster dated him? Did I ghost him on Tinder? No. I would've remembered those eyes. Wouldn't I?

Beck brushes my arm gently, and I manage a smile. But my mind is already chasing the shadow that just walked out of the room. Because Kage wasn't just pissed, he looked haunted. And I'm starting to think I'm not the only one running from something… or someone.

CHAPTER NINETEEN
LILA

The hospital smells like bleach and something sweeter, as if it's trying too hard to cover it up. Vanilla maybe. Or Thieves.

I hate it. I hate how familiar it's becoming.

I step into my mom's room, and for a moment, I forget how to breathe. She looks smaller today, as if this place is draining the life from her little by little. Literally, she looks so weak, like she couldn't lift something that weighs five pounds. Fragile, like a brittle plant left too long without water. And it's only her first day of chemo. But the moment her eyes find mine, she smiles like I'm the only good thing left in her fading world.

"Hey, sweetie," she whispers. I blink back the burn rising in my throat and force a smile. "Hey, Mom."

A framed photo catches my eye. It's of us at the beach, sitting beside her hospital bed like a forgotten memory. Her hair is windblown, her smile bright and carefree. I barely recognize her. But I remember that woman. And I know she's still in there somewhere. Aster practically launches across the room and pulls me into a hug.

"How did the interview go? We've been dying to know!"

I lean into her ear and whisper, "It was a shit show. Drive me home and I'll tell you everything."

Aster narrows her eyes, trying to read my face.

If only she knew. My body has whiplash from Beck and Kage, and I'm not sure if I need a therapist… or a cold shower.

I give her a tight-lipped smile and nod toward my mom, silently asking her to play along. "It was great, Mom. I got the job and I start tomorrow."

She exhales slowly, like even talking takes effort. "That's great, honey. I knew you would get the job. You have worked incredibly hard for this opportunity."

I move toward her carefully, like one wrong move might break her, and sit on the edge of the bed. "How are you feeling after your first treatment?"

"I'm feeling pretty good," she says, but her eyes lie straight to my face.

I take her hand gently, my thumb brushing soft circles over her knuckles. "It's okay to not be okay. This is hard and—"

Aster kneels beside her and takes her other hand, finishing my sentence for me. "We just want to be here for you. You've always been there for us. And we love you."

A tear slips down Mom's cheek. I wipe it away before it falls. "I love you girls. I'm so glad you have each other."

Aster and I share a look, silent but solid. She squeezes my hand. "I love you, sis."

KNOCK. KNOCK. KNOCK.

"Ladies, can I come in?" Dad's voice drifts from the doorway. He steps inside, holding a tray like it's sacred. "Grilled cheese and tomato soup. Your mom's favorite."

I smile, soft and bittersweet. God, I hope someday I have someone who loves me like that.

"Come in," Aster says warmly.

"Oh, honey, thank you," Mom murmurs. "But the chemo's made me so nauseous. I can't eat right now…"

"Mom, please try to eat. You need to stay strong," I say softly. "If you'd rather, I can pick up some protein shakes and bring them back tonight."

"I'm trying, darling." She pauses, looking down at her thin fingers. "Go ahead and bring them tomorrow, and I'll try… for you."

"Wait… you're not going home?"

"Unfortunately, not. The chemo trial requires inpatient observation. I'll be here for six months."

Six months.

This sterile, humming place. The bright lights. The quiet suffering. The too-white walls.

This is her world now.

Aster moves beside me and laces her fingers through mine. She doesn't say a word, but her touch says everything.

"Okay, Mom," I whisper. "We'll be here. Every step of the way." I smile, but it feels like cracked porcelain. My chest aches with everything I'm not saying, but at least she's fighting. At least she's still here. She is trying.

If I have to scrub Beck's floors for the rest of my life to keep her alive, I will. If I have to work under Clint and eat every ounce of pride, I will. If Kage wants to yell at me every day, I'll take it with a smile because she's my rock. And I'll do anything to keep her here with me.

❁ ❁ ❁ ❁ ❁ ❁ ❁ ❁ ❁

The second we hit a red light, Aster throws her head back and groans. "If you don't tell me what happened in that interview, I swear I'll crash this car into Beck's building."

"Girl," I mumble, slumping lower in my seat, "they saw everything in the maze. What I did to Clint. What I did with the Red Mask…"

Her jaw drops. "You're kidding. Wait, what did you do to Clint? When did you even see him?"

"I forgot to tell you. Clint was dressed up as one of the monsters in the maze. He decided to screw with me and basically called me worthless. Said I only made it this far because I use you. So I pulled the taser from my purse and zapped him once, and I was about to aim for the balls when he mentioned he could get me a job at Heartford's… so I let him email Beck."

Her contagious laugh echoes through the Mercedes, and I can't help but laugh with her. "Oh my gosh, Lila! That's freaking epic. Don't even think about feeling bad. He totally deserved it, and you know it. God, I only wish you'd done that to him in college!"

"Yeah, me too. But here's the kicker. Clint is supposedly their best employee… and now I have to work under him, and now he's my manager."

"What the hell! That doesn't sound like Beck!"

"Because it wasn't him. It was the one who shall not be named, or he might show up and make a scene."

She looks at me, confused. "Umm… who is that?"

"Kage. The grade-A asshole who hates me for no reason."

"Lila," she says, eyes wide, "I absolutely love you so much, but you have the worst luck of anyone I've ever met."

"You're telling me! I wanted to melt into the damn floor and slip out under the door."

"What did you say? Did you at least apologize?"

"No. I held my ground. And now I have to clean Beck's house once a week and work under Clint for a year."

Aster whistles low. "Damn. That's cold. How do these things always happen to you?" She's cackling now, full-on laughing like it's the best story she's ever heard.

"It's not funny," I say, even though I'm already laughing too.

"Just resign," she says, wiping her eyes. "My family will cover your Mom's treatment."

"No." I shake my head. "I need to do this. For me."

"I've never really asked… why does working there matter so much to you?"

She's right. She never has. And I never came up with a lie because I hoped I'd never have to. I'm a terrible liar. But I can't tell her the truth. Not about that night. Not about what really happened. It would destroy her. And if I had told her back then, her family might have gotten involved. He could have come after them. And if anything had happened to them because of me, I wouldn't have survived the guilt.

What do I even say…

"I had a distant cousin who was kidnapped," I say, keeping my voice calm. "They rescued her."

Her expression softens. "Oh wow. That makes sense. You want to help others the way they helped her."

"Exactly."

She doesn't know that it's because of that night. She doesn't know how badly I want to reclaim what was taken from me. And I will never put that weight on her shoulders.

She nods and grabs my hand. "Still… if they mess with you again, I'm kicking Kage's designer-wrapped ass."

I smirk. "I think you should date him. You've got the same energy. Hot. Wicked. Mildly unhinged."

She snorts. "We'd either kill each other or elope in Vegas."

I laugh. "Double date. You and Kage. Beck and I."

She rolls her eyes. "That sounds like an HR violation waiting to happen."

My phone buzzes in my lap.

Once.

Twice.

Three times.

I glance down.

UNKNOWN: *Good luck tomorrow, Princess. Try not to think about me too much. Will you be at the club this weekend? I want to finish what we started…*

My breath catches.

Princess.

The word hits me like a live wire. My heart slams against my ribs. Heat spreads beneath my skin like wildfire. I stare at the message.

Then reread it. And again. There's only one person I gave my number to today. Beck. It has to be him. The way he kissed my hand. The way he looked at me was like I was something he had been searching for. The way he made me feel like I mattered. But… he looked confused when he saw me, as if he didn't recognize me at all.

Could he really be the man in the red mask? Was it him in the pleasure room? My stomach twists. Because if it's not Beck… Then who the hell is it?

My fingers hover over the screen. Should I reply? Should I ask him? Should I confront him? Or should I admit what I already know?

Whoever this is… He's still watching. Still waiting. Still wanting more… More of me.

And I think a part of me wants to be wanted like that again.

CHAPTER TWENTY
LILA

The smell of coffee hits my nose. I inhale deeply, hoping it will kickstart my energy. I couldn't sleep. Not after that text. Not with the thought of him having my number and knowing my every move.

The Red Mask haunts my every thought, every breath I take. I've been near him four times now, and each time, his presence consumes me. Like smoke in my lungs, and I can't exhale. Like a fire that takes hold of every nerve in my body and refuses to let go. But last night, I ignored his message on purpose.

I wanted him to come find me. To get angry. To punish me. But nothing. No double text. No knock at my door. Just silence. Ugh… not exactly how I pictured my sleepless night.

Lying in bed, waiting for a masked, raging psycho to come stomping through the door. For his hand to wrap around my throat like a collar made of pure desire. For us to push and pull, claw and crave, knowing sleep was never part of the plan. Just sweat, teeth, and lips. All. Night. Long.

"Good morning. Welcome to Heartford Cypher International. Do you need assistance with anything?"

I snap out of my thoughts. The doorman, a kind, older man with warm eyes, smiles at me.

Sadly, he probably took this job because retirement no longer covers the bills. Between groceries, medicine, and rent, people are barely surviving. Inflation has gutted the middle and lower classes. In New York alone, homelessness has doubled in a year. Most people can't afford to stop working. So, we keep going. Not to live, but to survive.

Inflation is cruel like that, and it doesn't matter if we're young or old, healthy or sick.

I watched it happen to my parents as it took and took, until our home was gone and there was nothing left to steal but who we were. My heart breaks looking at his smile, because I see straight through it.

"No, sir, thank you, though. Today's my first day, and I'm a little nervous. Do you have any advice for doing well here?"

He smiles and gently pats my shoulder. "Darling, stay true to who you are. Because if you don't… they'll always find out what's buried deep within your soul."

The words send shivers up my spine. Each syllable sounds sinister.

They… Who? Beck and Kage? Someone else?

"Oh… well, ummm, thank you, sir. Have a wonderful day!" I walk away quickly, nerves prickling my skin as I try to shake off those chilling words.

Am I supposed to be scared? Should I fear them? Beck seems kind. He appears to be the type who would give someone the shirt off his back without a second thought. But Kage? Now that's a different story.

I reach the gold elevators and watch as the numbers tick down from fifteen to one. Each blink feels like a countdown to my own personal downfall. My stomach tightens. My heart climbs into my throat, making it hard to swallow. I've never been good at making friends, especially not at the Academy. Poverty made me invisible.

But I'm an adult now, so there's no reason to feel like I can't make friends… Still, the pain lingers like a bruise on my soul. Waiting to be rejected. To be ostracized by my peers.

Shit. I'm so pathetic.

The elevator opens, and I slide into the corner, hoping I'll blend into the gold reflection. I look down and press floor ten as it lights up. Then I catch a figure entering my peripheral vision. I shove my anxiety down. "Good morning!" I say, overly perky.

"Oh God, not you…" He mutters, stepping back as if he can escape, but it's too late. The doors close like a coffin lid. Perfect. Now it's just me and Kage… the asswipe.

"Don't you have a private elevator, so you don't have to associate with peasants?" I ask, turning to look up at this sexy, arrogant son of a bitch.

His green supernovas burn into mine. "I do. But unfortunately, maintenance is working on it. So, I have to ride with you." He looks me up and down like I'm a disease he doesn't want to catch.

But why is there a flicker of heat in my lower belly? Why do I want to touch him? No. Ew. Absolutely not. I'm not turned on by him. That would be an abomination, Lila.

I cross my arms. "What the hell is your problem?"

He freezes, then a slow, dangerous smirk curves at his mouth. He reaches behind me and stops the elevator. We hang suspended between two floors. The lights hum quietly above us, and the world outside fades away.

My heart freezes the moment the elevator does. Then it starts pounding like it knows exactly what's coming or what it's secretly hoping for.

He doesn't speak. He doesn't move. He just watches me. And somehow, that's worse. The silence stretches into something sharp. Something forbidden. I feel it all over my skin. Prickling. Tingling. Like the ground trembling before an earthquake.

Then he steps forward. Not fast. Not aggressive. Just slow and certain. Like he knows exactly what he's doing to me, my back presses against the mirrored wall. I try to hold still, but I can't. I feel every inch of his presence closing in on mine.

He moves like the Grim Reaper. Cold. Deliberate. Like he's here to steal something vital. Like a man who doesn't need to ask. Like a man who always gets what he wants. And right now, he's looking at me like I might be it. And I hate how much my body responds to him. My eyes drag down his frame before I can stop them.

The black Prada suit he's wearing outlines his every defined muscle. It hugs his chest, his shoulders, his thighs. But something is off with it… There are creases in the fabric near his chest, as if someone had clung to him. Like someone needed him the way I'm afraid I do. His shirt is white. Crisp. Clean. But the collar is open. The top button is undone, revealing just a hint of golden skin beneath. His tie hangs low, loose, and slightly crooked. It appears to have been tugged on.

At least one of us is getting some.

I swallow hard, the knot forming in my throat. His hair is a mess of soft brown waves, tousled just enough to look like it's effortlessly messy… or like someone ran their fingers through it while moaning his name. A flicker of desire pulses where it shouldn't.

He's probably married.

I glance down, searching for a ring, but his hands stay buried in his pockets.

Dammit.

His jaw is sharp, covered in the kind of stubble that would leave marks on your thighs if you let it. His lips are full, smooth, and unapologetic. But what draws me in most is the small freckle on the upper right side of his lip. They are parted just slightly, like he is already imagining saying something filthy, even though he hates me, even though he seems to live just to torment me.

His scent hits me next. Sandalwood and something warmer beneath it. Something masculine. Clean. Expensive. There's no smoke. No leather. No spearmint. At least I know he's not the Red Mask.

Thank God.

He doesn't touch me. Not yet. But he doesn't have to. The tension between us is already alive. Already throbbing in the space we haven't closed. I blink, trying to find my voice, trying to breathe. He stops just inches away. His eyes burn into mine. Green fire. Pure control. And I know if he so much as touches my wrist, I will come undone. Right here. Right now. In a gold elevator between two floors. And the worst part? I think he knows it.

I don't want him. I don't want him. I don't want him.

He cages me in with his arms, one on either side of my head, palms flat against the elevator wall. Not touching. Not speaking. Just hovering, like he's daring me to move first. His breath stays steady. Controlled. Mine's anything but that. My pulse is pounding in my ears. My skin buzzes.

This can't be attraction. It's fear. It has to be fear.

But fear doesn't make your thighs clench.

"You're my problem, Lila." The way he says my name is slow, like he's savoring it. It makes my stomach tighten. No one should sound like that. Not someone who looks at me like I'm beneath him. My breaths come shallow and uneven while the air is charged with tension. This elevator isn't just small. It feels like it's closing in around me. Like it's pressing me into him. Or maybe he's pressing into me without ever touching me. He's so close. Too close. If I leaned forward even an inch, my lips would brush the warm skin of his neck. And I hate that part of me that wonders how he'd taste.

I should back away. I should tell him to fuck off. Instead, I whisper, "What did I do to you?"

He leans in. His lips hover by my ear. Close enough for me to feel the ghost of his breath trailing along my skin. My pulse stutters. My knees threaten to give out. The heat rolling off his body is suffocating. Not just warmth. Pressure. I don't move. I can't move. Every nerve in my body is pulled tight. Screaming for contact. One inch. That's all it would take. One inch and I'd feel his mouth on my skin. And God help me, I want it. Just a little. Just enough to ruin me.

"You exist." He presses the button. The elevator jolts. We're moving again. It's not until the doors open that I realize I'm breathless. My chest is heaving. My body is trembling. My heart is a complete traitor. I shove his arm aside and step out. Like, I'm not seconds away from collapsing to my knees. Like I'm not drenched in confusion, heat, and shame.

As I walk away, I feel him watching me. Silent. Unapologetic. I don't look back. But then I hear him speak.

"Careful, Lila… You're starting to interest me."

CHAPTER TWENTY-ONE
LILA

My chest still rises and falls like I just stepped out of a sauna. Because, apparently, I did. Only it wasn't a sauna. It was an elevator. With him. The one I refuse to name. Because if I say it out loud, I might have an orgasm on the spot.

God, I don't even know what just happened. It felt like a daydream. Or a trance. Or maybe I stumbled into the damn Twilight Zone.

Did he hypnotize me? Use some kind of pheromone-packed cologne? That has to be it. It's the only explanation that makes any sense. Because what else could cause this kind of feral reaction from me? Here I am, spiraling over what just happened in that elevator, while he's probably already planning how to get me fired by the end of the week to avoid seeing my face.

But seriously, what did I ever do to him? I met him yesterday, and he's acting like I murdered his dog or betrayed his family name. Like we're sworn enemies from a past life. Like, I personally offended his entire existence just by breathing.

"Because you exist." What does that even mean? The way he said it... like my presence alone is enough to piss him off. Did I unknowingly wrong him years ago? Is he some forgotten rival from high school that my brain just decided to delete? God, who knows.

Whatever. I'm over it. I have to get it together and focus. Clint is my team lead now, which means I've got to establish one thing... and fast. He does not get to run all over me. Not unless he wants to get tased again, and this time in the balls, because I'm not backing down to him or Kage.

I roll my shoulders back and let the soft fabric of my purple ruffle tea dress grounds me. My cream Mary Jane heels click with confidence against the marble floors as I sway my hips and flip my half-up curls over my shoulder. The bow in my hair bounces behind me, delicate but proud. My pearl earrings catch the light just enough to whisper that yes, I'm here, and I'm not going anywhere, so deal with it.

I may not have grown up with money, but Aster taught me how to dress like I did. She always said the right outfit can build an entire illusion. Even when you feel like shit on the inside, put on the right dress and it becomes armor. A mask to cover every crack in your confidence. And right now, I need every layer of it if I'm going to outlast these men mentally.

I walk through the lower-level hallway, and it's just as extravagant as the upper floor where I interviewed. The lilacs are still floating from the ceiling like soft magic, suspended in time, defying gravity.

What is it with the lilacs? The gazebo in the maze. Beck's office floor. And now here. Wherever they are, they're breathtaking, and I get to see them every day. And honestly, I can't say I hate it.

I bite back a giddy smile and do a tiny invisible happy dance in my head. This is everything I dreamed of.

Well... almost everything. Minus Clint. And the one who shall not be named.

A gold plaque catches my eye ahead.

Cybersecurity and Intelligence Division.

Here we go.

I breathe in the lilacs, their sweet fragrance filling my lungs as I try to steady my pulse. My smartwatch vibrates at my wrist, flashing my elevated heart rate.

It's okay. You're okay, Lila. He chose you for this job, so you are enough.

I press a hand to my chest, exhale slowly, then grip the tall glass door handle and pull it open. And there he is. Clint. Perched like a smug little devil at the gates of hell. He leans back with frat boy body language and that same damn cocky grin.

"Well, well, well. Look what the cat dragged in."

I raise an eyebrow. "Don't start with me, Clint. You know I can whoop your ass."

He chuckles. "Yeah, sure. With a taser, maybe… which, if I remember correctly, is exactly how I ended up becoming your boss."

I shrug, grinning. "Work smarter, not harder."

Then I wink, to make sure he knows I'm not even a little sorry.

His smile stretches wider, but something behind his eyes flickers like he's actually almost impressed. "I'd love to bicker all day, princess, but we've got work to do. We're already behind."

Princess? What the hell. Did I hear that right? The Red Mask calls me princess. And now that I think about it, Clint was the first one to call me that in the maze right before I tased him.

No. No way. But what if he is? What if this is just one big game to him? A twisted little mindfuck?

Play it cool, Lila. Breathe.

I nod casually, pretending I didn't just short-circuit. He gestures for me to follow, and I fall into step behind him.

"So, this is my office," he says, opening the glass door to a sleek corner space. It's basically a luxury fish tank overlooking the skyline. A modern black desk sits at the center, equipped with three oversized monitors, a glowing mechanical keyboard, and a high-end mouse. A tall black computer chair waits behind it, looking like a throne built for someone who thrives on control.

Floor-to-ceiling windows stretch across the far wall, framing a stunning view of New York City. It isn't as massive as Beck's office, but it still radiates power and status. The final detail, the one that makes the space feel truly intimidating, is the pair of leather chairs positioned across from his desk. They are angled with just enough precision to resemble an interrogation setup, especially with the glass walls exposing everything to the entire floor.

Wow. What did he do to get this setup? Blow his "buddy" Kage under the boardroom table?

"And your desk is right across from mine," he adds with a smirk. "If you need anything like paperclips, sarcasm, or ego bruising, you know where to find me." He looks at me like I'm a problem he wouldn't mind getting in trouble for.

"Hey, hey, hey, don't make me get HR involved," I say with a wicked grin, teasing him.

"Oh, please. They wouldn't believe you over me. I'm the best employee at this company!"

I arch a brow and lean one elbow on the desk, chin in hand. "Well, Frat Boy… that was before I got here."

The office floor is spacious and features an open-concept design, with eight desks separated by low walls. I stare at my sad little cubicle. Two monitors. A keyboard. A mouse. And a row of empty gray shelves that haven't seen a hint of personality in years.

Ugh. It's giving corporate prison.

"Can I decorate this depressing box that I'll be trapped in for eight hours?" I ask.

"Sure, but only if you put up a shrine to me. Black and white photos work best. Really brings out my jawline."

I shoot him a flat look. "Are you always this arrogant?"

"Only with you." He smirks like it's a compliment.

I rub my brow, already exhausted. "I can't believe Kage stuck me with you."

Clint grins, full of himself. "Damn right he did. Bro always has my back."

I huff under my breath. "Probably because he knows you get off to his picture."

"What was that?"

"Oh, nothing." I smile sweetly.

I narrow my eyes, amused. "So, what are you teaching me today? Besides, how not to flirt?" I laugh at the witty remark.

"You wish, princess." My heart skips a beat at that word.

Not this again. Why is he calling me that? He literally called me a phony princess in the maze. Is he taunting me? Mocking me? Trying to get a reaction? Or is he the Red Mask, and it's not really Beck? Maybe this is exactly what he wanted. For me to overthink. To spiral. And unfortunately, it's working. Because now I can't stop wondering if it's just a nickname. Or if it's his favorite way of being an asshole.

He leans back in his chair, arms folded across his chest. "We have a lot going on right now with different undercover operations and rescues, but this week, you and I will be focused on planning the annual masquerade ball. It's a pretty big deal around here. Think royal ball-level fancy. Full black tie, designer gowns, champagne, music… the whole nine yards. Beck Heartford never holds back when it comes to spoiling his people."

My stomach flips.

A masquerade ball? Socializing? I don't even have a gown... I'm not ready for this.

"When is it?" I ask, trying to keep my voice even.

"Three weeks away from Saturday," he repeats. "So, make sure you've got a dress and some killer dance moves. Want me to be your date?"

"Hell no. I'd rather go alone."

"Suits yourself," he says, patting his chest. "But I'm a catch, Lila."

"Yeah, yeah, yeah," I mutter, smoothing the front of my dress and adjusting my hair. "Where is everyone?"

"In the conference room," he replies. "Wanna meet the team?"

"Please." I exhale, low and steady.

"You look great, by the way," he says. "They're going to love you. Just be yourself."

That throws me for a loop.

Why is he being nice to me? In the maze, he was cold. Pissed at me for lying, for being poor, and for surviving the game my own way. Did something change? Because I haven't.

I follow him down the hallway that branches off from our main office space. My heart pounds in my ears. My skin feels warm and flushed, but I am not panicking. Strangely, I feel okay. Safe even. Like I might actually belong here. Like maybe I have a real shot at making this something stable. Something good. Something mine.

Clint pushes open a door, and inside, seven employees sit around a large, modern conference table. Every one of them looks like they belong on the cover of a fashion magazine. Sleek. Polished. Expensive. Just like Jasmine, the receptionist from upstairs. And at the head of the table, dressed to perfection, is Beck.

Wow.

He's naturally stunning. The four men and three women seated at the table should look dull next to him. But they don't. Each one is sharp, poised, and intimidating in their own way. They don't just fit in. They own the space as if they were born to be there.

"Hey, guys," Clint says, casually confident. "This is Lila. It's her first day in our department, so please say hello and make her feel welcome."

I give a small smile and an awkward wave. It feels out of place, but I do it anyway.

"Welcome, Lila," Beck says smoothly. "Please, have a seat. We're in the middle of reviewing one of our biggest cases." His voice is calm and formal. All business.

Sir, your dick has been pressed against me. Let's not pretend we're strangers.

"Of course," I say sweetly, sliding into the empty chair and pulling out my notepad.

Beck rises from his seat. "We need to figure out how he's still running his ring from inside prison and who his top men are."

Everyone nods like they've been chasing this answer for months. "Any updates?" he asks.

A woman with ginger curls and oversized glasses adjusts her laptop. "I contacted officials in the United Kingdom, and we traced a phone line coming from inside the prison. It's registered to a gas station company based in London." She's giving full Daphne energy with the brains of Velma. She's the complete package. Beauty. Brains. Badass and I'm totally here for it.

"Good. Keep going."

Another team member chimes in. "SWAT rescued a sixteen-year-old last night. Her testimony confirms she was set to be trafficked by boat, headed for Europe."

I don't understand most of what they're saying, but I keep writing. Listening. Learning. Then Beck flips the whiteboard. My lungs lock. My vision tilts. Because there, pinned at the center of a chaotic web of newspaper clippings, mugshots, and blood-red thread, is a face I know too well.

Zev Volkov. The Wolf. That's what the media call him. The man who took me. His photo is old and grainy, but unmistakable. He sits like a king on a throne, a cigarette hanging from his lips, one leg crossed, chin tilted in arrogant control. A long scar slices under his left eye like a threat carved into skin. His eyes are lifeless. Cold. Black. Empty of anything human. His face pulls me back into the nightmare.

The board is in chaos. Red thread crisscrosses over maps, scribbled notes, shipping routes, and blurry surveillance stills. But it's him who locks me in place. My hands begin to tremble. Not from nerves. From memory.

I keep taking notes. Pretending. Breathing. But inside, I am unraveling. Because the last time I saw the Wolf, I wasn't sure I would ever escape. And now, I can't help but wonder if his men are still searching for me. Lurking. Prowling. Waiting for the right moment to take me back. To traffic me to Europe or worse…

Volkov keeps me for himself.

CHAPTER TWENTY-TWO
LILA

My nerves feel electrified, but this time, not in a good way. I'm on edge. Paranoid. Practically looking over my shoulder every time I turn a corner. I could barely sit still for the rest of the workday, and I couldn't bring myself to see Mom, but I did call to check on her.

The image of Volkov's face on that board is seared into the back of my eyelids, just like the fear tightening around my ribs. His thick Russian accent still sends shivers down my spine. It's fear. Raw, real fear. I'm scared of him. And worst of all, I know he knows I am, even from prison.

Right before Heartford's team stormed in, just as I was walking down the motel hall, Volkov leaned in, his breath hot and rancid on my neck, and whispered, "Run. Scream. Fight. None of it will save you. I will find you. I will find your family. And when I do… you'll beg me to finish what I started."

I was his last known victim. And he probably thinks I helped take him down. But I didn't. They had been watching him for months. I was just in the wrong place at the wrong time. And now I know he still has men. Somewhere. Waiting and watching, taking more victims, murdering anyone who doesn't play by their rules.

The clock on my nightstand ticks past 9:00 p.m.

Then 10:47 p.m.

Then 12:03 a.m.

I toss.

I turn.

I cuss into my pillow and seriously consider smothering myself with it just to shut my brain up.

"Dammit, why is time even a thing?" I groan, kicking the blankets off, then dragging them back up like they'll protect me from whatever monsters are out there. Or worse… in here.

I feel like a kid again, hiding from the shadows, hoping the dark doesn't reach out and grab me.

Only now, I know better.

The monsters don't disappear when you grow up. They get smarter. Crueler. Real. I lie still, ears tuned to every sound.

CREAK.

BOOM.

KNOCK.

SQUEAK.

Every little noise feels louder. Closer. Like someone's creeping toward me. Like, my walls aren't nearly as solid as I thought. "Maybe a little music will help me sleep." I turn on my Bluetooth speaker and let my playlist shuffle. Then I hear it. Screaming and then banging on the elevator shaft from a few floors down.

It's probably just stuck again.

I groan. "Go to sleep."

But I can't. Not with Volkov's face burned into my mind. Not with that voice still echoing in my head. Not with fear breathing down my neck. Before I can talk myself out of it, I grab my phone and pull it under the covers with me. My fingers tremble as I unlock the screen. The fear hasn't left. It's pressing on my chest like a weight. I need a distraction from the monster in my past. But what if the one I want to text... is darker? Worse than Volkov?

The Red Mask.

The Unknown Subject stares back at me like a loaded weapon. His first message is still there. Read. Unanswered. I opened it on purpose. I wanted him to see it. I wanted him to come after me. But he never did. And now that I know it's him, I guess it's time to add him to my phone, so I can be prepared before I open the following message.

I hover over the message icon, my thumb suspended midair, caught between logic and desire. Between danger and safety. My heart hammers in my ears. And still, I press send.

LILA: Are you awake?

Minutes tick by. Nothing.

Maybe he's asleep. Maybe he's pissed. Perhaps I'm insane.

Buzz.

My stomach flips.

THE RED MASK: I am. I thought about not texting you back since you ignored me.

I breathe out. Relief? Lust? I don't even know anymore.

LILA: I'm sorry. I've been busy, but this is an emergency… I need a distraction. Send me a dick pic or something. Anything.

There's a beat of silence.

God, what am I doing?

THE RED MASK: Tempting. But I'm working out, so no. What's wrong, Princess?

That name.

It sends a pulse straight through me.

LILA: I'm scared that someone from my past might come after me and hurt me... I can't sleep.

THE RED MASK: He can try, but he won't get close. He'd be dead before he reached your apartment door.

My brows draw together.

LILA: What do you mean?

THE RED MASK: I have cameras all over the outside of your building. And inside your apartment.

I shoot up in bed, dragging my blanket to my chest. My silk sleep dress clings to my thighs, the fabric cool against bare skin. No bra. No panties. I like to sleep freely. Untethered.

But now I feel seen. And I cannot tell if that is a good thing or a very bad one.

THE RED MASK: Relax. No cameras in the bathroom. I'm not a complete creep.

My breathing turns ragged. I should feel violated. But instead, heat coils low in my stomach. He's been watching me. And some sick part of me likes it.

LILA: What the hell?

LILA: Are you stalking me?

LILA: When did you install them?

LILA: How long have they been there?

I glance around the room, heart pounding. And then I see it. Tucked into the air vent beside my bed, barely visible unless you're looking for it, is the faint glint of a hidden camera lens.

Oh my God. That bastard can see everything. Every curve. Every soft sigh. Every night I lie in this bed, touching myself to the memory of a man I've never seen without his mask.

THE RED MASK: The night you cheated in the maze.

"Shit," I whisper. I sit up straighter and stare directly at the vent, arms crossed and lips pouting. "Remove them."

THE RED MASK: Hahaha. That's cute, but no.

I narrow my eyes, licking my lips. "Please, baby," I purr toward the camera, letting my voice drop into a slow, sultry tease. My clit throbs.

Soft music thrums in the background, heightening my arousal. The fire he sparks inside me grows hotter, wilder, until it threatens to blaze out of control.

THE RED MASK: Don't do that, Princess. I'll come over and spank you.

Oh? Let's test that threat.

I crawl to the foot of my bed, unhurried and controlled, aware of his eyes tracking my every move. I settle on my knees, poised like I could straddle anything he puts in front of me. My hands trail down my thighs, grazing the fabric as I lift the edge of my gown, higher, slower, teasing every inch.

The camera stares back like a dark, silent voyeur, and secretly I love being watched, as if I were made to perform for the ones I want… the Phantom and now him.

But tonight, they are not the temptation. I am.

I pause, spread wide just enough to tease my folds, lips parted, my heart thudding loud in my chest. The air vent stares back at me, and even though I can't see him, I know he's viewing me.

"If you don't remove the cameras," I whisper, letting my voice drip with a sensual touch, "you'll have no choice but to watch this every night… and never touch a damn thing."

THE RED MASK: Maybe that's how I like it.

I smile, slow and wicked. "What if I moan someone else's name?"

A beat of silence.

THE RED MASK: You better fucking not.

The message sends a jolt through me, hot and possessive and absolutely perfect. "Ooo, I love when you get feisty. You're making me so wet…"

But I want to push him. I need to. I want to taunt him. Break his control. If I can get him here or near me, I can find out who he really is. And once I do, I'll make him mine. But the second I close my eyes, they multiply… Kage's dominance. Beck's sweetness. Leon's touch against my skin. The Phantom's mystery. The Red Mask's breath against my ear in the pleasure room.

Yep, I'm a whore, but at least I'm honest about it.

I moan softly as my fingers trail between my thighs, spreading the heat.

I don't know which one of them I want worse. Or do I want them all? Hmmm. Can I have them all?

Kage flashes into my mind as my fingers circle my clit. The memory is fresh, still burning from the steamy elevator encounter this morning. The way our bodies were not touching, but it felt like his hands were all over my body. That cold glare. That fire. That unspoken dare. "Kage…" I whisper, louder this time. "Right there, yes…"

My fingers move deeper, slower. My other hand cups my breast, teasing my nipple until I gasp. Then… another image. The Phantom. Those haunting, icy eyes. That tattooed chest, slick with sweat. The way he watched me pleasure myself. The way I reacted, he reacted, and vice versa, as if we were wired the same.

"Oh God Kage… That's it." And finally… him. The one behind the cameras. The Red Mask.

I picture him at his high-tech desk, surrounded by glowing monitors casting a cool blue light across his mask. His fingers glide across a sleek keyboard, shifting angles, rewinding, zooming in. Surveillance feeds flicker like temptation on every screen. But the center one, the one he's obsessed with… is me.

Cheeks hot, legs parted, my fingers work in rhythm with my need. My other hand drifts lower until I gently slide into my entrance, stretching, filling, feeding the ache.

His jaw tightens. He leans back in his chair, unbuckles his belt, and pulls out his thick, pulsing erection. He grips it tight, stroking slowly, watching me with a hunger that borders on feral.

Wanting every part of me.

My body arches, caught in the fantasy of being surrounded by all three masked men. Their hands on my skin. Their breath in my ear. Their bodies are taking me apart, piece by trembling piece.

"Don't stop," I beg through clenched teeth. "Please. I'm so close."

I ride my fingers harder, faster, chasing the edge until the pressure inside me coils tight and ready to snap. My thighs tremble, my back arches, every nerve alive with heat.

And then I shatter. My body shakes, breathless, undone. A smirk tugs at my lips as my eyes flutter. Slowly, I slip my finger out of me and hold it up to the camera, showing just how drenched I am. Then I bring my fingers to my mouth and suck, slow and shameless, savoring every drop.

"Mmm… sweet like honey," I let it tumble from my lips. "And baby," I moan softly, dragging my nails across my own chest, "I hope you sleep like shit tonight."

I roll onto my side, back to the camera, smiling.

THE RED MASK: You're going to regret that, Princess.

I grin into my pillow, breath still heaving.

Let him come. No pun intended.

I want to know exactly what kind of monster I've just awakened.

And who's behind the mask.

CHAPTER TWENTY-THREE
LILA

I hate him.

That smug, manipulative bastard. He knew exactly what I wanted, and I played right into it like a naïve little puppet. I waited. And waited. And he never came. No punishment. No knock. Just silence. I thought I was taunting him. But really, he was the one taunting me. Watching through his perv cameras, probably smirking while I tossed and turned in a pathetic swirl of frustration. Until I finally shoved a pillow in front of the lens and flipped him off.

Take that, pervert.

I spritz myself with cotton candy perfume, slip on my white ruffled work dress, and lace up my heels. Grabbing my purse, I pause at the door. I glance left. Then right. I'm still on edge. Every man feels like a suspect. Could one of them be Volkov's? Could all of them?

I skip the rickety elevator and take the stairs, careful not to snag my hem as I descend one cautious step at a time. When I push open the grimy front door, I freeze.

Clint's leaning against a cherry-red Mercedes like he's starring in his own music video, sunglasses, arms crossed, wind flirting with his perfectly messy hair.

God, give me the strength to handle this diva.

"Hey, douchebag," I call. "You're not a pop star. Dial it back."

He slides his glasses down and smirks. "Thought I'd have to wait all day."

"I thought you didn't pick up trash," I toss back.

He winks. "Little did I know you were a treasure."

I hate that he's kind of charming. That smirk should be illegal. "Seriously, Clint. Why are you here?"

"It's supposed to rain," he says, shrugging like it's no big deal. "Figured I'd give you a ride. Didn't want your princess hair getting ruined."

I narrow my eyes. I don't trust him. Not completely. "What's the catch?"

"No catch. You seemed off yesterday. I was… worried." He shrugs again, then clasps his hands under his chin like a pleading schoolgirl. "Please?"

I sigh. "Fine. But if people talk, I'm blaming you."

"Fair," he says, already strutting over and opening the passenger door.

He swings it wide with a wink, and I can't help but roll my eyes at his arrogance. I slide into leather and gasp. It feels just like Aster's G-Wagon. Everything about it screams wealth. And maybe it is just me, but there is something about these expensive cars that feels sensual on purpose. Like they are designed to seduce you the second you sit down. Or maybe I see the world differently than the women who bury their desire because society tells them it's wrong. I used to hide that part of myself. But now I couldn't care less what anyone thinks.

"One day I'll have a car like this," I murmur.

"You will," he says easily. "I already know you'll work your ass off to get what you want."

Weirdly, his comment sounds sincere.

He hands me a bag. "Got you a bagel. And an iced caramel macchiato."

I blink, caught off guard.

He just assumed I would say yes to the ride. And he knew exactly what to get me.

Is that because he is the Red Mask and he's been watching me through the cameras? Or because we did kind of date for a few months… and he actually paid attention?

"You didn't have to," I murmur.

He smirks. "I know."

I take a sip, and it's perfect. My exact order from my favorite café down the street from my apartment. "How did you know?"

"Maybe the version of me in your head was conjured up before you actually got to know me. And maybe I'm not so bad…"

We pull into traffic, the city buzzing with people rushing to work. Horns blare in the distance, but when the rain starts, I can't help but feel at peace, like a little slice of heaven. But then I remember I'm with Clint.

"I should probably say this before it gets weird," I start. "I am truly sorry but… You know I don't like you like that, right?"

He bursts into laughter. "Lila, please. You nearly tased my balls off. I knew right then I didn't stand a chance with you."

We both laugh. "But seriously," I say. "Why the sudden shift?"

He goes quiet, gripping the wheel. "Because I judged you. Just like you judged me." He exhales slowly. "I said some really ugly things to you in that maze… and I regret it." His voice lowers. "You didn't deserve any of it. I was just pissed at the world, and you caught the worst of it. I took it out on you." He glances over. "I'm sorry, Lila."

My breath catches. "I was scared too, you know," I whisper. "That maze wasn't just a game for me. It brought back things I've been trying to forget."

"Yeah," he says softly. "Same."

We sit in silence, but it's not awkward. It's comfortable. Something soft and real is growing between us.

"So, you really want to be friends? Like you're not screwing with me?" I ask.

"Best friends," he says. "I need someone to keep me humble when I'm being a complete jackass."

"I'll keep you in line. Don't worry," I smirk.

He grins. "Good."

We turn into the employee garage, and all the warmth in my chest turns to fire as heat rushes to my cheeks.

Parked in front of the glass elevators is a Bugatti Divo, deep navy blue like the night sky. Kage steps out of the driver's seat while Beck gets out of the passenger side. They stand like Greek tragedies dressed in Dior, destined to ruin anything that gets too close. Beck is the sun. Glorious. Warm. Golden. But Kage...

Kage is the night.

All shadows and tension, he stands in a black button-down tucked into dark gray slacks, the sleeves rolled to his elbows like he is deciding whether to punish someone or fuck them senseless. His dark brown hair falls carelessly across his forehead, jaw clenched tight. And when he slips his hands into his pockets, those veins flex just enough to make my mouth water. His hands belong in a museum.

Or on my throat. There is no in-between. And he is glaring straight at me... well, at Clint.

Welp.

Clint mumbles under his breath. "Oh damn. They look pissed."

"What did we do?" I whisper.

Kage taps his polished shoe. Beck's jaw ticks. I grab the handle and push the door open. We step out. My knees wobble, and I can't tear my eyes from Kage. He's a walking red flag, and part of me wants to fix him… but the darker part of me wants him exactly like this. Cold. Dominant. Untouchable.

Clint tries to salvage the moment. "Morning, guys. Great day for a storm, huh?"

Silence.

Then Kage speaks, his voice low and sharp like a blade, slicing the air clean out of my lungs. "Why is she with you?"

"I… uh… I gave her a ride. It's supposed to rain…"

Beck crosses his arms slowly, voice cool. "You do realize it's against company policy to sleep with a coworker, right?"

My stomach drops.

Oh hell no.

Did Beck's sweet, golden-boy self really assume I was sleeping with Clint?

"Ew. I'd rather die than sleep with him. Did you forget I literally tased the guy?"

Kage's lip twitches. Almost a smile, but it fades back into his emotionless, hard, statue-like frame.

"Princess," Clint groans. "Can you not roast me in front of our bosses?"

My heart hammers in my chest from that one word.

Do not call me that in front of them. They really will think we are a couple.

Kage's body tenses. I can feel it.

"I told you I'd throw you under the bus if you keep calling me that," I say sweetly.

Beck chuckles, eyes gleaming. "So, Lila… your nickname is Princess?" His grin turns slow and wicked. "That's cute."

My stomach drops. That word. Again. But it sounds so sweet rolling off Beck's tongue.

Kage's breathing shifts. Subtle but there. His chest rises and falls like he's trying to hold something back. His eyes lock with mine. Ice and fire all at once. And I know that look. That is a man doing everything he can to hide his emotions. But wow, he looks irresistible. His body speaks in a language I shouldn't understand, but my thighs are fluent, and I am dripping for this man. *Good thing I wore panties today.*

Kage steps forward. "Since you two are such close friends, you'll be separated today." He turns to me. "Lila, you will be handling ballroom logistics on the 2/3 floor. Clint, come with me… Now."

He doesn't wait for a response. Just walks away. Lethal and beautiful. A thunderstorm in a tailored suit.

Clint grimaces. "Pray for me."

I watch Kage leave, still unable to take my eyes off him. He may hate me for whatever reason, but God, I would do anything to have a second alone with him. A single breath. A single look. A single chance. My pulse is thudding. My legs feel weak. And then I see it. He glances over his shoulder. Looking at me.

Did I imagine that… or did that really happen?

Beck steps beside me. "Don't take it personally. He didn't sleep much last night."

My throat tightens. Because maybe, just maybe, I'm the reason he couldn't sleep. Maybe he replayed every second in that elevator the same way I did. Maybe he wanted to text me. Touch me. Kiss me. Destroy me. Maybe I'm the thing he can't get out of his system. And if that's true?

I'll make damn sure he remembers me every time he closes his eyes.

We step into the elevator, and he presses a single gold button.

2/3.

I squint. "What does 2/3 mean? Why isn't it just the second and third floor?"

Beck chuckles. "This is going to sound over the top, but… we merged both floors to create one massive ballroom with cathedral ceilings. So… 2/3. It was Kage's idea."

I laugh under my breath. "That's a little extra, don't you think?"

"You'll understand when you see it."

Then, it hits me. This is the first time we've been alone since the Halloween party. Since the dancing. The grinding. The moment he made me feel something before I spiraled and bolted. That was almost five weeks ago. And somehow, that memory feels fuzzy now. Distant.

Does that mean I'm not into him?.

The elevator hums around us, and I realize I don't feel that same intensity with Beck. It's not fire and suffocation. It's calm. Comfortable. Safe.

Beck clears his throat. "This is the first time we've been alone since the party," he says, side-eyeing me with that slow, seductive grin.

I look up at him, and butterflies flutter somewhere in my stomach, but they're nothing like what I've felt before. Not the ones that choke me. Not the ones that possess me. Not the ones that consume me.

I smile politely. "I had fun that night. I tagged along with Aster. I swear I'm not a stalker."

He laughs, biting his lip.

I made him smile again. Isn't that better than the toxicity the Red Mask offers?

"I know… I looked into you before hiring you," Beck says softly. "Can I ask something?"

The elevator beeps. The doors slide open. We step out, and his fingers brush my arm. Warm. Smooth. Thoughtful.

"Why did you run that night?" he asks. "Why did you disappear?"

I pause. My stomach tightens. "Honestly? I don't have much dating experience, and when you asked me out… my body panicked. My brain spiraled. I had a full-blown anxiety attack. I just needed to breathe. I didn't want you to think I was crazy, so… I disappeared."

His gaze softens. He glides a finger down my arm, slow and gentle.

It's nice. Sweet, even. But it isn't electric. It isn't ravenous.

"I wish you'd told me," he says. His voice is low, almost regretful. "I would've understood. But I'm glad I found you in the maze."

Wait. What?

My pulse stutters.

"You… found me in the maze?" I ask slowly. He doesn't answer. The elevator dings, a soft chime that signals we've arrived. I turn around, needing air, and come to a halt.

The 2/3 ballroom spreads out before me like something out of a dream. It's divine. Like something God Himself sculpted with His hands. Heavenly. It's a perfect distraction from the truth crawling beneath my skin.

If Beck found me in the maze… then what mask was he wearing? And if it wasn't him behind the red mask… then who the hell was?

CHAPTER TWENTY-FOUR
LILA

"Welcome to the 2/3 floor! This is our company ballroom for events," Beck announces, his voice echoing through the vast space as he spreads his arms wide, reenacting the iconic Titanic scene. I stop in my tracks. Speechless.

It's breathtaking. Everything about this man's life is breathtaking.

I bet he had it easy growing up. Tuition covered at some elite academy. A future laid out like a red carpet, silver spoon in hand, a company waiting for him with a bow. No panic over rising bills. No graveyard shifts to keep the power on. No teenage years stolen by three jobs to keep food in the fridge. What a life that must be.

The ballroom looks like something plucked straight from a period film or a history book. Vaulted ceilings. Shimmering chandeliers. Intricate gold trim. Clouds and angels swirl elegantly across the ceiling, matching the same opulent aesthetic as Beck's mansion. Every inch whispers heaven on earth.

It screams royalty. Supremacy. The elite.

Perhaps Beck is royalty and no one bothered to inform me.

"Why didn't you mention you were royalty?" I tease.

He chuckles softly. "You think I did this? No, this was all Kage's work."

"Kage?"

"Yeah… I owe everything to him."

That's an odd thing to say. What does he mean by owe? What did Kage do?

Curiosity sparks, not for Beck but for Kage.

I clear my throat. "What do you need me to do up here?"

"To the right, there's a hallway with bathrooms and a storage room full of decorations, chairs, tables, everything you might need. I trust you to handle the decorating. Just let me know which flowers you want for the arrangements."

"Why would you trust me with all of this?"

He shrugs casually. "I looked over your transcript and resume. You ran multiple clubs in college, graduated valedictorian in high school, and…" His grin tilts, mischievous. "I asked Aster, and she said you live for this kind of thing."

"Hey, that's cheating!" I giggle. "You can't ask her!"

"Well, that's the perk of being CEO."

He gestures toward a cable near the sound system. "Also, feel free to play your music. Just connect your phone, and it'll play throughout the entire floor."

"Thank you, Beck. Seriously. For the job, for your kindness, for just being… you." I smile shyly, suddenly self-conscious.

Great. That totally sounded like I'm hitting on him.

"I swear I meant that in the most professional way possible."

He doesn't reply. Instead, he extends his hand toward me. "Would you dance with me?"

I glance around, giggling nervously. "We don't have music, Beck."

His hand remains patiently outstretched, waiting.

"Hey Siri, play 'Somewhere Only We Know' by Keane."

Dammit. How am I supposed to say no when he's looking at me like that, with this song playing?

It feels like a moment destined to become a core memory. Slowly, I place my hand in his, and he pulls me gently into his arms.

"Do you know how to dance?" he asks, smirk curling like a challenge. "Princess."

God, not that word again.

"Don't all princesses know how to dance?" I retort playfully, batting my lashes. He lifts an amused eyebrow. "I'm kidding," I clarify. "But yes, I know how to dance. I went to a fancy Academy, and unfortunately, dance lessons were mandatory."

"Oh, so you grew up in that life?" He sounds genuinely surprised.

"Something like that," I murmur vaguely. It feels oddly uncomfortable sharing details of my past with him, not because I'm ashamed, but because it feels too intimate. "The real question is," I say, tilting my chin up defiantly, "can you keep up with me?"

He chuckles softly, guiding our movements across the polished floor. His dark blue eyes hold mine, sensual yet safe. Comfortable, but not dangerous or dark like the Red Mask.

Beck isn't him. I know it. Even holding his hand feels different. Should I confirm it?

"You mentioned seeing me in the maze," I start hesitantly, watching him carefully. "But I don't remember seeing you."

"How could you forget, Lila?"

My heart pounds erratically. My thighs clench.

Could he actually be…?

"I was wearing black," he says, swirling me gracefully. The Red Mask was also in black. My pulse quickens with anticipation. "I was the one in the plague doctor costume… the one who took Aster."

My stomach sinks in disappointment. Beck is wonderful, smart, kind, handsome, dependable, but… he's not the one haunting my dreams.

He's not the one I want to make mine.

My body stiffens, and I know I need to shut this down before feelings take root and turn into heartbreak.

"Oh, right. I remember now—" My words are cut off by the sharp clack of designer shoes on polished floors.

CLICK.

CLACK.

CLICK.

CLACK.

"What the hell are you two doing?" Kage's voice slithers through the ballroom, low and predatory, sending chills down my spine.

Beck doesn't break stride. "We're dancing. What are you doing, Kage?"

His eyes are following our every move. "Trying to run a fucking business, but I have to babysit every man here from trying to get into her pants," Kage growls, nodding toward me.

Arrogant prick.

I halt abruptly, feeling heat rise in my cheeks. "Excuse me, are you implying I'm the problem?"

Kage stalks closer, deliberate and merciless, eyes narrowed with lethal intensity. "Keep your head down and get your shit together. If you're that desperate to get laid, go to a sex club. Or do you want me to fire you myself?"

"Relax, man. I'm not going to fire her," Beck begins.

Kage silences him by stepping closer, invading my personal space. His sandalwood cologne wraps around me, rich and inescapable, pulling me under like a tide I can't fight.

I tilt my chin up, matching his glare. "Hmm. Sex club? Do you think I'm some whore?" I pause, locking eyes with him, daring him to say yes. "First, you accuse me of lying about my story. Now, you're insulting me. Let me guess. You either hate women, or you and Beck are an item, and I'm just in your way."

And for the first time, his composure falters. Anger flashes in his eyes alongside something else. Something vulnerable and unexpected.

His jaw tightens as he leans even closer, his voice dangerously low. "Don't worry about coming to work tomorrow." He turns sharply and heads toward the elevator.

My stomach drops.

I've really done it this time. I said too much and let my other side get in the way. I need this job.

"Wait, Kage, please. I didn't mean—"

He cuts me off, not even turning around. "Be at Beck's house in the morning. Don't be late."

Even from behind, I can feel the smug satisfaction rolling off him.

"Thank you," I shout sarcastically as he enters the elevator. Kage turns slowly, his green eyes locked on mine, a triumphant smirk on his lips.

He's playing mind games, and this round goes to him.

As the elevator doors close, I exhale a breath I didn't realize I'd been holding. Beck rubs his forehead wearily. "I'm sorry about him. Kage can be… a lot. Even for me."

The moment has faded, but three things are now crystal clear.

Beck is not the Red Mask.

Kage is an infuriating tyrant.

And I'm utterly, completely mesmerized by him.

"I'm sorry that moment was ruined," Beck says with pure disappointment. I know I need to break this off, but honestly, my body is still humming from that encounter.

I feel like I have whiplash.

"It's okay... I... better get started so everything will be perfect for next week." Oddly, I want to be done with this conversation to get my mind off of all of this.

"Well, if you need anything, here's my number." He grabs my phone, enters it without asking, then lifts my hand and brushes his lips over my skin in a way that lingers.

Then he walks away, not before looking over his shoulder one last time, eyes tracing every inch of me as he steps onto the elevator. My phone feels heavier in my hand now, his number glowing on the screen like an offer I'm not sure I want.

I exhale, finally able to breathe again. "Shit... that was intense." My hands rake through my hair as I try to cool off. My skin is still tingling where he touched me.

I connect my phone to the ballroom speakers and set my playlist on shuffle. A slow, sultry rhythm pours through the room. I slip off my heels and let my bare feet touch the marble, my hips swaying, as the music peels away the tension wound tight in my chest, as I head for the supply closet.

The space is massive, with wire racks stacked with every imaginable kind of décor. I drag the boxes out one by one, and when I glance down, my faint reflection stares back at me from the polished floor. That's when it hits me.

If it weren't for the people in this company, I might not be here. That night could have ended differently. It could have ended me. But it didn't. I'm still here. Still breathing. Still alive. And even if decorating is not glamorous, it's more than I ever dreamed I would have. I'm grateful for another day of life, and it's because of this company.

I dig through each box, pulling out tablecloths, holding them up to catch the light as I try to imagine which colors will set the right tone for the theme. My hands sift through fabric, textures slipping between my fingers, but then one box in particular catches my eye. My pulse quickens as I slide it closer and lift the lid.

Costumes.

The clown suit Clint wore.

The plague doctor mask Beck had on.

Others I don't recognize.

The stack of employee masks sits neatly arranged. All accounted for except his.

A chill creeps up my spine, the air shifting heavy around me. I freeze, breath caught, as the ballroom lights flicker and dim.

Slowly, I turn.

And there he is. On the far side of the ballroom, cloaked in shadow like he was born from it.

Am I dreaming?

The Red Mask.

He wears a black turtleneck beneath a tailored suit, leather gloves fitted to perfection. His designer shoes whisper against the floor as he advances. It's eerie, yet he steals the breath from my lungs… and I haven't even seen his face.

We don't speak. We don't move. But the tension between us is unbearable. My body is fire, and he's the match.

The music pulses in the background, and my heart beats in rhythm with each step he takes. He's coming for me. No more games. No more teasing.

He stops close, so close I can feel the heat rolling off him, seeping into my skin like a warning. His chest rises and falls like he ran through a dream to get here. His voice is low, modulated. Smooth like aged whiskey, and I'm already drunk on the sound of it.

"Did you miss me, Princess?"

CHAPTER TWENTY-FIVE
LILA

My head spins. He's real. And he's standing right in front of me. Just this morning, I was spiraling, furious that he never showed. And now he's here, and I've already forgotten why I was mad in the first place. That's toxic, and I know it, but God, I missed him. The way our bodies pull toward each other is like magnets that can't stay away. And what wrecks me is that he doesn't fight it.

He gives in. Just like the night he kissed me, like he wanted it just as badly as I did.

"Yes," I whisper. No hesitation.

He seems stunned, like he didn't expect me to say it. Like, he doesn't believe I mean it.

His scent drapes over me. Sandalwood, leather, and the ghost of cigarettes. An addictive perfume I never want to escape.

It's him. It's always been him. But the question is… who is he? I know it's not Beck. It can't be Clint. He's with Kage.

Kage smells like sandalwood, and so does this man. But sandalwood is everywhere. It is not exclusive. It does not have to mean anything. Right?

I reach up and lay my hands on his chest. His heart is pounding. A human heart is beating beneath my touch.

"You're really real…" I whisper.

He lets out a low, dark chuckle. "You thought I wasn't?" he murmurs, his gloved hand grazing up the sides of my body with maddening precision. "Did you really think you dreamed up the entire pleasure room session all by yourself?"

"I thought maybe you were too good to be true."

He lets out a soft, humorless chuckle. "You think I'm good?"

"I think you're good to me." My eyes lock on his mask. "And I think you're what I want." He inhales sharply, as if battling his own demons, like he doesn't believe a single word. But I want to show him he's more than the shadows he hides behind. More than the ghosts that haunt him. Worth loving. Worth keeping.

"Take off your mask," I demand, my voice trembling, breathless from his presence.

The lights vanish, leaving us in total darkness. I can't see him, but I hear the soft rustle of fabric, followed by the sound of the mask hitting the floor. I audibly gasp.

He took it off. He took it off for me.

His breath brushes against my shoulder, warm and teasing, sending shivers skimming down my spine. He lingers there, so close I can feel the whisper of his lips just above my skin. The heat between us coils tighter. Hotter. Needier. I ache to kiss him the way I did before, to feel him melt into me all over again. *But if I do... will he vanish like a dream?*

The air between us is thick, charged with the unspoken.

"Why can't I see your face?" I whisper, barely able to breathe the words. Silence answers me. Only the music pulses softly in the background, and the sound of his breath fills the space between us. It is ragged and uneven, like we are sitting too close to the sun with no shade in sight.

And somehow, this shadow in front of me is my sun. Blinding. Burning. Impossible to touch. He blinds everything else in my life. When I stand near him, I start to burn.

The night in the pleasure room proved it. The moment our skin touched, it was like nothing else mattered. I didn't want to stop touching him. I still don't.

"Because I'm a monster," he whispers. His voice is no longer modulated but still hidden behind the mask. It is low and sad, like saying it out loud makes it real.

"Why would you say that?" I ask softly.

"Because it's the truth." He tilts my chin up, forcing me to look at him, even though I still can't fully see him in the dark.

His physical mask is gone. But in this moment, it's the other mask he's taken off. The one that truly matters. The emotional one. The one stitched together with shame and silence. The one he's hidden behind to survive. And somehow, it's not what he says that undoes me. It's what he doesn't.

He's letting me see the part of him no one else ever touches. And it wrecks me, because this vulnerability speaks louder than any confession. It's the most honest piece of him I've ever been given. And I don't even think he realizes it.

"Can I… touch you?" he asks, his voice trembling like he's afraid I'll say no.

"Don't ask," I breathe. "Just do." I don't see his face, but I feel him. The hesitation in his body. The way he lingers, like he wants to touch me but doesn't know how, just like the night at the sex club.

I reach for his hand.

He's still wearing his leather gloves.

"Can I take your gloves off?" I ask, my voice soft, an ache blooming in my chest like I can somehow help him by doing this.

He doesn't speak at first. Only the sound of his ragged breath fills the space, uneven and raw, like he's afraid of what might come out if he does. Then…

"Yes."

I start at the tips, slowly peeling the first glove away, finger by finger, until it slips from his hand and falls to the floor. I do the same with the other. And then… his bare hands are in mine. Rough. Callused. Large. They press against my soft palms, and the contrast is enough to steal my breath. I run my fingertips gently over his, tracing the lines in his skin like they're sacred.

"Cinnamon Girl," by Lana Del Rey hums through the speakers, sweet and haunting, like it's scoring this moment. I thread my fingers through his and guide his hands up, sliding them beneath my shirt. He trembles. His hands shake.

I place them on my hips, and he exhales, the sound broken and full of want, like touching me is unraveling him, but he's terrified of the connection, like it's something he's not worthy of. He caresses my sides, and I reach up, threading my fingers through his hair. The second I do, he lets out a shuddering breath, like I've touched something deep within.

Then his lips find mine, soft and tender at first, but it doesn't last. I kiss him back with everything I've been holding in. He groans and lifts me, and I wrap my legs around his waist. We devour each other like we are tasting one another for the first time. His mouth is spearmint, heat, and everything forbidden.

My hands tug at his hair, his neck, pulling him closer, deeper. But then… I feel it. A scar. Long. Raised and hidden in his hairline. My fingers pause against it, tracing gently. He stiffens, breath faltering, and I know I've touched something deeper than skin. Something carved into him long ago. Something that still bleeds.

"What happened?" I whisper. He doesn't answer. His breath hitches. His arms tense, like he's suddenly somewhere else. Somewhere darker. Somewhere that's a memory, and it's torturing him.

Oh God. What did I say?

"I… I'm sorry," I whisper. "I shouldn't have asked."

It feels old, like it's been there for years. Like it was carved into him when he was just a boy. Painful. Permanent. A wound that never really healed.

I let my hand fall away, voice barely a breath. "I won't ask again."

He doesn't speak. Doesn't move. For a moment, I swear he's still here. Still close. Still breathing the same air as me. But then something shifts. A quietness that wasn't there before. A presence fading.

He lowers me gently. So careful. Like I might break. I reach out into the dark, fingers searching for him.

"Baby?" I whisper the word, trembling from my lips. Silence. I step forward, heart racing.

The warmth drains from the air, replaced by a cold stillness that tells me he's gone, even before I reach for him. Only emptiness remains. A shadow swallowed by the dark. Just like before. Just like always. And I didn't even hear him leave. No word. No sound. Only the echo of my breath and the pounding of my heart. And there, on the floor…

His mask.

I move toward it slowly, every step heavier than the last. I kneel, brushing the cool surface with fingertips. It's the same one from the maze. From the club. From the shadows of every encounter that has left me wanting more of him.

But this time… he left it behind. Not hidden. Just left. My chest tightens. No note. No goodbye. Just the final piece of him, discarded like it meant nothing.

Was this my punishment? Did what we had really mean nothing to him? Is this the end? His way of saying he is done with me?

I press the mask to my chest, heart hammering beneath it, trying to convince myself this isn't goodbye. But it feels like he didn't just disappear… He left me here to feel like a fool.

My eyes sting as I stand alone in the darkness, the music still whispering through the speakers like a memory.

My heart aches for a man I've never even seen. A man I shouldn't want. A man who just walked away again, leaving me holding the mask that started it all. He's gone. And all I have left is the mask… and the hollow ache of wanting a ghost.

CHAPTER TWENTY-SIX
LILA

"Have you tried the strawberry protein shakes I sent with Aster?" I ask, phone tucked between my cheek and shoulder as I rummage through my bag, trying to get ready for work.

"I have, and I actually like them," Mom laughs. "The nurses mix them with vanilla ice cream. It makes it taste like a milkshake."

"Have you gained any weight this week?"

"Yes, honey. Three pounds. Please stop worrying and focus on your new job."

I cut her off, firm. "You are way more important than any job."

"I know. But you've worked so hard for this. Also..." Her voice dips, suddenly curious. "I was wondering about the fifteen million, so I did a little asking around..."

My stomach flips. *Oh no. She can't know about the wish.*

"Well," she continues casually, "a nice, handsome man came by and said it was a grant from the Heartford company. So, I want you to work extra hard, because they've been good to us."

"What did he look like?" I ask, trying to sound neutral.

"I don't remember much, pain meds and all, but he was very well-mannered. Kind. Handsome, too."

Beck. He must've stopped by. But why?

"That's... nice of them," I murmur, sliding on my tennis shoes. "Mom, I'm so sorry. I have to go. I'm waiting for my Uber to call. I'll see you in the morning. I love you bunches."

"I love you too. And hey, bring me a chocolate protein shake tomorrow?"

I laugh, loving how joyful she sounds. "Of course." I hang up and sigh.

Focus.

I'm going to clean Beck's house today, so I keep it simple: black tennis skort, black tank top, no makeup, hair twisted up in a claw clip. Nothing special. Nothing tempting.

BUZZ.

BUZZ.

BUZZ.

My phone vibrates in my hand. Text from an unknown number. Well. I know who it's not. The Red Mask. He left me last night without a word.

So, who the hell is this?

UNKNOWN: Change of plans. Come down.

My body locks up.

Is this… Volkov, the Wolf? Am I in danger? Should I call the cops? No. Calm down, Lila. He's in prison.

UNKNOWN: I'm waiting, Lila. I'm not a patient man.

My lungs seize. I glance at the air vent in the corner of the room, the one with the hidden camera. My voice barely escapes. "Are you still watching? If you are… is it safe to go with this person?"

A pause. I catch my reflection in the floor-length mirror and freeze.

God, I look insane. Talking to a vent and whispering to no one. What the hell am I doing?

THE RED MASK: Yes. You're good.

He answered. He's still watching. Which means, whatever this is between us… he feels it too.

I look down from my window and see it: midnight blue, sleek, commanding. An Aston Martin DBX is parked in front of my rundown building like it doesn't belong in this part of the city.

Is that... for me? What the hell? Is it Beck or Clint?

I untwist my hair and run a brush through the tangles until it falls in soft waves past my shoulders. I swipe on a little mascara and lip balm, just in case it is them and I have to attend a work conference or something, and just in case he is watching.

I take the stairs two at a time, heart racing. When I push through the dirty glass front doors, I stop dead in my tracks.

There he is. Not Beck. Not Clint. Not the Phantom. Not the Red Mask. Not Leon.

Kage. Standing there like every bad decision I want to make.

This is the sexiest man I've ever seen... and he hates me. So why is he here? To fire me for real this time?

He leans against his car with one hand in his pocket, a cigarette hanging lazily from the corner of his mouth like he's posing for a cologne ad. His hair is tousled like a young DiCaprio. His charcoal-gray Tom Ford suit is tailored to perfection, hugging every sharp line of his muscle. His black button-down is unbuttoned just enough to make my nipples harden. And his pants frame his thighs and…

Nope. Don't look. Don't look at the bulge.

My eyes drop anyway. And there it is. The outline.

I am so fucking horny for this man.

I try to channel Aster's confidence. Don't let him know what he's doing to you. But he probably already knows. He sees it every day when he looks in the mirror.

I run a hand through my hair and force a smirk, biting down on my bottom lip as I meet his gaze. His eyes are green, guarded, lethal, locked onto mine. "What the hell are you doing here?" I ask, fake attitude dripping from my voice.

The corner of his mouth twitches. It is not quite a smile, but it's something. I have never seen him smile. Who knows, maybe I never will.

"Change of plans," he says coolly. "You can clean Beck's house next week. I need you to be my personal assistant for the day."

I blink. "Where is your actual assistant?"

"She's in Europe for two weeks. Lucky for me, I'm stuck with you." His tone is flat and unreadable.

Oh. So she's a woman and not a man. Of course, she is…And she is probably sex in heels and smells like expensive floral perfume. *He probably knows her scent by heart, the way it clings to him when they're making out in his office and he's nibbling at her neck.*

Ugh. Damn her.

"So, I am getting paid, right?" I cross my arms and lift my chin, not backing down.

Kage smirks just a little.

"Yes. But being with me is the real reward."

The sarcasm is sharp, but I hate how much I like it.

"Oh, please. Get over yourself, rich boy." I yank open the passenger door and slide into the seat like I don't care that I don't belong in this car or in his world. But God, his car smells like him.

Sandalwood.

But beneath it are two other notes, faint but unmistakable. The scent of fresh leather clings to the seatbelt as I buckle in, and there's a trace of smoke in the air, like he lit a cigarette and put it out before taking the first drag.

All the same scents as the Red Mask. But somehow, they feel different. Or maybe I need them to be.

He climbs in beside me with the kind of ease that makes it hard to remember he is a jackass who hates me for no reason. But of course, I want those beautiful lips between my thighs and on my cli—

No. Chill, Lila... have some self-control. He hates you. Just get through the day without thinking about sleeping with your boss.

But my heart doesn't listen. Because maybe, just maybe, this is a chance. A chance to see who he really is beneath all that cold, unreadable exterior. And to finally put my suspicions to rest. To make sure he's not the man behind the mask. Even if part of me hopes he is. Even though I know he's not. Because why would he be?

He can have any man or woman he wants. So why would he waste his time on me? He hates me. I don't know why, but he does. So if he is the one behind the mask…

Was it to mess with me? To toy with my feelings for fun? Or worse, was it some kind of twisted charity? A pity project to make me feel wanted for once?

You are spiraling and jumping to conclusions. Do not judge him like you did with Clint, not before you actually get to know him.

"Do you smoke?" I ask, instantly regretting it.

Really, Lila? That's what comes out first?

He shifts in his seat, one hand still resting on the wheel. "No. Those cancer sticks are bad for you."

I glance over at him, studying the sharp line of his jaw. "You never smoke on occasion?"

He doesn't hesitate. "Nope."

His tone is short, sweet, and to the point. He still hasn't looked at me, eyes locked on the road like I'm not even sitting beside him.

I pick at a loose thread on the hem of my skort, pretending it doesn't bother me. "Cool. Just curious." Silence fills the car as we merge onto the highway.

RING.
RING.
RING.

Kage lifts his phone and turns slightly away, his voice dipping low. *"Hallo. Ja, ich habe sie gerade abgeholt. Nein, ich habe es ihr noch nicht gesagt. Ich schaffe das, hör auf, dir Sorgen zu machen."*

The words are sharp and fluid. German, I think. But I can't make out a single word. My chest tightens. He sounds different. More forceful, but smooth. Natural. Like it is his first language.

And the craziest part is he doesn't even have an accent. If I hadn't heard him just now, I would never have known he spoke another language. And when I thought this man couldn't get more irresistible, he proves me wrong. The confidence. The control. The power in his voice.

God help me. It makes him even sexier, and I didn't think that was possible.

His jaw clenches, hands gripping the steering wheel like he's trying to control more than just the car.

I glance at him, but he doesn't meet my eyes. Not yet.

"Ich liebe dich," he says, then ends the call with a flick of his thumb.

"Who was that? What were you talking about?"

And for the first time today, he looks at me. "If I wanted you to know, I would've spoken English," he says. His voice is smooth, but there's the faintest curve at the edge of his mouth now, and I see a faint dimple in his cheek. Not a full smile. Just enough to betray that he's amused. Like I've gotten under his skin, and he doesn't entirely mind it.

"Why am I not surprised? I knew you were talking shit about me. Nothing new." I roll my eyes. "So, what's my assignment today, Bossman?"

"We're meeting with Volkov's sister, Natasha. She helped us put him behind bars after he tried to force her into taking over the family business. Sex trafficking and prostitution. She wanted nothing to do with it, but he didn't take no for an answer. Eventually, she had her men contact us. Now she's a world-famous fashion designer and known as the ruthless sister. But in the past week alone, twenty-five girls have gone missing, and somehow Volkov might still be pulling strings from prison. We need to find out if she's involved."

"Does she live here in New York?"

"No. She lives in France, but she's renting a place on the outskirts of New York. We'll be spending the day with her, trying to get information and an update on him."

The more he speaks, the more I could listen to his sultry voice all day. The way his lips shape every word. The way his hand rests on the gearshift. Makes me imagine how they'd feel wrapped around my thighs, spreading me open, teasing until I…

He glances over at me with those lethal green eyes. "Lila?" he says in a low, smoky whisper.

"Mmmhmm?"

"Are you listening to me?"

Shit. I'm staring, and he knows.

"Oh, yes. I'm listening! Taking mental notes."

A deep, dark chuckle slips from his mouth, and a slow smile curves at the corner of his lips as his eyes stay on the road. "Oh, really? Then tell me one thing I just said."

He turns slightly, finally looking at me. And I see it. His eyes drop to my lips, just for a second. But I feel it everywhere.

Did he just look at me the way I look at him? No way. I must have something on my lip.

Heat rises to my cheeks, and I can't help but blush. "That's what I thought," he says, eyes flicking to my lips again before turning back to the road.

Wait a damn minute. He's doing it on purpose. Asshole.

"We've got about an hour's drive," he says, glancing at the navigation screen. "We'll stop at a rest area so you can change. You need to look the part. Before my assistant left, she picked up your sizes, makeup, and hair products."

She sounds like his little housewife. Bitch.

He checks the clock. "Shit. We're supposed to be there at ten, and we've got an hour. We're going to be late."

I stop him because he wants to play games, and I can do it too. "I'm not bashful. I'll get ready in here. Are your windows tinted?"

He doesn't answer. Just silence and tension. "Yeah. They're tinted," he says finally, eyes still forward.

"Great. Are you okay with that? I mean, you've probably seen hundreds of women. My body isn't anything special."

He says nothing. Just turns up the radio. "Good For You" By Selena Gomez pulses through the speakers, vibrating in my chest.

He hands me a floral duffel bag. "Here's what you'll need."

I peek inside. From the products alone, this bag must be worth at least $1,500.

Rich people and their essentials.

I shouldn't want to turn him on, but God, I do. He once said my existence was the problem, so I'll be damned if I don't become his favorite one.

"Are you sensitive to scented lotions?"

"No, why?" He says, staring straight ahead.

"Well, your assistant packed some in here. I usually put it on before getting dressed." He goes still. Not breathing. Not moving. I pull my tank top over my head, revealing a red lace bra that lifts just enough to make me look like I've got something to grab. I shimmy my skort down to the floorboard, my bare skin hitting the heated leather seat. My red lace thong clings to me. And in this moment, I feel sexy. Dangerous. Desirable. Something I've never let myself be.

I glance over and damn, it's exactly what I wanted to see. He's gripping the steering wheel like it's the only thing keeping him tethered to earth. Like if he lets go, he might do something reckless. Something sinful. Something I'd beg him for.

"Umm… are you okay?" I ask.

"Mmmhmm." He nods, keeping his eyes on the road.

I squeeze a bit of lotion into my palm and rub it along my legs, slowly, up to my hips, across my stomach. Deliberate. Sensual. I'm turned on. And I know he is too, just by how hard he's resisting the urge to look at me.

The music amplifies the tension. His chest rises and falls like he's struggling to stay in control. I gather my hair into a slick, chic bun, then add gold diamond studs and a simple necklace. But I'm not done yet.

"Does my hair look okay?" I ask, turning to him with a flutter of my lashes, my skin still dewy from the lotion, barely concealed in red lace.

He draws a slow, shaky breath, then turns to me, eyes dark, hungry, feral.

Time to step it up a notch.

I twirl the necklace around my fingers and bite my lip, just enough for him to notice.

"Does this necklace look okay?"

He swallows hard. Then I see it, he shifts in his seat, adjusting.

There it is.

A long, thick erection trying to escape his designer pants.

Oh, hell yes. I just won.

He leans in, close enough for his breath to graze my cheek. "Lila," he whispers, voice dark and possessive, "you better get those clothes on before I pull over and make you beg to cum."

Well, I thought I was winning until I heard those filthy words roll off his lips.

We lock eyes, and his gaze drops to my mouth. This time, he bites his lip and smirks.

Fuck me.

"You'll reach your destination in five minutes," the GPS announces, slicing through the tension like a blade.

I tear my gaze away, pretending I wasn't two seconds from crawling into his lap. "You wish," I mutter, rolling my eyes as I break the stare. If I keep looking at him, we will never make it to our destination with what I want to do to him.

I slip into the black knee-length skirt and matching button-down. I add a touch of blush, trace my eyes with liner, sweep on mascara, and finish with a pop of red lipstick. Just enough to look alive. Presentable. I slide on a pair of sleek black heels, and just like that, I feel polished. Powerful. Like I belong in his world. Even if it is only for a day.

I smile out the window as the GPS announces, "You have arrived at your destination."

He turns right through a gold gate that towers over the car.

Why am I not surprised...

"I thought she was renting a house?" I ask, blinking.

"She is."

"No," I say, staring up at the sprawling estate. "This is a damn castle."

And there she is. Natasha. She stands on the grand stone steps like a goddess carved from marble, pure elegance, poised and effortless. My confidence shatters in an instant. Suddenly, I feel ridiculous for everything I did in the car.

Because women like her? They're his reality. I'm just a girl playing dress-up in his world.

CHAPTER TWENTY-SEVEN
LILA

Kage steps out first, all sharp edges and cold indifference. Like he didn't have a raging hard-on ten minutes ago, and then he sees her.

Natasha.

She glides toward him like temptation wrapped in silk, her emerald gown clinging to every curve. Without hesitation, she lifts onto her toes and kisses him on both cheeks. Her crimson-tipped fingers graze his chest and linger... too long, too familiar. Not the kind of touch reserved for acquaintances, but one shaped by memory. By moans. By history.

Kage doesn't flinch. Doesn't resist. He leans in, his voice low and smooth, lips near her ear.

"Привет, красавица. Я скучал по тебе."

My breath catches.

Oh. So, he speaks Russian too.

Of course he does.

I don't know what he said, but it didn't need a translation. Not with the way she smiles, the way his tone drops like velvet, the way her hand curls around his arm like she's done it a hundred times. Like she belongs there. I feel it in my stomach. In my chest.

Jealousy, hot and bitter, is climbing up my throat. And the worst part? He hasn't even looked at me. Not once.

Then her eyes flick to me. "And this must be your personal assistant."

I part my lips to speak, but Kage cuts me off. "Until my main one returns from Europe, yes."

Ouch.

She scans me from head to toe like I'm a smudge on her marble. Her lips curl into a smirk that doesn't touch her eyes. She's sizing me up like I'm a clearance-rack tragedy that somehow wandered into Chanel.

Then she loops her arm through his like she's already won. And maybe she has.

Of course, she gets to touch him.

Kage has never touched me, not by accident, not by choice. Not even a brush of his fingers. Like my lower income bracket might rub off on his custom-fitted suit.

This is just like high school all over again.

He doesn't look back. Not once. Like I'm nothing. Like I'm invisible. And maybe I am.

Her auburn hair flows in perfect waves down her bare back. The emerald silk of her gown catches the light like it's flirting with it. She glances back with a knowing smirk. She knows she's perfect. She knows I'm not. And worst of all, she knows she could have him inside of her before noon if she wanted to.

My stomach knots. I can see it, her legs wrapped around him. His mouth on her throat. Her breathy little gasps as he grinds into her—

Lila. Pull yourself together. He's a man. Not yours. Never was.

I trail behind like an afterthought, heels clicking on marble, trying not to dissolve into the floor. I didn't expect today to feel like a public humiliation… but here we are.

The second I step inside, my breath catches in my throat. This isn't a house. It's a palace. Golden light spills through a chandelier so massive it could be its own solar system. The air smells like roses and old money. Like, even the oxygen is imported.

Two sweeping staircases curl up either side of the room, trimmed in intricate wrought iron, leading to an upper balcony that watches over the foyer. Pillars line the hall like silent guards. The floors are glassy, spotless, designed to reflect wealth. And in the center lies an ornate mosaic, so breathtaking I feel unworthy to even set foot on it.

Then I look up. A domed ceiling stretches above us, painted in gold and soft pastels, crowned by a skylight so exquisite it looks like heaven itself. My jaw drops.

How am I supposed to act normal in a place like this? I feel like I should be dusting the chandeliers, not walking beneath them in Target heels.

I'm out of my depth. If you've never seen *Anastasia*, don't bother. Natasha is that Russian princess. I half expect her to glide down the staircase in slow motion, birds chirping, a full orchestra playing as she sings an ethereal welcome. She doesn't wear a crown, but she doesn't need to. The house is her crown. Her throne. Her spotlight. And she knows it.

And me? I'm just the dirt on her shoes.

I trail behind them like a lost, homeless puppy. They walk in sync, heads tilted toward each other, laughter spilling from their lips like it's some private joke meant to remind me I don't belong.

Wait… Did he smile at her?

No. Worse. A full-blown, teeth-baring, dimple-showing, earth-shattering smile.

I thought Kage might have a dimple, but that?
Dammit.

Just one glimpse, one godforsaken dimple, and butterflies explode in my lower belly like they've been waiting for permission. He just keeps getting more dangerous by the second.

Natasha leads us into a parlor room, and I swear my jaw unhinges. Everything looks like it was plucked from a French royal estate, soft cream and gold furniture, antique pieces that scream wealth. The kind of beauty that doesn't try too hard because it doesn't have to.

Tall arched windows pour warm morning light into the space, casting a soft, golden glow across the floor. It feels like we've stepped into an oil painting.

I freeze near the doorway, too scared to sit. Afraid to wrinkle something. Afraid my existence might somehow scuff the rug.

She gestures toward a couch for him to sit on. And then she does the worst thing possible. She looks at me. Not like a guest. Not like an equal. Like I'm the help. Like I'm a butler waiting to be dismissed. I almost turn around and walk out.

Almost.

Instead, I sit down. Purposefully. Planting myself in her perfect room, refusing to disappear. A reminder to Kage that I'm still here. Even if he doesn't want me to be.

"Tasha," he says smoothly, and my stomach flips. "I'm glad to see you again. I enjoyed our last dinner. And dessert." He pauses, winks, then takes her hands in his like it's the most natural thing in the world. "But we need to discuss something serious. It's about your brother."

Tasha? He has a nickname for her, too? Perfect.

She sighs, dramatically, of course. "Well, if we're going to talk about him, I'll ask my chef to bring us some handcrafted coffee and pastries." She turns, hips swaying like an invitation. And he watches her every move.

Of course he does. Why wouldn't he?

"We don't have much time before she gets back," Kage mutters under his breath.

"What?" I blink, caught off guard. "What are you talking about?"

"Listen," he says, voice low and clipped. "I need you to disappear for a bit. Dismiss yourself and take the stairs up to the second floor. Turn left, third door on the right. That's her office. Take this." He slips a flash drive into my palm. "Plug it in. Download everything on her desktop."

I stare at him like he's grown two heads. "Are you insane? What if she catches me? She's Russian royalty. She'll have me buried in a forest or worse!"

"I'll pay you triple while you work for me. And I'll keep her occupied." His lips curve into a smirk.

Oh God. What does that mean? Occupied how? Talking? Flirting? Sex?

Ugh. I'm going to be sick.

"The fact that you know where her office is…" I narrow my eyes.

He shrugs. "What's it to you?" His granite green eyes stay unreadable. I cross my arms, pout already forming, but I don't answer.

Because he's right, what is it to me, and why do I feel hurt by that remark?

She re-enters, floating like she's weightless, a tray of delicate treats balanced effortlessly between manicured hands. "Now, let's begin," she says sweetly. "We all need the strong stuff today since we are talking about that criminal."

"Excuse me," I say, rising from my seat. "Could you point me to the restroom? I also need to step away for a moment to make a few company calls."

Her eyes light up like she is excited that I'm leaving.
Bitch.

She slides into the seat beside him, her hand settling on his chest. "It's in the foyer," she purrs. Her eyes linger as she rakes them slowly over Kage. "And honey… take your time. We have plenty to catch up on."

"Thank you, ma'am," I say, dismissing myself from this absolute nightmare.

Kage doesn't look at me. Doesn't even acknowledge that I'm here. He doesn't even blink.

I turn and walk out, but every step feels wrong. I don't want to leave. I don't want her touching him. I don't want him touching her. I don't want to imagine his hands roaming her body or the way she will lean in close, whispering in Russian.

I don't want to imagine it, but I do. The thought clings to me, vivid and cruel. My steps slow, each one heavier than the last, the hallway stretching ahead like a tunnel with no end. Just as I reach the grand staircase, my phone buzzes in my pocket. A text. From an unknown number.

UNKNOWN: Don't mess this up, Lila.

CHAPTER TWENTY-EIGHT
LILA

He really hates me so much that he won't even give me his number, just an unknown one to boss me around.

Wow. Noted, asshole. Screw him. I'll get this damn file downloaded and never look back. He and his Russian princess can roll around on their designer sheets for all I care.

I hear giggling from the parlor.

Gag me.

I slip off my heels, clutching them as I creep up the grand staircase, each step cautious. Silent. Hoping I won't get caught. Hoping she doesn't have cameras tucked into every corner of this palace. Hoping I'm not already too late, because if her brother is terrifying, I can't imagine what she's like when she's angry. And I don't want to find out what her bodyguards do to people who snoop.

The old wood groans beneath me like it wants to give me away. My breath catches as I freeze in place.

This is a terrible idea.

My heart pounds in my ears. The text replays in my mind.

Don't mess this up, Lila.

How about asking someone else next time, jerk?

But this isn't about him. This is about the twenty-five missing girls. Focus.

The scent of expensive perfume lingers in the air as I reach the top floor. It floats like a warning that she's been here. Her bedroom must be near the office.

Oh. That's how he knew where to send me. How to find her computer. He's been here before… in her bedroom.

It hits low in my gut. Hard. I reach the final step. My legs tremble with the fear of getting caught. I pause at the landing. Listening. Waiting. The only sound is her annoyingly perfect laugh echoing from the first floor, rising like smoke up the grand staircase. It wraps around me, a reminder that she's still downstairs… with him.

I glance down the hall to make sure I'm alone. And of course, my imagination betrays me. I picture their bodies tangled together. Hands fumbling. Clawing. Desperate. Her back pressed against the wall outside her bedroom. His mouth crashing into hers. That little breathy sound she probably makes when he kisses down her neck.

I can see her gown sliding off her shoulders, pooling around her feet. His hands gripping her thighs. Her fingers in his hair, pulling, guiding. Their moans echoing off the marble. He lifts her up and presses her into the doorframe. They don't even bother to close the door. Why would they? This is her house. Her world. Her body he's touching. Her name is the one rolling off his tongue. Russian. The language they share. It makes everything feel private. Intimate. Like, there's a whole world between them that I'll never be part of.

This isn't healthy. I should call Leon. He's hot. Nice. Wants me. He invited me back to the pleasure room, for God's sake. That's... something.

Something safe. Something real. Better than this twisted mess with a man who looks right through me. Who acts like I'm invisible.

I shake the thought out of my mind and finally spot the third door. The office. I reach for the knob, turning it slowly, careful not to make a sound. I slip inside and shut the door behind me, pressing my back to the wood.

My heart is sprinting, but it's not panic. It's wild and electric adrenaline pulsing through my body, hoping to make it through this day alive and not be killed. I let out a breath I've been holding since Kage told me to do this.

The room is dim and elegant. Built-in bookshelves stretch to the ceiling. In the center, a gold antique desk topped with white marble. Three massive monitors glow faintly in the dark.

This is it. The reason I'm in this mess.

I cross the floor on my tiptoes, trying to be light as a feather so the hardwood doesn't creak under my weight. I tap the power button. The computer blinks awake. I stare at the middle monitor, silently begging it to hurry. Please don't take long.

Then it pops up.

Password protected.

Of course.

I grit my teeth and start typing. Fast. I open a menu and run a basic bypass command. Lines of code flash across the screen. Wrong password. I try again, this time using a shortcut I learned in college. The screen glitches for a second. Then... click.

It unlocks.

The desktop loads with a dozen folders staring back at me.

I'm in.

RATTLE.

The doorknob jiggles behind me.

I freeze.

Another rattle.

Then silence.

My body shakes.

She knows. Should I get on my knees and beg for forgiveness? Shit, what am I going to do?

I look around to find somewhere to hide, but nothing. My spine snaps straight.

"Why is this door locked?" The voice was raspy, older, female, like she's smoked a pack a day since birth.

I jam the thumb drive into the port. Another voice joins. Younger. Maybe Hispanic.

"I don't know. Maybe she doesn't want us to clean it?"

Housekeepers. This is my luck.

The file starts downloading.

15%.

A clock ticks somewhere behind me. Each second bangs against my skull like a drum.

16%.

20%.

Come on, come on.

"No, we are not skipping this room again. Last time I did, she threatened to send me to Russia. I'll grab the master key," the older voice snaps.

My throat closes. The clock ticks louder. Too loud. Like it's echoing inside my eardrum.

29%

40%

51%

Breathe. Just breathe.

Sweat beads at my temples and slides down my back, soaking into the waistband of my skirt. My palms are slick, fingers slipping on the keyboard as I try to type faster. The computer blinks. Slow. Too slow. Like it's mocking me.

68%

76%

The keys rattle outside the door. The clock ticks faster. Or maybe it's just my pulse. I wipe my hands on my skirt, desperate to dry them, but it barely helps.

89%

93%

The metallic scrape of the key sliding into the lock rattles through the door.

No. No. No.

98%

I fling open the French doors, barely believing what I'm about to do. The sheer curtains whip around me, cold air slapping my cheeks and tangling in my hair. Inside, the doorknob turns.

100%

I rip the flash drive free, fling my black heels aside, and hurl myself over the balcony, grabbing onto the thick, vine-wrapped lattice clinging to the stone wall. The clock inside strikes. One brutal, hollow clang letting me know I'm out of time.

A sharp sting slices across my neck. "Ouch!" I slap a hand over the spot, feeling the hot trickle of blood. A rose thorn caught me. A clean slice across the skin, and the blood beads fast.

Triple pay, huh? I'm going to need more than that.

But then it hits me. I said it out loud.

Oh God.

Please tell me they didn't hear me.

I scramble the rest of the way down, my feet slamming onto the ground. And freeze because I see them.

Kage.

Her.

She's straddling his lap, her emerald dress bunched high around her hips. His hands grip her waist. He's not pushing her away. He's leaning in. And seeing it hurts worse than a thousand rose thorns tearing through my skin.

Of course, he would want her. Who wouldn't? I'm an idiot to think I was even half as attractive as her.

And thinking about him with another woman was torture enough. But seeing it? That's a fucking tragedy.

Turns out, jumping off a balcony wasn't the thing that hurt the most.

CHAPTER TWENTY-NINE
LILA

How could I be so stupid? To think I had a chance with him… To try and seduce him.

Disappointment and anger churn beneath my skin, eating me alive.

I wish I could say I still had the Red Mask.

But I think that's over. And the Phantom? He wasn't real.

Maybe I really do need to be admitted somewhere, to take a break from whatever the hell this past month has been.

My bare feet sink into the damp ground, each blade of grass poking at my shredded ego. I stand at the window, watching, forcing myself to take in every excruciating second.

He's nothing to me. So why does this feel like heartbreak? As if I'm losing something I never had.

Natasha leans in and kisses him. Full and seductive as she straddles his lap like she belongs there… and honestly? She probably does. This doesn't look like her first time being on top of him.

Push her away, Kage. Tell her to get off. Tell her you don't want her… that you want me.

At first, he stares at her with an unreadable expression. *Please don't do it.*

But then he kisses her back. Kage twists the dagger deeper, confirming what I already know. He wants women like her. Not me.

The kiss grows more aggressive, as if this isn't the first time. Like they've done this before. Like they're reuniting after being apart, craving each other in a way that makes my stomach twist.

My chest rises and falls, like I've been punched in the lungs and forgot how to breathe.

God, what I would give to be her right now. To be the one kissing him.

I watch her rock her hips against him, against what's likely a very eager erection, and nausea claws up my throat. I can't take it. I turn to leave, desperate to get back to the car and escape this hell I've walked into. Blood still drips from the cut on my neck, warm against my skin. And that's when I catch it.

His lips leave hers. Slowly. Dragging across her skin, down to her neck.

I hate how much I want him. How easily the knife in my heart dulls the second his eyes find mine.

His green, granite eyes open. And I freeze because it's like he read my thoughts, because now his eyes are locked on me. Feral. Possessive. Telling me not to leave. Burning straight through the glass.

Not again. This feels like déjà vu.

And despite every broken, bleeding part of me, a heat builds between my legs. A need for more. I'm frozen in place. I should move, I need to move. But he's staring at me like he wants to devour her. Or maybe me.

No, no, no, Lila, this will not be a rerun of the Phantom mishap.

His eyes grow darker, like he's speaking to me without a single word. His kiss turns aggressive. He grips her hips harder and harder, rocking her on his lap with a rough, desperate rhythm. His eyes never leave mine. Wetness pools between my thighs. My mouth goes bone dry. And the way he's responding by watching me… does he want me too?

I cross my legs, squeezing them tight, trying and failing to calm the throbbing pulse between them. Even with his mouth on her neck, I catch it. That tiny dimple on his cheek. He's smiling.

What the hell? Is this sick entertainment for him? Fine, Kage. Let's play.

I bite my bottom lip, my fingertips tracing a slow path down my mouth, over my chin, and along my neck until they pause at the swell of my breast. I hook a finger beneath my shirt and tug it lower, flaunting curves I barely have with the kind of confidence that says otherwise. My lips part. A soft breath slipping out, as if even my own touch might make me moan.

That got your attention.

I see him gulp, his Adam's apple bobbing, even as he sinks his teeth into her neck like there's no tomorrow.

And then I do the unexpected.

I press the back of my hand to the window and flip him the bird. Big and bold. Then I mouth, "I'm going to the car," and point in that direction. I add extra emphasis to the last word, mouthing, "asshole," like I'm spitting it at him.

Before I can see his reaction, I spin on my heel, cross my arms over my chest, and march away. Every step is screaming *screw you*. I sway my hips as I walk to the car, hoping he can see everything he's missing.

BUZZ.

My phone buzzes with a new message. I roll my eyes, knowing exactly who the text is from.

UNKNOWN: Did you like what you saw?

LILA: Just admiring how good you two look together.

LILA: And how tragically bad you are at kissing. Seriously, were you drinking from a water bowl or trying to kiss her? Hard to tell.

UNKNOWN: You sure you weren't imagining it was you on my lap, princess?

Really? He's trying to piss me off.

LILA: Don't call me that. Only Clint and Beck can call me Princess.

UNKNOWN: That's fine. I've got better names for you. None of them is appropriate for texting.

Shit. I know he doesn't mean it. He's just mad that I flicked him off, and now he's trying to tease me. But damn. That is so freaking sexy. And I can't help it… this man makes me weak.

I slam the phone face down in the passenger seat and drag my hands through my hair in pure frustration.

Then it buzzes again.

What now? Isn't he busy getting jerked off?

I snatch it up and freeze. It's not him. It's Leon.

This is what I need. Someone good. Respectful. Kind. Someone who actually wants me.

LEON: Will I see you at the club this weekend?

LILA: Depends. Will I get to kiss you again?

LEON: Only if you're a good girl.

Yep. This is exactly what I need.

LILA: Don't tempt me, Leon. How about Saturday? Aster and I will be there around ten.

LEON: Perfect. I will be waiting for an angel to walk through the door.

Butterflies swirl in my stomach. He called me an angel. That's adorable. Soft. Genuine. He's safe like Beck. And maybe, just maybe, that's what I need. The Red Mask and Kage are toxic. They make me feel vulnerable in a way I've never felt before. And that's the real danger.

I just need to get home. Clean up this damn scratch before it gets infected.

I lean down to hit the push-to-start button. And that's when I see him. The front door opens. He steps out. Natasha is standing there, waving like a damn homecoming queen.

"I can't wait to see you next time," she says, blowing him a kiss.

Ewww.

Kage glances at her with a polite smile before turning to me. His eyes pinning me in place. This gorgeous, arrogant bastard drives me insane, and the way he is prowling toward me now makes every step feel like he's savoring my heartbreak.

His smirk spreads across his face, knowing damn well what he's doing to me. *Oh, and now his one dimple.* That damn dimple flashes just enough to know it's there, just enough to drive me insane. And then, like it's nothing, he wipes his lips with the back of his hand.

His eyebrow lifts, waiting for my move, daring me to react.

Sir, you are asking for a game of chess you can't win.

He slides into the driver's seat effortlessly, red lipstick smeared across his neck. I can still smell her perfume clinging to his suit.

Man whore.

"So," I say, voice dripping with sass, "did you get the information you needed, or just your dick wet?"

He throws me a side-eye as he whips the car around, peeling out of the driveway. "I can multitask," he says smoothly. "Want me to show you?"

I roll my eyes so hard I'm pretty sure I see my own brain. "Oh, please. While you were busy getting laid, I was busy downloading everything onto this." I wave the flash drive in the air like a trophy. "But," I snap, my voice sharp and rising, "Because of the little situation you threw me into, I almost got caught. I could've killed myself jumping off the balcony. I could have broken my neck while you were busy playing tonsil hockey with your girlfriend!"

I pause, chest heaving, trying to catch my breath before I scream. "Oh, and a thorn slashed my neck. I'm bleeding everywhere with nothing to clean it up with, and I couldn't go back inside, or she would have known something was up."

I yank my collar down and show him the dried blood on my skin. "See? Hope your little make-out session was worth it. And to top it all off?" I add sweetly. "I had to watch you get nasty with Little Miss Russian Heiress." I smile brightly. "Which means you owe me five times more."

The car jerks to the side of the road before shuddering to a stop. Kage's grin spreads slow and wicked as his thumb drags over his bottom lip. He turns toward me, eyes animalistic.

"Okay, Princess," his voice drops, low and dangerous. "I'll meet that request. But are you sure there isn't something else you want… from me?"

His gaze lingers on my mouth.

I can't stop staring at his mouth. Plush lips I ache to taste, the freckle above them taunts me like it knows exactly how badly I want him.

Stay strong, Lila.

It's just a game. A way to toy with me. Or maybe I should do the unexpected. I stare at him, contemplating what to do.

What is my heart telling me to do?
Oops, too late. My body is in control.
I lean in close to his face and bite my lip.
It makes the Red Mask crazy, so why not try it on him?
"You know, Kage, I've been thinking about it." I lean even closer, and he stills. "I think

you're right… There is something that I want from you." I pause just long enough to make sure he's hanging onto every word, sliding my hands up his suit jacket to tease him a little, but I still can't read his reaction.

I lean in so close I could kiss him. Instead, I whisper low and seductive. "I want… your best friend," I smirk. Even though I really don't want him. I'm just trying to piss him off, but he doesn't need to know that.

The air in the car shifts. His body stiffens. I can feel the rage ripple off him, hot and wild and barely contained.

Good. I want him to feel what I felt.

RING.

RING.

RING.

Oh, that's not his phone ringing… It's mine.

Kage doesn't move. He glares at me, pure malice burning in his stare.

I clear my throat and answer. "Hello?"

"What's up, slut?" Aster's voice rings through the speaker, teasing. "You done cleaning Beck's palace?"

Kage cranks the AC to full blast, like he is trying to put out the flames rolling off him, and whips the car back onto the road toward New York.

"We'll talk later," I whisper into the phone, keeping my voice low. "I can't talk right now."

"Okay, okay, but listen. The guys called and wanted to know if we're hitting the club this weekend?"

Perfect. The timing is perfect. Just in time to piss him off even more. I want to rub salt on the wound.

"Actually," I say, flicking a glance at him, "Leon texted me earlier. Said he couldn't wait to see me this weekend, and I told him he could, but only if I get to kiss him again."

I watch Kage out of the corner of my eye. He's not just gripping the wheel. He's murdering it.

"No, you didn't!" Aster shrieks. "Oh my God, Lila, you little flirt! What did he say?" I smile sweetly and lean back in my seat, as if I'm not setting this car ablaze with both of us inside it. "He said only if I'm good. Aster, I can't wait to fuck him tomorrow. It's going to be amazing—"

I'm cut off mid-sentence. Kage yanks the phone out of my hand and throws it straight out the window.

"Hey! What the hell!" I shout, whipping around to watch my phone bounce down the road.

He says nothing. Eyes locked on the road, jaw clenched so tight I'm surprised he doesn't break his perfect teeth. His chest rises and falls, heavy and furious.

So, he can put me through literal hell, but I can't talk about hanging out with a guy?

I glare at him, seething. "Do you have any idea how long it took me to save up for that, you rich prick? Unlike you, I don't have millions sitting around!" I shout, the emotion cracking in my voice.

"I scrape by each month. I can barely pay my bills. Most nights, dinner is ramen noodles, but you wouldn't understand, would you!" His jaw clenches harder. But I can't hold it in. The tears blur my vision before I can stop them.

It's downright humiliating, breaking down like this in front of him. But he doesn't get it. It's a game to him. And yes, I was playing back. But this? I can't afford to buy a new one. He can throw money out the window, but I can't. That phone was everything. My connection to Mom. My check-ins with Dad. My emergency contact line in case anything goes wrong, especially where I live. And now? If I buy a new one, I won't be able to pay rent. I could get kicked out.

I hate myself for this.

I turn my face toward the window, biting my lip hard enough to taste blood, willing myself not to sob. Trying not to let him see how fragile I really am. How something so small could split me wide open.

CHAPTER THIRTY
LILA

I watch as my world stands still while New York City buzzes with life beyond my window. The nightlife glows, electric and endless, as I lie in bed where I've been since Kage dropped me off five hours ago. The rest of the ride was dead silent. Neither of us said a single word. All I could do was let silent tears slide down my cheeks as the trees blurred past the window. He shattered me with a single, thoughtless move. And I showed him exactly how brittle I really am.

Wow, Lila. You really are fragile. Nothing like Aster. Nothing like Jasmine. Nothing like Natasha.

I thought I was having fun playing his game. But maybe he took it too far. Or perhaps I did.

Either way, he doesn't have to think about money. Or consequences. Or people like me.

I flip over, facing the wall where the vent with the hidden camera sits. "If you're wondering why I'm rotting in bed," I say, my voice hollow, "it's because I've had a terrible day." My voice dips as I feel the tears threaten to break free. "But it's not like you care."

I feel insane talking to the vent. He's probably not even watching me. Why would he? He left his mask behind. That was his way of saying goodbye. And I know deep down… that was the last moment I'll ever see him. "Also… if you texted me, I don't have a phone anymore."

My voice cracks. "Or maybe you didn't text me at all."

The words fall out, broken, splintering the little strength I have left. A tear spills onto my pillow. And then another. And then I can't stop them. "I'm nothing. No one. Who could love a girl who can't even stand her own reflection?"

At that, my whole body caves in, and I sob into my pillow, drowning in it. Nothing but my cries and their echo in this tiny studio apartment. He's not there. He's not watching. He's busy with someone worth his time. Someone who isn't me.

The clock on the wall glows 7:45 p.m. Time doesn't care that I'm falling apart.

Maybe I should shower.

Mascara streaks my face. I smell like snot and rock bottom. But before I can move…

KNOCK.

KNOCK.

KNOCK.

I bolt upright, my heart pounding against my ribs. A cold wave of fear rushes through me. My body trembles, buzzing with panic.

Is it Natasha's guards? Did she find out I hacked her computer? Her brother, The Wolf? Is it his men? Well… if it were them, they wouldn't be knocking. They'd just barge in and kill me.

I glance down at myself. A blue satin nightgown clings to my skin, and my long blonde hair is twisted into a messy bun. I'm not exactly decent. Should I pretend I'm not home? But if I don't answer, they might break the door down.

"Who is it?" My voice comes out shaky, barely louder than a whisper. Silence. "Hello?"

There's no peephole. My door is so old, I can't even check if this person looks remotely safe.

Am I about to get kidnapped again? What will they make me do this time?

I slowly reach for the tarnished silver knob, trying to compose myself. My palm is slick with sweat. I can barely hold on. I crack the door open, keeping the chain in place. It's flimsy and useless, but it's all I've got. If someone wanted me badly enough, they'd rip it off and take me anyway.

"Are you Miss Anderson?" A teenage guy stands there, stoned out of his mind. Greasy hair. Pale skin. An unruly beard. A red cap and a matching collared shirt that resembles a local delivery service uniform.

"Um… I am. Is everything okay?" My voice is tight, but my heart finally starts to slow.

He doesn't seem like a threat.

"Everything's great. Just have a few bags and packages for you." I glance down and see five or six reusable grocery bags and two small boxes piled near the door.

"For me?"

"Yes, ma'am. Want me to bring them in?"

"No!" I cut him off, too fast. "Just… leave them right there. I'll get them. Um, thank you."

"You're welcome. Thanks for the generous tip and for using our services." He strolls down the stairs, whistling as if this were just another ordinary delivery.

I have packages? From who? Why? Am I still in danger? Could it be a bomb? Did he find a way to reach me from prison?

Inhale. Exhale.

"You're okay, Lila. You're not in danger." I shut the door and press my back against it, breathing slow and deep, holding a hand to my chest. "You're okay. You're not in danger." I whisper it again, trying to convince myself, trying to calm my fight-or-flight mode.

I've already had a pretty shitty day. But with the way things are going, I wouldn't be surprised if it were a bomb.

I unlock the door, slide the cheap chain off, and peek my head out, left and right.

Nothing. No one.

Well. Here goes nothing.

I grab the bags quickly and drop them inside, slamming the door shut and locking it again. Not that the lock makes me feel any safer.

I plop down in front of the pile, emotionally and physically wrecked. Tearing the first box open, I gasp. A brand-new phone. Top of the line. Shiny. Pristine. This thing probably costs three grand, way more than I could ever afford. The kind of phone someone with my status wouldn't even dare touch in a store. And sitting right on top of the screen, a sticky note, written in the most beautiful, clean handwriting I've ever seen: "Everything has already been set up. Your contacts and pictures have been transferred."

Short. Sweet. To the point.

Is this really... mine?

I rip into the second box, and my breath hitches. Bandages. Cleaning solution. Antibiotic ointment. Everything I'd need to treat the cut on my neck. The one I still haven't even cleaned because I came home and collapsed in bed and never moved. Another note is tucked inside: "I don't need you ending up in the hospital. Clean it up and be at work on Monday. Don't be late."

Kage? It must be. Could this be his apology? He didn't say sorry, but then again, neither did I.

I reach for the rest of the bags and halt. This isn't cheap instant junk. It's real food, fresh, expensive, too good for me. A note peeks out from between the bags, and a laugh slips from my lips before I can swallow it down.

"Throw the ramen away. That shit is bad for you."

I shake my head, muttering, "You sound like my mom."

My eyes drift back to the phone. The bandages. The groceries.

It's him. This is from Kage. He did this. But why? Is this an apology? A bribe to keep my mouth shut? Or just another chess move in a game where I don't even know the rules?

My stomach twists. I clutch the new phone against my chest, feeling the weight of it. And for the first time tonight, I can't tell if it's a gift or a loaded weapon, waiting to break whatever pieces of me are still left.

I guess I'll find out.

CHAPTER THIRTY-ONE
LILA

The sight before me will be imprinted in my mind forever. My watch buzzes, a sharp vibration against my wrist, reminding me that my heart is racing. But this isn't panic fueling my adrenaline. It's something else. Something forbidden.

The music pulses through the speakers, amplifying the tension in the air, making the scene before me feel even more exotic. The bedroom is drenched in deep, sensual shadows, where darkness and elegance intertwine. A towering black upholstered headboard dominates the space, its luxurious bedding a siren's call, luring anyone reckless enough to sink into its embrace.

On the nightstand, a crystal vase overflows with fresh, full, and almost too vivid red roses, which stand out against the moody palette. Above the bed, a skylight allows a sliver of moonlight and stars to seep in, casting silver streaks across the silk sheets. Velvet curtains cascade in dramatic waves behind the bed, framing the space like a stage because that's what this feels like.

A private performance.

This is a room built for secrets. A hideaway from reality. And at the center of it all, a blonde is on her knees in the center of the room, her long braid threaded with tiny purple flowers, a delicate gold tiara glinting on her head. She's dressed in a lavender strapless corset, a ruffled princess skirt hugging her curves as she takes him into her mouth, inch by inch.

She's beautiful.

And I'm wet. Soaking wet for what's in front of me.

She lifts her head, looking up at the dark silhouette as a low, masculine, haunting hum spills into the room. It slides down my spine like silk and leaves me desperate for more. I'm frozen, completely under its spell.

Who is she? Who is he?

She rises slowly, every movement graceful, as something sharp and electric stirs in the air. And then I see it.

She is me. There I am, standing before him. The Phantom. The man who feels like every wicked thought I've ever craved and every secret I've buried about myself. What I want in a man. What I ache for when no one's watching.

He watches me with a hunger so raw it steals the breath from my lungs. I take a slow step forward. He matches it. The tension between us pulls tighter, a thread straining to snap. I tilt my chin toward him, body quivering for his touch.

He leans in, unhurried and deliberate, his mouth hovering just above mine. So close I can taste the heat of him. So close I can feel his breath brush against my lips.

"Please," I beg silently. His hand lifts, brushing a strand of hair from my face with aching tenderness. A touch so soft it feels like a vow.

RING.

RING.

RING.

I jolt awake, blinking hard at the blinding daylight pouring into my studio. Disoriented. Shaking. I fumble for the sound, reaching blindly across the bed. It's not the alarm. It's a phone call. I squint at the screen.

Aster.

"Why do you always wake me up right before the kiss?" I mutter, voice rough and cracked.

"Uh, what the hell are you still doing in bed? It's two o'clock!"

"Making my deepest fantasies come true," I groan, dragging a hand down my face. "Since real-life dick is clearly off the table. I've been surviving on sex dreams until you cockblocked me in my sleep."

Aster giggles. "Oh, hun. That's about to change tonight. Do you even remember what today is?" She lowers her voice to a sing-song whisper. "Leooooon day."

My stomach drops.

Oh God. It's the day.

But something inside me stays numb. Heavy. Like I'm not ready. Like I'm watching myself from the outside. Like, I'm not even real.

Everything feels muted. Distant. I don't know how I am supposed to feel. Or if I even can. It's like I've left my own body. Like I'm floating. Disconnected. Desensitized.

"Ugh, do I have to go? I don't think I'm up for it today…"

"Something else is going to be up tonight…" Aster giggles.

"Seriously, Aster. I think I'm going to cancel. I don't even have anything to wear and—"

"I'm sending it over now. Be ready by 9:00 pm."

"No, I'm not wearing your slutty clothes—!"

CLICK.

"Hello? Hello?"

She hung up on me.

"Ughhh!" I groan, flopping back onto the bed in complete dramatic frustration. I turn my head toward the vent, where the tiny camera still blinks quietly. "I'm going back to the club tonight," I mutter. "If you're really done with me… don't show up."

I stare at the ceiling. "Let me get over your toxic nonsense," I whisper, like he's sitting right beside me.

These men will be the death of me.

I practically peel myself off the bed.

Why did I dream about the Phantom? Those crystal-clear blue eyes still linger behind my eyelids. He's not real. He can't be. But that hum… it was the same one I heard from the Red Mask. Maybe, deep down, I want them to be the same person?

It was just a dream, Lila. No reason to overanalyze.

I shuffle into my tiny kitchen, where the counters are stained and the fridge groans with age. I pull my hair free from its messy bun, my fingers catching in the knots. God, I need a shower. Maybe even a shave.

As if I'll actually get lucky tonight. Honestly, I've practically thrown myself at these men and still ended up alone. I hook my phone to the Bluetooth speaker and crank the only song that feels right, "Busy Woman" by Sabrina Carpenter.

The beat pulses through the space as I stomp around in my satin nightgown, barefoot and wild-haired, singing like a woman unhinged and ready for revenge. I open the fridge and freeze. It's full. Stocked with food like it belongs to someone else's life. I bite my lip, staring.

Kage. Damn him.

I grab strawberries and blueberries. Then, because I'm still me, I reach for the Honey Nut Cheerios. Add the fruit. Add the milk. I've lived like this for so long. It would feel wrong to eat anything else but cereal. But the fruit is a nice touch. One I could get used to.

A knock rattles the door. Sharp. Impatient. I open it to find Aster's assistant standing there, looking frantic and frazzled. Her long black hair is twisted up in a gold clip. Her tailored black suit hugs every curve. The white blouse beneath it is marked with a coffee stain, probably from whatever chaos her morning started with.

"Sarah, are you good?" I ask.

"She's got me running today, Lila."

"I'll call her and tell her to go easy on you. Maybe mention you looked really stressed."

She smiles. "Thank you! She's driving me nuts today. I think she's on her period, but have fun tonight… wear protection!" She gives me a wink and a wave before disappearing down the stairs.

I was expecting a shoebox or something small. Instead, it's a full garment bag with a note stuck to the hanger. "Break out of your cocoon and let your wings or legs spread tonight. Love, Aster."

I unzip it slowly, and my jaw actually drops. It's… a butterfly. Not just a top, a sculpted, iridescent butterfly molded in delicate pastels, like it was pulled straight from a fairytale rave. Its wings shimmer in purples, pinks, and opal blues, the colors shifting with every angle. Crystals and pearls snake up from the bodice, curling around an invisible halter that drapes over the shoulders.

It looks like it was made for a goddess with a grudge and a hit list of every man who ever let her go.

The skirt, if you can even call it that, is made of soft, pearled chiffon that hugs the hips with draped pearl chains and sequins that catch the light like stars. It's ethereal. Dangerous. Too beautiful to be real.

Too beautiful for someone like me.

I hold it up against myself and stare in the mirror. I look like I belong in a fantasy.

My phone buzzes. One new message.

THE RED MASK: *Wear it. I want to see you fly.*

He's watching. He knows where I'm going. Which means… he'll see me there.

CHAPTER THIRTY-TWO
LILA

Step by step, I make my way down the stairs to Aster. She's picking me up for a night full of unknowns. But I'm here. A little numb, but better. And honestly? The outfit helps.

My hair, usually wild and unruly, is twisted into an updo of soft curls piled on top of my head. I followed a YouTube tutorial, and it's definitely giving early 2000s vibes. To add a little more drama, I wove strands of pearls through the curls to tie everything together. A few strands spiral free, brushing my cheeks and neck to give it a romantic feel.

Hopefully, that's not the only action I get tonight.

My back is completely exposed, except for the delicate pearl and crystal strands that hold the top in placc. Thc butterfly bodice clings like it was sculpted just for me, fragile, feminine, and empowering all at once.

"Damn, Lila! Can I marry you?" Aster practically shouts, jaw on the floor.

"Stop. Don't blow smoke up my butt." I smirk. "And look at you! We're twinning. I love it." Relief washes over me. I won't be the only one in the spotlight tonight. We both will, and honestly, that takes the pressure off.

She twirls dramatically, her black butterfly outfit sparkling under the light. It's the same as mine, but darker, opalescent black with flashes of midnight blue. We're opposites. Day and night. Her short, jet-black hair is pinned up, threaded with black pearls.

"I guess we really are in sync," she says, grinning as she hooks her arm through mine.

Together, we walk toward her matte black G-Wagon, the moment unfolding like the first scene of a night made for trouble.

We hop in, and as the doors shut, I realize I haven't actually checked in on her in a while. Lately, everything's been about me. My job. My mom. My love life. Aster doesn't make it easy to ask how she's doing. She's the kind of person who hides behind jokes and shopping. She'll say she's fine with a smile and a wink, even when she's drowning. And honestly? I've let her get away with it.

"How are you?" I ask, glancing over. And this time, I really mean it.

She narrows her eyes. "I'm good… why? Do you know something I don't?" She pauses, then gasps. "Did Tom Holland and Zendaya break up?"

I snort. "Oh my God, no. If they ever break up, I swear I'm giving up on love entirely." She laughs, but I hesitate, then speak more softly.

"I just… I feel like I haven't been the best friend lately. You've been there for me with my mom, supported me through everything, and I've been so wrapped up in work and life that I haven't stopped to check in on you. To ask what's happening in your world."

She grabs my hand. "Lila, stop dragging yourself through the mud. You're always a good friend, no matter what's going on. Give yourself some credit."

I squeeze her hand, smiling. "Thanks, Aster… Now tell me the important stuff. Have you been on any dates recently? Anyone catch your eye?" She gives me a shy, almost guilty smile.

"What?" I ask, eyebrows shooting up.

"Well… if you must know… I think I like someone."

"No way. You? You've never had a crush on anyone in your life. I thought all your relationships were strictly no-strings-attached?"

"They were… are… I don't know." She says, her voice quieter now. "Until I met someone. The night of the Halloween party."

My heart stutters. "Was it Jack Sparrow?" I giggle.

"He was nice, but no. Do you remember the plague doctor who pulled me away from you before I lost? After he manhandled me, I was so turned on that I ended up making out with him. Hard. I flipped it, went full dominant, mostly because I loved the way he threw me over his shoulder." She pauses, her teeth catching her lip, eyes unfocused. "I shoved him against a bush, lifted his mask in the dark, and we devoured each other. God, he was into it." Her voice drops, breathless. "I can't stop thinking about that kiss, Lila. It felt… different. More."

Oh my God. The Plague Doctor… it was Beck. He confessed, and she has no clue. Should I tell her? Maybe I should, because honestly, she deserves someone like him. They'd be adorable together. He's a golden retriever, all warmth and boyish charm. And Aster? She's a hurricane in heels, unstoppable and wild.

"Aster, I'm so excited for you! Do you know who it is?" I play dumb because I need to know if she's even interested in him before I tell her.

"Sadly, no. I have no idea," she sighs, a dreamy look in her eyes. "But I'm hoping fate will let our paths cross again. I can't get him out of my head."

"I have hope for you. My love life might be six feet under, but you... You go after what you want!"

She smiles at me, unaware of the war happening inside my chest. I could never be that forward with a man. I'm too timid. Too scared of rejection. But she's not. I wish I could be more like her. Bold. Fearless. Unshakable.

We pull up in front of the four-story sex club that haunts my memories in the best way. Arm in arm, we step out in perfect sync. Yin and yang. Each stride feels like slow motion in a music video.

Aster tosses the keys to the valet with a wink, fully owning the main character energy she lives in. I flip my hair, letting them know I am just as hot and walking in with my baddie of a best friend.

"Aster, keep it in your pants," I mutter.

She smirks. "One of us has to get laid tonight."

I roll my eyes, but she's not wrong. Leon is about to forget every woman he has ever met the moment I walk in. The doormen open the pitch-black doors, looking us up and down as they should. If they didn't, I would have to file a complaint.

The place is exactly how I remember it. Bass thumps. Bodies grind. Pole dancers spin on elevated platforms. Waves of color ripple through the club, lights sweeping over every surface in a hypnotic rhythm. I glance down. Our butterfly outfits glow.

No… actually glowing. The wings catch the blacklights, shimmering as if crafted with bioluminescence. Every eye in the room locks on us.

"Did you really have to add that little detail?" I whisper in Aster's ear.

She grins with pure, wicked confidence. "I wanted to make sure we lit the place up."

Mission accomplished.

Heads turn. Conversations stall. We walk like we belong here, because we do.

The lounge is soaked in luxury. Black leather couches. Dim lighting. The scent of power clings to the air. It is full of elite businessmen with crystal tumblers in hand, each one convinced his money makes him a god.

But right now? They're drooling. Over us. Over me.

My eyes scan the room until I finally find him. Leon.

He catches my stare. I toss a playful wave and flash him a smile, because I am genuinely excited to see him again. Maybe I really can have something with him. And God, he looks divine. Jet-black hair, effortlessly styled, contrasts perfectly with his smooth, golden skin. That sharp jawline could cut glass, and when he smiles, all perfect teeth and playful danger, his eyes squint just enough to make my heart stutter. His black suit hugs his broad shoulders and trim waist as if it were tailored for seduction.

I swoon. But then I notice he is laughing, cutting up with a couple of other guys... And then I see it. My night crashes. Just like that. Over.

No, no, no. You have got to be kidding me right now.

There they are. Clint. Beck. And Kage. All seated around Leon like some kind of twisted royal court. Laughing. Drinking. Watching.

Kage's green eyes lock on mine, glowing with a slow, searing intensity. He lifts his glass and takes a sip of whiskey, unflinching. No hesitation. No mercy. His gaze drags over me like fire on bare skin, tracing every inch from head to toe. He makes no effort to disguise it. He wants me. And God help me, I want him too. More than I should. More than is safe. More than I've ever wanted anything. And that is the most dangerous part of all.

CHAPTER THIRTY-THREE
LILA

I glance at Aster, my face flushing so fast I feel it in my ears. "You have got to be kidding me…"

She grins like the devil herself. "You ready to wreck some hearts or get wrecked?" She throws me a wink. Dread rolls through me like a wave ready to take me under.

Act normal. You can handle this.

The air tastes like sweat, smoke, and sin. Somewhere above us, a woman moans. Long. Slow. Drenched in pleasure.

Nope. Absolutely not. Abort mission. I can't do this tonight.

We glide toward the table like we own it. But inside, I am a full-blown disaster. Category five. Screaming silently. My watch vibrates on my wrist. Sharp. Unrelenting. Buzzing like it knows I am about to fall apart. I am not panicking. Just anxious. Or excited. Or maybe I am actually panicking. Internally. Loudly.

Kage glances at the flickering screen on my wrist like he's reading my pulse. My thoughts. My unraveling. He sees straight through me, past the sarcasm, past the lipstick and lashes, into the fragile thing I fight to hide. He saw it when I shattered over something as stupid as a phone. Now he knows too much. He knows how breakable I am, and that makes it dangerous. Because he could use it. He could turn my weakness into another move in his fucked up game.

Aster, of course, is smooth as ever. Her voice drips like honey as she purrs, "May we join you boys?"

Before anyone can answer, she takes Clint's drink straight from his hand and sips it, slow, seductive, totally unfazed.

Clint stands and takes her hand like it's some old-Hollywood romance. "How about we grab a drink and hit the dance floor?"

She scrunches her nose. "Ew, Clint. Not even if we were the last two people on earth."

Leon turns to me, smirking. "You know them?"

I hesitate. "I… do. Beck, Clint, and Kage are my bosses at Heartford."

"You work for them?" He raises a brow.

"Yes…" I start, but he cuts me off, pulling me onto his lap like I weigh nothing. His hand settles on my thigh, and his mouth grazes my ear.

"How about you come work for me?"

Beck chimes in before I can breathe. "Absolutely not. You're not stealing my new hire. She's got wicked skills with code." He chuckles, sipping his drink.

But I barely hear him. All I can hear is the sound of my own heart, thrumming wildly in my chest, because I can feel him.

Kage. Staring. I see him in my peripheral, not even pretending to look away. His presence beside me is like static in the air. Buzzing. Burning. So close it hurts. So loud it drowns everything else out. I don't look at him.

Instead, I turn to Leon. I meet his warm brown eyes, soft and inviting, like I am slipping under a spell, and slowly wrap my arms around his neck. Then I kiss him. Right there. Right in front of Kage. It starts gently, a whisper of lips, but then it deepens, fast and hungry.

Leon's hands grip the bare skin of my hips, firm and possessive, just rough enough to send a shiver racing up my spine. It feels good to be touched. To be wanted. Not like the one beside me, who keeps his hands to himself, keeps his secrets, and couldn't even give me his real number.

Aster perks up. "See, boys? That's how you treat a woman. Screw this. I'm going to find a hot guy on the dance floor. You good, Lila?" Before I can answer, Leon cuts in.

"I'll take good care of her. You don't have to worry." Then he kisses me again. Deep. Claiming. Addictive. It feels nice. But the truth? None of this is for him. It's for Kage. And the rush that hits me when I sense him watching is intoxicating. Every. Single. Moment. His presence seethes with wrath and rage.

Why? He was all over Natasha. What is his problem? I feel like I have emotional whiplash from him hating me one second and buying me groceries the next.

Is this rage because he truly loathes me, or is it something else?

I exhale and glance around the table. Clint's mouth drops open. "Damn, Lila. You really did use me for the job!" He grins. "I tried to kiss you like five times and you dodged every single time."

"It's okay," Beck cuts in smoothly, cigar between his teeth. "She disappeared after we grinded at the Halloween party… then ghosted me." He smirks, sipping his drink with that wicked edge.

"Hey, hey, hey," I protest, throwing back a shot. "Since when is this the Crap-on-Lila Club? I can't help it if I'm irresistible." A laugh slips out of me.

Leon slides his arms around me from behind, lips brushing my neck. "Well, tonight you're not getting away from me."

My heart stutters. And strangely, I feel something. Excitement. And disappointment. Because I do like Leon, but he isn't Kage. He isn't the Red Mask. He isn't the Phantom. *I wish he were enough to drown out the others. I wish I wanted him the way I want them.*

Abruptly, Kage stands, raking a hand through his hair like he's dripping in charisma. "I need a cigarette… and some pussy," he mutters.

My jaw drops. "Why don't you just call up Natasha? And I thought you didn't smoke?" I snap.

He doesn't answer, grabs his whiskey, and rises from the leather couch. Beck chuckles. "Kage said he doesn't smoke?" His laughter deepens. "It's not his usual thing, but yeah, he definitely lights one up when he's pissed." He glances at me, then back at his friend. "Kage, what's got your panties in a wad?"

He says nothing, just storms out in silence. What the hell is his problem? Why lie about something as small as smoking? And did he seriously say he needs pussy? Right here. Right in front of everyone.

Typical man whore.

He walks away, no glance back, no hesitation. And I hate how much I want him to look back, to wonder if I'm watching him leave, to need me like I've been needing him. I ache to follow, but I don't, because I know he doesn't want me, and I have to stop.

Lila, get over it. Over him. The Red Mask. The Phantom. The fantasy.

He wants women like Natasha, polished and perfect, and this club is swarming with them.

I grab two shots from the table and knock them back, the burn chasing down the ache. "Who wants to dance?" I shout over the pulse of the music, hopping off Leon's lap like I don't care… like I'm not falling apart.

Leon stands, sliding off his jacket, and holy hell. He looks like sex and danger wrapped in designer fabric. His white shirt hangs half-unbuttoned, its cuffs rolled to his forearms, exposing his tan skin, thick veins, and a lightning tattoo that ripples up the length of his arm.

I blink. Hard. Because damn… that ink? It's hot. Raw. And completely unexpected. I've always had a thing for tattoos, but this one? This one hits different. I didn't peg him for the inked type, not with that charming smile and tender eyes. But this… this makes my stomach flip. It crackles across his skin like it has a pulse of its own, and I can't stop staring.

His strong hand reaches for mine without hesitation.

He pulls me onto the dance floor as the crowd pulses around us. Lights strobe and flare, purple, pink, and electric blue bleeding into a kaleidoscope of want. The atmosphere wraps around us like a fever dream, hot, dizzying, and heavy with lust.

The bass vibrates through my heels and settles low in my belly. Around us, bodies grind and sway like they are all chasing the same high. Neon shadows dance across his face as he pulls me closer, his body pressed flush against mine.

His heat rolls off him, his scent thick with cinnamon and spice, warm and intoxicating. The rest of the world disappears.

It's only us. Only this moment. The haze that surrounds us. And it feels like I am finally breaking free of the cocoon that has held me. The doubt. The heartbreak. The ache. This butterfly top is more than an outfit. Now I understand why Aster had it made for me. Tonight, I am done hiding. I am spreading my wings. I am ready to fly.

Leon's hands grip my waist, and I look up at him through my lashes. Without breaking eye contact, I guide his hands lower, sliding them over the curve of my ass. A bold move, but the smirk that curls across his lips tells me everything. He's into it. More than into it… I feel the hard outline of his erection press against my stomach, heavy and impossible to ignore.

Wow. He's not average… that's for sure.

I shift against him, and the heat between us spikes. He leans down and kisses me, soft at first, like he's asking if I'm sure. I answer by grinding just enough to pull a groan from his throat. His length throbs against me. My mouth goes dry. I try to swallow, but I can't. I'm so turned on, I feel weightless. Like I might float right out of my body. His hands trail from my ass to the hem of my skirt. His fingers skim my bare thigh, light as air but searing hot against my skin. Then he looks at me. Not with a question. With a promise. The kind that says he will ruin me sweetly, slowly, and make every hidden dream I've ever dared to have come true. I answer with a look so needy, so feral, he doesn't even have to ask.

His hand slides under my skirt, slipping beneath the edge of my panties. His fingers brush my entrance, hot and slick, aching for more. I grind my clit against the hard ridge of him, desperate for friction, for relief, for anything. Then one thick finger pushes inside. Slow. Gentle. Deliberate. My legs weaken, and I clutch his shoulders for balance, gasping as he curls it just right. Pleasure coils low in my belly. I bite my lip, barely holding back the moan rising like a tidal wave.

"I want you," I whisper. "Now."

His grin goes wicked. "That's all you had to say, Lila." He grabs my hand and starts guiding me off the dance floor, already pulling me toward the elevator. But then I hear it.

That hum. Low. Sultry. Hypnotic. The Red Mask?

My head snaps around, heart skipping. I scan the room, eyes darting through every shadow, but nothing.

Maybe I'm hearing things… or did we just pass each other? Was it just a memory? Or did someone else hum that same forbidden tune?

Leon keeps walking, unaware. Oblivious. He doesn't hear it.

Lila, stop. You're being crazy.

"WAIT!" Aster's voice slices through the music, sharp and relentless.

Aster, I'm going to kill you.

I freeze. Of course, she's about to cockblock me. Again. She's running now, full sprint in heels, chaos in motion.

"Come play with us! We're starting a round of truth or dare! We just ordered a round of shots!"

Neither of us responds. Leon looks down at me. I look up at him. And then Aster grabs my hand, ripping me right out of the moment.

Damn it. Not again. Leon fades, his warmth vanishing from my skin.

I was so close…

I glance back at Leon with a silent, "help me".

He gives me a soft smile, but it doesn't reach his eyes. We both know it. Whatever moment we had, it's gone, and it might not come again.

The disappointment fades the moment I see Kage. Sure, I wanted to go upstairs, but getting to watch him feels like a win in my book.

God, this man belongs in the Louvre.

He sits there like a masterpiece sculpted by Da Vinci himself, all brooding beauty and effortless arrogance. A brunette leans against one shoulder, a redhead curls into the other. A living, breathing pain in my ass. And yet I still can't look away. He pulls me in.

Every. Single. Time.

CHAPTER THIRTY-FOUR
LILA

"Kage, stop," the brunette giggles as he nibbles along her neck like she's his last meal. So much for my little victory. I thought this was a win until I ended up watching the three stooges in front of me… Him. The brunette. The redhead.

This is torture.

My stomach twists. My hands ache to touch him. And there he is, all over her like none of us are here… like I'm not right here, watching. Maybe I deserve it. I did the same thing with Leon.

I slide onto the couch beside Leon. His hand lands on my thigh, but I barely register it. Everything blurs at the edges. The music. The people. The noise. Because he's all I can see, it's like watching a car crash in slow motion as Kage licks the redhead like she is his favorite flavor. Kissing. Grabbing. Smirking and staring at me the entire time… Just like he did with Natasha.

He's taunting me, testing me. That bastard really loves to play games. The last time I let myself play along, he threw my phone out the window. I cried. I broke. And he saw it. But not this time. This time, I won't break. He thinks I'm weak. He thinks I'll bend the second he looks at me. He's wrong. I'm not the girl he can toy with anymore.

"Are you guys ready to play?" Aster calls out, flopping onto the lap of some eye candy she will probably break later.

"Yes," I say coolly, locking eyes with him as I toss back a shot. The burn slides down my throat, sharp and biting. Still not nearly drunk enough for this.

Beck sinks into the couch beside one of the girls Kage brought, but his eyes aren't on her. He keeps glancing at Kage, waiting for something. A nod. A look. But Kage gives him nothing. He is too busy watching me. His mouth is on another girl, but his eyes are glued to mine.

I furrow my brows, leaning into Clint, who is sitting beside me. "What the hell is going on? What is Beck waiting for?"

Clint leans into my ear, voice low and smooth. "I've heard… they share girls." My eyes snap wide.

Well. That was unexpected. But if I'm being honest? It's kind of hot.

The image flashes through my mind like a fever dream I have no business entertaining. Kage and Beck. Both of them are doing unspeakable things to me. I picture Kage pressing me into the mattress, wrists pinned above my head, his mouth trailing fire along my neck as he growls every filthy promise he intends to keep. And between my thighs?

Beck is on his knees, tongue precise and unrelenting, every stroke slow and sweet, like he has all the time in the world to unravel me. Kage leans in, whispering filth into my ear while Beck drags cries from my throat. Their hands. Their mouths. Everywhere. At once. One teasing. One commanding. Both are in complete control.

My thighs clench. A whimper nearly escapes. Heat coils low and tight in my belly, threatening to snap.

"Lila," someone calls. I blink, breathless, like I've just surfaced from underwater. "It's your turn to ask," Aster says, cocking a brow.

Right. Game on.

I tap my lip, pretending to think. "Hmm… Aster. Truth or dare?"

She tosses back a shot like it's nothing. "Dare. I'm not a little bitch."

Perfect.

I glance at Beck, then back to Aster. The air shifts. They both feel it. Something's coming. And neither of them has any idea what I'm about to do.

I smile sweetly. "Well, since you're so brave… I dare you to kiss Beck."

Beck stiffens. His brows shoot up. "Why are you picking on me?"

"What can I say? I like to keep things interesting," I say with a sweet smile that doesn't quite reach my eyes.

Aster rises from the guy's lap and struts across the room like the challenge was always hers to win.

Beck stands too, towering over her in front of the leather couch, and instantly, the tension between them is palpable, like fire and gasoline, and I'm about to watch it explode.

She reaches out, her fingers brushing his arm, and Beck's body reacts before he can even make sense of the feeling. Aster rises onto her tiptoes, and Beck leans in, meeting her halfway. The kiss starts off hard, playful, teasing. But then… it changes.

She softens. My badass best friend melts into him. Her hands slide behind his neck as his mouth parts against hers. This isn't just a dare anymore. It's not even close. He wants her. No…he feels something deeper. Her legs lift without thinking, wrapping around his waist, and he catches her like it's the most natural thing in the world.

I can't help but sigh in awe. I'm such a hopeless romantic, and this feels like a scene pulled straight from a chick flick. I catch myself smiling like an idiot because that's my best friend, and she found him. For the first time, I see Aster truly swoon, and it takes my breath away.

Clint lets out a low whistle. "Okay, okay. Get a room, you two."

They pull apart slowly, like gravity is still trying to hold them together. Aster grins, eyes locked on Beck's ocean-blue stare. Then I hear her whisper, "The plague doctor from the maze?"

Beck blinks. "Catwoman… from the maze?"

She nods, resting her forehead against his. "I've been thinking about you since that night."

His voice drops. "Me too."

Kage's voice slices through the moment. "Alright, lovebirds. Can we please get back to the game?"

Aster hops down, grabs Beck's hand, and pulls him toward the nearest leather chair. Her eye candy takes the hint and slips away without a word. She has her man now. Beck sinks into the chair, and she slides onto his lap, grinning like she just hit the jackpot.

Across the table, she mouths to me, "You knew it was him this whole time?" I nod, biting my lip, trying not to smile. "You sneaky matchmaker… thank you."

I blow her a kiss and make a cheesy heart with my hands. "Alright, Aster," I say, playful. "Since you went last time, it's your turn." She scans the circle, eyes glinting, playful and dangerous, before they settle on me.

Oh, shit. I did her a favor. That means she'll go easy on me… right? Right?

Her smile doesn't falter. But her eyes? Devious. "Lila," she purrs, "truth or dare?"

I toss back a shot like it's water and cross my arms. "Dare."

Aster leans forward, her chin resting on her hand, eyes glinting with mischief. "I dare you to seduce Kage."

My heart slams against my ribs.

Seriously, Aster? You cockblock me and then throw me into the lion's den. You must hate me.

But this is what I have wanted all along. While he was with other women, I was dreaming of touching him, teasing him, watching him come undone for me. And now it is real. I have the chance. His eyes burn into mine. He does not move. He does not speak. But I feel it. He is waiting for my response to the dare, waiting for me to back down, watching to see if I have the nerve to go through with it. Daring me to try.

My watch vibrates against my wrist.

Shit. My heart rate is spiking.

He glances down at the flicker on the screen like he already knows.

I can do this.

I will do this.

Slowly, I rise to my feet as Leon's hand slips off my thigh, and I never break eye contact with Kage. Then he speaks. His voice is smooth, cruel, laced with challenge. "Aww, Aster. That's cute. You really think she can seduce me?" He grins wickedly, arms still draped around the two women like he's already made his choice.

Show him what you're made of, Lila. He may have won the other day. But not tonight. Tonight, I win.

I take my time walking over, every step confident and unhurried, until I'm standing behind the leather couch where Kage lounges like a king among his playthings. "Revolving Door," by Tate McRae, throbs through the speakers. Every lyric hits like it was written just for me, syncing with emotions I've spent weeks trying to forget.

He's my bad habit. The one I swear I'll stop craving. But I never do. He's my own personal revolving door. No matter how far I run, I always end up right back here. Right back to him.

The beat pulses through me like a second heartbeat. The melody coils around the room, smoky and seductive, thick with tension. Like the song already knows what I'm about to do… even though I know I shouldn't. I lean in, slow and steady, letting my breath skim just beneath his ear. His arms are still draped around the women on either side of him, but I make sure he feels me.

Well. This won't do.

He smells like desire. Expensive cologne. A trace of cigarette smoke. And something darker. Something that is undeniably him. It takes everything in me not to thread my fingers into his hair and yank his head back to put my lips against him. I can't see his face, but I know his body. I know when he's bluffing.

He's too still. Too composed. Trying too hard to look untouchable. The song hums around us, and I wonder if he feels it too. This heat. This ache. This pull I can't shake. I go in for the kill.

My lips ghost along his neck, soft and fleeting, but it lands like a match to dry wood. Just enough to tease. Just enough to tempt. I do it again, slower this time, pressing a kiss that lingers against his neck. Skin to skin. A connection that feels as doomed as Gatsby and Daisy.

His body shivers underneath my lips. I let out a shaky breath. His body is reacting, but he's still holding back. Then I drag my lips against his skin, and I take it up to his ear. And just like that, it's electric. A live wire between us.

Every nerve in my body sparks to life. My skin buzzes. It's hot and dangerous and somehow achingly tender, like the space between us has always been waiting to ignite.

I don't press harder. I don't rush. I let the silence thicken.

This is everything I thought it would be… and so much more.

I reach down, slow and intentional, and gently remove his arm from the brunette beside him. She pouts, but I don't care. I take his hand in mine, letting our fingers brush as I guide it toward me. He doesn't stop me. His body is relaxed, but I can feel the tension coiled beneath his skin, waiting. With a gentle tug, I coax him to stand.

He rises slowly, watching me like he is trying to decipher my angle as I circle toward him. I step in front of him, finally taking in all of him. Every inch. The dim light kisses his skin, glowing golden and unreal. Dark brown hair, tousled and unruly, with strands falling carelessly across his brows. Full lips, slightly parted, marked by that single freckle above the right side. And when he smirks, that dimple appears… and every piece of me gives in.

His eyes. God, his eyes. Green and kaleidoscopic, sharp enough to cut through me and soft enough to ruin me. The dark navy button-down clings to every line of his chest, sleeves rolled just enough to reveal strong, veined forearms, masculine and defined. Those hands could tear me apart or put me back together. And I want both. His eyes meet mine, practically glowing. My breath catches.

I take both of his hands and thread our fingers together, then start at my chest and slowly guide his hands down to my hips. I let them settle there. His thumbs flex slightly. He still doesn't stop me, and that alone makes my pulse spike.

Is he liking this as much as I am?

I move in closer until our bodies are flush, chest to chest, heartbeats pounding against each other like a silent war. He towers over me, his presence dizzying. He stays rooted in place.

I rise up slowly, bringing my face just inches from his, like I'm going to kiss him. And that's when I see it. His lips part ever so slightly, like he's trying to catch a breath he didn't realize he was holding.

A slow smile curves on my lips. I have him. And honestly, I like seeing him like this… still, breathless, completely at my mercy. But instead of giving in and kissing him like I've imagined a thousand times, I decide to play.

I bite my lip, glance up through my lashes, and press my mouth to the side of his neck. Slow. Teasing. Letting my lips linger a moment too long. He stays perfectly still. So, I take it further. I flick my tongue across the warm spot just beneath his jaw. His breath hitches. I lean in closer, lips brushing the shell of his ear.

"Your move," I whisper. And then… the sound. A low groan from the back of his throat. Barely audible. But I heard it. And God, it makes me so wet for him. I smile, drunk on the power, and whisper against his ear, "Try not to moan. You've got an audience."

Before I can step back, Clint blurts from across the room, "damn, Lila, can you come do that to me?"

Kage doesn't even flinch. His voice is lethal. "Clint, shut the fuck up."

Did he just get jealous? Or is Clint just that annoying?

He stares straight ahead, like the stillness before a storm. A lazy smirk curls at his mouth like he's already won. "That's it? Hate to break it to you, princess, but I don't even have a boner."

I drift closer, my mouth hovering by his ear. "Well, since you weren't turned on at all, you wouldn't mind if I checked… to see if you're hard?" I close the distance, and his throbbing cock presses against my stomach. His jaw ticks, and he clears his throat because he knows I know.

Damn, Lila… That was bold. Dominant. Maybe this butterfly top really is armor.

I freeze. "Would you like me to keep going, since you're not turned on?" A low chuckle slips out of him, soft and entertained, but I see right through it. Our eyes lock.

He tilts his head, a faint smirk curving his lips. "Let's see what you've got, princess."

I take a breath before the adrenaline knocks me out cold. "Don't resist it... Kage."

"Don't listen to him, Lila. I'm turned on just watching you two, so I know he's hard," Aster yells over the pounding music in the background.

My body is an asteroid, burning and spiraling, seconds from collision. And he's the gravity pulling me in. The impact isn't coming. It's already here. I lean in again, close enough for my breath to drift over his lips. Whiskey and cigarettes. I hate both, yet on him, they are exactly what I crave.

Don't move too fast. He'll know you're down bad for him.

I lean in slowly, pressing my lips to his, testing the waters. He doesn't move, doesn't kiss me back. But he stills. My heart spikes, and instinct takes over before I can stop it. I lean closer, my voice dripping with seduction. "What did I say about resisting, Baby?"

Oh God. Why did I say that? I've only ever called the Red Mask that.

But that word... when I said it, I saw something light up in his eyes.

He liked it.

And I feel it in his touch, in the way his hands on my hips twitch like he wants to squeeze me tighter. Closer. I raise my hands and trail them up the back of his neck, finding that soft spot at his hairline. And I grab it. Hard.

I pull him down and kiss him again. This time it's not sweet. Not careful. It's feral. And he responds instantly. Teeth.

Tongue. Heat. His body tightens, his hands clamping hard on my hips through the thin fabric of my skirt. It isn't skin to skin, but it might as well be, because his grip will leave bruises. I fist his hair tighter.

"I knew you liked it rough, Baby," I whisper, catching my breath as I kiss his neck. Soft at first, then deeper. Sucking. Tasting. My lips find that spot beneath his jaw, and I hear it. The hitch in his breath. The faint groan escapes him. His eyes flick open and lock on mine, no longer unreadable.

"Princess, you have no idea what I'm capable of. I'll rip every moan from your throat and fuck you until you can't stand."

Oh.

I gasp, the sound raw and involuntary, as my wetness drips down my thigh from those words alone. His grin is full and wild, his teeth flashing, a dimple carved deep, his eyes lit with something unrestrained. My stomach bursts with butterflies. My breath comes fast and ragged, and I don't care that the whole room is watching. Not Leon. Not Aster. No one. This is what I have wanted since the day I met my sworn enemy. The man I loathe. And the man I yearn for.

My hands slide up, tangling into his hair. And I pause.

There. Under my fingers…

A scar. Raised. Jagged. Deep.

My brows furrow, and his do too when he feels my touch. There's a flicker in his eyes, something raw, as if I've brushed against more than skin.

I barely get to process it before Aster's voice cuts through the moment. "What did you say earlier, Clint? Oh yeah, get a room, you two. And Lila definitely won that dare."

Laughter erupts around us. I touch the spot again, and Kage pulls away. Suddenly. Too suddenly. Cold. Distant.

The warmth between us vanishes in an instant. His energy shifts, a door slamming shut inside him. He scoffs, eyes locking on mine. "Oh, Baby," he says, dripping with mockery and venom. "You actually thought that was real?"

My stomach sinks.

No, no, no.

Kage's smile drips with cruelty. "Oh, Princess. That's so… innocent of you. You really think it takes that little to turn me on?" My heart cracks.

Was I the only one in that moment?

"I mean," he continues, voice smooth and harsh, "you've probably only been with one person and it shows."

The table goes silent. And I feel it, the flush of heat crawling up my neck. Because he's right. And now everyone assumes or knows.

Aster jumps up. "Hey. No reason to be a dick. Let's go, Lila."

But I don't move. I don't blink. I keep my eyes on him. "Truth or dare?" I snap.

Kage pauses, brows lifting. "What?"

"I didn't stutter," I say, louder. "Truth. Or. Dare."

He studies me. The smirk is gone. "Truth."

We're face-to-face now. Breath to breath. I lean in. "How many people have you fucked?"

A low, dangerous laugh rumbles from his chest. His eyes darken to a deep green, nearly black. And for the first time, he looks angry. And maybe even a little impressed. "Oh, you really want to know?"

The table goes still. Tension thick enough to carve a name into. I wait. And then, with a slow, razor-edged smile that shows every perfect white tooth, he delivers it: "Five. Hundred. Twenty-one."

The sound fades. The room stretches and warps, no longer tethered to reality. My lungs forget how to work. My head spins like I'm seconds from blacking out. My pulse vanishes. My world tilts.

Five hundred twenty-one.

His eyes flick away from mine as he nods toward the two women still lounging in the booth. "And after tonight…" A cruel smile touches his lips. "It'll be five hundred twenty-three."

I don't speak. I don't move. I just break. The smirk on his lips only grows. I open my mouth, but not a single word comes.

The kiss. The heat. The spark I thought we shared… A joke. A fucking joke. And I was the punchline. My chest tightens. My body starts to shake, not from rage.

From panic.

The cold creeps up my spine. My vision narrows. *Breathe. Push it down. Hide it.* But I can't. This isn't nerves. This is real. My watch buzzes again… harsh and steady. Heart rate spike. Panic alert. I swipe at it, desperate, like I can silence the evidence that I'm spiraling. Because I am. I blink hard, trying to swallow it down, but it doesn't stop the ache clawing through my chest.

I was nothing but entertainment to him. A dare. A toy. A target. And now, in front of everyone, he's shattered me with one number.

I will never be enough for him. Not sexy enough. Not experienced enough. Not rich enough.

I blink fast. *Don't let them see. Don't let him see.*

But then our eyes meet. And that's when I realized he wanted this. He wanted to watch me fall apart. And he knew I would. Right here. In front of him. I look up at him through burning eyes. His smile hasn't moved. He's proud of what just happened. And that's when the words tear from me, raw and wrecked.

"You're a monster." A single tear slides down my cheek. He doesn't flinch. Doesn't blink. Just meets my eyes and whispers, "I know."

CHAPTER THIRTY-FIVE
LILA

"Hey, babe. Let's head up to our room. You're mine tonight," Leon says, slowly wrapping his fingers around my wrist, right where my watch is still buzzing.

"What?" The world rushes back in.

Kage is still standing there, beautiful and brutal, looking straight through me like I'm nothing. I tilt my head up to meet Leon's gaze, trying to understand what he's doing.

"Oh, right," I say quickly, pasting on a big fake smile. "I forgot that's where we were headed before we came to play."

Aster clocks the lie instantly but doesn't call me on it. She just smiles like she's in on the game. "Oh yeah, you told me you were staying the night when we were on the dance floor," she says, being the best friend she can be.

Leon pulls a gold key from his pocket and dangles it between us. "I even got the ultra-thin condoms," he says, shooting Kage a pointed look.

I press a hand to his chest. "Oh, we don't have to use those. I have an IUD."

That line wasn't for Leon. It was for the man behind me. I feel Kage exhale. The sound is sharp, heavy, and strained.

Good. He shattered my heart without flinching. Now he can choke on the pieces.

"Should I come pick you up in the morning?" Aster asks with a soft smile.

Leon cuts in smoothly, his arm slipping around my waist. "I've got her. I'll make sure she gets home safe."

I don't dare look at Kage. I keep my eyes locked on Leon, holding onto him like he's my anchor, the only thing keeping me from drowning in the hurricane Kage left behind. I slide my arm around him in return, leaning into his warmth.

"Well… goodnight, everybody," I purr, tossing the words over my shoulder. "Don't wait up for us. Oh, Aster, do you have my overnight bag and the lingerie I gave you?" I'm pulling this out of thin air, twisting the knife deeper, directly at the asshole who started this.

I hope it hurts. But knowing him? It probably doesn't. I bet if you cut him open, he doesn't bleed.

"I gave it to Leon's assistant," she says smoothly. "He took it upstairs."

"Thanks, pookie." I blow her a kiss, still in full performance mode in front of the truth-or-dare crowd.

Please don't see right through me.

Leon leans down and kisses me, sealing the moment. I close my eyes and let it happen, willing to play along just enough to make the lie believable and get out of here. When I pull away, I add, "Beck. Clint." A beat. "Kage… I guess I'll see you all bright and early Monday."

His name still sounds too pretty for someone so heartless. Kage looks up at me. His eyes are dark, unreadable, but there's something behind them. Something that almost looks like pain.

Hurt? Regret? Shame? I doubt it.

Still linked with Leon, we turn and walk away, step by step, arm in arm. And this time, I don't look back, because for once, he's the one left standing there. Not me.

My heart slows, and I feel my watch stop vibrating. It feels like a brick has been lifted from my chest, and I can finally breathe.

Leon hits the elevator button, still holding on to me. He doesn't say a word. The silence lingers as I try to process what just happened. We step in, and the doors shut. He lowers his arm from my waist in silence.

I look at him, and his eyes look sad. "Thank you for doing that, but…. Why?"

He still looks down at the ground. "Why what?"

"Why did you do that for me?" I say in a whisper.

"Because I had them when I lived in London."

"Had what?" I ask, trying to understand.

"Panic attacks." My breath hitches.

"How did you know?"

He looks up at me with sincerity in his eyes. "Because I see you for you." He takes my hand, grabbing it in a firm yet soft way. An unexpected tear slips down my cheek, and he gently wipes it away.

Leon is kind. He's grounded. He understands my panic attacks and still wants me, even after witnessing everything that just happened between me and Kage. But honestly, he deserves someone better than me. Someone whose heart isn't torn in two. Because no matter how hard I try, my feelings aren't all in for him. And he deserves more than the fractured pieces I have left to give. The elevator dings and opens onto the fourth floor, and he steps out, leading the way.

Wow. This place feels endless, like something out of the Titanic.

Everything is white and cream: the walls, the trim, even the ceiling. Every surface gleams with gold accents, framing the space like jewelry, impossibly elegant. Large mirrors hang between every door, catching the chandelier light and stretching the hallway until it feels endless.

Then, in the center of it all, I see a statue.

A woman stands nude, draped in a flowing sheet. Her body is both curved and strong, yet soft all at once. Across from her, a man kneels, just as bare, just as breathtaking. He looks up at her like she's the only thing that has ever mattered. The only thing that has ever existed. But she isn't looking at him. She doesn't see it. He is in love with her, and she doesn't even know. It's carved into his face. Real. Raw. Undeniable. It's breathtaking. And honestly? It's nothing less than what I thought it would look like.

God, what it would be like for someone to look at me that way. To be someone's whole being. To bewitch them in a way they can't understand. Ugh. I'm such a hopeless romantic. But whoever created this? They were, too.

The thick, rich carpet muffles our footsteps. It's patterned with pale gold that shimmers as we move. Above us, crystal chandeliers drip from the ceiling, casting a warm golden glow that dances across the walls.

Am I Julia Roberts in Pretty Woman?

I giggle out loud. I can't believe this is real. I gently tug Leon's hand, bringing us to a stop. "Leon, we played it off. You really don't have to give me a room. I can sneak out the back door…"

He cuts me off. "I had this room key for you before you even got here."

His beautiful milk-chocolate eyes soften, and my heart skips a beat. "You did?"

"Yes. I was hoping you'd want to stay with me tonight…" His eyes drop to the floor. "But now I know the truth."

"What do you mean?"

He glances toward the statue in the center of the hallway. "The way that man looks at the woman… It's how you look at Kage."

Me?

"No, no. You've got it all wrong. We hate each other. I could never—" I can't finish the sentence. Saying it out loud would be a lie.

For a moment, we're both quiet. Then Leon reaches for me, his fingers gently lifting my chin, coaxing me to meet his eyes.

"I may not be him," he says, voice low, British accent sounding sinfully smooth, "but you can pretend I am because you're the one I want. The one I think about. So maybe… maybe we can help each other forget the people who don't want us back."

"I… I don't want to hurt you," I whisper.

He smiles, soft and sure. "If I get even one second with you, even if your mind's somewhere else… I'll take it. I'll be grateful for every moment."

He steps closer. His hand rises, slow and intentional as his fingers brush against my cheek. The warmth of his touch sinks into my skin, melting through the cold I didn't even realize I was carrying. It's grounding. Tender. Almost like a promise.

This doesn't feel like a casual hookup. It feels like more. Or maybe we're both just reaching for warmth in this cruel world because I am broken. Heart-split. Humiliated. Emotionally gutted. And honestly? I want to feel something that doesn't destroy me.

To be touched. Wanted. Seen. And maybe Leon wants the same. Because at the end of the day, we're all just human. Craving connection. Meaning. A reason to keep going.

Besides, what's a body count of two compared to Kage's five hundred twenty-one? He's probably halfway through a threesome right now, forgetting I ever existed. So, screw it. Tonight, I choose escape.

I close the distance. I kiss Leon. Not for love. Not for revenge. Just the ache. The need. Two lost souls, colliding in time, just trying to feel something real.

CHAPTER THIRTY-SIX
LILA

Our lips never part as we stumble into the hallway, fumbling for the gold doorknob. We crash into the suite, but I don't bother taking in the view. I'm too focused on the way his mouth feels against mine. It's warm, eager, human. The most real contact I've had in a long time.

The red mask pleased me in the pleasure room, but I never got to touch him, not like this. This is what I needed.

I grip his button-down, ready for more. Leon pauses, just enough to catch his breath, fingers still tangled in my hair. "Do you know what you like?" he asks, voice low and rough.

"Um… what do you mean?"

"Kinks. Preferences." His gaze searches mine, waiting. "What turns you on?"

I hesitate. "I … I don't know. I've only ever been with one person, one time."

His smile is slow and wicked. "Oh, babe. Then let me help you find out." He steps closer, brushing my cheek with his knuckles. "There's a window in each room, a hallway where anyone could watch. Say the word and I'll close the curtain. Say nothing, and I'll leave it open. Tonight is whatever you want it to be."

I bite my lip, heart racing. "This whole night is about the experience, right? So… keep the curtain open."

His grin grows. "What about bondage?"

I laugh softly. "How about… next time?"

"Oh, so there's going to be a next time?" His British accent sends shivers down my spine. I lean in, arms around his neck, my lips brushing his.

"Only if you can please me, Mr. Amour." And then I can't wait any longer. I crush my mouth to his and let my human needs take control, and so does he. I'm nervous but grounded because it's Leon who sees me for me. I look to see if anyone is in our window, but nothing.

Good because I don't know if I'm ready for someone to see all of me.

The lights are low. And Leon's hands graze my stomach. "Turn around."

He's commanding. I didn't expect that, but I like it.

I do as he says and turn around. Pearl by pearl, crystal by crystal, my butterfly armor slips to the floor.

I've never thought much of my breasts. But under his gaze, they feel beautiful.

"Lila, you're … you're a goddess." His eyes glide up and down my body like he's taking in every freckle and flaw of me. My heart drops, and all I can do is smile.

No one has ever said or looked at me that way. The red mask said something similar, but I couldn't see him or touch him.

But this look he is giving me… it looks sincere. Honest. Pure.

Maybe I should be with him… He is rich, beautiful, and cares about my needs, unlike Kage. But then why do I still want him? The one who doesn't want me? Is this how Leon feels?

I don't cover my chest. I stand waiting for his next human move.

God, I really don't want to hurt him like Kage has hurt me.

A soft hum spills from the speaker. "Down Bad," By Taylor Swift's voice melts into the room as Leon slowly slips my skirt down as it hits the floor. "Shit, Lila." He looks down at me, voice thick.

I know my green eyes are dark, full of intent, because I like how I'm feeling right now. Without breaking eye contact, I reach up and pull the pins from my updo, letting my long blonde hair tumble down in waves. It slips over my bare shoulders, skimming the tops of my breasts. Soft and slow, just enough to make him stare. His breath hitches, and I smile, because I know exactly what I'm doing.

"Your turn," I say with a slow smile. I start at the top of his shirt, unbuttoning it one by one. I don't look up, but I can feel his eyes on me, heavy and unblinking. When I finally slide the fabric off his shoulders, my breath catches. Every muscle is carved like a statue, smooth and defined, exactly how I imagined. But what I wasn't expecting was the tattoo. The lightning bolt I noticed earlier wasn't just on his arm, it stretches across his chest, over his shoulder and down his back in jagged, breathtaking branches. I reach out and graze it with my fingertips, mesmerized.

"Do you have any more?" I ask softly, tracing the lines from his bicep to his spine.

"Nope. Just the one."

"What does it mean?" I keep touching it, taking in every twist and turn of lightning scattered across his skin.

"I got it because people always asked me what a panic attack feels like," he says quietly, voice steady but low. "This was the only way I could explain it. It starts with a single bolt, right in the center of my chest. A jolt that snaps through my nerves like static, lighting me up from the inside." His gaze drifts, like he's reliving it. "Then it spreads. Fast. Like lightning crawling beneath my skin, branching out until every part of me is buzzing. My body stops listening. My hands go numb. My breath shortens. My heart pounds out of control. My chest tightens like I'm going to have a heart attack. And then the fear comes. Not of dying, but of surviving it and having to go through it again."

He pauses, his throat working through the memory. "You're trapped. Inside your own body, watching it betray you. And no one can pull you out of it. So, you wait, praying it passes. A feeling I wouldn't wish on anyone…"

I place my hand on his bare chest and repeat what he said to me earlier because I know how it feels to go through it. "Leon, I see you for you."

He tilts my chin up, his lips crashing into mine. Hard. Desperate. Full of something unspoken. But all I can think about is the kiss I just shared with Kage downstairs. That kiss was everything I've ever wanted. So familiar. So dangerously close to the red mask. It was wild. Addictive. His lips were full and poisonous, laced with something I'll never be able to forget. They sent a shiver straight to my core.

Leon is the one touching me now. But my thoughts are still with him.

The lyrics swirl through the room, striking me with an ache I wasn't ready for. I'm down bad for Kage. But what if I can't ever have him? Not just for a night, but for the rest of my life. What if he lingers in the back of my mind forever, haunting me like the Red Mask and the Phantom, never mine, impossible to forget.

I'm obsessed with someone who will never see me the way I see him. And yet here I am with someone who sees me even when I'm looking away, just like the statue.

Leon brushes his fingers down my arms, staring into my soul like he knows I'm thinking about someone else. I let him go lower and lower, every fingertip brush leaving behind a need. I feel wetness between my legs. I pant, thinking about the one who doesn't want me. "I'm ready, Leon."

"Oh, are you? I want to take in every little moment with you, Lila… don't rush it."

"But…"

He cuts me off. "Sit on the edge of the bed."

"Okay, Mr. Amour," I smirk and take a seat on the luxurious duvet.

He bends down and kisses the inner part of my thigh, slow and agonizing. He kisses up to my freshly waxed mound.

I'll thank Aster later.

He looks up at my nervous face. Last time I was blindfolded, but this time I get to watch it all. He puts his mouth right on my clit, warm and hungry.

"Mmm, I might keep you around just for this." I giggle, my head falling back as a moan slips out of me, pleasure winding through every nerve. But even with my eyes shut, it's not Leon I see.

It's Kage.

His wild green eyes, that reckless hair, the kind of jawline that begs to be kissed and bitten all the way down to his sculpted chest.

Leon licks and sucks with slow precision, dragging bliss through my core, but I'm haunted by the one man who isn't here. "Mhmmm… yes," I breathe, the sound slipping out before I can stop it.

"Babe," he murmurs, glancing up, his voice rough and teasing, "if you keep making those sounds, I won't last long enough to take care of your needs." This man is entirely selfless, and yet all I hear is Kage's voice.

I look up at the window to see if we have any guests, and I freeze. *Am I hallucinating? Are my thoughts coming to life?*

Kage stands at the window, and he is completely unreadable.

Should I stop? Should I let Leon keep going?

The song bleeds into the silence, and I can't help but think it.

He could have had me tonight, but didn't want that, so fuck it. Then let me show him exactly what he's missing. He made his choice. Now I'm making mine.

I grip the back of Leon's hair and moan, but my eyes never leave Kage, just as he has tortured me before.

"Lay on the bed," I breathe, voice thin and charged.

"What?" Leon blinks, still kneeling.

I tilt his chin up, meeting his eyes. "I said… get on the bed. Now."

A feral spark flickers across his face as he strips off his suit pants, like a man who knows exactly what he's doing, until they're pooled at his ankles. His erection springs free, and I can't help but stare. My lips part instinctively because it's only the second dick I've ever seen, and this one looks absolutely delicious. Freshly shaved. Ready for me.

He leans back against the grand headboard, arms tucked behind his head, relaxed but watching me closely. There's heat in his eyes, but also something soft. He may be turned on, but he's still gentle. Still giving me control. I crawl toward him, dragging it out to make him sweat, every motion purposeful. Every movement is a performance. For Leon… and for the one I know is watching.

My skin glistens beneath the low golden light, shimmering like a marquise diamond waiting to be claimed. I hesitate. I've only had sex once. One guy. One forgettable night. I was on the bottom, and he finished in seconds. I glance down at Leon's thick, veined length glistening with a bead of precum.

I didn't think this through. I don't know how to do this. But I can't freeze now. I have to act like I know what I'm doing. They are both watching me.

I am the entertainment.

Kage has been with 521 women. If I did this to him, he'd probably laugh in my face, and I'd go down in history as the worst blowjob he's ever had. But Leon… he is different. He wouldn't do that.

I bend forward, letting my tongue glide along him from base to tip, tasting every drop. I arch my back, giving him a full view of my curves.

"Babe… that's it," Leon moans.

I glance toward the window. Kage's hand is pressed against the glass. Steady. Strained.

Good.

Then I see it. Another scar. Deep and jagged, slashing across his right hand.

Where did he get that? No. I don't care. Don't think.

I take him in my mouth, not entirely sure what I'm doing, but I get it wet enough to make it easy. Easy enough to slide right on top of him. Then I straddle his hips, guiding his length to my entrance. He hesitates, eyes searching mine.

"Are you sure?" he asks softly. "Since you've only—" I cut him off by sinking down, inch by inch.

Shit. That feels good.

"Damnit, Lila. You're so fucking tight." He grabs my face as he sits up, pulling me into a kiss. But he doesn't kiss me like this is a one-time thing. He kisses like he means it. He kisses me like I'm his world. Like I'm not pretending. Like, he's not second best. And maybe… just for tonight… that's enough.

I lock eyes with him through the window as I start rocking his hips, slow, steady, grinding until friction sparks against my clit. He's still watching. Sweating. Unmoving. Ruined. Just the way I want him.

My mouth parts as I move faster, harder. My hand slips to my breast, fingers twisting and pulling at my nipple, chasing the rush building deep in my core. "Oh, Leon… I think I'm about to—"

I ride harder, chasing the edge, eyes shut tight, a wave of heat rippling through me. Leon grips my waist and flips me onto my back, thrusting into me with steady, hungry power. I clutch the sheets, moaning as my orgasm tears through me, raw and overwhelming. And just as I fall apart…

"Oh God… Kage."

His name escapes my lips like a confession. One I can't take back. My body trembles beneath Leon as he releases inside me, groaning into my neck. His body collapses against mine, chest heaving, cock twitching inside me with the last pulses of pleasure. We stay tangled in silence, skin on skin.

So that's what real sex feels like… No wonder Aster keeps going back for more.

I turn my head, eyes drifting to the window. Empty. My breath catches. He's gone. Like a phantom slipping back into the shadows. As if he were never there at all.

CHAPTER THIRTY-SEVEN
LILA

"Sooo… how was last night? What happened after you guys went up?" Aster breaks the silence. I side-eye her as the elevator hums upward. "Bitch. Spill."

I sigh. "Well, Leon and I… did it."

She gasps, cutting me off. "Yes! Finally! Took you long enough to get laid. How do you feel? Are you sore?"

The elevator dings. "Like shit, Aster... I did something awful." The doors slide open, and a middle-aged couple stands there, waiting.

"Oh no! Did you queef?" The couple exchanges a horrified glance as they step inside, whispering to each other like we're contagious.

"Can you not say things in public that I don't even know the meaning of?" I whisper, trying not to laugh. "But if you must know… I said Kage's name when I finished."

Her eyes go wide. "Damn, Lila! That's like really bad."

"I know."

"Are you going to apologize or act like it never happened?"

I shrug. "I honestly don't know. We were doing it to do it… so did I actually do something wrong?"

"Not necessarily. But was he doing it to do it?"

I go quiet as we walk down the hospital hallway. "Well, if I remember correctly, he said something like… I may not be him, but you can pretend I am because you're the one I want. The one I think about."

Aster stops dead. "You did not! Leon never messes around with women unless he is serious! Do you not know what his last name means? It literally means lover."

I don't answer. Because I've zoned out. My mouth goes dry, and my heart starts pounding. Because we have arrived. Right there in front of me is my mom's hospital door.

Will she still look sick? Worse?

I reach for the handle. Aster notices me slipping into myself and nudges my shoulder gently. "We aren't done with this conversation," she says.

I nod, swallowing hard, and take a deep breath through my nose. I wipe my palms on my jeans. Suddenly, I'm twelve again, scared, small, standing outside a hospital room, pretending I'm brave. I'm not ready for what's on the other side. But I open the door anyway.

There she is sitting in the hospital chair, turned toward the window, staring out at the city skyline.

"Hey, Mom," I say, trying to steady my voice.

"Hey, sweetie." She doesn't turn around. Just keeps staring.

"How are you feeling?"

She doesn't answer. Doesn't blink. Then softly, she says, "Have you ever noticed how small we are? Just specs in the city. Specs in the world. Everyone's moving, rushing, surviving… while my world is falling apart." She pauses. My throat tightens. "And yet, nobody stops. The world doesn't pause for one person's tragedy. Not for cancer. Not for me." Her voice cracks. Tears roll down her cheeks, but she still won't face me.

"Mom…" I whisper. "Please don't talk like that."

"No, Lila. I'm serious. My little sickness? It doesn't matter. Not out there. Not in the grand scheme of things." Her voice sharpens, raw and rising. "Time doesn't slow down for pain. The world keeps spinning."

She's breaking. And it's breaking me.

Aster grips my arm, grounding me because she knows. She knows this hurts more than anything, seeing my mom grieving her cancer, slowly accepting that this might really be it… that she might leave us behind.

I walk over and kneel beside her, taking her hands in mine. "Mom, you do matter. Dad, Aster, me… we're your world. The outside chaos doesn't matter. Please… what's really going on?" Tears hit the soft pink robe Aster brought her. What once felt delicate and pretty now feels heavy beneath the weight of grief.

"I'm trying," she whispers. "But even with trying… I might not recover. I might not be here next year for Christmas."

Her voice breaks. And so, do I. My hands tremble around hers.

I'm trying to stay strong, to be what she needs. But how do you hold it together when the strongest person you know is the one falling apart?

Tears spill down my cheeks. My chin quivers. I don't wipe them away. Aster squats beside me, wrapping her arm around my shoulder. She doesn't say a word, just holds on as my pain bleeds through.

"I don't want to leave," Mom says, her voice raw and barely there. "I don't want to leave you guys behind."

"Don't say that," I whisper, wiping her tears as Aster quietly wipes mine. "Please don't talk like that. You're doing amazing. The doctor said the trial's working. Your lymph nodes are clearing up… that's huge. You have to hold on. We need you. I need you."

She gives me a small smile, but it barely reaches her eyes. Then, softly, like it physically hurts to admit, she says, "I'm also losing my hair." Her fingers glide through her blonde strands, and a small clump comes loose in her hand. She stares at it. It's like watching her confidence fall apart in slow motion. Delicate. Weightless. Like a feather drifting on the wind.

Aster gently breaks the silence. "I can get a real human-hair wig that looks just like yours!"

Mom shakes her head. "No, sweetie. You don't have to do that."

"I want to, Alice," Aster says, her voice full of warmth. "You're family, and I love you. It's the least I can do after everything you've done for me, after all the times you stepped in and were a mom when mine was away traveling."

She reaches out and takes both our hands. "I don't deserve you girls." She gives our hands a gentle squeeze.

"How about this week we come back and get you fitted for one?" she says softly. "I can bring my stylist."

Mom flinches. "No… I don't want anyone to see me like this."

Aster nods, already adjusting. "Okay. Then, how about just Lila and me? We'll come back, help you shave it, and bring a few soft caps to try on. I'll take your measurements then."

There's a long pause. Then Mom exhales slowly, and for the first time today, her voice doesn't crack. "I'm okay with that… It gives me something to look forward to."

The silence is aching. "Mom we brought you more shakes. This time cookies and creams anddddd our favorite mint chocolate chip!"
I say, trying to cheer her up.

Her voice is heavy with sadness. "Thank you, girls. But I'm really not feeling up for chatting right now… would you be okay if I took a nap?"

My heart breaks. She's depressed. She wants to shrink away and disappear.

"Of course. How about we get you to the bed and have the nurse bring your pain meds?"

She cuts me off. "No, I just want to sit here by the window. Could you recline the chair and grab my blanket?"

Aster grabs the fuzzy pink blanket from the bed and gently tucks her in as I lower the chair back. I lean down and kiss her forehead. "I love you, Momma. I'll call you later."

"Okay, honey," she whispers. As we leave, she doesn't look back. Her eyes stay fixed on the city, buzzing, busy, alive, everything she no longer feels. The hope, the light, the fight… all of it drained from her. What's left is only the shell of a woman who once lit up every room with just her smile.

This isn't her. This isn't Alice Anderson. Not the mother who built joy out of nothing, who made me feel safe and loved when the fridge was empty and the lights were off. Not the woman who cradled my head when I came home crying after being humiliated at the dance… left standing alone while everyone else danced around me.

I close the door behind us. And then I break.

I turn to Aster, sobbing into her shoulder, because I can't carry this alone anymore. "Why her?" I choke out. "She's already been through so much… It's not fair." My voice cracks, and the words unravel like everything else I'm trying to hold together. Aster holds me tighter, rubbing my back in slow, grounding circles. But even her arms around me can't stop the ache. The kind that settles in your bones when the person who once made everything okay is the one you can't save. And the worst part is, I don't know if I'll ever see her light come back.

CHAPTER THIRTY-EIGHT
LILA

The streets are buzzing with chaos. It's pure overstimulation to my already exhausted body. Anxiety coils in my chest, threatening to burst free, but I don't have time for it. I'm already running late, and the last thing I need is for Kage to have my head mounted above his fireplace like a damn trophy.

My eyes are heavy, bruised from a night of restless tossing and turning. I spent half of it replaying everything… Leon, Kage, the kiss, the sex. The emotional whiplash of it all. The other half I spent sobbing about my mom, spiraling into the kind of panic that tightens your chest until it feels like breathing is optional.

And underneath it all? The lurking fear that Volkov, the man who kidnapped me, is still out there. Hunting for me. Convinced I'm the one who put him behind bars. His final victim. His unfinished business.

At this point, my life is a literal shit show.

I push through the wall of bodies swirling through New York like a current I can't swim against. The noise is relentless. Too loud. Too fast. Too much. Every honk, shout, and step echoes like a fire alarm in my skull. My heart races. I feel the heat rise in my cheeks, the prickling chill that shoots down my arms to my fingertips. The panic is coming. Creeping.

I clench my fists.

Work is just three blocks away. You can make it.

I turn the corner fast, trying to outrun the rising tide beneath my skin. Then pain throbs through my left shoulder… and my ass?

I blink, dazed, and realize I'm on the cold, wet concrete, sprawled beneath the towering presence of a woman who looks like she just walked off a runway. Glowing hazel-gold eyes, designer heels, and dark brown curls that fall past her chest in tight, shiny spirals.

She's rich. That much is obvious. Her pristine black dress hugs every sensual curve as she hovers above me like I belong exactly where I've landed, the damn sidewalk.

That fall felt personal… like it wasn't an accident. And where's my purse?

She offers me her hand, her voice soft and honey-smooth. "Oh my God, I'm so sorry. I must've run into you while I was checking my phone."

I swat her apology away with words that come too fast and too sharp. "Hey! Maybe look where you're going next time…" I pause, giving her a once-over. "Miss Couture." The venom in my voice surprises even me. But it's too late. My nerves are frazzled, and my body reacted as if it were under attack. Fight or flight chose violence today.

She blinks, stunned. So am I. But then something shifts. Her expression hardens like she's recalibrating right in front of me. She bends down, now eye level, holding my old thrift-store college purse like it's something she scraped off her shoe.

"How about you stay on the ground with the dirt… where you belong," she says, voice calm and polished but cutting like glass into my confidence. A wicked smile stretches across her flawless face as she drops the purse in my lap. She doesn't hand it to me. Just lets it fall like she's tossing trash into a bin. I wrinkle my nose and squint up at her, too stunned to hide the disgust.

How rude. The whole thing feels calculated, aimed right at me. Maybe I deserved it after snapping at her, but something about this feels too intentional.

And then, of course, the sky opens. One drop. Two. Then a complete downpour.

Dammit. I forgot my umbrella.

She pops hers open like magic, shielding her perfectly blown-out curls, while I sit there, soaked and slumped like a drenched alley cat.

Of course. Just perfect. I swear the universe has it out for me today.

Her eyes never leave mine. That same slow, spine-chilling smile lingers like perfume.
She turns in her designer shoes and walks away. Heels clicking. Hips swaying. Completely unbothered by my presence. And she knows I'm still watching. She wants me to.

Do I know her? Does she know me?

I try to think back to my ex's girlfriends, and nothing rings a bell.

Well, at least the panic attack is gone.

Rain clings to my skin as I get to my feet. Soaked. Humiliated. Kicked when I was already down. My hair, my makeup, and my cream blazer… all ruined for work today. I take off running, as if I can outrun shame itself.

Please don't fall again. Please don't fall again.

I lift my purse over my head in a pathetic attempt at coverage, praying my mascara isn't streaked down my face and staining my blazer. On top of that, I'm already ten minutes late. When I finally reach the building, the elderly doorman, the one who greeted me on my first day, rushes out with an umbrella like he's about to save my life.

But honestly? There's nothing left to save.

"Thank you, sir. I really appreciate it," I say as he shuts the heavy glass door behind us.

"You're welcome, Ms. Anderson."

I smile. His kind spirit doesn't belong in a place like this, not with people like Kage. "I'm sorry… I don't know your name."

"Davey. Call me Davey," he says with a warm grin.

I take his hand, worn and weathered like he's lived a hundred lives, and squeeze it gently, hoping he feels how much that small gesture meant to me. "Davey, do you like coffee and bagels?"

"Of course. What New Yorker doesn't?" he chuckles.

"Good. I'll bring you some tomorrow, I promise! I hope you have a great day."

"You too, sweetheart."

I hurry off, desperate to avoid being twenty minutes late in the first month of working here. Then I see it. Both elevators are blocked off with orange cones, each marked by a laminated sign swinging slightly from the door. And my reflection? Horrifying. Soaked hair. Smudged mascara. Wrinkled clothes. I look like I lost a fight with a car wash.

I step closer and read the sign. "Elevator under maintenance starting at 8:00 AM. Please use the stairs down the hall to the right and then the third door on the left."

"Really?" I huff and cross my arms, pouting. The universe isn't just kicking me today. It's body slamming me on repeat like we're stuck in an MMA cage match. I groan and head for the stairs, rainwater squishing and squeaking in my heels with every step.

Perfect. Now, I'll be late and smell like sweat.

I yank the heavy stairwell door open and stare up like it's Mount Everest.

Each echo of my soaked heels sounds more pitiful than the last. I glance at my watch. My heart rate's at 160 bpm, not from panic this time, but because I'm actually working out. My thighs are burning. My dignity's on life support.

I let out a breathless gasp and clutch the railing, one slip away from tumbling back to square one. "Finally," I gasp, dragging myself up the last step.

Clint is never going to let me live this down.

My arms shake as I pull open the tenth-floor door. I step into a hallway I don't recognize, breath still shallow from the stairs. White walls. Polished marble floors. Outer glass panels stretch along the edge, framing the city like a moving portrait. It's quiet up here… too quiet. I glance around, confused.

This isn't the floor I usually enter from. Oh wait. I'm on the wrong one. Eleventh, not tenth. Figures.

My heart drops. Kage's office. All glass. Wide open. And I freeze. My knees give out from the climb.

I hit the floor hard, landing on them with a gasp, palms braced against the marble as I struggle to catch my breath. Rain drips from my hair. My chest heaves from climbing the stairs, lungs burning from the desperate sprint to make it on time.

But none of that matters. Because through the glass wall of his office, I see her. Her back is arched, her arms wrapped tight around his body. Her black dress hugs every curve as if it were designed for seduction. She moves against him slowly, deliberately. Like she knows him. Like she's done this before.

I don't see her face. But I don't need to. It's her. Miss Couture. The woman who dropped my purse in my lap like I was filth. The one who watched me fall and smiled. Who walked away while I sat drenched in the rain. And of all the people to witness me like this, it had to be them…

She's here. In his office. With her hands on him. And he is letting her touch him.

Two hands press against the glass on either side of her head, just like he did with me in the elevator. I can see the scar on his right hand, clear as day. I can't hear what they're saying, but I don't need to. The scene speaks for itself. He's doing what he does best. Taking women to bed like it means nothing. Like this isn't the first time. My stomach twists.

Of course, she's his type. The kind of woman Kage would touch. She's elite, polished, and cruel. A flawless reflection of him. A match made in hell, two monsters draped in beauty.

She leans in and presses a kiss to his neck just like I did to him at the club. And when she shifts, tilting her head just enough, I see him. I'm still on the ground, knees bruised against the cold marble. Soaked. Trembling. Frozen.

That face. Those dangerously unreadable green eyes. And they're locked on mine. Piercing. Still. Unshaken. Like I'm not real. Like I'm a dream he's been trying to forget, and now I've come back to haunt him.

CHAPTER THIRTY-NINE
LILA

How do I keep ending up in this situation? Does my body crave chaos… or just him?

His green eyes burn through the glass wall, glowing like embers straight into my soul.

Great. I look like shit in front of him after the circus of a morning I've had.

And to top it off, I'm on the ground while she stands there, flawless from head to toe. Meanwhile, I'm mascara-smeared, heels squishing, a full-blown disaster. The kind of chaos he'd never want. A truth I really need to accept. I should be chasing someone in my league. Someone who deserves me. And even though I want him… he doesn't deserve my attention. Or my love.

He doesn't smirk. Doesn't blink. Just furrows his brow like he's… concerned?

For me?

Why? Because I look like a drowned rat sitting on the floor? Because I'm interrupting whatever this is? Or maybe… maybe he's remembering the last time we saw each other when he shattered me in front of everyone at the club during that twisted little truth or dare game.

I haven't seen him since. Since I found out he's a man-whore with a body count of five hundred twenty-one. And that was days ago, so let's be generous and round it up to five hundred twenty-four, thanks to Miss Couture. And let's not forget, he saw me with Leon… well, I think.

I told myself I had imagined it, that I had dreamt it. That I didn't moan his name while someone else was between my legs. But I did. Because all I could think about… was him.

But he wouldn't waste his time watching me. Not when women like her line up just to be chosen by him. To be touched by him.

I rip my gaze away.

I don't want to be here. I'm not watching this time. For my sanity, I can't. I'm done. I have to be. I don't want to want him. Correction, I can't want him because he's not good for me. He never was. He belongs with someone like her. Or Natasha. And I have to be okay with that… if I plan to survive this job.

I pull myself up off the marble, trying to steady my legs and walk without looking back. I need to escape. His gaze. This hallway. This whole moment.

Weirdly, I'm not panicking… well, not exactly. I think I'm getting used to the chaos. But I need a second. Just one second to breathe, to reset, because if today keeps unraveling like this, I won't even make it to lunch.

I reach for doorknobs like I'm playing survival roulette, just trying to find somewhere… anywhere to hide.

It's like I can't escape that Halloween night. No matter how far I run, it's still chasing me. Ever since I saw the Phantom, my life hasn't been the same. I'm still lost in the maze. Still searching for an exit from this nightmare.

Finally, one opens. I slip inside and close the door behind me.

Janitor's closet.

I let out a dry laugh. Of course, this is where fate dumps me. The light flickers overhead. The smell of bleach and Pine-Sol clings to the air, thick and punishing. I try to take a deep breath, but I cough hard. The chemicals burn my throat. Even in here, I can't catch a break.

I slide down the wall until I hit the floor, knees to my chest, arms wrapped tight. I bury my face like a child shielding herself from playground bullies… only this time, the bully is me.

I'll never be enough.

But I whisper to myself anyway, "Pull it together, Lila. You've got a masquerade ball to finish. You've got parents depending on you. Debt to pay off. A job to keep." It all weighs heavily on my chest.

But one day… one day I'll be able to say it was all worth it. You don't have time to be heartbroken over a crush. Someone out there will love you… the real you. Mess and all.

A tear slips down my cheek. The doorknob rattles.

Oh no.

My heart launches into my throat. Adrenaline spikes, making my pulse skip and stutter. I try to hide, but there's nowhere to go.

I'm trapped.

I flip the light off and hold my breath, crouching low in the shadows. The door creaks open. A large shadow steps inside and shuts it behind them. The closet goes still. Silent.

What is happening? Is someone else hiding, too? Or did I just get caught?

I cover my mouth, desperate to silence my breathing as I disappear into the shadows.

"Are you okay?" a low, sultry voice asks, smooth but concerned.

Kage. What is he doing in here? This isn't the kind of room he just… hangs out in.

The lights are still off, but the moment he speaks, I don't need them. He lit the match inside me. I don't reply. I'm still in shock, unsure if he followed me… or if he was meeting one of his women and didn't expect me to be in here.

Maybe I can slip out. My eyes are more adjusted to the dark than his.

I see his silhouette. Broad. Sharp. Framed by that tailored black suit. I move with caution, trying to slide past him without making contact. My fingers grip the doorknob, ready to yank it open and run. But then his hand catches my wrist. Strong. Tender. But trembling and scorching against my skin. His breath is shaky, like it hurts him to touch me.

"Lila," he says, voice low but firm. "Answer me. Are you okay?"

So, he does know it's me. And that commanding tone again... God, he makes me weak. I'm his, and he doesn't even know it.

"Why do you care?" I snap as I yank my arm free, even though every part of me aches to stay. I want him to pull me closer. I want to bury my face in his chest and cry until the weight of all the pain I've been carrying finally lifts, even if just for a moment.

His outline drifts nearer, silent but impossible to ignore. The tension is deafening. He's inches from me, and I can barely breathe. I'm going to pass out from his presence alone. This feels familiar. Like the moment with the red mask... when I was left shattered, alone, clutching nothing but his mask.

He left. And Kage will too.

I fumble for the light switch, needing something... anything to ground me. But the second my fingers touch it, his hand covers mine.

"Don't," he breathes. Just one word. A whisper against the dark. Then softer, "I... I won't be able to say what I'm about to."

His voice is low, rough, and timid. My heart races so hard I can feel it in my ears. Our faces are inches from one another. His breath is cool mint, tinged with smoke. It's dark, but the air between us is electrified, like lightning striking a metal rod.

"What do you want to say, Kage?" I whisper.

"Don't do that."

"Do what?"

"Say my name like that…" Our breaths are ragged. His words steal every ounce of oxygen from my lungs. His hand trembles as it hovers over my neck. "Can I… Can I t-touch you?"

"You never have to ask my permission." His fingertips brush my neck, sending goosebumps rippling down my spine. His slight touch has me emotionally on my knees.

"Dammit, Lila," he growls, voice cracking. "I'm unraveling… waiting for your existence not to matter, to loosen its grip around my throat." He freezes, grazing his fingers over my collarbone. "But another day comes, and I'm wrecked all over again, wrecked from the inside out. I'm clawing at myself, trying to fight it. To fight myself. To fight you. But you… You're making it impossible."

He glides his fingers down, then pulls his hand away like it burns him.

"No." I grab his hand. "Finish." I place his palm on my chest, where my pounding heart waits for the heartbreak I know is coming. His breath shakes, and my chest rises and falls beneath his hand.

"Every breath you take is my enemy. Every heartbeat is a call I can't outrun. Every touch lights a furnace inside me, a burning reminder that I'm not worthy of you. And your scent is imprinted in my blood, leaving me high, aching for another dose of you." He slowly lifts his hand from my chest, and I see his trembling fingers grip my chin. His thumb drags across my lips. "And those lips, the ones that kissed me. No, made love to my tongue. They've wrecked me, Lila. Tell me… do you enjoy this? Watching me fall apart? You exist… and it's fucking destroying me. Every second you're here feels like a blade carving me open. And still, I crawl back for more. More of you. More of the unintentional pain your presence brings."

He pauses, chest heaving, then leans into my ear. "I'm fighting relentlessly to escape you. And I can't. I wish I hated you for that… Princess, you are my undoing."

Those words. They settle over me like ice. I lean in closer, my lips brushing the shell of his ear, and murmur, slow and deliberate:

"Kage…" I let his name roll off my tongue, a taunt. "How about… You fuck off."

It's easier to push him away than admit I want to believe him. That I want to believe someone like him could ever want someone like me.

He pulls back, startled. "Stop playing games with me, asshole." I yank the door open and step into the hall… head pounding, every nerve screaming that I need to get out of here. But as the door swings shut, his voice curls around me, low and dark, a twisted promise that lingers in the air.

"Oh, Princess… you sure do love a good chase."

CHAPTER FORTY
LILA

Well, I thought this day couldn't get any worse. But somehow, it just did. I mean, I wish he meant the things he said. I wish every word he said were real, but ever since he spun around in that chair during my interview, all he's done is torment me.

And what did he mean by "Oh, Princess… you sure do love a good chase"?

The only person who's ever chased me is… No. No way. Kage wouldn't be that cruel. To play those games and pretend none of it mattered. If he did, he'd have to be completely soulless.
But he's Beck's best friend so that he would have been at the Halloween party… right? There's no way he's the Red Mask. He couldn't be. It's not possible.

I shake the thought from my head and stomp down the stairs to the correct floor. I shove the heavy metal door open and practically sprint down the hall, running from what just happened or maybe, if I'm being honest, from the entire past few days. I finally reach the office.

Clint is waiting, arms crossed, foot tapping. That smug bastard grin stretched across his face like he's been rehearsing a monologue just for me. "Well, well, well. Look what the cat dragged in." He freezes, giving me a once-over in complete shock. "Damn, Lila. You look like shit. What happened?"

I cut him off before he can get another stupid word out. "Don't start with me, Clint. I'm not in the mood, and I swear, if you piss me off today, I'll tase you."

"Woooah, sweetheart, let's not get crazy this morning." He smirks. "But I do have to ask… why are you an hour late?"

"Why don't you ask that prick, Kage?"

His grin widens like he knows something I don't. "What?" I snap.

"I saw the way you two looked at each other at the club. You can't fake a kiss like that. Were you two up all night, finally banging it out?"

"You're really asking to get tased this morning." I shoot him a glare sharp enough to kill a man and reach into my bag like I'm actually considering it.

He calls my bluff and stands there with his arms crossed, clearly waiting for some kind of confession. But there is nothing to tell. Kage likes to play games and sleep around. "Clint, we both know he's a man-whore and a walking STD. I'm going to pass."

He shrugs. "I guess you're right… But you know you always have me." He winks like he's doing me a favor.

I roll my eyes and head to my desk, letting out a breath as I catch sight of the fresh flowers Aster dropped off this weekend after we visited Mom. I haven't had a chance even to decorate my gray, drab desk because so much has been going on, but Aster came to the rescue, ready to cheer me up. And she never disappoints.

I can't believe my eyes. It's beautiful. The once-boring cubicle is now a soft, dreamy haven. Gold-framed pictures of me, Mom, Dad, and Aster are arranged across the walls, each one capturing different moments of our lives.

A tear slips down my cheek. They line the space like a quiet reminder of why I keep going every day. Them. My home.

Two computer monitors are framed in gold. A light pink mouse and keyboard tie it all together. The mat underneath is adorned with pink and gold flowers, pulling everything into a perfect, gentle harmony. Soft lights drape overhead, brightening the dark cubicle. My name, "LILA," written in elegant cursive, stands proudly against the backdrop, and for a moment, I almost forget everything that's gone wrong today.

My desk is L-shaped, complete with a plush pink chair that looks as inviting as a hug, exactly what I need right now. The soft touch soothes me, healing a tiny piece of my broken spirit. I inhale deeply, the scent of the pink peonies masking the damp, rain-soaked scent clinging to my clothes.

On the gold pinboard is a sticky note from Aster: "Kick ass soul sister. I love you. Kisses," signed with her signature, a delicate aster flower.

I smile, really needing that this morning. She outdid herself, as always. I open my drawers and find a beauty kit tucked inside. Makeup, deodorant, perfume, a hairbrush, and mouthwash - everything I need to salvage the mess I am today.

"Aster, you are heaven-sent," I murmur. Then, a bag with my favorite snacks, topped with a sticky note: "You can thank me later." I laugh softly.

"Good morning, team! Be ready in five minutes. We've got a meeting about the Wolf." Clint's voice echoes through the office.

My throat tightens at the sound of his name. My smile fades, dread twisting in my gut. I'm going to have to get used to hearing his name if I want to work in this department. I can't let the fear of him rule me forever.

Besides, he's in prison… right?

My hands shake as I swipe on lip gloss and throw my hair into a high ponytail. My heart stutters, skipping again and again.

Dammit, not these things again.

The flip-flop in my chest unnerves me. They say it's just anxiety. The cardiologist has checked me, but that doesn't stop the fear clawing at my insides. The feeling that I'm going to die at any moment.

I grab my clipboard and pen, forcing myself to act composed. From this awful day to the skipped heartbeats, I'm internally a mess. My legs tremble in my heels as I slide into a chair at the large conference table.

Ugh, I hope Kage isn't the one leading this meeting today. That would be the tip of the iceberg.

The same coworkers from the first meeting take their seats, notes and files in hand.

I can't wait to finally contribute something meaningful to the team instead of just prepping the ballroom for Saturday.

"Alright, team, let's begin," Clint says, his professional tone switching on. "We've located a few of the girls who were kidnapped. We're going to do a rescue operation tomorrow. Sage and Kelley, you'll be helping the rescue team." They nod, focused and determined. "What else do we have? Any updates?"

"Yes," someone says. "The cops arrested one of the suspects who was relaying information from inside the prison. We think that's how Volkov's been working from behind bars."

"I'll talk to the law enforcement team to see if they've questioned him yet," Clint replies.

Sage speaks up. "The police also suspect there's a rat in the company leaking information to Volkov."

Clint grips the table like the comment pissed him off. "I'll talk to Beck and Kage about it. But if there is a rat, I hope they know those two don't mess around. Any other updates?"

I clear my throat. "Did you guys find anything on the hard drive from Natasha's computer?"

Clint and the rest of the team exchange confused looks. "Huh? Who's Natasha?"

My pulse spikes.

They would've checked the drive. They would've known. Unless… they didn't even know it existed. Unless he never told them.

"Ah… Kage took me with him—" I stop myself, scrambling, unsure if I should even mention it. "Sorry, guys. I'm running on no sleep. Must've dreamed it." My heart skips again from the stress, leaving me breathless.

Clint lets out a light laugh. "We've all been there. Once we wrap up, Lila, head down to the ballroom and finish everything for Saturday."

"Okay. Will do," I reply softly, praying I didn't just blow everything. But my mind won't stop racing.

Why did Kage hide Natasha? Why didn't he tell them about the hard drive?

My heart twists, dread building in my chest. There, in the window of the conference room, I catch a shadow that freezes me in place. His granite-green eyes meet mine, unreadable and cold. He doesn't smirk or give anything away. Kage slowly turns, his dark brown Armani suit sharp and controlled, his hands slipping into his pockets as he walks away. He disappears, silent as ever, but the damage is done.

And now I don't know what terrifies me more. That Kage is hiding something, or that the man I've let into my heart is possibly helping the same monster who once tried to tear it out.

CHAPTER FORTY-ONE
LILA

This day will never end. It just keeps getting worse and worse. "Ugh, I'm so tired of this place," I mutter under my breath. I look up at the hospital, wishing Mom weren't here, but at least she's still getting treatment.

"Lila! Wait up!" Aster calls from across the crosswalk. I turn to see her jogging towards me. I don't say a word. I honestly don't have an ounce of energy left to respond.

"Whoa, what happened to you today?" she asks, concern clear in her voice.

"I don't want to talk about it," I say quietly, wrapping my arms around her neck. I inhale deeply, breathing her in. Aster's hugs are different. Not the kind people give out of obligation, but the kind that hold you up when you're falling apart. The kind that says, without words, I've got you.

I needed this one more than I realized. Aster pulls back, her eyes scanning my tear-rimmed face like she's piecing together every shattered part of me.

"Are you sure you want to do this today?"

"I don't want to do it at all," I admit, "but I need to be here for her."

Aster slips her hand into mine as we walk through the hospital's front doors into the dim, sterile lobby. "Well, I'll be here for you," she says softly, giving my hand a gentle squeeze.

I glance at one of the patients sitting nearby with her family. She looks pale, frail, barely hanging on. When she smiles, her lips are almost the same shade as her teeth. Chemotherapy has stripped her completely… her hair, her color, her confidence. Is this what Mom will look like after we shave her head? Am I ready for that? Can I handle seeing her like that? Am I strong enough?

I haven't seen her since Sunday. Since the day she sat by the window, quietly watching the world move on while she stayed behind, fighting to stay alive.

"So… how are you and Beck? What happened after Leon and I left?" I ask. The elevator dings, and we step inside, heading straight toward the heartbreak waiting for us. Two older women in their fifties join us. The air turns awkwardly silent.

"Well, if you must know," Aster starts, completely unbothered, "I went back to his house, and I thought we were just going to fuck…" Both women gasp at her sailor's mouth. Aster? Doesn't even blink. "But it was different, Lila. I think we actually made love. And you know me… that's not my style!" She clasps her hands together like she's in a romance movie, eyes sparkling with the memory.

I grin. "I'm so happy for you. You deserve that kind of love. So, are you two, like… official now?"

"He wants to be," she says, then sighs dramatically. "But you know me. I've never been the committed type. I prefer my monthly orgies."

The women beside us nearly choke. Aster flashes them a dazzling smile.

The elevator can't open fast enough.

They whisper back and forth, but Aster doesn't care. She's unapologetically her, and that's what makes her so special. The elevator doors open, and we leave the gossiping women behind.

"Well, I support you no matter what you choose. But know, if Beck breaks your heart, I will break his face," I tease, and we both giggle.

"Duly noted. But honestly, that's not even the most exciting part. After you and Leon went upstairs—"

"Huh? What do you mean?"

"After you and Kage had your spat and you went upstairs with Leon, Kage got sloppy drunk, told the girls to get lost, and then got into a fight with Leon's personal assistant!"

"Oh my God, why didn't you call me? I would have come down and gotten him—" I stop myself before I finish the complete sentence.

"That's why I didn't. If he was acting out because of how he treated you and what he lost, then I wanted him to grovel in his self-pity."

"You're an evil genius," I say with a laugh.

Aster throws her head back, her signature evil laugh echoing down the hallway, her eyes glittering with mischief.

"Okay, chill. That was actually scary," I say, caught off guard.

Our laughter fades as we reach Mom's hospital door. We freeze, and Aster grips her bag, knowing what's inside. The hair clippers.

The object that will break Mom more than she already is. My heart races, and for a moment, I almost ask Aster to stop, to wait, to turn back. But there's no turning back from this. "Are you ready?" Aster whispers, her hand trembling on the door handle.

"As I'll ever be," I breathe out.

Inside, Mom sits in the recliner, watching the sunset sink slowly over the city. She looks like she hasn't moved in days. Her hair falls out in patches, bald spots scattered across her scalp.

Dad sits across from her, watching the love of his life suffer day after day, completely powerless to stop it. But he's still there, step by step, even as she pushes him away. That's what love is. The hardest part isn't loving someone who's dying. It's loving someone whose death could be stolen at any moment.

"Hey, kiddo." Dad stands and pulls me into a hug.

"Hey, Mom. How are you feeling today?" I ask, but she doesn't take her eyes off the city skyline, just a void, vacant stare.

"I've been better," she says softly, her expression unchanged.

I step closer, breaking her line of sight, and bend down so I'm face-to-face with her tired eyes. "Momma. I'm right here. Dad is here. Aster is here. We're all here for you. Please," I plead, reaching up to gently cradle her face. "Please don't push us away."

She slowly lifts her frail hand, placing it over mine. "I'm sorry, honey. I'm not trying to push you away. I feel detached, like I've already accepted my fate and now I'm just waiting for it to happen."

Her cold, delicate fingers brush against my cheek. "And that's okay," I whisper. "But don't forget why you're fighting so hard to stay alive." A small tear escapes, rolling down my cheek. She wipes it away with her thumb.

As always, she's the one taking care of me when it should be the other way around.

"You always help bring me back to earth," she murmurs, her lips curling into the first genuine smile I've seen in two weeks.

Aster's voice echoes through the room. "Well, Alice, are you ready to kick cancer's ass?"

We giggle, and the sound makes Mom and Dad laugh too, filling the room with warmth. "They did say the lumps in my breast are looking good, and the cancer in my lymph nodes has decreased tremendously," Mom says.

I throw my arms around her neck. "Mom, that's amazing!"

Every ounce of her smile radiates pure joy. "It is, but I hate that I have to shave my head."

"I told you I'm getting you a wig made. Once we shave it, I'll measure everything and get it started tomorrow," I say.

"Aster, I told you, you don't have to do that," Mom protests.

Aster cuts her off, sass shining through. "And I told you I want to. You're my family. Practically my second mom. I love you, and it's totally happening."

Mom rolls her eyes, knowing she won't win this one. Aster's too stubborn. Dad stands and ruffles his hair. "How about I grab us a few pizzas while you ladies get started on Mom's hot girl makeover?"

We giggle as he leans down and presses a sweet kiss to Mom's pale lips, like it might be his last. Aster pulls a chair from the table while I take Mom's hands and gently help her up.

"Take it easy," I whisper. "We're not in any rush."

"I am," she says softly. "This hair holds the past, and I'm ready to move forward to your future. The new hair that grows will be the hair my grandchildren braid during makeovers. The hair that flows in the wind at your dream wedding. I'm ready." She settles into the chair, determination shining in her eyes as Aster wraps the cape around her neck.

"Here, Lila," Aster says, holding out the clippers. "You should be the one to cut your mom's hair. The strands that fall will be everything you two have overcome."

My hands tremble as I take them. "Mom, are you sure you're ready?" I ask, my voice breaking.

"Honey, are you?" she counters, her voice calm and steady.

Tears roll down my cheeks. "I'm trying to be." I flick the switch. The soft hum fills the room like a heartbeat, steady and inevitable. Mom reaches behind me, her frail hand wrapping over mine.

"I'm ready, sweetie," she whispers. And together, she guides my hand as we cut the first line, her tears falling faster than the hair. This isn't just her battle. It's ours. And I swear, cancer won't take her. Not while I'm by her side.

CHAPTER FORTY-TWO
LILA

I practically killed myself getting the entrance done, but somehow I pulled it off. We step out of the elevator onto the 2/3 floor, greeted by a walkway scattered with rose petals. They guide us toward the heart of it all, a towering gazebo framed by gold pillars and drenched in deep red roses. Tiny lights are threaded through the blooms, mimicking a night sky.

Romantic, but not too sweet. That's why I added black velvet curtains on either side of the arch. I needed something darker to balance the beauty. Something mysterious. Something that reminded me of him. The Phantom of the Opera was my muse. Because of the Halloween party, that room, that moment, was when everything changed. The unraveling. The ache. The shift I never saw coming.

Maybe I imagined it. Maybe I filled in the blanks with fantasy. But even if I did, the Phantom changed something in me. Something permanent. The roses. The gold accents. The shadows. The lights that flicker like stars. All of it traces back to that room. The one I wasn't supposed to find. The one I slipped into to breathe. And I did.

But not in the way I expected, I hid in the dark and watched him. The man in the black and gold mask. That night rewired something inside me. And now I've designed this space with him in mind.

I wanted to give this night the same unforgettable energy that the room gave me. Not because I want others to experience what I did. But because I hope they feel something real. Something they can't explain. Something they'll never forget.

Past the enchanted walkway, a photo booth waits with soft lighting and a velvet backdrop. A professional photographer stands ready to capture every masked fantasy. Beyond that, another rose-covered arch leads into the ballroom.

I'm still scrambling to finish that part. Beside me, Beck's breath catches.

"Lila, this is incredible. This is going to be an unforgettable masquerade ball." His voice softens, filled with something that almost sounds like awe. "I knew I picked the right person."

"Well, technically, Aster picked me. But yes. Yes, you did!" I grin and nudge him. At the mention of her name, I see something shift in his expression. Like the air just turned heavier. "Beck, you know I want you two together, right?"

He raises an eyebrow. "You sure? I thought it might be weird. After what happened between us."

I burst out laughing. "Oh my God. We danced. We grinded for maybe ten minutes. That was it. Besides, I've got a few other people on my radar."

He smirks. "Kage?"

I groan. "No! Why does everyone keep saying that? He's such a dick."

Beck laughs harder, flashing that annoyingly charming grin. "They all say that and then they come crawling back for more." The word **all** lands like a gut punch. "As your friend," he says, his tone softening, "I'd honestly steer clear of him. He's loyal, and he's my best friend, but…"

"But?"

Beck's expression shifts, something darker settling in. "His past is heavy. And so is his soul. Just… be careful if you really, deep down, feel something for him." My stomach twists.

A dark past? What is that supposed to mean?

But it would explain so much. The coldness. The mood swings. The way he can look right through me like he sees all my secrets and still couldn't care less. I want to ask more, demand answers, but the words that come out are softer than I expect.

"What kind of dark past?"

Beck doesn't smile. Doesn't flinch. "One you don't want any part of," he says, eyes locked on mine. And for once, he isn't joking. For some reason, that only makes me want to know more.

Why is he the way he is? What is he hiding behind those eyes? What have they seen to make his past so dark? And if he's the one sneaking around, leaking information to the Wolf... then maybe this isn't just about closure anymore. He spoke Russian with Natasha. That wasn't a coincidence. That wasn't nothing. Catching him could get me answers. Maybe even a raise.

"Maybe I'm darker than you think," I say with a smirk.

Beck turns to me, completely serious. "I mean it, Lila. Please don't get caught up in his past. As my girlfriend's best friend, I don't want to see you get hurt."

I start to reply, but my voice catches. I was only teasing before, but that response was unexpected. I nod slowly as he places his hands on my shoulders and pulls me into a hug.

"Trust me," he says. "You deserve someone who can love you with their whole heart. And that's not something he can give. Kage doesn't love himself, so he can't love you."

A silence falls between us. Heavy and full of things I'm not ready to unpack. Then Beck steps back with a sigh and checks his watch.

"Damn it! Aster's going to kill me if I'm late for dinner reservations."

I force a smile. "Go. Save yourself."

He chuckles, already walking away. "Wrap things up and catch a cab, okay? And text me when you get home."

"I will," I say, watching him disappear down the hallway. And just like that, I'm alone again. But the words he left behind are still with me, echoing louder than I'd like.

Ugh. Emotions are so damn fickle.

But I can't shake what Beck said.

"His past is heavy."

Was he a criminal? Is he still a criminal? Maybe I should find out… No. I couldn't. If I got caught, I'd be fired.

But it's late. The office is empty. I could copy everything from his computer and go through it later… No, Lila. That's crossing a line.

I flip the lights off, grab my bag, and head to the elevator… when I hear it. A hum. But not just any hum, the one that lives in my dreams. The hum of him. The Red Mask. My chest tightens.

I'm being delusional. There's no way he's here. Besides, I have his mask at home.

I wait. And wait. But the elevator never comes.

"Ugh, not again. They must be working on them," I mutter, rubbing my temple. I stumble through the dark toward the stairwell, finally finding the door that leads to the only lit space on this floor. The moment I swing it open, the sound hits me… soft at first, then rises. A haunting hum echoes up the stairwell, swirling around me like the oxygen I need to breathe. Beautiful. Tragic. Familiar. My heart stutters. My hands tremble.

I know that sound. I can't believe it. He's here. He's really here. Maybe I can finally see him… Without the mask.

Then footsteps. Heavy. Measured. Definitely male. Each one echoes up the stairwell with eerie precision.

"Red Mask?" I call. They stop. Dead silence. "Hello?" I start walking, then running. Desperate to know if it's really him or if I'm just a lunatic chasing shadows. Heavy footsteps pound the floor, running away from me.

"Hey… wait up. Please." No response. No footsteps. No hum. Nothing. Only silence and the ache of not knowing.

He's gone.

I glance up and freeze. I'm standing on the stairs that lead to Kage's office. My heart thuds in my chest. *While I'm here… maybe I'll just swing by. Not to do anything crazy… maybe copy his hard drive.*

I grab a black thumb drive from my bag and slide it into my bra. *Totally normal behavior.* I stand at the knob, debating.

This is a terrible idea.

But my body takes over, flinging the door open to the dimly lit hallway. "Okay, where was his office again?" I mumble, turning corner after corner… until I see it. Him. The breath leaves my lungs.

Kage's office lamp glows softly, casting golden light over his skin. Angelic. Carved from marble. His eyes stay locked on the computer screen, jaw tight with focus. No humming. No movement. Not in the stairwell. Just working, like nothing happened.

Was it him humming? It sounded like the Red Mask… but maybe I just heard what I wanted to hear.

My stomach yearns for the truth.

Did I imagine it? Am I losing it?

And yet... that sound is still echoing in my bones. And the worst part?

I'm not sure if I want the answer.

CHAPTER FOUR-THREE
LILA

That hum… It felt familiar. It felt like the Red Mask.

I watch him from the shadows, clenching my thighs without meaning to. My clit pulses at the sight of him.

How's it even fair that I can look at someone and immediately be turned on? He doesn't even know I'm here, and I'm already wrecked. Shit… I'm down bad for this man, and now I want him even more because I shouldn't have him. Because of his dark past. Because he might be the enemy.

I stand in the dark, clinging to the corner of the wall, trying to stay hidden. Just observe. But then our eyes connect. Through the shadows. Locked across the space between his office and the dim hallway where I'm frozen like a thief caught in the act. His office is glass. Clear. Exposed. The only thing separating us. One fragile barrier keeps me from him.

How did he know I was here? Can he read my mind? Did he feel my presence like I sense the Red Mask when he is around?

His face is unreadable. Completely blank.

Maybe he doesn't actually see me. Perhaps it's just a coincidence that we locked eyes.

He sits up straighter, adjusting in his chair, then lifts one hand and curls his finger to come here. A silent command. A dominant one. Not just into the room. To him. He doesn't speak. Doesn't blink. Just waits.

Oh, shit. What do I do? He knows. He has to know I was about to snoop.

A bead of sweat slips down my back. I'm nervous he might fire me. Or worse. If he's tied to Volkov's men, he could do more than fire me. He could kidnap me, ship me off to Europe, and no one would ever know.

I slowly step out from the shadows and make my way toward his office, trying to act normal. His face doesn't change, but his eyes glow with something forbidden. I tuck my hair behind my ear and smooth my skirt, doing my best to look put together even though he can see every nervous gesture. I raise my hand and knock on the glass door before gently pushing it open.

Breathe, Lila.

"What's the point of having a door when your whole office is completely see-through?" I say awkwardly, trying to crack a joke.

He doesn't smile. He turns his head toward me. "Lila, why are you up here?" His voice is deep and commanding.

He didn't call me princess. That alone tells me he is serious. Don't let him see through you. Lie. Lie. Lie.

"Well… to be honest… I felt bad about how I acted in the closet, and I just wanted to say… I'm… I'm sorry."

He doesn't look convinced. "Yeah, I don't believe you." He motions to me with his finger again. "Come here."

Oh no… I like where this is going.

I step closer, closing the space between us while he stays perfectly still in his chair. I stop right in front of him, heart pounding, waiting for his next move. His fingers drift to his chin, then slowly trace across his lips like he's deciding what to do with me. The way his eyes drag down my body and return to mine makes my breath catch. That single gesture sends a wave of heat through me. Then he rises.

Now we're face-to-face. So close I can feel the warmth of his breath. Just mint today. No cigarette. The tension between us is so thick I can almost taste it, just like it was at the club. The air tightens, heavy with the memory of everything that happened. Last time, it ended with me saying his name while someone else was inside me. But maybe this time, it'll be him. Maybe this time, I'll scream it while he's the one making me come undone.

"Tell me the truth." He closes the distance between us, leaning down until his lips brush my ear, his voice low and sinful. "Why. Are. You. Here?"

He's irresistible. That much is clear. But what I won't tolerate is him talking to me like I'm stupid. Yeah. I'm not down with that shit.

"Oh, Kage, you want to know why I'm here?" I say, voice soaked in seduction as I trace my finger along the edge of his sharp, clean-shaven jawline. His Adam's apple bobs. Like swallowing me down suddenly became a challenge. I trail my fingers down the column of his throat, watching goosebumps rise over his skin like he's trying and failing to stay unbothered by my touch. I lean in, letting my lips barely brush his ear. A soft, intentional accident.

"I was just checking," I whisper, voice playful and lethal, "to see if you were up here being a slut."

He leans in closer, his mouth at my temple, breath warm and smug. "Why, princess? Are you jealous?"

"Oh, jealous of STDs?" I snort, flashing a dangerous smile. "Not in the slightest."

There's no space between us now. I feel the rise and fall of his chest against mine, every breath slow and loaded, like he's trying not to come undone. His heart pounds, wild and erratic, just like mine. Maybe we bring that out in each other. Perhaps it's attraction or anger. Or it's cosmic. Like the planets have aligned, and the universe is holding its breath, waiting to see which one of us will break first.

"Wow. You're really fired up after work," he murmurs, a dark chuckle slipping past his lips like his own wicked mind amuses him. "Let me guess… haven't gotten off in a few days? Leon not doing it for you?"

I narrow my eyes, making no effort to hide how deeply he's gotten under my skin. "Oh, please. You wish you could add me to your list." I cross my arms, chin tilted high.

"Princess, I don't have to fuck you to please you."

The nerve. The arrogance. And God, the way it makes my thighs press together. Of course, he turns it into a game. Every conversation with him feels like foreplay. And the worst part? Each word makes me want him more.

I let out a dry laugh. "Really, tough guy? You think you're that good?"

His gaze doesn't waver. He lifts a brow like he already knows the answer. "I don't think. I know." He stands there, unreadable and smug, waiting for my next move.

Shit. My panties are soaked just picturing his mouth between my legs, those hands holding my hips down while he ruins me. I want to slap him. I want to ride him. And I don't know which urge is stronger.

I freeze, not sure what to say. And of course, he sees it.

"You're thinking about it." He grins. That dashing, devastating smile I rarely get to see. "It's all over your face."

Of course it is. How could it not?

"No," I snap, glaring at him. "I was just wondering how many women are waiting for you at home. So maybe don't worry about whether I'm getting off."

I turn on my heel to leave, waiting to wake up from this dream, when his hand catches the fabric of my blazer, his fingers curling around it and stopping me in place.

"Please don't." His voice is quiet, almost pleading.

I look back at him, and for a moment, I forget how to breathe. He isn't smirking. He isn't playing games. He's just standing there, eyes cast down, like he's afraid of what happens if I walk away.

"Don't leave," he says again, barely above a whisper.

This is a terrible idea. You're going to end up heartbroken again.

But I don't move. He reaches for me, gently, and leads me to his desk.

With one hand, he slides the keyboard and mouse aside, clearing the space like he's making room for something more than just my body. Like he's making room for a moment he doesn't want to forget.

His gaze shifts from the marble floor to my eyes, and something behind them feels pained. "Can I… can I touch you?" he asks, almost quietly.

I blink. "Why do you always ask permission?"

He doesn't miss a beat. "Because I don't touch what doesn't want me to." His gaze doesn't leave mine. "So… yes, you want me to touch you, or no?"

Something in me cracks open. The way he says it. It's more than just consent. It feels connected to his past, the one Beck warned me about. The one that's left scars, I haven't yet seen. This moment feels heavier than it should. Sad. Personal.

"Yes," I whisper.

He smirks. "Yes, what?"

I roll my eyes. "Shut up. You just wanted me to say it out loud."

I cross my arms, trying to look annoyed, but I can't help the full smile that breaks across my face. And then he smiles too. Not his usual cocky grin. A real smile. Soft and fleeting. Like it snuck out before he could stop it, and then the unexpected happens.

He laughs. Out loud. And it's music to my ears. Beautiful. Raw. Real. A sound I've never heard from him before. I watch something shift in his eyes, like a weight he's been carrying just lifted, even if only for a second.

God. I made him laugh. And now I want to make him laugh forever.

He steps closer, still smiling, and wraps his arms around me, lifts me like I weigh nothing, then sets me gently on top of his desk, his hands lingering just long enough to make me forget how to breathe.

"If you must know…" His voice lowers, warm and intimate. "I've never done anything in this office with anyone. This is a first for me."

My heart swells. Not from lust, but from something more profound. Because it feels like a secret, like he's giving me a piece of himself no one else has seen, and in this moment, he doesn't feel unreachable. Or broken.

Just… human.

CHAPTER FORTY-FOUR
LILA

This is everything I ever wanted. I used to daydream about him touching me. About being the only thing on his mind, even just for a moment. But now that it's actually happening… I'm nervous.

What if I take my clothes off and he changes his mind? What if he doesn't like the way I taste? He's been with hundreds of women… There has to be someone better than me. Someone tighter. Prettier. More experienced. What if he laughs? What if he tells someone? I want this to be just as unforgettable for him as it is for me, but can I really trust him?

My heart stammers as I look at him. "Kage… do you think this is a good idea?" I ask, swinging my legs from the edge of his dark cherry oak desk, feeling smaller than ever. He plants both hands on either side of me, leaning in, his perfect lips inches from mine, that maddening smirk teasing every inch of my sanity. And let's not forget that perfect beauty mark above his lip. It makes me want to rip his clothes off in 1.2 seconds.

"Well, I told you… I don't touch what doesn't want to be touched. So, if you don't want this—"

I cut him off, dragging my fingertip slowly up his chest with a wicked grin. "Ooooh, is the tough guy backing out? Can't live up to his own words?"

He grabs my hand, the one resting on his chest, and brings it to his lips. My fingertip grazes the curve of his mouth, soft and slow, and my body reacts before my brain can catch up. Then he inches closer. And closer. So close, I'm terrified he'll feel how badly I want him.

My throat is dry, raw like sandpaper, desperate for him like I haven't had a sip in days. My emotions are a traitor.

I know I shouldn't be doing this. He's not good for me. But I can't stop. I won't stop. Damn him and his magnetic energy.

"Lila, don't do that."

"Do what?" Then I realize, I'm biting my bottom lip, eyes locked on his mouth like it's the only thing I want in this world.

"Bite that bottom lip," he whispers, his voice deep, dirty, and commanding. "That's my job."

His gaze drops to my mouth like he's already picturing me gagging on him.

And hell, maybe I will. But not without a little attitude first.

"Oh really?" I tease, running my tongue across my bottom lip as my eyes lock onto his. "Then what's taking you so long?"

I want this. I want him. But to him, this is just a game. A game he's played with five hundred and twenty-three other women. I'm just another number.

And yet… he laughs. Again.

God, he's laughed with me more than once tonight. It feels like an intimate moment. And somehow, it doesn't feel like a game. It feels almost normal. Like he's not the smug asshole who fucks and forgets. Just like he would do with me.

He closes the distance, his breath teasing my lips, and I don't look away. "Princess," he murmurs, voice carved straight from temptation. "I don't think you can handle me."

"Oh, please," I scoff, rolling my eyes as heat coils in my belly. "Get off your high horse, Kage."

He doesn't move. His green granite eyes sparkle with mischief. And then, slowly, with a hesitation that nearly breaks me, he cups my face with his bare hands, like he's deciding to touch something he knows he shouldn't, even though I already gave him permission.

"Just don't fall in love with me," he says quietly, no smile in sight. And it feels like he means it. Like it's a warning. Not a joke. Not a tease. A truth. And it hurts. It breaks something soft and stupid inside me.

Why can't I fall in love with you? What are you hiding, Kage?

The words sting. They sink deep. My heart drops straight to the bottom of the ocean. Some part of me knows he's not good for me, that he is dangerous. That I should pull away. But I don't care.

I want to fix him. To hold him. To love every part he tries to bury. To care for him in the dark, where no one else has dared to go. I want him to be mine. More than the Red Mask. More than the Phantom. I want Kage. Not just now, not just tonight. I want him as my past, my present, and every part of my future.

"Only if you promise not to fall in love with me," I whisper, the heat between my thighs making it hard to speak. He looks down at my lips before leaning in and kissing me. The kiss is soft and unhurried, tender in a way that catches me off guard. Our lips come together like a broken vase being gently pieced back together. We're the fragments. He and I are the broken parts, slowly learning how to fit. This moment feels like a memory I will cherish forever. Even if I fall in love one day, I know I will still remember this.

This kiss. This feeling.

My whole body comes alive with something that is different. It's not just lust, not the usual rush of need and hunger.

It feels deeper. It feels like a connection. Like my heart is recognizing something it has been missing.

Every nerve in my body is awake. I can feel everything. His breath. His hands. The weight of the moment pressing down on my chest in the most beautiful way. Then I feel a sudden vibration against my wrist. My watch is buzzing. My heart thrums against my ribs, fast and unrelenting. I glance down just as his eyes follow mine. The screen flashes. Heart rate alert.

Are you serious? Right now? In front of him?

His smirk spreads slowly across his face, not just in his mouth but in his eyes too. He knows exactly what it means.

That he is making me nervous in all the best ways.

"Are you good?" he asks, his voice low and smug. Heat rushes to my face, and I stumble over my words.

"Yeah… I'm good. It's just, um, my alarm. To call my mom. You know, check on her."

"Oh, really?" he chuckles. "Let's see if we can make it go off again."

Before I can process the words, his lips crash against mine. His mouth is full and intense, claiming mine with purpose.

He made the first move. That means he wanted me.

He is rough in all the right ways. The way his fingers tighten in my hair. The way his bare hands rest on the nape of my neck. The skin-to-skin contact sends a shiver through me, grounding me in something that feels both raw and intimate. And his taste is pure addiction, a flavor I want to savor for the rest of my life. Then something shifts. He softens, and the kiss slows. It becomes gentle. It becomes something else entirely.

I want to believe I'm special. I want to believe this kiss means something. But deep down, I know he has done this before. He knows exactly what he is doing. He has been with so many women. Please don't fall for him. Don't fall for this.

A moan slips out of me. His tongue slips between my lips, like an apology for the kiss we shared at the club. The one where he said he wasn't turned on. The one where he made sure everyone knew I had only been with one person. The one that made me feel small. Like I wasn't enough for him. Like I wasn't experienced enough to keep his attention.

But something about this moment throws me off in the best way. It is warm, which surprises me, considering how cold he is emotionally.

Our tongues move together in a rhythm that feels too good to be new. It reminds me of the times I've been with the Red Mask, but this goes deeper. Like he is giving me something he has never given anyone else.

This is probably what he does with all his skanks.

His hands slide out of my hair and grip my back, pulling me closer, as if we are not already pressed together, as if he needs to feel every inch of me, as if anything less would not be enough. And because of it, I can't breathe. I can't think. I can only feel. Then he tugs my hair back and breaks the kiss, trailing his lips down my neck. I gasp and wrap my legs around his waist. And that is when I feel it.

Oh God. He is hard. Wait, not just hard… Ginormous.

The way he presses against my clit makes my head spin. It's not just the size… it is the texture, the pressure, the rhythm. It's Kage. It is better than anything I have ever felt. Every grind hits a nerve I did not even know I had. My hips move on their own, chasing the sensation, desperate for more.

What the hell is that? It's him, but… not just him. There's something there, and whatever it is, I never want it to stop.

"Keep teasing me like that and I'll bury myself inside you so deep you'll feel me for days." He hisses, his voice low and wrecked.

Please.

I feel the rush of heat between my thighs, sudden and uncontrollable. My panties are soaked. My breath comes in shallow pants, sweat beading along my chest as his mouth drags lower, licking and nibbling down the curve of my neck. Then it slips out of me, soft, breathy, desperate.

"Kage..."

He pauses and gently lifts my chin with two fingers. "Yes, princess."

Our breaths intertwine, fogging the glass of his office.

"I want your mouth," I whisper. "Between my legs… Now."

He smiles again, but this time the look is darker. Almost sinister. Without saying a word, he slides me closer to the edge of the desk. His hands lift my skirt, achingly slow, like he wants me to feel every inch of anticipation. He begins at my knee, pressing his lips softly against my shaved legs. Then he kisses higher.

His mouth continues its path up my thigh, his tongue dragging along my skin just enough to make my breath hitch in my throat. "Take your underwear off," he growls, his voice thick with hunger and control.

I tilt my head to meet his gaze, letting my voice turn soft and teasing. "I'm not wearing any," I say, savoring the way the power shifts between us.

Then I bite my bottom lip, not because I'm nervous but because I want him to see what he is doing to me.

His eyes darken immediately. "Fuck, Lila," he breathes. He pushes my skirt up and over my hips, exposing everything to him without hesitation. But then he stops moving. He doesn't say anything. He just stares. At me… all of me.

He looks at me like he has never seen anything so raw and beautiful in his entire life. "It's nothing you haven't seen before, Kage," I whisper, trying to sound calm, even as my heart races. "You've seen plenty of pussy."

But he still doesn't speak. He keeps staring, my legs spread for him, like he's committing every detail to memory in case he never gets this again. Then, gently, he guides me back until I am lying flat on the desk. I stare up at the ceiling, wondering if I'm dreaming. If maybe I'm still in my bed, lost in some fantasy, I won't remember when I wake up. He touches me as if I were something rare. Something fragile. Like, I am breakable in the best possible way. And maybe that is what makes him so addictive.

His mouth starts again, kissing up my thighs, like he wants to kiss every space on my body.

"Just know if you don't do a good job," I murmur, half-joking but completely serious, "I've already got someone lined up for when I leave."

I mean the Red Mask. Because the way his tongue moved still has me crumbling every time I think about it.

He chuckles darkly. "You won't be thinking about anyone else once I'm done with you."

Then his mouth is on my clit. Rough. Vigorous.
Whoa.

His tongue moves slowly, controlled, like he wants to drag this out until I break. His teeth tug gently. Not painful. Just right. Then comes a sharp pinch to my clit. My hips jerk. It isn't pain. It's the kind of tight, building pleasure that hurts only because I want more.

"What was that?" I gasp, eyes fluttering open.

He smiles up at me, dimples flashing, teeth white and sharp. "A binder clip... clamped right on your clit." My mouth parts in shock, but before I can speak, he keeps going. "Let me guess. You don't even know what you like and dislike, considering you've only been with one person."

"Um... two now."

"Oh, right. Leon. I almost forgot." He smirks, cocky and unbothered. "Let me teach you a little something." His mouth lowers, tongue sliding down to my entrance, and my entire body shudders.

He knows exactly what he's doing. Too well. The way his tongue moves is familiar. Not the same, but close. It reminds me of the Red Mask. The rhythm. The confidence. He can't be? He would've already told me.

"Princess," he growls against my skin, "you taste like something I've craved my entire life. I've never been satisfied with the women I've been with. Not until I tasted your sweet cunt."

It is filthy. Crude. Vulgar. And somehow, it still feels intimate. Is that his game? Make it feel personal so I fall harder?

His tongue moves between my folds with unrelenting need for me. It pulls me under, dragging me into a haze of pleasure so intense I forget how to think. Then I feel it. Something tightens around my ankle.

What the hell?

My eyes fly open. He is holding a thin phone cord in his hand, wrapping it around my ankle and tying it to the drawer pull beside the desk. My chest rises and falls in sharp, frantic waves.

I can't move. I am entirely at his mercy. This could be bad. So bad.

"If this is one of your games," I breathe, "and you leave me here like this… so help me, I will murder you myself."

He cuts me off before I can finish the threat. "Relax and let me do my job." He ties my other ankle to the opposite side of the desk, spreading me completely open. His voice drops to a whisper, thick and private, like a secret he only wants me to hear. "Because the second you come, those pretty legs of yours are going to want to close. But I'm not letting you run from it. You're going to feel everything, Lila. Every wave. Every twitch. Every release. And your body will never forget it… Never forget me. I will be the only thing your body wants."

I can't even respond. All I can do is nod at his words as he ties me down.

God, I really like this. No. I love it.

He makes me feel powerful and completely exposed at the same time. Tied down and spread wide on his desk, yet somehow more in control of my body than I have ever been. He rolls his sleeves up to his elbows, revealing forearms slick with sweat, veins prominent and pulsing beneath his skin.

He runs a hand through his hair, pushing it back as beads of sweat gather at his brow. Then he pops open the top button of his shirt… and freezes, like a thought just caught him mid-motion. Something important. Something he's debating whether to act on or ignore.

Whatever he was thinking, he shakes it out of his head and starts back devouring me, drinking me like I'm the water to cool him off. He swirls and licks between my folds, the clip on my clit painful, but in a good way. Then he slides a finger inside me, and I moan. Slow at first, then deeper, faster. I can't help but squirm on the desk. It feels too good. Like if I come, all the weight and stress I've been carrying will finally break free. Like, release could mean more than just pleasure. It could mean peace until it builds up again.

"Please."

"Oh? You already want to cum?"

"Yes," I say, completely breathless.

His thick, masculine fingers pump in and out, making me moan louder. I open my eyes, and it's his stare, his face, the phone cord, the binder clip. That pushes me over the edge. My body is finally releasing what I couldn't with Leon. But he doesn't stop. He keeps going. He removes the clip and starts swirling his tongue again… licking, nibbling, sucking my clit while still finger-fucking me slowly and agonizingly.

I run my hands through his hair. It's soft and coarse at the same time, just like him. He devours me.

"Yes, Baby… you're doing so good."

Shit. I did it again. Why do I always do this? Is baby just my default word for intimacy? Is it special… or do I give it away too easily?

He hisses, "If you keep talking like that, you're going to have to finish me off."

The thought alone sends a wicked shiver down my spine. I can't help but picture myself stripping him down, inch by inch, watching every muscle tense beneath my fingertips. I want to tease him the way he's teasing me now. I want to take my time. Drag it out. Make him beg.

I imagine my mouth wrapping around him, savoring the weight of him on my tongue. The taste. The sound of his breath hitching. The way his hand might tighten in my hair as he guides my movements. And just like that, I break. Again. Sweat clings to my skin. My legs tremble uncontrollably. I want to close them, but I can't.

"Kage, I can't…" I gasp, barely able to breathe. "I can't go again. I'm going to black out."

But he doesn't stop. He slides two fingers inside me again… and then clamps the clip back onto my clit. My body jerks from the overstimulation. And then… he does the unexpected. With his fingers still moving inside me, he slides his thumb into my ass.

"Hey! What the—"

He cuts me off before I can finish. "Trust the process," he says, never breaking eye contact.

God. I don't think he's looked away from me once.

"Start rubbing your clit," he commands. "Right where the clip is."

I freeze.

Can I really do this? In front of him? Is that weird?

"This is already too much," I whisper, barely able to get the words out.

He leans in closer, his voice low and unshakable. "Then tell me to stop." His eyes stay locked on mine, searching, daring me to speak. His tone deepens, thick with authority and something darker. "Tell me to stop touching you, and I will. One word."

He is giving me the choice. But God, he knows I don't want him to stop touching me. I stay silent and let my actions speak for me.

I take the binder clip off my clit and start rubbing it. My hips shift against his hand, hesitant at first, testing the edge of restraint. I start with slow, circular motions, teasing myself, but then I feel my hips shift, searching for more. His breath hitches, a sharp intake he tries to swallow down. I move again, harder this time, chasing the friction I crave. His fingers press deeper, stroking in sync with my rhythm until control unravels and I'm grinding against his palm, lost to the heat, the ache, the need.

A low moan slips from him as he watches me, his control cracking at the sight of me coming undone in his hand.

His eyes burn with hunger, locked on mine, drinking in every tremor of bliss that ripples through me.

It feels incredible. His fingers. My fingers. The pressure. The clip. His thumb. I have never felt this high. Never this consumed. This is what Aster means when she says sex is a drug.

"I want to be inside you, Lila… more than anything." Those words spill from his mouth so freely that they pull a scream-moan from my throat before I even realize it. The way he says my name makes it sound like it matters. Like I matter.

But then he pulls away. Just like that. Probably the same way he does with everyone once he is finished, leaving me empty, severing the connection before the string has a chance to tighten, before either of us can risk getting attached.

My body is still trembling, still quaking, and honestly, I am not even sure I can stand.

I sit up, disoriented, barely able to process what just happened. My hair is a mess, my makeup is smudged, and sweat clings to my chest in sticky little trails. He looks at me while untying the cord and flashes a wide, white smile like he didn't just ruin me in the best possible way.

"Don't look at me like that," I mutter, tugging my skirt back down, flushed and shaky.

He smirks, that look on his face saying everything he doesn't. I glance down at the pool of slick cum on his desk. We both burst out laughing. Not just a little laugh, but full-on, bent-over cackling.

"Where the hell did you learn that?" I ask between gasps.

He shrugs, looking down at the floor. "From the women I've been with." My stomach twists in a tight knot.

Right. The women. The hundreds of women. That is who he is. And maybe… maybe I can be one of them because he knows exactly what he is doing. And now I feel lighter, emotionally.

I walk toward him temptingly, placing my hand over the hard length still straining beneath his pants.

"I want more from you," I whisper. He gasps as I blurt out, "Sleep with me."

"You don't want that, Lila," he says, softer now. "I'm a walking STD. Remember?"

"You know that I didn't mean that…" I whisper. "But that doesn't mean we can't help each other out!"

He chuckles, turning away and gathering his things like the moment between us never meant anything. "No," he says firmly. "I can't do that to you."

"But I want this. I want to learn. I want to know what my body can do… and I want it to be you. I want to feel that again. The way you touched me. The way you made me fall apart."

He doesn't even look back. "No." His voice is sharp. Stern. Final.

"But you literally said you wanted to be inside me."

He cuts me off. "Forget everything I fucking said. Drop it," he snaps, raising his voice as he turns to look out the window.

And I am glad he does. Because if he had looked at me in that moment, he would have seen everything I was trying to hide. He would have seen me standing there with my arms crossed, my heart cracked, and my pride bruised. He just made me feel like the most powerful, worshiped woman in the world.

And now I feel discarded. Unwanted. Why? Why is he acting like this now?

"So you can sleep with every woman in New York City, but not me? Wow. Got it. Message received."

I grab my bag and storm out, slamming the door behind me. The glass rattles. So does something inside me. A single tear slides down my cheek.

I knew I wasn't good enough for him.

I run into the dark, down the stairs, away from him, away from my own stupidity. Beck warned me, and I didn't listen. I know I will never outrun what just happened. Not the way he made me feel. Not the way that moment will replay in my mind again and again until it destroys me. Not the truth I can't admit out loud.

That I fell for him long before he ever told me not to.

CHAPTER FORTY-FIVE
LILA

I open the door to my shitty apartment and let my bag drop to the creaky hardwood floor. I cried the whole way home. It was incredible with Kage, but I was already attached. And when he rejected me again, it cut deeper than I expected. It feels like my heart is bleeding. My chest hurts. The tears behind my eyes haven't dried yet, which means I can cry more. And I probably will.

Why do I do this to myself? He warned me. Beck warned me. How could I be so stupid to think I would be different to him? That I could fix him? What's crazy is that I broke my own heart by imagining a future he never promised. He told me not to catch feelings, and I did it anyway. This is my own fault… my own hell that I have created in my mind.

I slowly undress at the door, trying to shed the night like it never happened. But the scent of him, spearmint and sandalwood, still clings to my skin. I want it gone. I want him gone. My naked body feels exposed now. Insecure. Thoughtless.

I cover my breasts as I walk toward the shower, ashamed. I turn the hot water on and let the steam build, warming the icy bathroom. The heater in this shithole barely works, but for now, the rising steam wraps around me like a false comfort.

I step into the water and close my eyes as it pours over my skin. And still, I imagine him. His kisses. The way it all felt so natural, so right.

"Hey Siri, play Taylor Swift." My phone shuffles, and of course, it lands on "I Can Do It With a Broken Heart."

Perfect.

I sink to the floor of the shower and wrap my arms around my legs, pulling them to my chest. I start making up my own lyrics in a sad, off-key tone.

"I am so obsessed with Kage, and he runs from me like I've got the plague." I let out a bitter laugh.

I'm losing it. I've officially cracked.

I hear my phone vibrate on the counter…

Maybe it's him. Maybe he's apologizing. Maybe he's about to show up and fuck me into oblivion.

I shoot up and grab the phone, breath catching. But when I see the screen, everything inside me drops.

THE RED MASK: Are you okay?

I throw my head back and laugh.

Of course. Not Kage. Just the other dick in my life. The one who dropped his mask and left me in the dark with nothing but questions. Wow. They have more in common than I thought.

I slam the phone down on the bathroom vanity, hard enough to make the bottles rattle.

Maybe he saw it on one of his creepy little perv cams. I hope he did. I hope it pissed him off.

I grab a towel and wrap it around my goosebump-covered body. I'm cold. But inside, I'm seething with anger.

I am so sick of these punk ass men.

If you want someone, tell them. If you don't, leave them the hell alone. My phone buzzes again. Ugh.

THE RED MASK: I can see you're ignoring me.

I snatch it up and stomp to the bed, making sure he sees me crawl under the covers completely naked. Let him look.

THE RED MASK: Okay, you're pissed. Valid.

LILA: What do you want? Why are you still watching me when you dropped off the face of the earth?

THE RED MASK: Because I can't have you, but I care about you. So, this is all I can do. Sit. Watch.

I sit up with a huff, exhausted from these mind games. *I just want honesty. The truth.*

LILA: Why can't you have me?

THE RED MASK: Because I don't deserve you.

LILA: Isn't that my decision?

I wait, picking up the phone, then putting it back down. Waiting again. When finally…

THE RED MASK: It was never your choice to carry the weight of who I am.

The words gut me. Not because they're cruel. Because they're heartbreaking. Because some part of him truly believes them. He doesn't think he deserves me. He doesn't believe he's worthy of love or connection. He says it like he's already lost. Like he's made peace with being alone forever. I grip the phone tighter, my jaw clenching as a wave of frustration rises in my chest.

LILA: Cut the shit. Who are you?

For a moment, there's only silence. The kind that presses into your ribs and steals the air. Then the reply lights up the screen.

THE RED MASK: A walking nightmare.

He probably expects me to be scared enough to run, but the past few weeks have been scarier than anything he could say. I laugh at his vagueness because I'm over it. Over him. Over Kage. Over all of it.

I toss a pillow over the vent camera and roll my eyes, slinging the blanket over my head. That's when I hear a knock at the door.

What the hell? Who could be knocking at 12:30 a.m.?

I stumble to the dresser, grabbing the nearest clothes. My legs are shaking.

I probably shouldn't open the door, but what do I have to lose? It's not like anyone would care.

My phone vibrates again on the bed. I ignore it. Because if he cared, he would be here. And if something were wrong, he would let me know. He has cameras everywhere in this building. I grip the old doorknob and turn it.

At this point, if it's Volkov or his men, maybe they'll put me out of my misery.

But my expression twists into a frown when I see what's waiting on the other side. A man stands there, holding a massive vase of roses. The arrangement is so big I can't even see his face behind it. They're beautiful. But completely eerie.

This is precisely what I meant. Receiving flowers at this time of night is scarier than anything else.

Are they from Kage? Maybe an apology for being an ass. Maybe Leon is trying to ask me on a date in the most dramatic way possible. Or maybe… the Red Mask.

"Special delivery for Lila Anderson?" he asks.

"Umm… thanks. Do you know who they're from?" I try to sound casual, but my voice gives me away.

The man is tall and broad-shouldered, with skin as dark as midnight and a presence that makes my stomach twist. There's a slow, sinister curl to his lips.

"There's a card," he says. "You'll have to find out."

He hands me the flowers. I take them. "Thank you… Sir."

I shut the door behind me, making sure to lock it, then rush to the bed with my heart pounding. But when I grab my phone, my breath catches. My smile fades into a stern frown. My wristwatch buzzes again with an alert. My limbs go cold. Panic grips me.

THE RED MASK: LILA, DO NOT OPEN THE DOOR! HE COULD HURT YOU.

I drop the phone. Everything spins. I lunge for the flowers, tearing through the bouquet with shaking hands and no breath in my lungs. And there it is. The note.

SNITCHES GET STITCHES, LITTLE BITCH… OR A BULLET.
YOUR DECISION.
YOURS TRULY, VOLKOV.

CHAPTER FORTY-SIX
LILA

The bag is ripped off my head, and the darkness swallows me whole.

Who did that?

I look around frantically, but I can't move.

Where am I? The last thing I remember is walking down the back alley... I was late for work. And now I'm here.

The air is thick with humidity. It is damp, disgusting, and suffocating. It clings to my skin like oil, making me feel sticky and sick. The scent of sweat, stale liquor, and blood hangs in the darkness. It wraps around me, heavy and unrelenting, choking every breath with decay. I'm somewhere I'm not meant to be. Somewhere I need to escape. Somewhere death lingers.

And then I hear footsteps. Each step squishes against the floor, wet and deliberate, as if he wants me to hear him coming for me. I cannot see the ground, but I pray it is not blood. His presence moves closer. It is thick, suffocating, and undeniably evil. I can't see him, but I know he is here. He is watching me, even in complete darkness, because his soul can see what mine cannot.

What does he want with me?

This is how he emotionally breaks his victims. He traps you in a room he knows inch by inch, while you know absolutely nothing. He creates fear by controlling the space around you. He wants you scared. He wants you blind. He wants you helpless. He wants you begging. It's sick. It's twisted. And it's working.

"Hello, beautiful." A thick Russian accent growls from the shadows. His voice is rough, gravelly, and far too close. I don't speak. I can't. My heart races inside my chest. My legs are trembling beneath me, barely able to hold me up from the fear. But if I sit down, there is no telling what I might sit in. Sweat slips down my temple as I stand shackled and shaking. "My boys did a good job picking you."

His breath brushes against my face. He is close. Far too close. Then his fingers brush against my arm. They are rough and calloused. My stomach twists, and bile rises in my throat.

I just wanted to go to work. I just wanted to help my parents. I didn't ask for this. I don't want this.

"You're a pretty thing. Maybe I'll keep you for myself," he whispers. Then I feel it. A kiss. His scruff scrapes against my lips, and the liquor on his breath makes me want to gag. A violent shiver shoots down my spine. My body reacts before my mind can catch up. I slap him. The sound cracks through the air like a whip.

CLAP.
CLAP.
CLAP.
"Earth to Lila? Are you listening?"
Clint's voice cuts through, his hands clapping as he tries to pull me back into the meeting.
Oh no. I zoned out. I was lost in a memory I wish I could erase. A nightmare that still lives inside me. Like it happened yesterday.

"I'm sorry," I say quickly. "I was up late working on the masquerade ball and didn't get much sleep." I try to play it off, even as the note replays in my head.

I can't tell them. If I do, snitches get stitches.

"I saw it this morning. It looks amazing for tonight," Clint continues, smiling. "Do you have anything to add to the meeting?"

I try to focus. "The team rescued some of the girls that were taken, and a few of Volkov's men are in custody… but we're sure he's still in prison, right?"

Clint lets out a light laugh, as if it's a silly question. "Oh, Lila. There's no way he's getting out of that place. He's locked in tight. No one else is going missing on his account."

I wouldn't be so sure of that.

I nod anyway.

"Okay, meeting dismissed!" Clint announces, clapping again. "And don't forget about the masquerade dance tonight. It's going to be a ball." He grins like he's proud of the pun.

I scrunch my nose in disgust. "Really?"

"Lila. Ball-room?" he adds, clearly entertained with himself. Everyone turns away, collectively annoyed. Classic Clint. He catches up to me as I grab my things to head to Aster's. She's booked her entire glam squad for us. Yes, us. She's Beck's date. Me? I'm going solo.

"Are you going with Kage?" he asks.

"That prick? Hell no."

"Ooooh, tough crowd. What'd he do?"

"Exist."

The word lingers. Familiar. It's exactly what Kage said in the elevator the day after we met.

RING.

RING.

RING.

My phone goes off, and I jump like I've been shot.

"Whoa, you okay? You seem… off. A little jumpy?"

"Oh, you know… I'm just on my period," I say casually. Guys will believe anything if you blame it on your period.

"Ohhh. That makes sense."

I roll my eyes. No, it doesn't. Not even close. He opens the front door for me like a charming gentleman. Too bad he's not.

"Bye, loser. See you tonight," I say with a smirk.

"Hey, watch your tone. I'm your boss," he shoots back, flashing a grin.

"Not outside those doors." I wave, spinning off in the opposite direction. But I freeze in front of the building.

Oh crap! I forgot my phone went off.

1 MISSED CALL – MOM

My stomach flips.

Please don't be bad news.

I quickly redial. "Hey, Mom, I'm so sorry I missed your call—"

She cuts me off, sounding perkier than she has in days. "Hey, honey. I just wanted to hear your voice and let you know the doctor came by. I'm officially scheduled for the double mastectomy next week!"

Relief floods through me. "That's amazing, Mom. I'll be there. I'll make sure I'm off."

"I already spoke to your boss and he said you could have the week off!" she chirps.

"…My boss?" My brows knit. "I'm confused."

"Well, I forgot to mention it, but the CEO has been visiting me every other day."

I blink. "Beck?"

"I think so. He said he runs Heartford Cypher International. He's been bringing us dinner, snacks, and even helping with my medications."

My mouth goes dry.

Beck has been visiting her? Why wouldn't he tell me?

"Oh… I wonder why," I murmur, trying to piece together what the hell is going on and why I'm always the last one to find out.

She continues, her voice warm. "Probably just checking in on your progress. He's such a good boy. He told me all about his past… You should think about going after that one. He's got depth."

"Mom, he's dating Aster."

"Oh well. She's always had good taste."

I frown, the puzzle pieces refusing to fit. "I can't believe he didn't tell me."

"You should talk to him tonight. Lila, he sits with me for hours. Playing cards. Doing puzzles. Just talking. He's really helped me through this."

"Damn, Mom. Should I book you two a hotel room?"

She laughs. "No, sweetie. It's not like that. It feels like he needed a mom, and I needed a son."

My chest aches. "Well, if you're happy, I'm happy. I'm glad you made a friend."

"I did. But I love you and just wanted to share the good news before your fancy masquerade. Go have fun."

"I love you too." I hang up and stare at the phone. Beck never mentioned visiting my mom. And something about what she said doesn't add up. The dinners. The medications. The stories.

Why didn't he tell me? And why didn't Aster? Did she even know?

I glance toward the lobby windows, a chill creeping down my spine. Something is off. And now my mom is involved. I do not like this. Not one bit. Whatever is going on, it stops tonight.

CHAPTER FORTY-SEVEN
LILA

"You've got to be kidding me, Aster." My jaw drops as I stare at the sleek black limousine pulling into her driveway. We are standing at the front door of her massive mansion, and I cannot help but feel like I don't belong. She's begged me to move in more times than I can count, and there's more than enough space.

But this kind of life? It doesn't feel like mine. Still, with everything happening with Volkov, I have been thinking about it. But moving in would only make her a target, too, so I don't know where to run.

"You know I like to go all out," she says with a shrug. "But this was actually Beck's idea."

Right on cue, he pops his head out of the sunroof and yells, "Wow. I've got two smoking hot dates!"

"Babe, don't tempt us," Aster teases, biting her lip as she eyes me up and down. "You know we've… experimented with each other. I was her first kiss!"

"Oh my God," I groan, whipping my head toward her. "Aster, we said we'd never talk about that again!"

Beck's eyes widen. "Holy shit. The both of you? Together? Sheesh. I'd die a happy man." He slips out of the limo in a tailored black suit, holding the door open for us like some cocky prince charming.

"I'm teasing, Lila… or maybe I'm not." Aster winks at me and slides gracefully into the leather interior.

"Oh, please let that happen!" Beck's voice calls from inside, dripping with mischief. "Just once. Let me have a threesome with you two."

I roll my eyes as Aster sticks her hand out to me dramatically. I take it. "I'm done talking about this."

She kisses my hand in a playful gesture. "Are you sure, pookie? Because you weren't saying that when I showed you how to—"

"Aster!" I cut her off, heat rushing to my face from embarrassment.

"Okay, okay! I'm done." Then she turns to Beck and kisses him like no one else is in the car, and the two of them start being disgustingly adorable. Beck looks unreal. Which, I guess, makes sense. He is the CEO, after all. His black tux and crisp white shirt are sleek and classic, but I can tell they are custom. The fabric alone probably costs more than my rent. The bow tie sits perfectly at his throat without a wrinkle or flaw. It's effortless perfection. His skin is sun-kissed, like he has spent the week surfing in Hawaii—even though this is New York City.

Maybe he has a boat. Maybe he sails. Or maybe he steps into a tanning bed between meetings.

His dark blonde hair is streaked with golden highlights that somehow make his ocean-blue eyes even sharper. And when he flashes that too-white, too-perfect smile at Aster, the fantasy clicks into place. He looks like he belongs on a yacht. Not in my world. And neither does Aster. She is breathtaking, like one of those women in the high-end fragrance commercials. The kind who rides bareback on a horse down a sunlit beach.

Yeah. That is Aster. Her jet-black hair falls in loose, glossy curls, and her smoky eye makeup makes her golden-brown eyes glow like embers. And that dress, it's a showstopper. A floor-length halter gown made of liquid gold, laced with diamonds. It's soft and feminine, but dangerously powerful. It dares you to touch her. But only a fool would try.

They fit into the same world. They seem to have been born for it. And me?

I have never really belonged anywhere. But they let me in. They want me here. And for now, that is enough.

"Want to join?" Beck asks, giving me a wink.

I blink, realizing I have been staring while he and Aster make out. I was utterly lost in thought. I smile and let out a soft laugh. "Not this time. Actually… I have a question."

They both turn to look at me. "This is going to sound crazy, but… by chance, have you been visiting my mom?"

Beck tilts his head, his brow creasing in confusion. "Your mom? Where is she?"

Aster answers for me. "She's in the hospital. She got accepted into a cancer trial."

I stare at Beck, confused. "She's been there since you paid for her treatment…" I freeze, watching him, still seeing that same confused expression. "Umm. Didn't you?"

He sits up straighter, his eyes narrowing slightly as he processes what I just said. "Lila, if I had known, I would have paid for it. But I didn't. I didn't even know your mom was sick."

I want to argue. I want to accuse him. But all I can do is stare, because his eyes, those ocean-blue eyes, hold nothing but honesty. I turn to Aster. "Was it you? Or your family?"

She shakes her head. "Lila, you know I would have told you. Especially something like that. I know how you feel about charity."

My heart sinks. "Then who has been visiting her? Who paid for everything?"

A heavy silence fills the car.

"Let's figure it out tomorrow," Aster says gently. "Tonight, let's just have fun. Let loose, Lila! She is being taken care of, and that is what matters most."

"Yes," Beck agrees, placing a hand over mine. His touch is warm and grounding. "I will get my people on it first thing in the morning. I promise."

I nod slowly, watching the sincerity curve into his faint smile. "Okay then," I say, holding out my hand. "Give me the aux cord so I can get this party started."

"Absolutely! That's my girl." Aster laughs, pouring us all shots like she is working as a bartender in the back of a limo. "To whatever the hell happens tonight."

We clink our glasses and throw them back. The liquid fire burns down my throat, and it feels good. So unbelievably good. Like for the first time all day, my nerves finally shut up.

"Please turn on our normal jams," Aster grins. "Beck won't judge us. And if he does, I'll punish him later."

She slides her hand slowly up his inner thigh, and I see it. A switch flips in him. He smirks. "Oh, I'm definitely going to judge you."

Honestly? It's hot. Like… really hot. And if they let me watch? I'd totally say yes.

Is that weird? Probably.

Am I going to ask? Absolutely not.

Aster opens the sunroof, leans back with her arms spread, and flicks on the limo's colorful interior lights. "Think About Me," by Jxdn floods the space, the bass pulsing through the leather seats.

And just like that, the night begins. "Hell yeah, this song's killer," Beck says, clearly surprised by our music choice. The lyrics hit a little too close to home.

I want to know where Kage is. I want to know if he is thinking about me the way I am thinking about him. How do I ask about him without sounding desperate?

I yell over the music, trying to sound casual. "So… I haven't seen your boyfriend. Is he not going to be up your butt tonight?"

I'm talking to Beck, but really… I'm fishing. "Nah," he says with a shrug. "Kage doesn't come to stuff like this. He's in Paris this weekend."

Of course he is. Rich bastard. And he's probably sleeping with every French woman he can find or having threesomes. Or orgies.

Jealousy churns in my stomach, sending bile up my throat. I don't want him touching anyone but me. Yet I have seen him with four different women, and it doesn't get any easier.

I crank the music louder and knock back another shot.

And who knows, if Aster and Beck ask me to join them again… I just might say yes. If Kage wants to play around, maybe I should, too.

Aster and I scream every word like it's our anthem, like it'll rip him out of my head. But it doesn't. Kage is still there. In every lyric. Every thought. Every ache. No matter how loud I scream the words, he's louder.

I throw my head back, eyes closed, trying to forget, trying to feel anything else. But the truth is, even with the lights, the liquor, and the limo, I'd still choose him. Even if he never chooses me.

CHAPTER FORTY-EIGHT
LILA

This feels like déjà vu. Except this time, I'm not the same girl who walked into that Halloween party. That night changed everything. The way I feel. The things I want. My future. All of it.

I stand in front of the floor-to-ceiling windows in the Heartford Cypher International lobby, admiring Aster's handiwork once again. But tonight feels different. Because I am different. Back then, I was shy. Insecure. Letting fear call every shot. But now? I feel beautiful. Powerful. Wanted.

I'm no longer hiding who I am. I've stepped into her. The woman I always dreamed of being. The skin I used to wish for.

My long hair is pinned and twisted into a high, romantic bun, with soft curls spilling loose around my face. The bright blonde strands catch the light, glowing against a full face of makeup. My green eyes shimmer, lined in black, smoked with shadow, and winged with glitter into a fierce cat-eye that commands attention. Burgundy-red shadow smolders beneath, making the green burn even brighter. My cheeks glow with a rose-colored shimmer, sculpted and warm. And my lips are dark red, glossy, and completely unapologetic.

Oh, and the dress? It is beyond anything I imagined. A passionate red, just like the roses I chose for the ballroom. I wanted to stay on theme with the decorations, and Aster had been dying to have this design made. Now that I am wearing it, I am blown away. It's mesmerizing.

The deep crimson ball gown features a sweetheart neckline that dips into a subtle V, giving my small chest the illusion of curves I do not have. The fitted bodice is refined, cinching at the waist before cascading into a full, flowing skirt with a daring slit that reveals my leg.

But what I love most are the long matching gloves. They make me feel like I just stepped out of an 1800s royal gathering. The kind where a man was not allowed to touch your hand without gloves. And last but not least, a velvet choker hugs my throat, reminding me that I would not mind if a hand took its place tonight.

Kage's, of course.

I feel regal. Unforgettable.

"Hey, you ready to go up?" Beck asks, his voice edged with concern.

"Huh? Oh. Yeah." I snap out of my thoughts.

"Good. I want both of you on each arm when we walk in. I want to feel like it is a cinematic moment in a James Bond movie."

Aster rolls her eyes, placing her arm in his, and I cannot help but laugh. "Wait. I have our masks," Aster shouts, digging into her bag. "Here it is!" she says, handing me a piece that looks like it belongs in a museum.

The mask is unreal. She is practically my fairy godmother, dressing me up and making me feel like a princess. But this mask says something else. It is not sweet or delicate. It is intoxicating. It draws people in.

Deep crimson velvet forms the base, with delicate black lace curling over the edges like rose vines. Sparkling red crystals trace the mask, catching the light with every turn. At its center, a single crimson gem glows.

It's dramatic. Enchanting. Dangerous. And somehow… it feels like it was made for me and made for this exact night.

"Holy shit, Aster," I breathe, my mouth open in shock.

"It felt like you," she says softly. "You have the biggest heart. That's the large crimson gem in the center. It burns with warmth and love, even when you try to hide it. But there's another side to you... Something darker. Untamed. Fierce. That is the black." She pauses, her eyes searching mine. "And the crystals… they're the parts of you you've worked so hard to keep intact. Bright. Unbreakable. Even after everything life has thrown at you… You still shine."

I can barely speak as I fan my face with both hands, tears pooling in my eyes. "I love you and…"

She cuts me off. "Don't you dare mess up your makeup! That took Franny two hours!" She starts fanning my face, too.

We laugh as the tears dry up without ruining my foundation. Then she steps closer and places the mask over my face, adjusting the fit gently. We stand there in front of the elevator mirror, staring at our reflections.

"You look beautiful, Lila. And screw Kage. He does not deserve you."

And for the first time… She is right. He doesn't deserve me. Beck walks over and places a hand on my shoulder.

"You know… she's right. He's my best friend, but honestly?" He shrugs. "I think he's blinded by his own stupidity. So once again, the offer stands… You can always come join us." He winks.

I throw up my arms and roll my eyes. "Not this again." Aster cackles as we step into the elevator. She presses the button for the 2/3 floor, and for the first time, my watch stays silent. Surprisingly, my heart isn't racing. Not from nerves. Because for the first time in a long time, I know I look good.

No. I look unforgettable. And tonight, I could have anyone I want. I take a deep inhale and slowly exhale.

"All right, guys," I say, straightening my spine. "Let's do this damn thing."

The elevator doors slide open. Beck steps out first, and we follow. Me on one arm, Aster on the other. The room stills. People freeze mid-step, mid-sip, mid-sentence. The masks may hide our faces, but there is no hiding who Beck Heartford is.

The whispers ripple instantly.

"Is that him?"

"That's Beck."

"Wait, who's with him?"

"Who is she?"

They don't know who I am. But they will.

We walk through the rose-draped gazebo archway into the ballroom. The doormen swing the grand doors open. A wave of gasps and silence washes over the space like a spell. It feels cinematic.

The string quartet and piano begins playing "Wicked Games," by The Weeknd. Each note moves with grace. But beneath the beauty, something stirs. A chill that crawls across my skin.

I almost laugh. *Why am I not surprised this song is playing.* My whole life has felt like one giant game. A cruel, beautiful, twisted game. But then, my smile fades. Across the ballroom, past the soft candlelight and spinning couples, I see him. Ice blue eyes. Locked on me. Unmoving. Unblinking. A smirk curls at the corner of the mouth I can see. My stomach drops.

No. No, it can't be. He wasn't real. He was just a hallucination… a product of a panic attack. But then I see it. His mask. Black. Custom. Etched in intricate gold roses, exactly like the Phantom from the Halloween party. My breath catches in my throat.

It's him. He's here. He's real. And he's watching me like he's been waiting for this moment. The ballroom spins around me, blurred faces and glittering lights melting into the background. But all I see is him. The Phantom.

Frozen in place, I can't move. I can't look away. Not from those eyes. Not from that smirk. Not from the mask that haunted my dreams.

This can't be real. This can't be happening. And then he tilts his head. Just slightly. Like a dare. Like a game he's been waiting to play. And before I can even breathe, he disappears into the crowd. But then I hear it. That hum.

A low, haunting melody seeps into my bones. It winds through me like a siren's song. Gentle. Dangerous. Each note pulls me deeper, wrapping around something I thought I had buried. My breath catches again.

But that hum... it doesn't belong to him. The Phantom never hummed. That sound... it came from the Red Mask. The one who stalked me in the maze. So why am I hearing it now? Is he here too? The Red Mask? Both of them? Are they together?

My heart stutters. The music coils tighter around my ribs. My eyes scan the ballroom. I turn in place, dizzy like I'm stuck on a carousel I can't escape. Every masked face is a mystery. Every glance, a question. Every man… could be him. I feel it. The heat. The pull. He is here. Both of them are. Somewhere in the shadows, watching my every move, playing a twisted game of cat and mouse, waiting for the moment to strike, calling me back into the game.

And just like that, I forget how to breathe. My watch buzzes at my wrist, a jolt against my skin. But this is not fear fueling my pulse. It is adrenaline. It's the thrill. The chase. And I cannot help myself. I am already lost in it and lost in it with them. *Lost in the chase.*

CHAPTER FORTY-NINE
LILA

"Damn, Princess," a voice says behind me, low and playful. "You look like a candy apple. Sweet, shiny, and irresistible. I wouldn't mind taking a bite out of—"

I spin around, already smirking. "Clint."

Of course it's him. Only he would flirt like a pervy fairytale character. Typical Clint. I cut him off before he could finish the sentence. "Remember, you're my boss," I say, fluttering my lashes with a sweetly sarcastic smile.

He throws up his hands in mock innocence. "Hey, I'm just here to support female empowerment one compliment at a time." Then he bows with a dramatic flair, like I'm royalty. "May I have this dance, my lady?" he asks, holding out his hand like a true gentleman.

Which he is not.

"That's actually cute, Clint. Maybe if you don't talk, it'll stay that way," I mutter, placing my hand in his. He brings it to his lips and kisses it sweetly. Then he licks it.

Spoke too soon.

"Mmm… just as tasty as a candy apple."

"Ughhh, you're disgusting." I yank my hand away and wipe it on his tux. "Are you going to keep being ridiculous, or are you going to dance with me?" I huff.

"Princess… are you asking me to dance?"

"You're annoying," I grumble, turning to walk away. Someone grabs my wrist and pulls me back. "Clint, I swear I have a taser tucked in this dress just for you," I snap without looking, already prepared for his next joke.

But then I freeze. Because it's not Clint, it's him. The Phantom.

He towers over me, his hand still around my wrist, black leather glove firm and unyielding. That same custom black mask, etched with gold roses. That same unnerving stillness. And those ice-blue eyes locked on me with a feral glare. My breath catches. My chest rises and falls too fast. Flashes from that night hit me like a drug I never knew I craved.

The way we touched ourselves from across the room, the way he watched, the way I came undone just by his response to her, and the way his head tilted back in pure bliss with his large tattoo sprawled across his chest.

My mouth goes dry just thinking about it. I'm parched for him. Thirsty for the idea of my lips wrapped around him.

"Hey, man," Clint's voice breaks the haze. He steps forward, clueless. "We were about to dance…" He eyes the Phantom up and down, wrinkling his nose. "And you are?"

I've never heard the Phantom speak.

I thought he was a hallucination. A shadow. A ghost. A figment of my imagination.

But then he says, in a voice low, dark, and devastatingly real, "none of your fucking business, wise guy." He doesn't look at Clint. Not even for a second. His eyes stay glued to mine. Like I'm the only thing that exists.

"Umm… Lila, you know this guy?" Clint's voice is cautious now. Protective.

"Yeah, Lila?" the Phantom taunts, his voice low and dangerous. "Do you know me?"

The truth is, I don't know him. I have no idea who he is. I thought I made him up. But every inch of my body remembers him. And that terrifies me.

His gaze roams over me, slow, filthy, possessive. It's not just a look. It's a claim.

And the worst part? I'm okay with it. Clint's still waiting for my answer, tense at my side.

I finally speak.

"Oh yeah… we know each other. From the Halloween party."

Clint hesitates. "Okay, well… if you need me, text me."

"She won't need you." The Phantom cuts him off without breaking eye contact. "Thanks anyway."

The Piano starts playing, slow and ghostly. It's "Candy Necklaces," by Lana Del Rey, but not like the version I know. This one is stripped down. Raw. Sorrowful. Every note feels intimate, like a dance with fate. My fate. All three of the men that I can't escape.

We stop in the center of the ballroom, and I freeze. He's standing so close I can smell him, something clean and completely addictive.

"Did you miss me?" he murmurs, his voice low, almost careful, like he needs the answer more than he wants it. I stand there, silent, staring at him in pure shock. "You look… delicious," he says.

My lips part, but no words come out. Because yes.

God, yes.

But I'm too stunned to speak.

The mask is more intricate up close. Black velvet carved with gold roses. It hides most of his face, but not the sharp cut of his jaw… not the curl of one side of his mouth. And those eyes. Ice blue. Piercing, sparkling like they know exactly what they're doing to me.

He takes my waist, controlled and deliberate, his touch achingly sensual even through the leather gloves. Then he lifts my arm, places it on his shoulder, and laces his fingers with mine. We begin to move. And I swear I'm not dancing. I'm floating. My breath comes in shallow bursts. My thoughts tangle.

Why do I feel this way about him... about the Red Mask... about Kage? I'm not boy crazy. That's never been me. But there's something about the three of them, something I can't sever. Can't untangle. Can't let go of. I want all of them, in different ways. I wish I knew what that meant...

We move in perfect sync, the music swirling around us. The tension between us is suffocating, just like it was with Kage. Just like it was with the Red Mask. The same weight. The same intensity. Heavy. Loaded with unspoken words and unanswered questions. He stares at me like the rest of the world doesn't exist. And I stare right back. His movements are calm like this means nothing to him.

But me? My every nerve is lit. And I've never felt more alive. I swallow, trying to steady my voice. "Where did you learn to dance?"

His eyes flicker with something soft. Almost wistful. "My mother used to dance around our apartment," he says quietly. "She'd blast old records, close her eyes, and pretend she was somewhere else. A ballroom. A stage. Anywhere but there."

I blink. "She sounds like a dreamer."

"She was." He nods, a hint of a smile tugging at the corner of his mouth. "She took community classes when she could. She said it helped her escape reality, if only for a while. Eventually, I begged her to teach me. I wanted to be the one to dance with her."

A beat passes. The music swells. "You're really good," I say. "I bet she's phenomenal now."

That smile fades. His gaze drops. He looks... pained. Like I just touched a bruise he hides beneath the mask. "Yeah," he says softly. "She is." Something in his tone sounds final. Heavy.

I hesitate before asking, "Did she ever get the life she wanted?"

His jaw clenches. A pause. "Unfortunately, no. But I'm living the life she always wanted for us."

Us?

My chest tightens.

Who's us? Does he mean… himself and her? Or… me?

Before I can ask, he leans in close enough that his breath brushes my ear. "But let's not talk about me," he whispers, a smirk ghosting across his lips. "Let's talk about you. Tell me, Princess… have you thought about me since that night?"

Lie.

Lie.

Lie.

And how does he know my nickname?

"No," I say, forcing a scoff. "Why would I? Honestly… I thought it didn't even happen."

"Oh really?" His smirk deepens. "So, you're telling me you haven't dreamed about me? Not once?"

Before I can answer, he lowers his head and presses a soft kiss to my neck. My skin ignites. My face flushes. Heat spreads up my throat and down between my legs like wildfire.

"I have better things to dream about," I manage to whisper.

But he cuts me off. "You don't remember?" he whispers. "I do. Every second of it. The way you moaned. The way you moved under the sheets. The way you called my name. The cameras see everything …Princess."

My eyes widen, pulse crashing in my ears. "What… what do you mean?" I breathe, the floor tilting beneath me.

He doesn't answer. Instead, he spins me once, twice, pulling me closer with every turn. And then I hear it. The string quartet plays it like a haunting lullaby.

"I requested our song," he murmurs, tightening his grip around my waist. "I know how much you love it."

I blink, heart skipping. Trying to figure out what he means by our song. "What are you talking about?"

He doesn't explain. Instead, he leans in closer, and this time he hums the tune playing. So close, I can feel the vibration of it against my skin.

Where have I heard that before?

And suddenly… everything clicks. That song. That voice. That night in the maze.

Oh my God. The song he is humming is The Phantom of the Opera. The melody that echoed through the maze. The hum that brushed my skin. If I had recognized it then, I would've known. I would've known he was the Red Mask. The answer was there all along. In the music. In him.

My knees go weak as the truth slams into me.

They are the same person. The Red Mask is the Phantom. The Phantom is the Red Mask. The maze. The music. The pleasure room at the club. The night I touched myself, thinking it was just a fantasy. It wasn't. It was him. He was never a dream. Never a shadow. He was real. Every version of him pulled me in. And I let him. But this is messed up. This whole time, I thought I was losing my mind.

Falling for three different people. Questioning everything, I felt. Everything I wanted. And he let me. He watched me spiral. Watched me ache. And said nothing.

I am still angry. Angry that he left his mask behind. Furious that he made the choice for both of us. Enraged, he decided he was not good enough for me without even asking what I wanted. I've spent weeks falling apart over him. Tonight, I choose to stop.

I step back, my shoulders tense, my voice cracking with fury. "Am I a fucking joke to you?"

He does not flinch. He does not blink. "No," he says softly. "You are not, Lila."

"Then tell me. Why?" My voice cracks. "Why would you do this?"

"I promise I'll explain everything… just not now."

"Then when?" I cross my arms, tapping my foot, every second stretching longer than the last.

He looks down, dragging his hands through his hair like he's the one who's frustrated. Then he reaches for my hand, his thumb moving in slow, gentle circles against my skin. "Trust me, I want to tell you. But…"

His voice fades like the words are stuck in his throat. I pull my hand away, take a breath, then say what I've been avoiding. "I can't do this anymore. Not with you. Not with anyone." Another breath. This one deeper. Sharper. "I deserve better than this. Better than you."

"There you are!" Aster laughs as she grabs my arm and pulls me away from him. "Beck has someone he wants you to meet. It's a guy and he's totally hot and super sweet."

"Okay, let me finish dancing, and I'll come find you guys."

My heart's breaking open, right here on the dance floor, and she has no idea.

"Hurry, because if you don't grab him, I might just ask him to have a threesome with me and Beck. But I doubt he'd enjoy that nearly as much as me and you." She winks and walks off, laughing, while I force a smile so she won't know anything's wrong.

I spin on my heels, heart pounding, ready to demand answers. But when I turn around, he is gone. Like water slipping through my fingers, I try to hold him, but he disappears every time, vanishing like he was never mine to begin with.

And I am left standing there, hands empty, heart shattered, soaked in the echo of what almost was. And the worst part? I can't even cry, because deep down, the ones I love always leave me behind.

CHAPTER FIFTY
LILA

My heels clink against the filthy concrete as my dress drags behind me. I'm walking through New York City at ten o'clock at night in a custom gown, practically begging to be robbed or kidnapped. But it's Friday night. All the taxis are gone.

Since my dick of a man ditched me and left me to wander the streets alone? Yeah. Why the hell not? Tonight, it should have ended differently. Aster, my fairy godmother, dressed me up for a ball. I should have been the one to run from him like Cinderella. Instead, he left me. I should have danced the night away, caught in a whirlwind of magic. I should have dropped something behind so he would come after me. But the only thing I left behind was my heart.

RING. RING. RING.

INCOMING CALL - MOM

Finally. Someone to talk to.

I swipe the screen and press the phone to my ear. "Hey, Mom," I mutter, my voice low as I step around a pile of trash bags on the curb. I sound as drained as I feel.

"Hey, honey," she says warmly. "You sound bummed. Didn't you have fun tonight?"

I glance around at the blur of passing headlights, wondering if one of them could be him. Or maybe someone new. Someone who doesn't leave me with emotional whiplash. "It was okay," I say, adjusting the strap of my dress. "Nothing special. Just the usual chaos."

"I'm sorry… Maybe tomorrow will be a better day."

"It will be." A soft smile creeps in, the first one I've felt in hours. "I'm coming to see you."

"I can't wait!" she says, her voice instantly brighter. "Did you ask Beck about me?"

I pause at the corner of the block, staring up at a flickering streetlamp as it blinks overhead. A chill runs down my spine. Something feels off, like something bad is already happening… or about to.

"Umm… yeah. And weirdly, he had no idea what I was talking about. I'm trying to figure out what's going on."

"What? That doesn't make sense… I literally saw him yesterday." Her voice tightens with confusion. "Do you believe him?"

I rub my forehead as the headache creeps in. "Honestly, Mom? Yeah. I believe him. He's like a golden retriever in human form. Sweet. Loyal. Too honest for his own good." But then my heart skips.

Wait. Could it be Volkov? Would he really go after my parents to get to me? No. No. He wants me. Not them. He wouldn't. Would he?

"Mom," I say, suddenly tense, "can you describe him for me? Any distinct features?"

"Of course. How could I not? He's stunning." She giggles.

"Mom. I'm serious. Focus!"

"Well… he's tall and masculine. Great build. His voice is smooth as honey. And his smile? Bright white. He has a deep dimple on one side."

I freeze. "Wait. A dimple?"

"Yeah. It pops out when he beats me at gin rummy!"

Dimples are common. I try to remind myself of that. But I know for a fact Volkov doesn't have one. So, it can't be him.

"Okay… what else?"

"His hair is dark brown. Wavy, but neat. And his eyes are bright green. They light up when he talks about his mom."

Green eyes. Brown hair. A dimple. My pulse starts to race. No. This can't be happening.

"Anything else?" I ask, my voice barely above a whisper.

"Oh, and he has a little freckle. Just above his upper lip."

My stomach twists so hard I almost double over.

No.

No.

No.

It's Kage. He has been playing me. All this time. But this? This is different. This is unforgivable. Mess with me all you want. Lie to me. Toy with me. Break my heart a thousand times. But not her. Not my mom. Not the woman fighting for her life. This isn't a game anymore. He has crossed a line.

Just wait until Monday. I'll be in his office first thing. I will be cool, calm, and collected. And then I will tear him apart piece by piece. If he brought some French girl back with him? She can have him! I am done playing nice.

"Mom," I say through gritted teeth, "stay away from him! He's dangerous!"

There is a pause. "Honey," she says slowly, "I really don't think we're talking about the same person…"

"I'm serious. He puts on a facade! Don't let him fool you. He's in Paris right now. He gets back Sunday night. I'll talk to him Monday."

"Are you sure he's in Paris? Because he is supposed to swing by—"

"Mom, sorry to cut you off, but I just got home and I've got to walk up all these stairs…You know I can't talk and exercise at the same time."

She laughs. "Okay, sweetie! Call me when you're on the way tomorrow."

"I love you, Mom." I stare up at my rundown apartment building, wondering why I'm still here.

Volkov knows where I live. His men brought me flowers. I'm not safe anymore. I really need to start searching for a new place to live.

I climb the dirty stairs, each step heavier than the last, my dress dragging behind me like regret. The regret of ever walking into that bedroom on Halloween night. The glitter is gone. The night is over. And I'm not the girl everyone saw on the dance floor. They probably thought I was some celebrity on Beck's arm. But I'm not. I never was.

The city hums outside, but in here, as I walk barefoot up the stairs to my apartment, there is only silence. Silence… and a heart that wanted too much.

My heels dangle from my fingers. My hope is still out there somewhere, bleeding on the ballroom floor beneath a velvet mask. And I am left with nothing but quiet and the kind of loneliness that seeps into your bones and stays.

My phone buzzes.

THE RED MASK: *YOU CAN'T STAY THERE.*

THE RED MASK: *LEAVE. NOW.*

It's him. The Phantom. Or should I say the Red Mask? Who cares… he's the same asshole who keeps leaving me. Why should I listen to him? He's done nothing but break me, repeatedly.

But my stomach twists because something felt off when I was walking home. Each step toward my apartment feels heavier, like an anchor dragging me down. My legs begin to shake.

I am scared.

I stop in front of my door, and I can't believe what I'm seeing. It has been kicked in. The frame is splintered, the lock shattered. The door hangs open for anyone to see.

I have to go in. My whole life is in this one room.

"Hello?" I whisper. "Anyone there?"

The door creaks open, and my breath catches. Tears sting my eyes before I even step inside. My apartment…

It's destroyed. Ransacked. Furniture overturned. Glass shattered. Groceries ruined. Drawers ripped out and dumped across the floor. And scrawled across the wall in red spray paint that drips like blood down my beige wall:

I WARNED YOU.

Then across the massive floor-to-ceiling window, in thick, black, dripping paint:

WHEN I GET OUT… YOU ARE MINE, LILA.
YOURS TRULY,
VOLKOV

My heart slams against my ribs.

I have to leave this apartment. This city. Maybe even this country. But I can't go to the police. I can't tell a soul. If he finds out… he will go after the people I love. I have to be smart. But where can I go? Not a hotel. I can't afford it. Not the hospital. That puts my parents at risk. Not Aster's. Beck is there, and that puts them in danger too. I'm out of options.

My hands tremble. Sweat clings to every inch of my skin. I drop to my knees and yank my pink duffel bag from under the bed. I'm shaking so badly I can barely hold anything, but I start grabbing clothes, handfuls of them, stuffing them inside. I rip my charger from the wall and toss it in. I probably won't be coming back. Whatever I need must fit in this bag.

I rush to the bathroom, snatch my toiletry bag, and shovel in every cream, lotion, bottle of body wash, shampoo, and conditioner I can grab. Still wearing the damn ballgown, I throw on socks and shove my feet into sneakers.

If I need to run, I need to be ready. There's no time to change. They could come back. They could already be watching. Where is a safe place to hide?

Then it hits me. I grab my phone and call. It rings. And it rings again.

"Lila? You good?" Beck's voice is calm. Soft. Innocent.

"Yeah, I'm good. Just got home. But would it be okay if I came to clean your place tonight?"

"Tonight? It's late!"

"I had an energy shot after the party, and I'm wide awake. Besides, I still owe you."

"Of course. You're welcome anytime. There's no one there, and no one will be dropping by to interrupt you! Kage is in Paris."

I sigh. *I do not need the reminder.*

Beck continues. "When you get there, just enter your Social Security number into the keypad. You're already in the system."

If I weren't terrified, I would yell at him for having my social. But now is not the time. I will save that for next week... If I'm still alive.

"Got it. Where are the cleaning supplies?"

"They're downstairs, in the closet next to the pantry. And if you get hungry, feel free to help yourself. There are plenty of guest rooms, so please stay over."

His sincerity makes my throat tighten. *Why can't every guy be like him?* "Thank you, Beck."

"Of course. Call me if you need anything."

In the background, I hear Aster giggling and shouting, "I love you! I'll see you at the hospital in the morning!"

My smile fades. My heart aches in silence. "Love you guys. Text me the address, please." I press the end button.

For a moment, I stand there. Numb. Dissociated. Lost.

Why can't I have that? A normal life. A real relationship. Peace. Happiness. The kind of quiet where you can actually sleep without fearing what tomorrow might bring.

Everything around me moves in slow motion. My watch keeps buzzing from my heart rate, but I can't even panic. I don't have time. I have to move. I have to get out of here. But I'm not just running. I'm carrying the weight of a past that never let go. And now? That past isn't just haunting me. It's hunting me. And this time, I don't know if I'll survive it.

CHAPTER FIFTY-ONE
LILA

I never thought I would return here, but here I am, standing in front of the eerie mansion. The same one I didn't even want to step foot in on Halloween night. And yet, I find myself practically running toward it. Tonight, it's the only haven I have. I glance over my shoulder, watching the Uber disappear through the iron gates, making sure he actually leaves.

I can't trust anyone right now. The good news is that no one can get in without Beck's permission. But what if the monster is already inside? What if he is behind the gate with me? What if the gate is not keeping danger out but locking me in? I am safe.

At least, that is what I keep telling myself.

You're safe, Lila. You can finally breathe.

Not a single light glows inside. The dark silhouette of the mansion is cast beneath the full moon. It looms over me, imposing and cold. I steady my breath, clutch my bag tighter, and walk toward the front doors. The same ones held open by masked men the night of the party.

I punch in my Social Security number, still unable to believe Beck even has it. Not that he would want to steal my identity. Not that anyone would. A sharp click echoes as the bolt releases.

It worked.

I push open the heavy doors. They creak with age, the sound slicing through the silence and echoing across the acres that surround the home, sending a jolt of fear through me. Inside? Silence. Pure, undisturbed silence. Oddly, it's refreshing.

I flip on the lights and freeze. The decor, once hidden beneath Halloween decorations, is now fully visible. And it's magnificent. Antiques line the halls. Exquisite sculptures and paintings, probably originals, adorn the walls. Everything is trimmed in gold, framed by towering mirrors and grand chandeliers. It feels royal, just like the ballroom at the company. It leaves me speechless. However, it doesn't feel lived-in. It doesn't feel like Beck.

There's nothing personal. No framed family photos. No warmth. Nothing sentimental. It's an emotionally empty mansion. Not a home.

I glance up at the grand staircase, the one burned into my memory. The one I ran up that night, desperate to escape the panic attack. The one that led me into a room that changed everything.

What if that had never happened? Would Beck and I be together right now? Would it have worked out? Would I be spending the night in his bed instead of wandering his house like a ghost?

I reach for the custom wooden handrail, my fingertips gliding over the smooth finish as a thousand memories flood back.

Him. That night. That room.

I hesitate as I take one step after the other, climbing the stairs and making my way toward the hallway lined with towering doors. I reach the top and pause, my eyes sweeping across them.

Which one is it?

I try the nearest doorknob. Locked. Another. Also locked. Not just any locks, either. These are fingerprint scanners. High-tech. High-security. The kind you can't pick with a bobby pin or wedge open with a credit card.

Hmmmm. Where the hell is a guest room? Maybe the third floor. Probably where Beck's room is, too.

But then it hits me. The room that the Phantom was in… That door. The one I pushed open by mistake. The one where I found him. The one I convinced myself wasn't real. I need to see it again. I need to see the room where everything started. The room that sparked this obsession. It's technically a guest room, so unlocking it to put my stuff down for the night counts as following instructions… right?

Please don't be locked. Please don't be locked.

I turn the knob. Locked. A fingerprint scanner flashes at me, waiting.

Shit. Maybe, just maybe, he added my fingerprint to the system.

My hands are shaking as I lift my thumb to the pad, glancing over my shoulder like I am about to get caught. I brace for the red light. For the error message. For the rejection. But it never comes. I hear a soft click.

It worked. Who would have guessed! So, most likely, all the keypads open with my fingerprint. Wait. How did he even get my fingerprint?

Lila, save that for another day. Not tonight. You can yell at Beck on Monday, right along with Kage.

I push the door open. A dim light glows from inside. The room feels light and airy. I turn the corner, the same one that hid me that night, and there it is. It is all real. All tangible. Just like I remember, the lamp still casts a soft, warm glow in the corner. The balcony door is slightly ajar, allowing a gentle breeze to drift through.

Someone must have forgotten to close it.

Everything looks exactly the way I've replayed it in my head a thousand times. Moonlight streams through the skylight, casting a silvery sheen over the silk sheets. They shimmer like liquid silver, pulling me in.

I reach out and run my hand across the bedding. It's soft, familiar, and comforting. Something about it feels like home. I set my bag on the bed and unzip the dress, slipping out of it like I'm peeling off the final layer of tonight's chaos.

I will have to return it to Aster tomorrow. It is her favorite. And with my apartment destroyed, I barely have a closet to store it in.

Still in my bra and panties, I cross the room and open the double-door closet, expecting something grand. I carefully drape the dress over my arm. I can't let it wrinkle. It is too perfect.

No wrinkles. Please, no wrinkles. I have no idea how much this thing costs.

The closet is massive. Rows of tailored men's clothing stretch from wall to wall. In the center stands a custom-built island displaying watches, ties, sunglasses, and colognes. Everything is pristine.

What is all of this? Maybe it is his overflow. His extras. He is rich, after all.

But something feels off. It does not feel like storage. It feels used. It looks like someone has been in here today. There is no dust. No untouched surfaces. No stale air. Everything is perfectly arranged… yet lived in, as if someone comes in and chooses from this collection daily. And whoever it is? They were here recently.

Is this Beck's room?

I pick up a few colognes, sniffing each one. None of them smells like Beck. Curiously, I walk deeper into the closet, fingertips brushing across the delicate fabrics.

Okay. Yeah. I guess I am snooping now. Wait. No. I am assessing what needs to be cleaned. Totally different.

I grab a hanger, carefully drape the ballgown over it, and slide it between two suits. That is when I see it. Tucked behind the clothes, hidden in plain sight, is a corkboard. A memory board.

I set the dress aside and step closer, heart thudding in my chest. The photos are old. Faded. Their edges curling, as if they have been there for decades. Two boys at a playground. One dark-haired, serious, protective. The other blonde, younger, is clinging to the older one with a smile that screams trust. A woman appears in several of the pictures. Beautiful, but broken. Her eyes are glassy. Her smile is forced, as if she's trying to be okay for her kids.

Then I spot one of the three together. The older boy stands tall, arms around the younger and the woman. A family. I stare at it, my brain buzzing.

Is that? No. It can't be.

It looks like Kage and Beck. But that would mean…

I glance at another one. This time, it is not a photo. It is a drawing. Crayon on yellow craft paper. A little blonde boy holding the hand of an older boy with brown hair. Above their heads, in scribbled handwriting: "I love my big brother."

Breathing suddenly feels impossible, my vision growing foggy as none of it makes sense.

They are not just best friends…They are brothers. And this is no ordinary guest room. This is Kage's room.

The truth slams into me like a freight train. Kage is the oldest. He was at my interview.
He stood silently through every big decision. He gave the orders. He bossed Beck around. Kage is the CEO. He didn't lie to my mom. But why did they both lie to me?

I stagger back, vision spinning. The walls feel like they are closing in on me. My skin turns clammy. My stomach twists. I bolt for the bathroom, barely making it to the toilet before I throw up everything I ate tonight. My stomach heaves. My body trembles as I cling to the rim, completely a mess.

When it finally stops, I stagger to the sink and grip the counter with shaking hands. I catch my reflection. Pale. Wide-eyed. Completely wrecked by this awful night. And then I glance down, and there it is. Confirmation. His sandalwood cologne. His spearmint toothpaste. His contact lens case. His razor.

Kage Heartford. This is his room. *This whole time… I have been in his room.*

I grip the sink tighter, knuckles white.

What is happening? Why are they hiding this? Why pretend they are just coworkers? Why lie about something so big? Are they working with Volkov? Are they manipulating me? Or is the truth something worse? Something I have not even begun to see yet? Beck warned me about his brother. But why?

My mind spins with questions. I don't know what's real anymore. What's true. Who to trust. And maybe that was the point all along. To confuse me. To break me. To lure me here, trap me behind these iron gates.

Now I'm locked inside. Alone. A sitting duck in the monster's room.

He's in Paris. But even thousands of miles away, I can still feel him. In the walls. In the shadows. In me. And something tells me he's already on his way back.

CHAPTER FIFTY-TWO
LILA

The numbness creeps up my spine and crawls into my arms. My fingers tingle. My chest tightens. I'm seconds from spiraling, but I can't lose it now. I have to stay sharp. I need to know if they're working for Volkov. Or maybe Heartford Cyphers Internationals is a polished front for something darker. Something bigger. Maybe I've walked straight into the center of a trafficking ring hidden behind a multibillion-dollar company. If I'm right, and this house is what I think it is… then I'll be the next girl possibly sold and never seen again.

I glance around the familiar room. Just minutes ago, I was buzzing with butterflies. I've been dreaming of being back here since that seductive night. But now it feels wrong. Off. Like I'm waking up from a fantasy and realizing it was a nightmare all along. But I am here, which means I'm in the perfect position to find evidence. Something that finally tells me who they really are. Anything. A clue that proves the truth. They both live here. There has to be something hidden in this house.

Hmmmm. Where would the office be?

I throw on a cropped tank and biker shorts, then pull up a pair of long socks. I let my hair down, and it falls in a messy tangle around my shoulders. I look casual. Innocent. Just a girl cleaning. But just in case, I slide a flash drive into my bra.

If I find a computer, I want to be ready. I need to know what twisted secrets these two brothers are hiding.

I walk the halls with a steady pace, keeping my eyes sharp. I look for anything. A cracked door. An unlocked drawer. A hidden passage. But every door is locked. Every hallway is silent.

Then I see it. Another staircase tucked behind an arch. A third floor.

Damn! This place is massive.

I glance left and right to make sure I am still alone. But something shifts beneath my skin. It feels like I am being watched. Maybe I am just paranoid. Maybe it is my anxiety from all the stress piling up. Volkov's flowers. My vandalized apartment. Kage visiting my mom. Kage and Beck are brothers. Kage is the CEO.

This world I have been dropped into feels like a lie. A beautiful, seductive, dangerous lie. And I cannot trust anyone.

I step off the last step as I enter the third floor.

I hear something... What is that?

Muffled music. The floor beneath my feet vibrates with a slow, rhythmic pulse.

Music? Where is that coming from? Oh, God... What if I am not alone?

Kage is in Paris. Beck is at Aster's. Unless they have another sibling hiding in this house. Another dangerously sexy relative they have conveniently kept a secret.

Lila, no. They could be criminals. Villains. Monsters. But the truth is, those are the sexiest damn brothers I have ever seen.

I follow the sound to the end of the hall, where it thrums low and steady behind a door. A deep crimson red door.

No. Not that color. It's the exact shade of red.

My breath catches.

It is the same color as the door from the night I was kidnapped. Why? Why is it here? This is the only door in the entire house that looks like this.

My heart pounds in my ears. My throat tightens. It's hard to swallow. What if there is someone inside? What if they have a bodyguard in there, slaughtering someone for them?

Cutting them into tiny pieces, ready to toss the remains into a pig pen. My brain spins with possibilities.

Open the door, Lila.

I glance around for something, anything, to use as a weapon. That is when I see it. A Roman soldier statue towers in the corner of the hall like it's guarding the damn place.

Of course. Kage is so extra.

In its hand is a long, ancient-looking sword. Something straight out of a museum or a Julius Caesar reenactment. I step closer, gripping the handle, and wiggle it free from the statue's grip.

Shit. It's heavy. I really need to work out more.

I try to lift it, nearly tipping over in the process, and I can't help but laugh under my breath. I probably look ridiculous. But at this point, I don't care. I need protection. Just in case there is a psycho behind this door, I steady my grip on the sword. My hands tremble as I reach for the red door. The bass from the music pounds in sync with my heartbeat. The rhythm is hot. Heavy. Almost… seductive.

I have to know.

I grab the golden doorknob and crack the door open inch by inch, the metal hinges creaking as I peek inside. Sword raised. Breath caught in my throat. But nothing lunges. No shadow. No scream. No masked man. Just… a gym.

An elite, private gym straight out of a luxury magazine. I lower the sword slowly, confused. The music is now clear, the lyrics dancing through the speakers.

Someone must have left it playing.

I lean the sword against the wall and let out a breathless laugh.

Geez, you are losing it.

"Hello?" I call out softly. "Is anyone here?"

The silence that answers is worse than any scream.

Okay. Focus. How do I turn the music off?

Black matte walls. Gold fixtures glowing like candlelight. Sleek mirrored panels stretch floor to ceiling across the far wall. The space smells faintly of cedar and something yummy. Masculine. Maybe sweat. Maybe testosterone.

I like my men sweaty and… salty.

I wipe my forehead as sweat drips down my temple, the weight of tonight pressing in from all sides. Just seconds ago, I was sure I was about to walk in on a murder scene. I scan the room and spot a stainless-steel mini fridge tucked under the sink.

Jackpot.

I crack it open, grab a water bottle, and chug half of it like I just ran a marathon. When really, I am just panicking and imagining hot brothers working out in here. This room is straight out of a frat boy's Pinterest. Guys would kill to have this setup. The ceiling lights cast a soft amber halo over everything, making the dumbbells, bench press, treadmills, and punching bag look strangely inviting. Like I might actually work out here…

Spoiler alert… I won't.

I freeze in place when I see it. A half-full water bottle rests in the treadmill's cup holder. Condensation still clings to the plastic.

Someone has been here. Recently.

My heart skips. Then it hammers. I scan the room again, every muscle locked in place. And then I hear it. A moan.

CHAPTER FIFTY-THREE
LILA

What the hell was that?

"Hello?" I call again, louder this time. No answer.

Just the pulse of "Call Out My Name" by The Weeknd flowing through the speakers. The sound is slow, smooth, and sinful. It slithers around my throat, making everything feel darker, heavier. I barely breathe. My feet feel like cement. My lungs? Barely functional.

What kind of moan was that? Was it pain? Was it pleasure? Was it muffled? Like someone with tape over their mouth?

My mind spirals.

Kidnapping. Torture. Sex. Secrets.

I don't know which scenario terrifies me more.

I swallow hard.

I need to wake up from this nightmare. But I'm wide awake, still searching for the exit to the maze.

I scan the room, desperate for a moment to anchor myself, and I spot a set of tall glass doors leading to the balcony. I slide one open and step into the cool night air. It rakes across my skin like icy fingers. I inhale, deep and slow, searching for any sign of life, but there is nothing. No movement. No voices. Just me… and the nonsense in my head.

I stare at the dark horizon, replaying every possible scenario, each one darker than the last. I turn to go back inside. That is when I see it. A clear glass sauna door, tucked into the far corner of the gym, practically hidden behind the mirrored wall. My lungs beg for air.

Oh my God.

Steam swirls behind the glass, thick and hazy and alive. The sauna is on. Someone is inside. And then I hear it again. Deep. Rough. Masculine. Definitely human. Definitely not in pain. And definitely not innocent.

No. No. No. Not again. Dammit! Why does this always happen to me?

My body tightens. My clit throbs with heat. And instead of turning away, I stare. I can't stop looking. I will not stop looking. Something about this is pulling me in, like my desire is louder than my fear.

Yep. My kink is voyeurism. Officially.

I step closer, heart pounding in my chest like a warning, telling me to stop, to turn away. But I ignore it. I get a little closer, trying to see something. Anything. Anyone.

No one is supposed to be here. So who the hell is? Do they have a sexy cousin? A secret friend with zero shame?

The glass is so fogged that I can barely make out anything. Just the silhouette of a man. He is lounging back, movements deliberate, head tilted in pleasure, touching himself. My thighs clench. The wetness between my legs soaks through my panties.

Do not do it, Lila. Do not touch yourself.

But the music thrums. The lyrics are sensual and raw, sending goosebumps up my arms and down my spine. This feels like a game. A dirty, twisted, intimate game… with myself.

This is not the time. It is 2:00 a.m. There is a stranger in this house. And here I am. Soaking wet. Panties ruined. Playing Peeping Tom. I should leave. I should run. I should be calling the police or at least pretending to be a responsible human being.

But instead… I stare. The steam rises just enough. And that is when I see it. His hand, wrapped tight around his cock, stroking, slowed and controlled. Every movement is laced with pleasure, like he is savoring the tension.

God help me… I have never seen anything like this. Not in real life. Not in this kind of proximity. Not like this.

I gasp, quietly, but I can't look away. I track every slow pull of his hand, every subtle shift in his body, like I am hypnotized. But something catches my eye. Something shiny.

Wait. What is that? Maybe jewelry? Maybe metal of some sort?

I squint. And that's when I realize there are piercings. Up and down his shaft. A Jacob's ladder. My lips part in silent shock.

Oh, great, now my standards are broken beyond repair.

I've never seen one before, but Aster once told me they are heavenly. Heat pulses between my thighs. My body practically begs me to keep watching.

His moans deepen. The rhythm of his hand grows more urgent. And suddenly, I am panting with him, matching his breath, matching his heat. But I am still holding back, still restraining myself, fighting the desperate urge to touch myself.

Then he stands and braces himself against the glass. I can't see his face. But across his chest, slick with sweat, is something I can see. A tattoo. Large. Intricate. Sprawled across his heart like a memory etched in ink. I don't move or breathe because I know that tattoo. The sadness in it. The emptiness. The elegance wrapped in loneliness. Just like the night of the Halloween party. This is him. This is the Phantom.

I stare, not because of his muscles. Though God knows, those alone are worthy of worship. But because what I could not see that night is now completely, unmistakably clear. Etched across the center of his chest is a detailed rendering of the inside of the Majestic Opera House in New York City, where The Phantom of the Opera once came to life.

The seats are empty, the stage deserted, like a memory frozen in time. It is cathedral-level beauty. Arched domes. Carved molding. A chandelier inked with such delicate precision, I can almost see it glint. Every seat below is empty. Every detail feels like mourning. It spans over his chest, positioned perfectly over his heart. The chandelier is the centerpiece. It hangs exactly where his pulse beats.

This is not just a tattoo. It's a secret refuge carved into skin. And somehow, it makes him even more untouchable. Like the Phantom is carrying an entire world I was never supposed to see. Then his hand slams against the glass. His pace quickens.

"Yes. Oh God, yes." My blood turns molten. "Right there, Lila." My eyes snap open wider.

Did he just call my name? No. I must have imagined that. I had to.

But then it happens again. "Lila. You're such a good girl."

My breath catches so hard it hurts. My lungs forget how to work. Every muscle in my body stiffens like I've been turned to stone.

He said it. He said my name.

Adrenaline floods my veins. Heat rushes straight to my thighs, my core, my trembling hands. I watch, paralyzed, as he swirls his thumb around his tip. His strokes become faster. Rougher. Then comes release.

He finishes right into his hand. The shadow of his head tips back. Sweat glistens across his skin as he pants from inside the sauna. And yet, I feel like I am the one trapped behind the glass door. The sauna presses in around me, thick with heat and heavy silence. It wraps around my skin like his presence, deliberate and suffocating. I am smoldering, breathless, flushed from the inside out. Like, I am the one being devoured. Not by steam. By him. Needing. Aching.

To see his face. To know the truth. To finally unmask the man who haunts me. The Phantom. The red mask.

I force myself to turn away. To leave. To not get caught again. Not like this. But then I hear it. The sauna door creaks open. A rush of steam rolls out. It curls around my legs like the eerie fog in the haunted maze.

Do not turn around.

Do not turn around.

Just go.

But I can't. Not when I have come this far. Not after chasing this shadow through every twisted path, every aching memory. Not when I am this close to finally seeing the man who made me feel whole. Like I belonged. Like I was seen. Wanted. Craved. Accepted.

I turn, and my heart cracks.

No.

It shatters.

Because standing in front of me, a towel slung low on his hips, chest glistening with sweat, breath shallow from release, are those eyes. Those ice blue eyes. Locked on mine. Equally stunned. Equally exposed.

Kage.

The Halloween party. The night I walked in on the Phantom. It was his room. The night he chuckled at me, watched me finish, and let me leave like it meant nothing. He knew. This whole time, he knew.

He steps toward me, but I instinctively back away.

"Lila, I can explain."

I keep moving.

My hand searches blindly behind me for the door, for a way out, for air. But his words from the maze echo louder than my heartbeat. "You never turn your back when you are being hunted."

I won't turn around. My eyes refuse to leave his. Not now. Not after everything.

Tears sting the backs of my eyes.

This was not a love story. It was a game.

No.

A fucking joke.

"Lila, please."

I stop, frozen, staring into the eyes I have looked into a hundred times. Just behind green contacts. And now? There is no mask. No darkness to hide behind. Just him.

Kage.

I have questions. My voice is flat. Calm and stripped of feeling, numb to the pain that's been tearing through my chest since the moment I saw his face. His jaw tenses.

"Did I walk into your room at the Halloween party?" I ask.

"Yes." His voice is steady. His face gives me nothing.

"Was it you in the red mask in the maze?"

"Yes."

"Was it you in the pleasure room with me at the club?"

He hesitates, but only for a breath. "Yes."

Tears roll down my face. "Was it you who was watching me on the cameras in my apartment?"

"Yes."

"Was it you in the ballroom when you left me alone in the dark, heartbroken?"

"Yes." His body stays perfectly still. I search his face, but I still cannot tell what he is thinking.

"Was it you who danced with me at the masquerade party tonight?"

"Yes."

My voice breaks on the next one. "Kage… are you the Phantom?"

He meets my eyes. He doesn't blink. "Yes."

The lump in my throat swells so thick, I feel like I might choke. I have been manipulated. I have been toyed with. I have been hunted. And then, the final question. The one that burns the loudest. The one that rips the floor out from under me. Last question.

I whisper, "Are you the man in the Red Mask?"

He doesn't flinch. He does not lie. "Yes."

My knees buckle as they hit the hard floor.

Warm blood seeps from the cut, but even that pain is nothing compared to what Kage has done to me.

How can I loathe the man who broke me and still yearn for him to be the one to put me back together?

***The chase may be over…
But the pain is only beginning.***

**Continue the journey after the
Epilogue with a sneak peek of Book
Two in the Lost series:**

Lost in the Pain

EPILOGUE
<u>NIGHT OF THE MASQUERADE BALL</u>
KAGE

God, she looks divine tonight. Her hair's pinned high, revealing the delicate line of her collarbones, the very ones I want to trace with my tongue until I reach her sweet, lush lips.

The crimson ball gown clings to her every curve, and my dick strains in the middle of the crowd. I shift my stance, palming myself, desperate to hide what she does to me.

Pathetic? Maybe. But if she noticed, I'd turn her laughter into moans within seconds.

Sadly, I've never truly desired sex. For me, it's always been tied to numbness and dissociation, a body conditioned since I was sixteen to perform but not to feel. I accepted that long ago. But when I look at her, my cock twitches in my pants. It's new. It's sharp. It gives me hope that sex isn't only a weapon or a transaction but something more.

More of it.

More of her.

More of us.

And I'm more than willing to let every pulsing throb remind me she isn't an empty fantasy. She isn't a ghost I cling to while I move through another body. She isn't a dream. She isn't an illusion. She's real. And I need her to know that I'm real too.

I watch her as she admires the ballroom that she brought to life, oblivious to me prowling in the crowd, waiting for her to acknowledge my presence.

I wasn't going to do this, but I had to bring the Phantom back to remind her of what she can't forget. To remind her of who awakened her desires. Because the truth is, she awakened mine, too.

I want her to notice me, to feel her body stiffen under the chandelier's lights. To see her fight the pull between us, knowing she can't forget me any more than I can forget her. I crave that resistance. It proves that what I feel is real.

But then I see it, her gaze is locked on me.

Thank God, because I would hate to have to punish her here.

Those green, doe-like eyes burn through the black and red mask. They carry fire. Vengeance. She's pissed I'm here. *I've pushed her too far already. I always do.*

I've watched her, not as a stalker but as someone who cared. I needed to know where she was, who touched her, and if she was safe. Call it obsession. Call it protection. Either way, I won't let the monster who ruined me touch her.

Because of Volkov, that murdering psychopath, the moment I was ready to tell her who I really was… was utterly shattered. I had made my decision that morning when I saw her with Clint, and I knew I had to do it when Beck took her in his arms and dared to dance with her.

But the second her fingers brushed my scar, Volkov came roaring back, a ghost I could never bury. He was in my head, reminding me of everything I wanted to forget. He was dragging me back to a childhood that broke me piece by piece.

I didn't want her to see that. I didn't want her to watch the walls I had fought to keep standing collapse in front of her, exposing the pain I swore I'd never show.

So I left. I disappeared. I severed the cord between us. But something about her keeps me coming back… Always. I left that other mask behind to stop hiding, to give her the real me. Yet here I am again. New mask. Same story.

I smirk as her face goes still, her eyes locked on me like I'm the ghost from Halloween night. A low chuckle slips from me, barely audible, because in a way, I guess I am.

The thought twists inside me, and my lips curve into something darker.

I can see it in her gaze, the memory flickering back to life, pulling her straight into our night. The night everything changed. The night love struck like a bullet, piercing straight through my ice-cold heart.

The room where she set me on fire and rewrote my fate.

She wears her facade well tonight, but I know my Princess.

I call her that not because she was dressed as Rapunzel at the party, but because of the battles she's fought and survived. That's what makes her royalty. She doesn't need a man. But God, I hope she wants one. I hope she wants me even if I don't deserve her.

Lila is the reason for my being.

The words written within my pages.

The heartbeat in my story.

She's perfect. I'm not perfect for her, but everything in me wants to lock her away in that tower I found her in and keep her all to myself.

My Lila.

My need.

The one thing I never believed I could have...

Until she walked into my room.

<u>A Love Note Just for You</u>

I want to take a moment to thank you for all the love and support you've shown this book. Writing has always been my passion, but it wasn't until July 2024, while I was sitting on a balcony by the beach listening to the rhythm of the waves, that the words finally began to pour out of me.

What I never expected was how deeply this story would connect with so many of you. Readers have reached out to share how the themes of sex trafficking, mental health, panic attacks, and cancer mirrored pieces of their own journeys, and how they've found themselves in Lila's story.

At first, I was nervous, afraid it would be seen as just another sex filled romance, but instead, I've learned that it has touched hearts and started conversations that truly matter.

So, thank you from the bottom of my heart.

You've changed my life in ways I never imagined. I didn't even think I would publish this story, and now I can't picture my life without it. I'm so grateful to everyone for trusting me with your time, your hearts, and your emotions.

Thanks to your encouragement and kindness, I look forward to sharing what comes next. As a thank you, here is a special sneak peek of *Lost in the Pain*, Book Two in the Lost Series.

Kisses and hugs,
Danni Marie

PROLOGUE
<u>14 YEARS AGO</u>
KAGE

"Did you brush your teeth?" I ask frantically, darting around our ragged apartment.

"Yes."

"Did you lay out your clothes for school tomorrow?" I force a smile, trying to cheer Beck up, but the sadness in his eyes speaks louder than his words.

"Yes. Stop worrying about me… I'll be fine." He stares down at the filthy carpet beneath his bare feet. "I'm always okay when you're gone."

"I know," I sigh, glancing at the clock on the stove. *Fifteen minutes late already. Dammit.*

I throw on my clothes, drag my fingers through my hair, and brace myself for the hell waiting to consume the next eight hours of my life.

"By the way," I call out, "I grabbed Mom's favorite flowers from the market today. Can you put them in some water and set them on the table?" I pause, feeling the tears that threaten to break free. "It feels like a little piece of her is still here with us when I smell them in the kitchen…"

His face falls as he struggles to hold it together. "I… I will…" I step closer and press a kiss to his forehead. "Ich liebe dich. Lock the door behind me."

I tilt his chin until his eyes meet mine. "I love you too," he whispers. "Be careful, please." He looks away, not meeting my eyes. "I'm scared I'm gonna lose you the way we lost Mom."

I cup his jaw, trying to soothe his fear even though I can't promise him that my fate won't end the same way as Mom's, because deep down, I don't know if I'll make it back.

"I'll be home in the morning," I lie, with a shaky smile.

God, I wish I didn't have to leave him. I wish I could curl up with him on the couch and shield him from the cruelty waiting outside our door. But wishes don't keep the lights on or put food on the table.

I close the door behind me, sealing him in, and pray that the rusty chain will keep the predators out.

He's just a boy. My boy. With so much life left to live… a life that doesn't involve Volkov and his men.

I sigh, hoping he'll be okay tonight. A glance at my watch tells me I'm already twenty minutes late.

Shit!

The dingy walls blur as I take off running, trying to salvage the time I've lost. I fling the stairwell door open and race down until my feet hit the concrete of the bottom floor.

It has been a year since he murdered Mom, and I took her place. Since then, our lives have been anything but easy.

The night we lost her was the same night I lost my virginity to Emily… and it destroyed me. I didn't just lose Mom that night, I lost myself. Whatever humanity I had vanished and never came back.

That twisted, sick woman made my body react, but even when the blood rushed to my dick, I didn't want it. I didn't want any of it. She smirked like my hard-on was proof, like I couldn't deny her.

I wasn't turned on.
I was scared.
I had no choice.
And I didn't want her.

But she kept pressing closer, her voice dripping in my ear, telling me I wanted it, telling me my body was craving her touch. My own body became my worst enemy. I hated that I couldn't stop it. I hated that she made me question myself. Made me wonder if maybe she was right. If maybe… I really did want it.

The shame burned hotter than the blood in my veins, and I knew I'd never be clean again.

I didn't want my first time to be like that.

I wanted it to be special.

But who the hell would want me now? I'm disgusting.

I repulse myself.

Mom always said to wait until you're ready and to give 100% of yourself to the right person, but I can't even give 1% after the men and women I've been with.

None of it was by choice.

How pathetic.

That night, I came back to the apartment with my clothes drenched in sweat, sex, and the stench of other bodies. All I could do was scream. Not quiet sobs, but guttural cries that tore out of me like the sound you make when your best friend's murdered right in front of you.

Beck woke up and, of course, asked what was wrong, forcing me to relive the memory of watching Volkov kill my mother again and again.

And thanks to him, we barely get by now. We live off ramen and whatever I can scrounge from the trash behind local restaurants.

Beck doesn't know what I do for work, only that it leaves me hollow in every way.

When I drag myself home at six thirty in the morning, he always has breakfast waiting and the shower running, like he's trying to wash away the weight I carry.

One day, he'll put it together. He'll see it the way I did with Mom. But if he never has to do what I do, then maybe breaking myself to save him is the only thing that makes this life worth living.

Prologue to be continued...

To P, my soul sister…

Thank you.

If it weren't for you, this book would still be sitting unfinished. It would be just another dream I let slip away, another story I convinced myself I wasn't worthy of telling. You believed in me before I ever believed in myself. Where I saw only flaws, you saw potential. You held my hand through every wave of doubt and whispered, "Keep going," when I was ready to quit.

You were there for it all, cheering me on, listening to my scattered ideas, reading every messy draft, and reminding me how to believe again.

From the moment we met, we bonded over our shared love of dark romance. We giggled and squealed over fictional men as if it were second nature.

I had no idea I was meeting the real-life version of my favorite kind of heroine. Fierce. Radiant. Brave. And exactly the kind of friend my heart had been waiting for. I didn't just find a reading buddy. I found my person. My soulmate. My constant reminder that I'm not alone.

Life is hard. It drains you. Wears you down in ways that feel impossible to carry alone. But with you in it, everything feels a little lighter. A little softer. Like maybe I don't have to be strong every second of every day, because I have someone beside me who holds me up without even trying.

Watching you chase your dreams, as you bring life into the world and protect the women who carry it, inspires me in ways I'll never be able to fully express. You show up, fully and fearlessly, for the people you love. And every single day, you remind me what real strength looks like.

So, thank you. For holding my glass mask when my hands were too tired to carry it. For celebrating every little win and for seeing the magic in me when I forgot how to look for it myself.

This book exists because of you. And even if I never sell a single copy, it will still be a success because it helped me find my voice and it brought me back to myself. And most of all, it brought me even closer to you.

I love you.

Always and forever, D.

ABOUT THE AUTHOR

Danni Marie is a southern author and advocate for mental health who writes to encourage others to love themselves and embrace every emotion without shame.

Living with panic attacks herself, she pours her truth into every story she tells. The heroine of her debut novel, Lila, reflects her own journey, which makes the book deeply personal and raw.

Her love for storytelling began in middle school with poems and lyrics, and what started as a dream has now become her first published book.

She is an extrovert at heart who loves people, music, traveling, and turning thrifted treasures into something new. She treasures her family, the joy of cooking, and dreams of one day living by the ocean, where she can spend endless days on the balcony writing and pursuing a full-time career as an author.

Her debut novel is the beginning of a dream she once thought was impossible, and the first of many stories she longs to share with the world.

Contact Information

Email: Booksbydannimarie@gmail.com

Tiktok: DanniMarieBooks

Instagram: DanniMarieBooks